Matchmaker, Matchmaker

Marjorie waved her hand. "Blackmail, extortion. I daresay, what's the difference as long as my mother doesn't know about it? How exciting this shall be. Clandestine meetings. Romance. I really should be paying you," Marjorie said with an impish grin. Mr. Norris's expression was so startled, Marjorie laughed again.

"You have no idea how utterly dreary the life of a spinster can be," she said. "I want to travel, to see the world, to have adventures. Do you know, the only place I've ever been is to Paris and for the sole purpose of being fitted for gowns? A spinster's life is tedious."

"Lady Marjorie, if you don't mind my saying so, you are not the picture of any spinster I have ever seen."

"Nevertheless, I am at the age when most young women are married."

"How old would that be, ma'am?"

"Twenty-three."

Mr. Norris raised one eyebrow. "Indeed. Perhaps, whilst we are looking for a wife for me, we might find a husband for you."

More historical romance from Jane Goodger

The Spinster Bride

JANE GOODGER

LYRICAL PRESS
Kensington Publishing Corp.
www.kensingtonbooks.com

First Electronic Edition: February 2015
eISBN-13: 978-1-60183-163-7
eISBN-10: 1-60183-163-3

First Print Edition: February 2015
ISBN-13: 978-1-60183-228-3
ISBN-10: 1-60183-228-1

Printed in the United States of America

This book is dedicated to everyone who urged me to keep writing. Thank you.

Chapter 1

Marjorie Penwhistle came to the startling realization, on the fifth of May in the year of our Lord eighteen hundred seventy-four, that she was destined to be a spinster. That she was, in fact, *already* a spinster.

She had been overlooked.

As she stood in the ballroom next to her mother, she noticed an odd phenomenon. All the young swains who used to hover around her were now hovering around Miss Lavinia Crawford. Marjorie was, by London society standards, quite old to not be married. At twenty-three (and very nearly twenty-four), she was, of course, still lovely, but there were lovelier—and younger—women, fresh to the marriage market, full of laughter and life while Marjorie had to admit she was a bit . . . jaded.

"Miss Crawford seems to be drawing quite a crowd," she said to her mother. One look told Marjorie that her mother had noted the same thing.

With eyes narrowed, Dorothea Penwhistle, Lady Summerfield, said, "They'll stop flocking around her once she opens her mouth to speak. I have never heard such a high-pitched screeching sound come out of a young lady's mouth."

Marjorie chuckled and her mother looked pleased by her reaction. Miss Crawford did, indeed, have a voice normally found in a ten-year-old child, but, despite her mother's comment, the young men by her side didn't seem at all bothered by it. Marjorie pressed her lips together, earning a sharp look from her mother. She forcibly relaxed her mouth, turning it up into a pleasant smile meant to convey both confidence and feminine charm. It was a smile she'd practiced in front of the mirror any number of times, with her mother by her side offering suggestions.

Marjorie had been the rather miraculous product of two exceedingly homely people. Her long-dead father (some said her mother had killed the man with one of her lethal looks) had been short, fat, and balding, with a bulbous, cratered nose and plump lips. His one pleasant feature, deep gray eyes rimmed with blue, Marjorie had inherited. Dorothea had been his perfect match—a sturdy, square-jawed woman with iron gray hair (even in her late twenties), and small brown eyes dominated by strong, thick eyebrows that needed trimming once a week.

Marjorie was slightly taller than her father and her mother, and had been blessed with a lovely face, thick dark curls, and a trim, feminine figure that, until this season, had attracted a large bevy of suitors. She knew her lack of beaus perhaps had as much to do with her age as the fact she'd rejected nearly everyone who had approached her. The pool of suitable men was rapidly dwindling, thanks not only to her pickiness, but also to her mother's insistence that she marry only a title. It was quite known among the *ton* that unless one had a lofty title (a mere baron would never do—at least not until this point) one did not approach Lady Marjorie Penwhistle and ask for even as much as a dance. If Marjorie were honest, she'd enjoyed her discerning reputation the first two years after coming out, but was weary of it now. She wondered if her mother were even aware that Marjorie was no longer the belle of the season.

"She's rather like a delicate canary surrounded by hungry cats," Marjorie said of Lavinia in her mother's ear, gaining her a grin.

It was easy to please her mother. Marjorie need only breathe to make her mother happy. She knew her mother believed Marjorie was the product of her own hard work, a piece of art to proudly be put on display. Marjorie loved her mother dearly, but often found herself disliking her. The burden of always being the good child, the beautiful one, the charming and special one, grew tiresome. If she were the golden child, her poor brother George was the pariah. George, with all his wonderful imperfections, bitterly embarrassed their mother.

Sweet George, who didn't have a mean bone in his lanky body, was the object of Lady Summerfield's scorn. And so, as much as Marjorie loved her mother, she disliked her, too. Disliked the way she treated her beloved brother, the way her eyes turned cold when he walked into a room.

Something was off about the young man sitting across the card table, but Charles couldn't quite put his finger on it. It was more than his unruly and rather horrifyingly red hair or the strangely intense way he was looking at his cards. The young man, who could be no more than twenty years of age, kept losing—mostly to him. And yet, his expression never altered, even when his older friend lost. He didn't sweat or swear. He didn't engage in any of the banter the others exchanged after a disastrous hand, the kind of verbal volley that was meant to announce to the others that losing five hundred pounds in a single hand was merely a drop in the bucket. It looked as if he didn't truly care whether he won or not.

And Charles had yet to meet a man who truly didn't care.

Hand after hand, the young man stared at the table or at his cards as they were dealt to him. He played poorly, mostly because he never looked around him, didn't bother trying to see if his mates were telegraphing the kinds of cards they held. Sir Robert, for example, would pull at his untamed eyebrows when he had a particularly poor hand, and sit stock-still when he had a very good one. Lord Hefford would clear his throat when he was a bit excited about his hand; Lord Pendergast would slouch. And the young man's friend (he couldn't recall his name even though they'd been introduced) tugged on his collar when his hand was particularly bad. Their tells were easy to pick up if one were actually looking.

But the young man had no tells, for his expression never varied. Charles knew this because he stared at the young man hand after hand, watched his eyes darting over his cards. He knew how to play, that was certain. He bid well when he had a bidding hand. But because he didn't look around, he had no idea what the other men held. And that's how Charles won hand after hand, until the young man realized, much to his surprise apparently, that he'd accrued a debt of nearly twenty-five thousand pounds. It was an enormous sum. A devastating one. And yet . . . surprise was as far as it went when the men were finished and the damage totaled, as if the young man had taken a bite of something that looked sweet and found that instead it tasted sour. Such a curious reaction.

Charles knew very few men—particularly young ones—who would not have vomited after losing such a stunning amount of money. Or started to weep. Instead, the young man said with resignation, "Oh, dear. Mother will be very angry."

The game broke up and Charles eyed the young man carefully. He'd heard of men taking drastic measures after losing such a sum, and he hardly wanted to feel guilty after the fellow committed suicide. Charles pulled him aside so as not to humiliate the fellow.

"Sir, do you need time to settle your debt?" he asked the younger man. Charles studied his face for any signs of distress. There were none.

"I lost a total of twenty-four thousand, five hundred and seventy-five pounds," the young man said, bobbing his head slightly in cadence to his words. "I owe *you* twenty-four thousand, five hundred and thirty-two pounds. I have thirteen thousand, two hundred and twenty-two pounds in my account at Baring's."

Charles grimaced. "So, you do need time."

"I need eleven thousand three hundred and ten pounds in order to make good on my debt to you."

"Of course." Charles furrowed his brow. Something wasn't quite right. The man obviously was intelligent enough to do high figures in his head, but it was the manner in which he was speaking that told Charles that he was a bit of an odd duck. "And do you have that amount?"

"No." That word was said with the same inflection one might use to refuse a drink of water.

"Allow me to introduce myself. I am Mr. Charles Norris." The man continued to stare just off to Charles's right side, not meeting his eyes, though he did dart him a look or two. The young man held out his hand and the two shook.

"I am George Penwhistle, Earl of Summerfield."

Charles's brows shot up and he took a moment to consider. "Your sister is Lady Marjorie?" He remembered meeting Lady Marjorie and her bulldog of a mother at a house party last fall. Lady Marjorie's name, which had appeared on his list of potential brides, had a large and definitive "X" by it. Her mother not only frightened him, but she also insisted with a ferocity he'd never seen—and that was quite the statement—that her daughter only marry a titled man. Alas, Charles, a second son of a viscount with a brother who already had three strapping male children, was quite far down the list of heirs.

George smiled for the first time. "Marjorie is my older sister," he said enthusiastically. "She is two years, nine months, and two days older than I."

"I see." Charles was beginning to see very clearly, indeed. Though the man demonstrated keen intelligence, something wasn't quite right. Charles hadn't been back in England long enough to be privy to all the gossip, but now that he thought about it, his fellow card players had seemed a bit reticent about welcoming Summerfield to their table. He could not take money from this man, for he obviously didn't have all his wits about him.

"I'll tell you what, Lord Summerfield. I'll forgive your debt if you do me one favor. Wait here."

Five minutes later, when Charles returned with a sealed envelope, Summerfield was standing precisely where he'd left him. He fleetingly wondered how long the young man would have stood there if he hadn't returned. "Give this to your sister, will you? It is a matter of vital importance."

Marjorie wished her brother were here. Instead, he was out with their cousin, Jeffrey, a nice enough chap if you liked sullen men who constantly complained of their lack of funds. Ironically, the two were playing cards at their club. Marjorie gazed around the room, then halted when she saw the familiar shock of her brother's bright red hair. Next to her, her mother stiffened, and Marjorie's stomach twisted, to see the object of her thoughts walking toward them.

"Good God, he's not even dressed," Dorothea said with horror.

"He's dressed, dear Mother, just not properly." Marjorie gave George an affectionate smile. He was wearing an informal suit with a bright green vest and mustard-yellow cravat. His hair, never truly tamed, was particularly messy, as if he'd been out in a windstorm.

Marjorie left her mother's side to intercept him and lead him away from their parent. "I wasn't expecting you this evening, George," she said, looping her arm affectionately around one of his. "And from your dress, I don't believe you were, either."

"Mother is going to be so angry, Marjorie," George said, swallowing thickly. He sounded frightened to death.

Marjorie felt the blood drain from her head, and she pulled him into a hall for even more privacy and to get away from her mother's prying eyes. "What's happened, George?"

"I like playing cards at school. I'm good at it, too. I almost always win because I know what cards there are. I keep track of what's left, you see."

"You gamble, George?" Marjorie asked, dreading what was to come.

"Only for a few pence at school. But I went to the club—it's Wednesday, you know."

Yes, Marjorie knew what day it was and also knew that on every Wednesday George went to his club without fail. However, she'd never known him to join a card game.

"I saw Lord Hefford and Lord Pendergast and asked if I could join their game. A Mr. Norris was there, too."

"Charles Norris?" Marjorie asked, with the feeling of dread growing. She'd met Charles Norris during a house party. The boisterous Mr. Norris had briefly pursued her dear friend Katherine Wright, now the Countess of Avonleigh.

"Yes. Charles Norris. He won a lot of money from me."

Marjorie could feel sweat forming along her hairline as her trepidation grew. Surely Mr. Norris would not take money from George. Then again, perhaps he hadn't noticed that her brother was slightly . . . off. Oh, she adored George, but she worried about him in social situations. He was brilliant researching law, which was why he was a solicitor, but he'd never be an effective barrister. He was, to say the least, awkward. "How much money did he win, George?"

"Twenty-four thousand, five hundred and thirty-two pounds."

What little blood was left in her head drained away and Marjorie actually swayed. "Oh, *no*, George." She knew it wasn't the loss of money that was the most important thing, it was that *George* had lost the money. If it had been Marjorie, her mother would have forgiven it, would have even laughed at her daughter's silly folly. But this was George and he would never be forgiven. It was simply another flaw that would never be overlooked, another reason for her mother to claim he was not worthy of the title. How many times had her mother said aloud that she wished she could petition the House of Lords to remove his title? Even Lady Summerfield knew that was a nearly impossible task. But losing such a sum? It would simply add fodder to her claims of incompetence. Poor George would not fare well in any public hearing.

"It's all right, Margie. He said he'd forgive the debt. He gave me this note to deliver to you."

The relief she felt was nearly as strong as the fear she'd experienced just moments before. Perhaps Mr. Norris was a good, fair man who realized George likely didn't understand the enormity of what he'd done.

Marjorie took the note, suspecting it was simply an explanation of the evening's events.

> *Please meet me at my townhouse 25 Bury St. immediately so that we may negotiate the terms of the dissolution of your brother's debt.*
> *Yrs.*
> *Charles Norris*

The dread came back in force. Immediately? It was nearly one in the morning. She couldn't possibly . . .

Oh, she would have to, drat it all. Marjorie looked up at George, angry with her brother for putting her in such a situation. And frustrated that he seemed so completely oblivious to this fact. "George, I am very, very angry with you."

"You are?"

"Yes. You are never to gamble again, do you understand me, George? *Never.*"

George ducked his head, his pale, freckled cheeks turning scarlet. Marjorie instantly felt remorseful, for she couldn't remember the last time she'd raised her voice to George. Using a softer tone, she said, "This was very bad of you, George. He has not forgiven the debt but has requested a meeting. Thank goodness he's asked to see me and not Mother."

George couldn't know how very improper such a request was, and if she felt she had a choice, she would have refused. But how could she? If Mr. Norris did not forgive the debt, her mother would surely take steps to remove George from society. Why would any gentleman demand to see an unmarried woman in his townhouse at such a disreputable hour? For all his flaws—and Marjorie had noted quite a few in their brief acquaintance—she had thought him to be a gentleman.

She tried to remember what she did know of the man, but came up with a woefully small amount of information. If she remembered correctly, he was the second son of Viscount Hartley, and a diplomat of some sort who'd recently returned from somewhere.

She gave an inward shrug. She'd no doubt find out more about his motives in a few minutes, for his home on Bury Street wasn't far from where she stood now. If it weren't for the hour, they could have walked.

"You will accompany me to his townhouse, George, but wait in the carriage. If I do not return outside in twenty minutes, you are to knock loudly on the door and demand entrance."

George, with his head still down, nodded.

"I'm not still angry with you, George. Well, perhaps a bit. But I will have that promise from you about gambling. Never again, George. It's clear you have no talent for it."

"I was a champion at school," George said. "I won six pounds, seven pence."

"But those were boys. You were playing against men tonight who have been gambling for years. No more, George. Promise."

George looked up. "I promise, Margie."

Marjorie smiled. "Good. Now let's call your carriage. It's likely not blocked in as you just arrived."

Marjorie, with much protestation from her mother, finally was released from the ball after pleading a dreadful headache. She admonished her mother, who was having a grand time with her dear old friend, Lady Benningford, to stay and enjoy the evening.

"I'll see you in the morning, Mother," Marjorie said, kissing her mother on the cheek. "You have fun. When was the last time you had a good time just for you?"

Dorothea smiled at her fondly and let her go, noting aloud that Marjorie did look a bit peaked and perhaps that explained why so few young men had shown an interest in her that evening. Marjorie forced herself to agree with her mother, even though she resented her mother's ability to bring every conversation back to their quest for a husband.

Once in the carriage, seated across from her brother, Marjorie tried to remain calm. Those words in the cryptic note nagged at her—

"negotiate the terms." What on earth could he mean by that? Her imagination suggested every scenario from her hand in marriage, to her virtue, or one of her family's properties. But if he wanted a property, couldn't he have negotiated that with George? Her brother was the head of the family and quite capable of such a negotiation.

Oh, God, would he want . . . favors? Her stomach twisted as she tried to recall anything she could about Charles Norris. He was a gentleman—at least he had been raised that way. His brother, heir to the viscountcy, was a highly respected man with an excellent reputation. She tried to recall Mr. Norris from when he'd pursued Katherine. Mr. Norris was large, boisterous and . . . handsome. He was appealing if one liked large, boisterous men. And, frustratingly, that was all she could recall of him. He'd gone to a cricket match with Lord Avonleigh and her friend Katherine. She remembered only because she'd been seated not far away and she'd found him rather overly enthusiastic about the game whilst trying to teach Katherine all about it.

"What was Mr. Norris like? What was his disposition?" she asked. "Was he nice?"

"Oh, yes. He smiled at me and that meant he liked me. Didn't it?" George asked uncertainly.

"I'm sure he was quite happy after winning that sum of money," Marjorie muttered.

"No. I don't think so. That's why he is giving the money back. He asked me if I had the money, and I told him that I only have thirteen thousand, two hundred and twenty-two pounds in my account at Baring's. That means I need eleven thousand three hundred and ten pounds."

"That's still quite a sum," Marjorie said. "What exactly did he say to you?"

"He said, 'Sir, do you need time to settle your debt?' and then he asked me to give you the note."

Marjorie furrowed her brow in thought. She supposed the only way to find out Mr. Norris's intentions was to meet with him. She just wished it wasn't at this hour of the early morning.

In short order, the carriage pulled up in front of the townhouse on fashionable Bury Street, not far from St. James's Square. The streets were deserted, but well lit by gas lamps hissing in the quiet of the night. With a deep sigh, Marjorie stepped down from the carriage, ignoring the concerned look of their footman, and walked up the steps to the front door. Twisting the bell, she stepped back, clutching her fists to her stomach in a desperate attempt to squelch the sick nervousness settling there. She barely had time to collect herself when the door opened to a tall Indian man wearing a traditional dhoti and white turban.

"Lady Marjorie, please come in. Mr. Norris is expecting you."

"Lovely," Marjorie said, stepping into the dimly lit entry hall.

"This way." The servant walked down a long, dark hall, which only added to the trepidation in her heart. She thought she heard a strange grunting sound coming from the direction of their path, and she stopped dead.

The man turned toward her inquiringly.

"I . . . Are there no lights?"

"Ah, forgive my rudeness. I am used to walking these halls in the darkness and quite forgot you are not familiar with this house." He pulled a match from his pocket and lit a wall sconce. "Better, no?"

Marjorie smiled. "Much better, thank you."

"Now we can contin—" His sentence was interrupted by a very loud and very foul curse. "Nighttime can be difficult for Mr. Norris," the Indian said cryptically, before continuing down the hall.

"Perhaps another time would be better?" Marjorie called after him.

He turned again, smiling pleasantly. "This way, my lady."

With a sigh of resignation, Marjorie began walking toward the end of the hall, stopping when the man knocked softly at a door, which showed a dim light underneath. Here they would no doubt find the loud and foul-mouthed Mr. Norris.

"Goddamnit, Prajit, if she ain't here yet, leave me the fuck alone!"

"Perhaps I should come back at a more respectable hour, sir?"

Charles spun around from his spot by the fire where he'd stood, hoping the warmth of the flames would soothe the agonizing pain shooting through his leg. He muttered yet another curse, clenched his jaw, and forced a smile, which even he knew probably made him look like a madman.

"Lady Marjorie, I apologize for the lateness of the hour, but I wanted this resolved as soon as possible."

Through the haze of pain, he was aware the lady was dressed for a ball, and he had enough wits about him to realize she'd been pulled from said ball to attend him. "And I apologize again for taking you from what I imagine was a pleasant evening."

"Perhaps more pleasant than this," she said, raising one brow in her lovely face.

Now that she was in front of him, he realized he remembered her quite well. It was rather difficult to meet Lady Marjorie Penwhistle and not remember her. She was, in fact, every Englishman's fantasy of what an English woman should look like—if one preferred dark-haired beauties as opposed to blondes. Her complexion was near perfection, creamy and smooth with the slightest blush along her delicate cheekbones. Her nose was small, her chin perhaps a bit strong (a gift, no doubt, from her mother), but she was in no way mannish. Her eyes were dark, and in this light, he couldn't tell if they were dark blue or perhaps brown. Her entire countenance gave her an air of authority and intelligence—and coldness. No, he wasn't the least bit attracted to her.

She would be perfect for him.

Chapter 2

"Please sit down, Lady Marjorie."

She hesitated, not wanting to be put at a disadvantage, but realized she was already so at a disadvantage she might as well do as he asked. Or rather demanded, even if politely. She sat and looked at him expectantly, fear trickling down her spine.

They were in a small room, crowded with furniture and books and things that had been collected, no doubt, from his travels. Foreign and frightening-looking things filled the room, things that would be fine for a museum but were a bit off-putting in a parlor. And at the center of this small room was a large man standing by the fire as if he were some sort of medieval king. His hair was an odd color—neither blond nor red nor brown, but somewhere in between and with shots of all of those colors streaking through it. At the moment, it was rather unkempt, tousled one might say. His eyes—a brooding dark brown—were staring at her. One hand was fisted tightly on the mantel, and when he saw her look curiously at that white-knuckled fist, he carefully loosened it and shoved it into one pocket.

"Your brother has told you what happened this evening?"

"Yes, he did. Though I'm not certain George fully understands the scope of his debt."

"He knows how much he owes me."

"Oh, yes, he does," she said agreeably. "But he doesn't fully understand the repercussions of accumulating such debt. My brother is frightfully smart about certain things. But he struggles with the intricacies of society."

"He's a pleasant young man, but a bit of an odd duck. I did notice that."

Marjorie smiled. "Yes, that's about right. Why have you asked me here, sir? Surely you don't think I can come up with the amount he owes."

Mr. Norris took a step away from the mantel and let out a low sound, his face contorting in pain. Marjorie stood and started moving forward, but he held out a hand, staying her. "Get out, Prajit. I am fine. For God's sake."

Marjorie turned to see his manservant standing at the doorway, his expression filled with concern. He backed out and silently closed the door, leaving them alone again.

"You are injured?"

"In Ghana. The Ashanti War."

Marjorie nodded. Even though she knew very little about the war, she and everyone else in England had heard about General Garnet Wolseley and his efforts there. "Did you meet General Wolseley?"

"Indeed, I have met him. Impressive man and a great strategist. Extremely . . . efficient."

Something in his tone told Marjorie the discussion of the short-lived Ashanti War was ended. "I am sorry for your injury and grateful for your service, but I would like to know why I am here."

"I need a wife."

Marjorie sat back down, her knees giving out from under her, unable to stop the audible gasp that escaped her mouth.

"Not you, you ninny."

Even though marriage to him was the last thing she wanted, Marjorie couldn't help but be slightly insulted by this last. "I continue to be confused as to why I am here, sir."

"As you wish," he said, though it seemed to Marjorie that he'd rather not do as she wished. He seemed more like a man who expected her to do as he asked, simply because he asked it. And obviously, he was correct, for here she was in the middle of the night just because he'd requested a meeting.

He gave her a level stare that even in the dim light of the room was intimidating. So when he finally began his explanation, Marjorie was nearly stupefied with surprise.

"When I was twenty-five, I decided I wanted a wife and marriage and children and everything that went along with the sort of sedate life that my parents have. So, I set about finding the female who would best fill that role. I found her immediately. Fell in love—like that." He snapped his fingers.

"Things did not work out?" Marjorie asked, stating the obvious.

"She was in love with one of my best friends. You may know her now as Lady Willington." Marjorie nodded. "Licking my wounds, I headed for India. And fell in love again. And again. All with women who were either completely inappropriate or held their affections elsewhere or were, let us say, less than enamored with me. After ten years away from England, I returned home and found yet another girl I felt I could love."

"Katherine Wright."

He smiled thinly. "Indeed. I've come to the conclusion that there is something wrong with me and I require assistance."

Marjorie began shaking her head before he could get the proposal out of his mouth.

"That is the deal, Lady Marjorie. I will forgive your brother's debt if you manage to find me a bride this season. *This* season."

"But it's impossible," she blurted, and immediately regretted it, for the man looked quite put out by her words. "I didn't mean that it is *impossible* to find you a bride, but that it is highly unlikely if you have been unsuccessful in *ten years* that I will be successful in two months! The season is already in full swing, sir. And isn't this blackmail?"

"Extortion, actually. But let's not put such an ugly word on what could be a mutually beneficial agreement." He gave her a thin smile. "Look at me, ma'am, and tell me what you see. Am I delusional? Am I a monster and I have yet to realize it? Is there something about me that is distasteful or repugnant? Have I an odor?" He was smiling slightly and she could detect no emotional hurt in his eyes, so she was quite certain he didn't believe any of these things.

Marjorie looked at him and shook her head. "You are a fine-looking man. Above average, really. And you are wealthy, if I recall?"

He nodded, his expression, if possible, growing even darker. "Exceedingly."

She stood and stepped closer to him and took a delicate sniff, smelling only a very nice and subtle cologne, one that, if she were honest, drew her to him, not the opposite. She looked up into his square-jawed face, noted his firm but sensuous mouth, his straight nose with its small cleft, his prominent brow over dark brown eyes, and could find nothing that would be at all off-putting to a woman. Indeed, he was far more handsome up close than she'd noted before.

"You're actually quite good-looking. Perhaps it's your personality. Or perhaps you are simply targeting the wrong women."

He smiled broadly. "Yes," he said with enthusiasm. "That's it. And that's why I need your help. I keep picking the wrong women and with your help I shall pick the right one."

Marjorie returned to her seat. "Why me? Surely you have friends who can help you. I don't even know you, your likes or dislikes. What sort of woman you want."

Mr. Norris shook his head as if these details were of no consequence. "I have been away from England for ten years. I don't know anyone, particularly young women. My friends are all married and rarely attend social events these days. Too busy having children," he said with no small amount of derision.

"You don't care for children?"

He looked momentarily confused by her question. "Of course I like children. But they should have been *my* children. I was the one who wanted to get married, not them. But here I am, ten years later, the last of us to marry and I was the first to announce my intention of getting married."

Marjorie winced as this last was said quite loudly. "Have you always been so loud?"

Mr. Norris sat down heavily, one hand clutching his thigh—the one Marjorie supposed was the injured one. "I am trying to control that tendency," he said softly. "But when I feel passionate about something, I tend to get a bit loud, yes."

"Thunderous would be a more apt description," Marjorie said with a small laugh. "You might frighten your future wife away."

Marjorie was slightly amused to see him clench his jaw in frustration. She stifled a yawn right before the door opened again, revealing her brother and Prajit.

"It's been twenty minutes, Marjorie."

Marjorie stood. "So it has." Turning back to Mr. Norris, she said, "I agree to your terms. If you don't mind, sir, I would like to meet with you soon to discuss our agreement."

"I'll call on you tomorrow."

Marjorie was immediately filled with alarm. She could already picture her mother ranting on and on about how she should not encourage the untitled Charles Norris. She would likely try to bodily remove Mr. Norris from their home should he dare show any interest in her. Of course, Marjorie could never explain the arrangement she had with him.

"No, we'll not have the privacy we need. I know what we can do. When George goes to the Christy collection, he can take me along and we can discuss things there."

"And what, pray tell, is the Christy collection?"

"Antiquities and whatnot. Cavemen and their rocks. What does it matter? We're not going to look at them but to meet discreetly. It's on Victoria Street, Westminster."

"I have the guide," George put in. "It's in our library on the third shelf from the top, tenth book in from the right."

Marjorie smiled. "That's wonderful. The deception is complete," she said, laughing.

Of course, Mr. Norris frowned. "I don't much like the idea of lying to your mother. I never lie."

"Says the man who is blackmailing me. And you won't be lying to her. I will."

"Extorting."

Marjorie waved her hand. "Blackmail, extortion. I daresay, what's the difference as long as my mother doesn't know about it? How exciting this shall be. Clandestine meetings. Romance. I really should be paying you," Marjorie said with an impish grin. Mr. Norris's expression was so startled, Marjorie laughed again.

"You have no idea how utterly dreary the life of a spinster can be," she said. "I want to travel, to see the world, to have adventures. Do you know, the only place I've ever been is to Paris and for the sole purpose of being fitted for gowns? A spinster's life is tedious."

"Lady Marjorie, if you don't mind my saying so, you are not the picture of any spinster I have ever seen."

"Nevertheless, I am at the age when most young women are married."

"How old would that be, ma'am?"

"Twenty-three."

Mr. Norris raised one eyebrow. "Indeed. Perhaps whilst we are looking for a wife for me, we might find a husband for you."

"Titled husband. My mother actually mentioned to me this very evening that the Duchess of Marlborough had been feeling ill, and wouldn't it be oh so terrible if she were to perish, leaving an opening for her replacement. This, sir, is what I am up against on a daily basis. But if you want to take on the task of finding me a title, please do."

He smiled, then grimaced, clutching his leg.

"Mr. Norris was injured in Elmina on January twelfth of eighteen seventy-four," said George. "Three other men, Patrick Gilwood, Sir Elmer Huff, and Benjamin Fredericks were killed. Patrick Gilwood died of his wounds three days after the battle."

Mr. Norris's jaw dropped just a bit. "That is precisely what happened. How . . ."

"I read the newspaper account on January twenty-fourth. It was on page two of the London *Times*," George said.

"He has a rather impressive memory for things he's read. He's a brilliant solicitor. He adores anything to do with history."

"But a rather terrible card player," Mr. Norris said, a note of warning in his tone.

"Don't worry, sir, George will not be playing cards again."

"Good. And what time shall we meet at the exhibition?"

Marjorie turned to George. "You go on Thursday, do you not, George? What time?"

"Tomorrow is Thursday. I go to Hyde Park at one and then the Christy collection at four."

Marjorie explained. "Oh, yes. That's right. Perhaps at four then, George."

Her brother nodded his head in agreement.

"It'll be fine, George. I'll be there, won't I?"

"I have to go to Hyde Park on Thursday at one."

Marjorie could feel her cheeks flushing slightly. She adored George, but she also knew his behavior could be a bit off-putting to most people. Well, all people, if she were honest.

"Yes, and after that, we'll go to the exhibit. You don't really mind if I come along, do you, George?"

George pressed his lips together, something he did when he was upset. "Okay. After I go to Hyde Park at one o'clock."

"Good. Then we can meet tomorrow just past the hour?"

Marjorie knew the exchange with her brother was odd, but Mr. Norris's expression showed nothing. "I look forward to it, Lady Marjorie. Lord Summerfield."

"It's a rock," Marjorie said, frowning at a small piece of flint lying on a bit of velvet inside a glass case.

"Ah, but it's a rock once held by an ancient hand, Lady Marjorie. And if you look closely, you can see how it was shaped. Do you see those angles?"

Charles watched with no small amount of impatience, as the skeptical lady peered—unimpressed—at the pieces of flint. George, on the other hand, seemed fascinated by them and kept referring to his guidebook.

What an odd pair these two were, Charles thought. Lady Marjorie, the self-proclaimed spinster, wore a delightful royal blue dress that turned her eyes bluish-gray. It was surprising to see such a lovely color looking back at him when he'd thought she perhaps had dull brown eyes like his own. He wondered, not for the first time since he'd met her, why she'd been unable to find a husband. Yes, she wanted a title, but there were plenty of those to be had in England.

He hadn't found her shrewish. Indeed, she was rather delightful with a penchant for smiling and finding delight in the unusual. Then why . . . ?

"I have to go home at six o'clock."

It was, perhaps, the fifth time her brother had said that, and each time Lady Marjorie gently acknowledged him. And that was when he realized that the fact she was unmarried perhaps had nothing to do with her, but everything to do with her younger brother.

"You're protecting him," he said softly, looking at George, who hovered over a display across the room. "From whom, I wonder?"

She looked at him, startled, then sent an affectionate look toward her brother. "My mother," she said finally. "If I'm not around, she would crush him. Perhaps not on purpose, but she would crush him. He needs me. I understand him. I know he's brilliant and loving, but I'm afraid all she sees is . . ."

"An embarrassment," Charles supplied gently. When he was a younger man, he might have judged him the same. He'd been a bit close-minded back then, but he was a changed man now. The years had mellowed him and made him far more tolerant and understanding than he'd once been. So he was a bit surprised by Lady Marjorie's fierce look.

"He is not an embarrassment," she whispered harshly.

"You misunderstand, my lady. I don't believe he is, but I wonder if that is how your mother feels."

Her face immediately softened. "Oh. I do apologize. I tend to, as you said, be very protective of George." She let out a soft laugh. "My mother is more than embarrassed by him. I fear sometimes she wants nothing more than to strip him of his title and see him spend the rest of his life in an asylum. As long as I am breathing, that will not happen. And that's why I am here, sir. Because my mother can never find out that he lost all that money."

Charles smiled gently at her. "My dear lady, never show all your cards. You don't know me and yet you just told me your greatest fear. You have given me power over you, more power than I had previously."

Her brows snapped together and he laughed aloud. "No fear, please, my lady. It is a cautionary tale only. I will protect your secret"—he gave her a bow—"with my life, if need be. But I thought it necessary to point out how foolishly naïve you are."

She tilted her head, her eyes snapping, but he could see a small smile tugging at her rather lovely mouth. "I begin to see now why you are as yet unmarried, sir. You are far too blunt."

"I am not this way with women I'm courting. I'm a complete idiot when it comes to most beautiful women."

"So good to know you are completely immune to my charms," Lady Marjorie said dryly.

"While your charms are considerable," he said, unable to stop his eyes drifting to her mouth, "I am, as you say, completely immune." Even as he said the words, he realized, somewhat surprised, that he was lying.

"Wonderful."

"Would you rather I become completely besotted and have my heart broken yet again?"

She smiled, her eyes turning to lovely half-moons. "I very much doubt your heart has ever been truly broken, sir. And I also very much doubt you have ever truly been in love."

"Are you saying, my lady, that I don't know what's in my own heart?"

She tilted her head in thought. "Who would you die for?"

"My sister," he said immediately. "Perhaps my mother and father."

"And me. Don't forget, you just told me you would guard my secret with your life." She seemed far too delighted to recall this fact. "You give your life much too easily, sir. No doubt you would die for any woman who agreed to dance with you. I can see that was not a very clarifying question."

He grinned down at her uptilted face, noting her smug expression. "That is my problem, you see. I give my heart far too easily."

"Which again proves my point. You are infatuated. Not in love."

"I believe that's what I've been saying all along, madam. And it is your job to steer me away from women who are inappropriate, uninterested, and unavailable."

They spent the next hour touring the museum and making plans for their operation. It would be difficult, they both acknowledged, to carry through with their scheme when Marjorie's mother was in attendance. The operation would have to be clandestine. They would pass notes, whisper words in passing, secretly meet. Charles was charmed by how enthusiastic Lady Marjorie was. She seemed to carry no resentment that all this had been forced upon her by his extortion.

"I know!" she said, clutching his arm. "We shall have a spot where we can leave a note. I can give you instructions, and you can respond or let me know which party or ball you'll be attending that evening, and I can make certain I am there. Or at least I can try." She steepled her hands and pressed them against her lips, eyes shining with excitement above them. "I have the perfect place," she announced. "Behind our townhouse, there is a wall separating our garden from the mews. There's a narrow lane back there that is accessible to anyone. Near the gate there is a loose brick where I always keep a key to the house for George and me in case we ever need it. When we go out without Mother we use it all the time. I don't like waking servants up, you see. We can leave the notes there." She clapped her hands like a little girl about to open her birthday presents.

Charles had had enough excitement in the last ten years to last a lifetime, but it was clear this young woman led a rather sedate life. He hoped whoever married her gave her a bit of excitement once in a while.

"How often should I check this brick?" he asked.

"Every day. I shall write every day. Won't it be fun?"

"Only if you find me a wife. Then, indeed, it shall be quite fun."

Marjorie's smile slipped a bit, almost as if she'd forgotten what all this note-passing was about. "It will not be as easy for me as you seem to think to find you a wife. What if you become enamored with someone I know you should not? How can I possibly dissuade you if you do?"

"I will simply have to trust your judgment," he said, wondering if it would be a simple thing at all. He knew himself quite well at this point, and he knew he was giving her a difficult task. "In the process, perhaps we will find you a husband as well."

Marjorie shook her head. "I very much doubt you will have success where my mother has failed. Finding a husband has been her province for forty years, starting with her own hunt."

Forty years earlier

Dorothea Stockbridge knew when she looked in the mirror that she was no beauty. Her mother called her handsome, and she supposed she was that. She did have a rather mannish square jaw and her figure could be described as square as well. The only way she could show off her waist was to tie her corset excruciatingly tight, which she had her maid do on a regular basis. Still, for a girl lacking certain physical charms, she did all she could to look her best. She wore the latest styles, whether they flattered her or not, dressed in the finest materials, the most expensive lace. She adored hats and was rather proud to be a trendsetter in that department. The bonnet she wore now, for example, had an outlandishly large brim decorated with tiny florets, and she was constantly having to hold it to her head, for it was rather breezy. The large satin ribbon tied beneath her jaw fluttered against her cheek as she walked down Regent Street with her best friend, Mary Marshall, Lady Benningford. They were shopping, of course. But what Dorothea was truly doing was looking for Lord Smythe, a man she'd been impossibly smitten with for the past four years.

Dorothea was unmarried, of course, and at an age when most women had children and a home. At age twenty-eight, she was so long on the shelf she was considered dusty. But even at that age, she continued to have hope that someday she would marry, would have her own home, and perhaps children (though her mother hinted she was already far too old to begin down that road). And Lord Smythe, ever so polite, ever so attentive, was her last hope. He always asked for a dance, and the two of them had strolled together in more gardens than she could count. While he'd never expressed any feelings toward her other than friendship—they shared an interest in botany—Dorothea allowed herself to imagine that he did have them.

"He always goes to Briggs on Wednesdays at two o'clock because that's when the new shipment of books arrives." This wonderful tidbit had come from Mary. And so that's where the two of them were heading.

Dorothea knew Mary felt sorry for her, but she hid it well most of the time. She saw Mary's look of hesitation each time Dorothea would mention Lord Smythe. She knew she had no chance with him, not when there were so many other far younger and far prettier girls to pick from. But she couldn't stop her heart from wanting what it wanted. Four years of wanting. Four years of lying in bed at night, staring at the ceiling, and wondering if there were any hope at all that he was doing the same about her.

Regent Street was busy this time of day, with men going about their business and women out for a stroll and shopping. The wide street was quite filled with traffic, the sounds of carriage wheels loud against the pavement, and brick walkways that stretched between the side streets. They'd just crossed Hanover Street when Dorothea spotted a dear old friend holding the hand of a small child. As she watched, her friend bent down and tapped the child on her nose, then kissed the child's cheek before straightening and turning away from them.

"Oh, look, Mary, it's Lenore," she said, pulling Mary along so they could catch up.

Mary dug her heels in, resisting. "We can't, Dottie," Mary whispered harshly. "We can't acknowledge her. You know that. It would be embarrassing to her, not to mention what it would do to our reputations."

Dorothea stopped in her tracks. "Of course," she said with sad resignation. "I wonder how she is doing."

"How do you think? She married a *land steward*, for goodness' sake. I thought they were living in the country on his farm. I wonder what she is doing in London?"

Dorothea watched as her old friend got lost in the crowd of pedestrians and then disappeared from sight completely. "Perhaps she's reconciled with her family."

"I hardly think that," Mary said. "Besides, did you see what she was wearing? I'm surprised you recognized her at all, but it was Lenore."

"She has a daughter," Dorothea said, unable to keep the wistfulness from her voice.

"Yes, and no doubt they have a grand time churning butter together and milking cows."

Despite herself, Dorothea laughed. "I still can't believe she eloped with that man. I cannot imagine how her parents felt about it all. I remember, at the time I was so angry that she hadn't told me. Surely I could have convinced her to abort their plans. And her sisters are all unmarried, you know. Did she not think of how her actions would affect them?" Dorothea shook her head. "I think I'm still angry with her."

"It was most shocking at the time. The daughter of a duke running off to Gretna Green to marry a land steward. What could she have been thinking? And him. What a scoundrel to lure a young girl like that. He must have known they could not remain with the family. What did he think, that he would live with the family, eat meals with them?"

Dorothea remembered that behind the anger she'd felt that her friend hadn't confided in her, was the thought of how romantic it had been to run off with the man you loved. That Lenore was so very much in love she was willing to give up everything to be with him, land steward or no. Now, however, she realized how very foolish Lenore had been. Her parents had cut her off completely, as had her friends. Who were Lenore's friends now, other tenant farmers' wives? What on earth did they talk about?

"Here we are," Mary said, wrapping one arm around Dorothea's. "Shall we buy a book?" Mary gave Dorothea an impish smile.

They entered the bookstore and were immediately hit with the wonderful scent of beeswax and books. The clerk looked up as they entered and gave them a polite smile. Dorothea immediately headed to the section on botany toward the back of the store, and clutched Mary's arm tighter when she saw the familiar form of Lord Smythe. He was simply beautiful.

The sun streamed through a window high above him, hitting his golden yellow hair and creating a halo of light around his head. He looked up and saw the two coming toward him and gave Dorothea a smile. She very nearly swooned.

"Good afternoon, Lord Smythe," Mary said. Thank goodness, because Dorothea could not bring herself to utter a single word. Her stomach was aflutter and she could feel her face flushing bright red.

"Lady Benningford, Lady Dorothea." He nodded, looked down at the book he was holding, and then with slight hesitation, said, "The latest *Revue Horticulture* is available. Lovely pictures of roses in it."

"Oh?" She was breathless, could hardly move. But Mary gave her a subtle shove in his direction and she forced herself to walk toward him, her eyes on the journal. If she looked up at him, she was quite certain he would see the rapt adoration in her face.

"Here, you take this. There are other copies." He handed her the periodical and Dorothea took it as if she were taking a rare object.

"Thank you," she said, daring to look up at him. She smiled, hoping she looked at least a little pretty, and he smiled back.

"Will you be going to Ascot this year, my lord?" she asked, rather proud, under the circumstances, to have introduced a new subject.

He darted a look to Mary and back to her. "Of course. I have a horse racing this year. Emilius. Finest horse I've ever owned. Keep an eye out for him, will you?"

He gave her a wink and he might as well have given her his heart for the fluttering that occurred.

"I shall be rooting wholeheartedly for Emilius," Dorothea gushed.

"Good, then. Perhaps I'll see you there. If you will excuse me, ladies, I must be on my way. Good day."

Dorothea moved aside, letting him pass, clutching the periodical to her breast. When he'd gone, she turned to Mary and whispered, "Did you hear that? He'll look for me at Ascot."

Mary smiled. "He did not quite say that," she said gently.

Dorothea refused to have her mood dampened by the truth. "No matter. *I* will look for *him*."

Chapter 3

Hebert ball. Saturday.

Marjorie looked down at the cryptic note and smiled. How fun it had been to pull the brick out and find that small bit of paper there. "Hebert ball. Saturday," she said aloud, mimicking his baritone.

Pulling her pencil from her pocket, she wrote: *Yes. And I have a list.* She stuffed the note back in the hole and walked, smiling, through their garden and into the house. She did, indeed, have a list. At the top was Miss Susan Mitchell, daughter of Sir Robert Mitchell. Nineteen. Pretty. Wealthy enough to attract lower titles, but, as far as Marjorie knew, had no great aspirations. Then there was Penelope Richardson, daughter of the third son of the Baron of Werington. She'd gone through at least two unsuccessful seasons—she had a rather large nose that had a tendency to drip—but she was intelligent and pleasant enough. At the bottom was Lavinia Crawford, placed there only because Marjorie liked Mr. Norris far too much to subject him to such a ninny.

It was a good, solid list, but Marjorie frowned. Knowing men as she did, she feared the first time he laid eyes on Miss Crawford, he would be as smitten as every other man in London. She wasn't awful, but there was something about the girl that Marjorie just didn't like. Perhaps it was because the same men who used to hover over her were now hovering over Miss Crawford. Marjorie shook her head, not liking where her thoughts were going. If she were truthful, she couldn't imagine being married to any of the men who'd tried to court her or had even asked for her hand. So why was she jealous of a silly girl?

Because you were once that silly girl, that's why. Truth be told, she missed being the center of attention, having her dance card filled before the orchestra played a single note. She missed men good-naturedly fighting over who had the honor of bringing her in to dine. The entry hall filled with flowers. The morning post filled with entreaties to take her riding on Rotten Row.

Was she so shallow?

She let out a soft laugh as she made her way to the front of the house. Of course she was.

"Were you out in the garden at this time of night?"

Marjorie's hand flew to her chest. "Mother, you nearly frightened me to death. And yes, I was. It's a lovely evening."

"The night air isn't good for your complexion, my dear. I was just about to look for you so we can discuss the Heberts' ball. What were you thinking of wearing?"

"The new blue, I think. It's been so warm lately, I cannot imagine wearing anything other than silk."

Dorothea walked into the main sitting room and Marjorie followed. It struck Marjorie then, as it had many times in the past, how empty their house seemed. When her brother was home, as he no doubt was, he stayed in his rooms poring over books of history. Marjorie knew he was avoiding their mother, just as she knew her mother was just as glad to not have him underfoot. Once her mother had finally accepted that Marjorie was to remain unmarried, their outings would no doubt lessen in frequency. Was this to be their life? Sitting by a fire stitching or reading? It was unlikely her brother would marry (he'd shown little interest in the opposite sex after one unfortunate experience) or that her mother would remarry. The thought of spending her remaining years in an empty house was depressing. Perhaps she could travel as she'd always longed to do. Find a group of spinsters and tour Italy and France.

Perhaps, if she were successful in finding Mr. Norris a wife, she could become a professional matchmaker. She sighed aloud.

"What a mood you're in tonight," her mother said, looking at her sharply after she sighed.

"I'm just tired this evening." She forced a smile. "Do you think the blue will do?"

"Of course. It is one of your lovelier gowns. It quite flatters you. But . . ."

"But?" Marjorie prompted.

"Blue is Miss Crawford's signature color. If you wear it, everyone will believe you are trying to outshine her. Or worse, copy her."

"You cannot own a color, Mother. And that gown was very dear. What a waste if I'm never allowed to wear it. Am I not permitted to wear any of my blue gowns? I wore a blue day dress yesterday. People must have been shocked."

Dorothea gave her a chastising look, then shook her head. "Burgundy. You may wear the blue when we can be assured Miss Crawford will not be present. Even then, it is a risk."

Marjorie knew there was no changing her mother's mind, so she acquiesced. "As you wish."

"What I wish is for you to try a bit harder this season, Marjorie. It was all well and good to turn down everyone when you were the Incomparable of the season. But you are no longer that girl."

Her mother rarely spoke so harshly to her, and Marjorie was slightly taken aback. "I know that, Mother."

"Do you not want to marry?"

"I do. But we are running out of titles, are we not?" Marjorie asked, laughing. Her smile faded when she saw her mother's expression.

"I know why you have turned everyone down and I want it to stop. Immediately."

Marjorie felt her face flush and her stomach twist. "I don't know what you mean."

"Your brother. It always comes down to him. Lord Kingsley said this about him, Lord Whitsford said that about him. I don't care what they say, what they do, or even if they have him committed. The next man who proposes to you will be given a positive answer. Do you understand me?"

"Don't you mean the next title, Mother?"

Dorothea's eyes narrowed. "That's precisely what I mean." Her expression softened. "Darling, I know how difficult this has been for you, but it's time to stop. You'll be twenty-four in a few months. Do you realize what that means?"

"Don't say it, because it isn't true. Not yet at any rate."

To Marjorie's horror, her mother's eyes filled with tears. "If you have not found anyone this season, you will have been passed by."

Four men had proposed to her, including a baron (rejected out of hand) and two viscounts (onerous and old), so Marjorie hardly thought that qualified as being "passed by." She'd actually considered accepting a proposal from Lord Whitsford until she overheard him say, "She'll do as long as that idiot brother of hers isn't about."

Her brother would *always* be about, because without her he would be lost.

"I'll try very hard to find a husband, Mother. I promise."

Marjorie felt even more depressed by that promise than by the prospect of never marrying at all.

On the night of the Hebert ball, Marjorie arrived wearing her burgundy gown, and noticed immediately that Miss Crawford was indeed wearing blue. And then she noticed Mr. Norris, standing off to the side, staring at Miss Crawford. Drat. He would have to set his eyes on the one girl he probably couldn't get—not with her immense popularity. Half the young bucks were already in love with her. It was only a matter of time, if what Mr. Norris said was true, before he would fall for her. From what she'd learned, Ruthersford was already negotiating with her father.

"Blue," her mother said.

"Yes, I noticed. How on earth did you realize it's what she always wears, though?"

"It is what I do, darling. I notice things. For example, I notice that Lord Wentworth is here tonight. It's the first time he's been in public since his wife died last year."

"Which one is he again?"

Dorothea nodded slightly, indicating the right side of the room. "He's talking to Lady Hebert."

Marjorie scanned the right side of the room until she saw a tall, slim man with a pleasant face and slightly receding hairline speaking with their hostess. She had a vague recollection of meeting him, but that was the extent of her knowledge of the man.

"Rank?"

"Marquess. Wealthy. A lovely townhouse in Mayfair. Huge estate in Leeds. Five children." She frowned. Marjorie knew her mother was thinking that her daughter would not mother a future marquess. "Still, it's a fine title."

"What of the man?" Marjorie asked, pointedly.

Dorothea waved her hand as if the question were inconsequential. "I've never heard a word against him."

In other words, her mother knew about as much of him as Marjorie now knew. And five children! Just the thought made her slightly queasy. Oh, she had no doubt she could care for and love five of her own children, but could she come to love someone else's? And could they come to love her?

"I'm going to the refreshment table, Mother. Would you like anything?"

"Some punch would be nice. I think I'll give my regards to Lady Hebert."

Marjorie gave Lord Wentworth one more look before heading to the refreshment table on the opposite side of the large room. She was not one to believe in love at first sight, but she couldn't even imagine kissing the man, never mind marrying him. But if he were kind, if he would care for George, then perhaps she could marry him. Certainly a man with five children could not be too awful.

"You're looking lovely this evening."

Marjorie turned to see her cousin, Jeffrey. "Not in the card room yet?" she asked sweetly. She blamed Jeffrey for bringing George to the club where he'd lost all that money to Mr. Norris. If he hadn't, she would not be in her current predicament. She had little doubt the only reason Jeffrey had brought George with him was so he could use a bit of her brother's cash.

"Not yet," he answered agreeably. "Aunt, you look quite dashing this evening."

Dorothea beamed a smile and gave Jeffrey a small curtsy. "Why thank you, Jeffrey. Please be certain to ask Marjorie for a dance, will you? Her card's not yet full."

Marjorie shot her mother a look of disbelief. In the five years since she'd come out, she'd never missed a dance because a man hadn't asked her. If she did miss one, it had been her own choice.

"Of course," Jeffrey said with a small bow.

"While I appreciate the grand gesture, cousin, I doubt it will be necessary."

"Necessary?" he asked with mock confusion. "It would be a pleasure and nothing more." Even as he said those words, he glanced casually at Miss Crawford, who had a small flock of men around her. Marjorie felt the heat of anger and a bit of embarrassment touch her face. Had she become someone to be pitied?

"She reminds me a bit of you," Jeffrey said, then leaned toward her so Dorothea couldn't hear what he said. "Well, as you were five years ago. Like bees to honey until the next pretty flower comes along. And she is quite the pretty flower."

Marjorie lifted her chin and pretended his words had no effect. She'd never liked her cousin, and that dislike had only grown after his father's death. For with that death, Jeffrey came within one relative of obtaining the title he so obviously coveted. He'd never said anything overt; it was just a feeling Marjorie had when he and her brother were together. It wasn't *what* he said that was so grating, but rather *how* he said it—that derisive, condescending tone. And it was also the way he looked at George when he thought no one would notice, with a coldness and disgust that was palpable.

Marjorie had even mentioned it once to her mother, but Dorothea had dismissed the observation out of hand, making Marjorie feel as if she'd imagined everything. Her mother was fond of Jeffrey and would hear nothing against him.

The orchestra had not yet begun playing, and the ballroom was crowded with people milling about. The noise and the heavy perfume in the air were already giving Marjorie a slight headache. As she made her way to the punch bowl, she was stopped numerous times by acquaintances, mostly friends who were long married and looked upon her with either pity or curiosity. And, sometimes, a bit of envy.

"I thought this might be your destination."

Ah, Mr. Norris.

"Yes. And I see you've already found someone to catch your eye. Miss Lavinia Crawford."

"The blonde surrounded by drooling boys? No. I haven't the stomach to face that sort of competition."

They stood side-by-side, facing the wall. He gathered small sweets on a plate while she carefully ladled two glasses of punch. Anyone casually looking at them would not know they were conversing.

"You have a list?"

"I do. I'll put it in the wall this evening. I hadn't a chance to earlier. You'll be happy to know it's a rather long list."

She turned to spy her mother, who had her back to her, then faced Mr. Norris, who was looking down at her with a small smile on his nicely sculpted lips. My, he was a good-looking man, and she couldn't fathom why he'd been unsuccessful in his bride hunt, if looks were any consideration. His deep brown eyes swept her face, stopping briefly at her mouth, and Marjorie was shocked by what she saw. He had the look of a man who wanted to kiss a woman. She took a small step back, alarmed.

"What are you doing?"

"Admiring you. You're quite lovely this evening, Lady Marjorie. And your mouth is rather meant for kissing, is it not?"

She was stunned. "Are you drunk?"

"Sober as you are." He raised an eyebrow as if questioning her own sobriety.

"But you told me you weren't attracted to me." It was an accusation.

"I lied."

Marjorie tilted her head and gave him a look of mock anger. "This won't do, then. If you're attracted to me, then I might thwart your plans. You'll fall in love with me and that won't do at all."

"Just because I want to bury my face between your breasts and stay there for a fortnight doesn't mean I want to marry you." This was said dryly.

Marjorie opened her mouth, stunned. If any other man had said those same words to her, she would have slapped him across the face. But it wasn't what Charles Norris had said, it was how he'd said it, as if one couldn't take anything he uttered seriously. And yet, she knew he was probably speaking the truth. So, instead of slapping him as she should, she laughed.

"You are awful. No wonder you're not married."

"Good God, do you really think I'd say such a thing to a woman I was courting?" He looked truly outraged.

"But you said it to me."

He shook his head. "Entirely different. You are not a candidate to be my wife and we are not courting. We're more like . . . business partners."

She lifted her chin slightly. "Do you often look at your business partners as if you'd like to kiss them?"

Grinning, he turned back to the refreshment table, then let out a low, but audible and very foul, curse.

"Sir, I would recommend you curb your language if you think to attract one of these fine ladies," she said, looking at him with concern. She couldn't imagine the kind of pain that would cause such a man to seize up and curse aloud in a ballroom.

"I wouldn't use that sort of language in front of a woman I was courting," he said through gritted teeth.

That statement was beginning to get a bit tiresome. "I'm starting to feel affronted, you know. I am a lady. An *unmarried* lady." Marjorie knew she should be insulted. Couldn't fathom why she wasn't, but she thought she *ought* to be and should point this out. She found his casual disregard for her endearing, actually. How strange.

He gave her a curious look. "Do you want an apology?"

"I think I do."

"You're not certain?"

She bit her bottom lip and was slightly dismayed to see his gaze drift down to her mouth and linger. "Stop doing that. If I'm to help you, I cannot worry that you're going to pounce on me at any moment."

"But I want to pounce on you. I would very much like to ravish that lovely mouth of yours." His words said one thing, but his eyes quite another. He was simply playing with her, delighting in shocking her. She found herself laughing again.

"Mr. Norris, please do try to resist my charms and put all that energy to finding a woman who is actually interested."

His expression immediately changed, became more serious, as if she were a secretary reminding him of an important meeting.

"Very good. Who is on the top of your list and is she here this evening?"

Perhaps Charles had not completely shocked Lady Marjorie by his behavior, but he had certainly shocked himself. Never in his life had he spoken to a woman the way he'd spoken to her. It was the oddest thing, almost as if crossing her off his list of potential brides had freed him to act as he wished. Had he really told her he wanted to bury his face between her breasts? And had she truly *laughed*?

It was a bit of a problem that he was so physically attracted to her. When he'd first developed his plan, he'd thought she was perfect because he couldn't recall being attracted to her. She was pretty, yes, and her mother was one of the most frightening people in the *ton*, but he supposed he'd been so enraptured with Miss Wright, he hadn't really given Lady Marjorie a serious look. And he knew the futility of courting her, so why look at her at all?

Now, though, she was standing next to him in a gown cut to make a man think things he oughtn't—never mind say them aloud. If anything, he was glad she was aware of his attraction. Hiding such a thing was difficult, and now that they'd had a good laugh about it, they could carry on. Perhaps he could even get that kiss one day. Just the thought of her soft lips molding to his sent a sharp surge of desire coursing through him.

"The lady on the top of my list is Miss Susan Mitchell."

"I'm not familiar with the name." Actually, given that he'd been out of the country for ten years, he would probably be unfamiliar with most names on her list.

"Her father is Sir Robert Mitchell. They are quite wealthy and he is related in some way to the Duke of York."

Charles scanned the room. "Where is she?"

"The girl in pale yellow. Brown hair. She's standing next to an older lady in lavender, her grandmother I think. By the orchestra."

There she was, the first possible Mrs. Charles Norris. She was a tiny girl—and she *was* only a girl. A flat-chested, skinny girl. She could be fifteen. "How *old* is she?" he asked.

"Nineteen. She is a bit petite, but this is her second season."

"She won't do. Not at all."

"Too young?"

"Too everything. Who's next?"

Marjorie looked about the room and suddenly jerked. "It's Katherine." Across the ballroom Charles saw Katherine Wright, the American girl he'd been a bit smitten with, but who was now married to his friend, Graham Spencer, Lord Avonleigh.

"I really have no interest in courting a married woman," he said, teasing Marjorie. But she was so distracted by seeing her friend, she apparently didn't immediately understand his quip, but then looked up and gave him a brilliant smile. Clever girl.

And then Katherine spied them and began walking their way. He'd been more than smitten with Katherine before realizing—yet again—that she was in love with one of his friends. Looking at her now, he felt nothing but a bit of embarrassment that he'd made such a cake of himself. Thank goodness most of his friends were married, or he'd no doubt fall in love with their intendeds.

Charles looked for Marjorie's mother, saw her frowning their way, and decided to remove himself from Lady Marjorie's company. My God, her mother would have made a fine general.

"I'll let you two ladies become reacquainted," he said, and left Marjorie before she could protest, but he did think he heard her say beneath her breath, "Oh, bollocks." God, she made him smile.

Marjorie watched Katherine and her new husband, the Marquess of Avonleigh, formerly known as the Miserable Marquess, walk toward her. The pair looked decidedly happy and were fairly glowing with good cheer. Perhaps Katherine had forgiven her for nearly driving the pair apart.

"Hello, Lady Marjorie," Katherine said pleasantly, but Marjorie's stomach twisted. Katherine had never called her "lady" anything.

"Please, may we talk privately?" Marjorie asked, feeling very nearly on the verge of tears. Although their acquaintance had been brief last year during the little season, they'd become fast friends—until Marjorie had betrayed their friendship in an ill-conceived plan to "save" Lord Avonleigh from Katherine. Marjorie's mother had convinced her that Katherine had been scheming to trap Lord Avonleigh into marriage. Dorothea had forced Marjorie to tell Lord Avonleigh her suspicions. And though, to be perfectly honest, it had appeared that Katherine was indeed trying to trap Lord Avonleigh, it turned out Marjorie had been terribly wrong.

"Go on, Katherine," Graham said. "I'll keep Norris occupied while you two talk."

Marjorie led Katherine from the crowded room and into a small hall. When the two women were alone, Marjorie spun around and said, "I cannot say how sorry I am for what I did. I am so glad to see that you are happy together. It was my mother. I mentioned, in passing, what you'd said to me after you'd been caught with Lord Avonleigh. I only spoke because she'd seemed so enthusiastic about a match between the two of you. I could not have predicted her reaction. She was incensed and demanded that I tell Lord Avonleigh what you'd said to me."

"It's all right. Everything is fine now and we're very happy."

"You didn't plan it, did you?" Marjorie said, remembering how Katherine and Lord Avonleigh had been caught quite publicly in a compromising position.

Katherine shook her head. "No. I didn't."

"I *knew* you didn't. But . . ."

"I understand. Graham and I never were very discreet. It was bound to happen. And now we're both very glad it did."

"Oh, that's wonderful," Marjorie said. "I was going to write, but I didn't know quite what to say."

"Please, you are forgiven. You only did what you thought was right. And what of you? Are you here with Mr. Norris?"

Marjorie looked slightly taken aback. "No," she said quickly. Then, "Yes. No. Well, yes."

Katherine laughed. "Which is it?"

"Yes. But we're not courting. It's a long and very ridiculous story. I find him extremely onerous, as a matter of fact."

"He *is* handsome. And rich."

"No title," Marjorie pointed out with a laugh. "And besides, he's no doubt already half in love with someone else."

"There is always Lord Mandeville," Katherine said, referring to an ancient widower.

Marjorie laughed. "I'm so glad you're not angry."

"I *was* angry," Katherine said. "But that lasted only until Graham came to his senses."

The two women returned, arm in arm, to the ballroom. Katherine immediately spotted Graham and led Marjorie to her husband, who was still talking with Mr. Norris. It appeared as though Mr. Norris had said something to make Lord Avonleigh angry.

When the two women reached the men, Mr. Norris said, "Lady Avonleigh, did you know that your husband once made a mockery of me for having the audacity to fall in love?"

"It does sound like something he would do."

"What in heaven's name did you do to him, my lady?" Mr. Norris asked.

Katherine looked up at Graham, her eyes shining. "I made him smile."

"If that is all that's necessary, I should have been long married by now," Marjorie said. Katherine did look so happy, so much in love, and Marjorie couldn't stop the small twinge of envy she felt. Would she ever love anyone like that? Would a man ever look down at her the way Lord Avonleigh was looking at his bride?

Marjorie saw her mother frowning at her, but Marjorie knew her mother approved of Lord and Lady Avonleigh, in spite of their inauspicious courtship. She was no doubt tolerating the presence of Mr. Norris because he was a friend of Lord Avonleigh.

When the first waltz began, Lord Avonleigh asked his wife to dance, and the two drifted off together, looking dreamily into each other's eyes.

"He didn't even want to get married," Charles said, sounding a bit mulish. "And there he is, looking like a besotted fool, dancing with his lovely wife. Doesn't he know it's not the done thing?"

Marjorie laughed. "Don't worry. We'll have you looking at your wife like that before the season is through. Right now, though, my mother is staring daggers at me for being so brash as to talk with a man without a 'lord' in front of his name. Off I go. I'll look for the next note. What fun."

No doubt Charles wouldn't get a chance to speak with Lady Marjorie again, a thought that made him slightly depressed. He scanned the room, his gaze stopping at every young thing in a skirt. God, they all looked the same. Hair carefully curled, white or pale-colored gowns, hovering by mothers and looking hopefully about the room for a potential suitor.

Miss Lavinia Crawford was, by far, the most beautiful girl of the bunch. Though he'd at first crossed her off his list, he gave her a second, long look. At least she didn't look like a girl. She filled out her gown in a lovely way that stirred his imagination. She might have all those boys hovering around her, but he wasn't a boy and perhaps that would make all the difference.

And so, Charles convinced himself that he could win Miss Crawford's hand. He smiled at the way she tilted her lovely head. Such a charmer, she was. She had her bevy of boys acting like puppies begging for a treat. And she was a treat. Just lovely. The sort of woman he'd imagined himself with. They'd have blonde-haired children with her lovely blue eyes. He imagined they must be blue to match that white-blonde hair of hers. And, good Lord, she had the smallest and most intriguing little mole right above her lip, like the beauties of the last century who'd put false ones on their faces. Like Marie Antoinette.

Decision made, he began moving toward her, feeling himself grow more and more entranced by her with every step he took. She laughed, and it was, if not delightful, the sort of laugh that made one want to join in.

"Oh no, you don't." The words issued from a female to his left. Lady Marjorie.

"What am I doing?" His eyes were still on the lovely Miss Crawford.

"From that ridiculous look on your face, you are falling in love with Miss Crawford and Ruthersford is already in negotiations with her father. He's a viscount." She added this last with emphasis.

"I am not falling in love. Do you think me that great a fool? I haven't even spoken to her yet." He finally looked down to see Lady Marjorie looking at him the same way his old governess had looked when she was very displeased.

"You have engaged me in a mission to stop you from attaching yourself to the wrong woman. Miss Crawford is the wrong woman."

As if drawn like a flower to the sun, he turned his head to again drink in the sight of Miss Crawford. "We shall see," he said, and moved past Lady Marjorie with determination. He thought he heard her make some sort of sound behind him, but he knew she wouldn't give chase.

"I quit."

Now that did stop him. Cold. He turned slowly, trying to hide his irritation. "There is the small matter of a debt."

He watched as she set her jaw. Then she took a few steps closer, looking about to make certain no one was curiously watching them. "How can I hold up my end of our evil bargain if you will not hold up yours?" she asked, her voice just above a whisper. "You gave me very specific instructions. Miss Crawford is practically engaged. And her mother—"

"Wants a bloody title. Yes. Don't they all," Charles completed for her. He let out a harsh breath, then turned, steeling himself instantly against the slicing pain in his leg that always seemed to catch him unawares. Even after all this time. "I'll have one dance from her," he said, wondering if he could even manage a dance with his leg beginning to act up.

"I suppose one dance won't cause too much harm," Lady Marjorie said. He hated the resignation he heard in her voice, as if he were such a dolt that he could fall in love after a single dance.

Marjorie watched him walk toward the beautiful Miss Crawford with a sense of dread. She liked Mr. Norris and had no wish to see him make a fool of himself. She removed herself to the opposite side of the room, where she could watch his ruin from afar.

He was taller than the other swains hovering about Miss Crawford. And his hair, that glorious red-blond-golden hair, made him stand out even more. The moment he walked up to the group, they parted, welcoming him. Marjorie watched as, curiously, one by one, the other men departed, until it was just Mr. Norris standing with Miss Crawford, until he bowed over her hand, obviously requesting a dance. It was impossible that the girl still had room on her dance card, but she nodded, pulling out her little pencil and writing in his name before shyly looking up at him.

"He's Charles Norris." Marjorie's ears perked up at the mention of his name, said with breathy awe. To her right was a small group of young debutantes, tittering and giggling, and at the moment gazing with rapt longing at Mr. Charles Norris. Oh, goodness. Perhaps finding him a bride would be easier than she'd thought.

"My father says he's a war hero. He has the most romantic limp. Have you noticed?"

"And he's so tall."

"Why does Miss Crawford get all the attention?" This from a girl with plain, mousy brown hair. Marjorie stifled a smile. What a stir the two of them were making. They were a striking couple, though she didn't know how he could stand to listen to Miss Crawford's squeaky little voice.

"If you ask me, he's far too old. And no title, you know."

"He doesn't look old to me. And he is the son of a viscount. You can't discount that, you know."

How did they all know so much about him? And that's when Marjorie realized something she should have noted before. Charles Norris was the talk of the *ton*: the mysterious war hero who'd returned to England after a ten-year absence. They were all creating a romantic lead in their little play of love and marriage. How fortunate. Instead of him having to pursue the lovely ladies of the *ton*, they would be pursuing him. He'd find a bride in no time and her brother's debt would be forgiven. And maybe the rumors about Ruthersford weren't true. Maybe Miss Crawford could be won by Mr. Norris.

Marjorie looked about the room until she came across the frowning visage of Lady Hawthorne, Miss Crawford's mother. The baroness was staring at her daughter, who was gazing up in rapture into the face of a certain Mr. Charles Norris. Oh, my, thought Marjorie, Lady Hawthorne does not look very pleased with this development. No doubt she'd been basking in the glow of her daughter's success—until now. Marjorie tried to recall who had been hovering about Miss Crawford before Mr. Norris had ploughed into the group. She mentally ticked each one off, realizing quite quickly that nearly everyone had either been titled or was the heir to a title. How disappointed Lady Hawthorne must be.

Marjorie made her way over to the frowning older woman and walked by casually, hoping Lady Hawthorne would make eye contact with her long enough to force a greeting—and perhaps some conversation. Lady Hawthorne was a bit thick about the middle, but it was obvious where her daughter got her great beauty. Marjorie promenaded about the ballroom, pretending to be interested in watching the couples dance a reel, and walked directly to where the lady still stared at her daughter. Marjorie was about to despair that the woman would never tear her gaze away from the pair when she turned and saw Marjorie, and nodded.

"Good evening, Lady Hawthorne," Marjorie said with a bit more enthusiasm than was called for, given that she didn't know the woman well.

The lady nodded pleasantly. "Good evening." Marjorie suspected the woman had forgotten her name.

"My mother, Lady Summerfield, was just noting how lovely your daughter looks this evening. What a success she is this season."

Lady Hawthorne smiled. "Thank you. She is a lovely girl." The older woman turned, giving Marjorie an assessing look as if recalling who she was.

"She is speaking with Mr. Norris. A fine man," Marjorie said, praying she didn't sound rehearsed. But she needed to find out if Miss Crawford was already engaged—or nearly so.

"I've yet to meet the man," Lady Hawthorne said sourly. "Do you know him?"

"Not well. Only that he is the second son of Viscount Hartley and that he is a war hero. I've heard nothing that should cause a mother concern."

"And what would you know of a mother's concern?" Lady Hawthorne asked, turning her head slowly and making Marjorie's face redden.

"Only that I have a mother and I know what concerns her."

Lady Hawthorne nodded slowly. "I have the same concerns, I believe." Her eyes narrowed as she watched her daughter laugh.

"Given your daughter's great popularity, I am certain she will be settled soon. Everyone thinks so."

"And they would be correct."

Marjorie bit her lip, wondering if she could be so bold to ask about Viscount Ruthersford, who in truth, was on her own mother's list of possibilities. Marjorie didn't like the man; she found him cold, but that didn't mean he wouldn't make a fine husband for someone. She rather liked the idea of having him crossed officially off her mother's list of possible suitors. Though the list was getting rather sparse these days.

"Mother was thinking of inviting Viscount Ruthersford to our ball in two weeks."

Lady Hawthorne turned sharply to stare at her. Then she smiled, like a chess player acknowledging a crafty move. "Of course, your mother may invite whomever she wishes to her ball. That is the twenty-third of May, is it not?"

"Yes."

"I've just sent our regrets today, I'm afraid. We've other plans. And I do hope you are not too disappointed to learn Ruthersford will also, no doubt, be sending his regrets."

A surge of triumph and something that oddly felt like relief swept through Marjorie. "I'm so pleased for you all," Marjorie said.

And, because nothing was official, Lady Hawthorne gave her a curious look, as if she hadn't the vaguest idea what Marjorie was talking about. "I'll be more pleased after tomorrow," Lady Hawthorne said after a long silence. "If you'll excuse me, I do need to speak with my daughter. Good evening."

Engaged! The chit was engaged. Just when he thought he might have found a charming—well, charming looking—potential bride and the very next day she announced her engagement. What rotten luck.

Charles, flush from what he'd thought was his success and rather carnal images of Miss Crawford lying beneath him, stared at the *Times* in utter dismay two days after the Hebert ball. He'd sent her a sinfully expensive bouquet of flowers and received a pretty little note of thanks that same afternoon. And then, not a day after, he'd seen the notice. Viscount Ruthersford, the cold fish, had managed to snare her.

Charles led his horse down the darkened lane that ran behind the Summerfield London townhouse, a note tucked in his front breast pocket. The invitations he'd been receiving should have been heartening for a man bent on finding a bride. But those stacks and stacks of cards only depressed him. He wanted a wife, but this chase, this dance one had to do to get a wife, was downright wearying. Perhaps that's why he'd been such a failure at finding a bride. He wanted it to be easy. To meet a girl, point a finger and say, "You're the one." And she would, of course, swoon as she said, "Yes, I'll marry you."

Wasn't that the way it'd been done in years past? Arranged marriages were so much more practical.

It was a warm evening, and the lane was filled with the fecund smell of spring, rich, moist and so very English. It was good to be home, to be able to breathe in without getting a lungful of dust. Even the rather ripe smell of the mews made him smile because it was all so wonderfully familiar.

He stopped by the gate behind the Summerfield townhouse, his hand immediately going to the brick, sticking out just a bit, hinting of its compartment. He pulled it out and felt inside, smiling when his hand touched a small bit of folded paper. His note said only: *Covent Garden Opera. Tuesday.* He'd wanted to write more. To acknowledge that she'd been right about Miss Crawford, perhaps. But he'd never been one for notes and such, and so left it simple.

He hoped she could attend Covent Garden. The evening was not a full performance, but a reception for patrons of the opera house who would be granted a private performance by the great Adelina Patti. He was going in his brother's stead, for the future Viscount Hartley was staying in his family's country estate in Northumberland. God knew he envied his brother. Not for his title, but for his happiness with his family. It seemed all his life people had been waiting for his brother, who'd always been sickly, to die. Instead, as he entered adulthood, he seemed to thrive and grow stronger, leaving behind whatever childhood ailment had plagued him. Robert had always been strong in spirit, if not in body, and Charles was nothing but happy for him. But visiting Robert and his wife was a bit like torture. Did they have to seem so utterly content? So completely happy with their three rough-and-tumble boys? It seemed to Charles that life was passing him by and one day he'd wake up and be one of those old bachelors whom people pitied—or avoided.

The note in his hand could be his salvation, the promised list of possible brides.

Even though it was too dark to read, he could immediately see she'd written quite a bit more than he had. Apparently, she was one for notes and such. Smiling slightly, he pressed the paper to his nose and breathed in, smelling nothing more than paper and ink. Then, feeling foolish, he tucked the paper in his pocket, the same one that had held his own note just moments before, and replaced the brick.

> *I did warn you about Miss Crawford and I do hope your heart, given it is so vulnerable to a pretty girl with blond hair, was not too engaged. As she is now. Engaged, that is. I've come up with a list of women I believe would be potential candidates, but after going through it I am not entirely pleased with it. You did indicate that you didn't want a girl right out of school and it seems as if several on my list are so terribly young. Would you consider instead a young widow? Or are you bent on someone young and innocent? Or simply someone who likes cricket as much as you do?*
>
> *As you can see, I am a bit at wits' end as to what you are looking for in a bride. I would ask that you create a list of characteristics that please you and, based upon that list, I shall create one of my own.*

Why must this be so complicated? It needn't be, he supposed, if he were simply looking for someone to give him heirs. But an heir didn't matter, not to someone fifth in line to the title. He wanted what his parents had, what his brother had. He certainly did not want what his sister had, a passionless life of monotony. Charles frowned. Poor Laura, she'd been so in love with her foolish husband when she was nineteen. At twenty-nine, she was childless and imprisoned with a man who continued to dote upon his horrid mother more than he'd ever doted upon Laura.

Flinging Marjorie's letter aside, he sat down at his desk, turned up his lamp, and set about creating his list of attributes.

> *Pretty.*
> *Intelligent.*

He stopped, feeling more depressed than he had in some time. Good God, he just wanted to not be so damned lonely all the time. To sit at breakfast with a woman who smiled at him. To turn to her in bed and draw her close and bury his nose against her sweet-smelling hair. That's what he wanted. He supposed one word summed it up. Love. He wanted to love someone who loved him.

Charles stared at his woefully inadequate list for a moment before he forged ahead.

> *Honest.*
> *Not a child.*
> *Must like children.*
> *Must be caring.*
> *Must like cricket.*

He smiled after that one and could picture Marjorie doing the same.

> *Must like the country as much as London.*

It wouldn't do to have a frivolous wife bent on spending all his money on gowns and such.

And then, the most important thing:

> *Must not want a title.*

There. That ought to do well enough.

Chapter 4

Forty years earlier

"I saw Lord Smythe earlier today," Dorothea said, then daintily took a bite of scone. Her mother insisted, despite Dorothea's completely undainty form, that she act dainty and feminine at all times.

"Oh?" Dorothea's mother gave her a sharp look, then pressed her lips together. "I do believe it is time you gave up on that front, my dear. I hear he has begun courting Lord Orford's daughter, Matilda."

Lady Matilda was a simpleton whose only concern was making certain that every curl was in place. While Dorothea was just as meticulous in her appearance as Matilda, it was not all she thought about. She was quite certain the girl's head was vacant of any thought other than her lovely appearance.

"I simply mentioned seeing him," Dorothea said, looking down at her plate.

"Very well." Her mother placed her fork aside, an indication that she had something of import to say. "Your Aunt Frances is getting on in years. The last time she was here, we talked about perhaps having you live with her. Keep her company. She's so isolated out there in Ipswich."

Dread fell heavy and hard on Dorothea's stomach. Going to live with a widowed aunt was tantamount to completely giving up on any hope of securing a husband.

"When you were thinking?"

"I thought you could leave the beginning of next week." Her mother indicated a letter by her plate. "She's quite lonely and is very much looking forward to seeing you."

"But Ascot's only two weeks away. I did so want to attend this year. And it's the middle of the season. I cannot possibly go now, Mother."

Her mother looked away, giving her head a subtle shake. "I do not mean to be cruel, Dorothea, but I believe that particular ship has sailed. You are twenty-eight years old, my dear. It is time you come to accept that you will never marry. There is nothing at all wrong with spinsterhood. Why, some of my dearest and happiest friends never married. You haven't had a single prospect in ten years. To continue as you have been is to deny your circumstances."

Dorothea swallowed heavily. It was true. No man had ever courted her, even though she had a sizeable dowry. It was not so unusual to be passed by, but Dorothea had never truly thought it would happen to her. "Lord Smythe—"

"For goodness' sake, Dorothea, Lord Smythe has no more interest in marrying you than he would one of his hunting dogs."

Tears flooded Dorothea's eyes, and her throat hurt so much it felt as if someone were squeezing it. "That was cruel, Mother."

Her mother's eyes softened. "No, my dear, it's the truth. And it's high time you understood that. You are a good girl, kind and gener-ous. But not every kind and generous girl finds a husband." She picked up her fork. "You should probably begin packing tomorrow."

"How long will I be gone?" Dorothea asked, her voice small. She cleared her throat. "I need to know how long I'll be gone so I may pack properly."

"I'm sorry, I thought you understood. You'll be living with your aunt. Indefinitely." Her mother laughed at Dorothea's expression. "My dear, she's seventy-five. It won't be forever."

But it would be forever. If she were gone for years, Lord Smythe would surely forget about her. She might not get back to London at all and by the time she was back, she'd be—oh, God—in her thirties. Dorothea stared at her plate, her food now untouched. "May I at least stay until after Ascot? I promised Mary I'd attend with her."

"Until past June the fourteenth?" Her mother let out a heavy sigh. "Your aunt will be disappointed, but I suppose so."

Some of the sadness left Dorothea. She still had one more chance to see if Lord Smythe loved her even a little.

Chapter 5

"The opera? I thought you didn't care for the opera." Dorothea paused in the act of spooning an oversalted consommé into her frowning mouth.

Marjorie had expected that reaction to her request that they attend the special performance at Covent Garden, and was ready with the only response she knew would sway her mother.

"It's a special evening, Mother, with a light supper before the performance. You know that only draws the highest levels of the *ton*. And I hear Lord Wentworth will be there. I think you were right. I think he may be ready to remarry."

Dorothea gave her daughter a level look, almost as if she were trying to read the sincerity of her daughter's request, and Marjorie used all her learned poise not to squirm. "And I suppose there will be others," her mother said, finally, and then beamed a smile. "I'm glad to see a bit more enthusiasm, my dear. I had all but given up hope that you even cared to find a husband. But unfortunately, I cannot attend. Lady Benningford has invited me to a reading and as I have already accepted, I cannot change my plans."

"Oh," Marjorie said, feeling a deep stab of disappointment. She'd been so looking forward to discussing Mr. Norris's list with him and matching it up with the women on her list.

"So disappointed," her mother said, looking at her thoughtfully.

"Can it be that you actually have developed a tendre for Lord Wentworth?"

Marjorie gave her mother a wan smile. "It's not just that, Mother. I suppose I was looking forward to attending an amusement that Miss Crawford will not be attending. I do so want to wear blue. It suits me best."

Her mother let out a laugh. "That it does, my dear. All right, then, let me see if your aunt can attend with you."

"Aunt Gertrude?" she asked hopefully. Gertrude was a lovely old lady and the worst possible chaperone. Once her aunt found old friends to gossip with, Marjorie could disappear for hours at a time without being questioned.

"Of course, Aunt Gertrude. Do you think I would trust you with any of your father's sisters? Doddering old maids, the lot of them."

Marjorie rushed to her mother's side and gave her a kiss on the cheek. "Thank you, Mother, I adore Aunt Gertrude. We shall have a wonderful time. And I know she loves the opera—even if I do not. But this is not an opera, it's a solo performance by Adelina Patti."

"Yes, I know. She is exquisite. But I saw her just last year. I'm not too heartbroken. And you have never heard her sing, have you?"

"No, and I am looking forward to it."

"I cannot wait to hear about your evening. I do hope you will sit next to someone worth sitting next to during dinner."

"My mother would kill me if she saw me right now," Marjorie said with a laugh. She sat between two ineligible men—Charles Norris and Lord Ruthersford, who seemed not to have warmed a single degree since his engagement to Lavinia Crawford. The former smiled down at his plate, the latter ignored her completely. She almost felt sorry for Miss Crawford now that she was no longer on the marriage mart and would have to spend the rest of her life with Ruthersford.

"You seem to have a streak of deviltry in you, my lady."

"Oh, much more than a streak, I can assure you. Alas, there have been woefully few times I have been able to express it." She leaned a bit so that she could see her aunt and waggled her fingers. Her aunt smiled back at her and immediately turned away to speak to her dinner companion, an old friend of her late husband. This evening, the building's narrow lobby had been turned into a dining room of sorts, with three long tables set up to accommodate the elite crowd. Aunt Gertrude had warned her not to expect much from the meal, as it was being prepared in a restaurant next door and brought over by an army of servants. Apparently, the famous soprano had requested "the least odiferous items" be prepared so that her olfactory sense would not suffer.

"I have the list," she said in a whisper. "I'm afraid, after seeing your requirements, it's rather short."

"I didn't know I was being so particular," he said.

"I assume you are looking for someone a bit older, and being a man, you probably would like her to be somewhat attractive. Here." She reached beneath the wide lace ribbon at her waist and pulled out a small bit of paper. She laid her hand, palm up, upon her lap and indicated with a small nod that he should take it.

She should have known better. Mr. Norris looked from her face, to her lap, where she held the paper, and back to her face, raising an eyebrow in such a suggestive way that she felt an awful heat envelop her. Awful, because she knew what that heat meant and she had absolutely no intention of ever feeling *that* sort of heat when she was with Mr. Norris.

"You are insufferable."

"I am a man. A man who has just been invited to lay his hand upon a lady's lap."

"I did no such thing," she said, trying to sound and appear angry but failing miserably. She made a fist, crumpling the bit of paper, and placed it unceremoniously on the table next to his dinner plate. But before she could snatch her hand away, he laid his palm upon hers, warm and large, for just a small moment before releasing her.

Oh, goodness. What had just happened? A surge of something electric made her let out the tiniest gasp and her face flushed red. It was instantaneous. She prayed he interpreted that gasp and flush as anger, but was sorely disappointed when she looked at him through her lashes and saw the most irritatingly smug expression on his lovely mouth. *Lovely mouth?*

"I beg you to stop, Mr. Norris."

He raised his brows innocently. "Stop what, Lady Marjorie?"

"Taunting me," she said with a bit of exasperation after briefly searching for the correct word. "This is not a game to me." She did *try* to sound angry, but, blast the man, his smile only broadened.

"You are enjoying yourself immensely."

Marjorie pressed her mouth together, desperately trying not to smile. "Perhaps," she relented.

"There is no 'perhaps' about it. And, my darling girl, I find I am enjoying myself immensely as well. Who knew finding a bride would be so much fun?"

Oh, yes. The bride. Marjorie felt herself deflate just a tad at the reminder of why they were sitting together.

He brazenly opened up her note at the dinner table and scanned the list.

"Are any of these ladies here this evening?" he asked after a moment.

"Two. Miss Elizabeth Vincent and Miss Petunia Peterson."

"I can't marry someone named Petunia."

"She's very nice."

"I don't like petunias."

Marjorie looked at him in disbelief. "Who wouldn't like petunias? They are a lovely flower. Very colorful. And very much like their namesake. She's the girl sitting next to Admiral Clarkson."

Marjorie watched with some consternation how his expression changed when he saw Petunia. She *was* a lovely girl, with a country-fresh look to her. Her dark blond hair gleamed in the gaslight, and her eyes were an unusual shade of green. She was *so* lovely, in fact, Marjorie wondered why, at twenty, she was still unmarried. She came from a good family, had a significant dowry, and Marjorie had never heard any scandal connected to her. These were all the reasons she'd added Miss Peterson to her list. But now that she thought of it, there had to be *something* wrong with her. Something niggled at the back of her mind. Perhaps she was a dimwit?

"I suppose," Charles said slowly, "that I could get used to the name. I could give her a nickname. Pet or Tuni or some such thing."

"You cannot call your wife 'Pet.' It's demeaning."

His gaze was still on Petunia when he said, "Then Nia. One of her syllables can certainly be used as a name." He sounded slightly irritated.

"Nia isn't too awful," Marjorie said, wondering suddenly why she'd included the girl on her list and refusing to wonder why she suddenly *didn't* want the girl on her list.

"And who else is here from your list?"

"Miss Vincent. She is sitting at the far table, so I'm afraid you won't be able to get a very good look at her."

Charles strained his head a bit to spy the far table. "What color hair does she have?"

"Reddish."

"No. I will not marry a red-headed girl."

"But you're a bit red-headed," Marjorie said.

"I am not. But I was as a lad, and I can tell you that I suffered for it. And with a red-headed wife, I'd most assuredly have red-headed children, and I'll not have anyone call my son or daughter Ginger." He let out a gusting sigh. "So I suppose tonight I should concentrate on Miss Peterson."

And that's what he did, with a gusto that Marjorie found a bit amusing and Miss Peterson seemed to find a bit frightening. The group had perhaps an hour before the concert began, during which many of the men went outside to smoke a cigar and sneak a sip or two from their flasks. Miss Adelina Patti did not allow smoking in the building when she was performing.

Charles did give the men who were outside enjoying their cigars a look of longing, but then asked Marjorie for an introduction.

"I have to stand by my aunt for now. Mother has too many friends here and it wouldn't do for one of them to mention I'd been at your side all evening. My aunt and I will make our way over to Miss Peterson, and then you can join us and I can make introductions."

He nodded and moved off without a word, leaving Marjorie to find her aunt. She found Gertrude sitting in a corner with two of her dearest and oldest friends, and Marjorie felt a twinge of guilt that she would have to drag her aunt away.

After greeting the older women, Marjorie said, "I'm sorry, Aunt, but Mother insists that I mingle at these events, as tedious as it is. Would you mind walking about with me? Then I will safely return you to your friends."

"My goodness, there's no need to apologize to me! I raised three daughters, you know. Of course you know. They're your cousins!" She let out a laugh as she stood up.

Marjorie was well aware of her cousins and of their marriages to well-placed men—all titled and all rather nice. Her mother would never admit it aloud, but Marjorie knew it bothered her mightily that her sister had managed to get *three* daughters married and she'd not succeeded in getting even one down the aisle.

Her aunt scanned the room, no doubt homing in on all the eligible men. "Pity," she said softly.

"What's a pity, Aunt?"

"Oh, nothing." But her aunt's eyes were trained on someone across the room. Marjorie followed her eyes and felt her face flush. He did look rather magnificent standing in that group of older men. It was almost as if he were thrumming with vitality while the other men were mere husks of humanity. Even from across the room, she could hear his laugh, booming and unself-conscious. "Are you certain your mother won't even consider a man without a title? There's that very nice Charles Norris. He *is* the son of a viscount, you know. Very well-heeled family. His mother is lovely. Perhaps your mother would consider—"

"No, Aunt. She won't."

"Lord Ruthersford . . ."

"Is engaged." Marjorie walked sedately toward where Miss Peterson stood with her mother and father.

"Yes, yes. I thought I remembered reading something about that. Pity you were seated between two ineligible men."

"It sometimes happens," Marjorie said happily. "It's not often I get the chance to relax and enjoy a meal rather than put myself on display."

Her aunt chuckled. "Ah, I remember those days. It can be wearying, dear, I know."

The two chatted amiably, but Marjorie was always aware of Miss Peterson—and Mr. Norris. He had the subtlety of a cannon, and she could feel him watching her progress toward his possible future wife. As Marjorie walked by Miss Peterson, she pretended to be bumped and fell lightly against the younger woman.

"Oh, I do apologize," she exclaimed. Then she put on a brilliant smile. "Miss Peterson, how are you? And Mr. and Mrs. Peterson. I haven't seen you all since . . ." She pretended to search her memory. ". . . the Halford ball last season. You remember my aunt, Lady Southbridge."

"The Halford . . ." Mrs. Peterson said, her face turning an alarming shade of red. Mr. Peterson cleared his throat loudly and tugged at his collar. "Of course," Mrs. Peterson said, darting a look at her husband. "We've been . . . traveling abroad."

"In Italy," Petunia added cheerfully if a bit overbrightly. "And other places. We had a wonderful time, didn't we?" She turned to her parents, who seemed mortified, but by what, Marjorie couldn't begin to guess.

"It is good to see you, Susan," her aunt said warmly, grabbing Mrs. Peterson's hand and giving it a squeeze.

Mrs. Peterson gave a tremulous smile, seemingly grateful for the kind words. And leaving Marjorie completely confused. She racked her brain for any tidbit of information she might have heard about the Petersons. Had someone died? Had they lost their fortune? *Something* had happened since the Halford ball, that much was certain.

"Did you enjoy Italy?" Marjorie asked, not knowing what else to say.

"It was . . ." Petunia looked at her mother as if seeking help for the right word to describe Italy. ". . . lovely. Yes, lovely." Petunia had said the word lovely, but she might as well have said "dreadful" if Marjorie correctly read her look of utter discomfort. And that's when Mr. Norris walked up to the group, looking like an eager puppy.

"Mr. Norris," Marjorie said, pretending surprise. "This is my aunt, Lady Southbridge. Mr. and Mrs. Peterson and their daughter, Miss Petunia Peterson."

Charles bowed to the ladies and shook Mr. Peterson's hand.

"We were just discussing the Petersons' recent trip abroad," Marjorie said, gamely forging ahead with the plan. "You have something in common with Mr. Norris, Miss Peterson. He's just returned from being abroad, as well."

"Oh?" This from Mr. Peterson, who looked suddenly delighted to meet Charles.

"Yes. I've spent the last ten years in India. And Africa."

"Mr. Norris was injured in the Ashanti War. He served under General Garnet Wolseley."

"You don't say," Mr. Peterson said, looking even more delighted, which seemed a strange reaction upon hearing someone had been injured. "So you've been away."

"I returned only a few months ago," Charles said. "I'm a bit lost in society. I'm hoping to find someone to guide me." Marjorie nearly winced when he looked at Petunia as he said those words. Good Lord, couldn't he be slightly more restrained with his attention?

"I'm certain my daughter would be more than happy to fill that role," Mr. Peterson said with unexpected enthusiasm. Petunia stiffened, then dropped her head, and Marjorie got the distinct feeling the gesture wasn't one of shyness, but of something else. Misery?

And then it hit her. Marjorie remembered what she'd thought at the time had simply been a vicious statement. She'd heard it only once and dismissed it completely, given the source. She'd been at a supper more than a year ago, and Priscilla Montgomery had said something about Petunia, implying that Petunia seemed a bit unusually plump, but only in the middle and wasn't that an odd place to gain weight when one was so thin. The other girls gasped and giggled, and Marjorie hadn't given it another thought. For one, Priscilla had always been nasty and was known for spreading false gossip, and for another, Marjorie hardly knew Petunia and hadn't really cared to hear such gossip.

She surreptitiously looked at the girl's stomach and saw nothing but a thin, flat waistline. But when she raised her eyes, she looked directly into those of Mrs. Peterson, who looked—it could only be described in one word—horrified. Marjorie gave the older woman a bland smile to put her mind at ease.

"Would you mind very much if I called on your daughter tomorrow? Perhaps we could take a turn 'round Rotten Row."

"Well, Petunia, would you like that?" asked a beaming Mr. Peterson.

"Yes. That would be quite lovely. Thank you, Mr. Norris." But the girl looked like she might burst into tears at any moment.

Marjorie quickly worked out the scenario, and gave an inward sigh of defeat. This girl would never do for Mr. Norris.

Twenty minutes later, Charles was hoping to get Marjorie alone. He wanted to thank her. She was a matchmaking wonder. Petunia, despite her unfortunate name, was perfect for him. She was even lovelier up close than from afar and seemed to be an intelligent and calm girl, one who would be a wonderful helpmate and mother. He'd already pictured the two of them watching their children play around their feet. Why, he'd give his old chum John Willington a run for his money on the number of children they'd have. John had five (and counting) and Charles wanted more. More and more. And they would spend their days in the country, watching their children grow and thrive and . . .

"She's in love with someone else."

Marjorie had come up behind him as he was lost in his fantasy.

"You are a walking, talking bucket of ice cold water," he said darkly.

"As I am certain you were already walking down the aisle with Miss Peterson, I thought I'd let you know immediately that she is not the girl for you."

Charles gave a huff of disappointment, but he was beginning to trust her judgment. God knew he couldn't trust his own.

"What makes you say that? How do you know? And if she's in love with someone else, how did she end up on your list?"

She gave him a cheeky smile and he couldn't help but smile back. "You were so busy coddling up to her father, you didn't notice that the idea of going riding with you made her terribly sad."

"She was not sad," he said. "She smiled at me. More than once."

"Fine. Go riding. You must anyway, as you've already asked her. But do pay attention this time."

The Petersons lived in a lovely, if modest, townhouse in Leicester Square. It was a warm, blustery day, and the sun shone weakly through the cloud-filled sky. He cast a worried look at the clouds, giving a small prayer that it would not rain.

He was a nervous wreck, as he always was when he was about to begin courting a woman. No matter how many times he chastised himself for acting like a boy, the thought of being alone with a woman always made his stomach roil, his hands sweat. He gave the doorbell a sharp twist and stood on the landing, hat clutched in one gloved hand as he tapped a beat against his thigh.

To his surprise, Mr. Peterson, smiling widely, opened the door. "Good day, Mr. Norris, good day." He stepped back, welcoming Charles into their house. Miss Peterson stood just beyond her father, a vision in a soft yellow gown, and Charles's heart expanded. Lady Marjorie had to be wrong about her. She could not be in love with another man if she were smiling so happily at him.

Charles gave her an elegant bow, ignoring the small stab of pain in his leg. Damn and hellfire, it would not trouble him this day.

"Do you mind if I take a look at your cattle?" Mr. Peterson asked, and went out the door without waiting for an answer. The small group, including a plainly dressed woman Charles assumed was Miss Peterson's maid, followed him out, Miss Peterson trailing a bit behind. Charles eyed the statue of George I sitting on his fine steed in the center of the square and wondered if Mr. Peterson had chosen the square because of the statue.

"Fine pair," Mr. Peterson said. They were from his brother's stables, as Charles hadn't been inclined to buy his own horses. He wanted to wait until he purchased a home and had a bit of permanency to his life. A home, a wife, some fine horses—what else could a man ask for?

"They're from the Hartley stables. I'll pass on your admiration to my brother. He's an excellent judge of horseflesh and I hope to get his opinion when I buy my own pair."

"Petunia sits an excellent horse," Mr. Peterson said grandly, and the object of his praise ducked her head. Charles liked a shy girl, he decided instantly.

"Shall we go, then?" Miss Peterson lifted her head and smiled brilliantly at him. By God, he knew she was the one that very moment.

Charles helped first Miss Peterson, then her maid, into the carriage before climbing in himself. They were silent as they rode down Piccadilly, and Charles racked his brain to come up with some bit of conversation. Why did he become so tongue-tied around women? He wasn't that way with his sister, but he could hardly imagine Miss Peterson as his sister. And he'd had no problem with Lady Marjorie. Why, then, was coming up with something witty to say so difficult?

"What was your favorite part of your trip to Italy?" he said, remembering she'd been abroad.

Her face heated instantly. "The weather. It was sunny and warm nearly every day."

Charles looked up at the milky sun, struggling to make an appearance through the clouds, and frowned. "The sun was my least favorite part of India and Africa," he said.

She darted a surprised look at him, then lowered her eyes as if confused by his statement. Their pace to Hyde Park was terrifically slow because of traffic, and Charles suddenly wished he'd suggested a different sort of outing. Beside Miss Peterson, her maid had dozed off, no doubt lulled to sleep by the soporific movement of the carriage.

He gazed at Miss Peterson, who seemed to studiously avoid looking at him. The light and brilliance she'd shone with when he'd first arrived seemed to have disappeared entirely. She hadn't smiled once since the carriage had pulled away from her home. Even Charles's quip about a gentleman wearing bright purple making him long for grapes failed to produce a smile. Lady Marjorie's words came back to him, and try as he might to push them aside, it soon became obvious that Miss Peterson wished she were any other place on Earth than sitting in his carriage on the way to Rotten Row.

She was lovely, yes, but she seemed to be enveloped in a cloak of sadness, now her parents weren't hovering over her with hysterical cheerfulness, that showed itself in spades. He wondered, had Lady Marjorie not mentioned anything, if he would have seen how very unhappy this girl was.

He did try to make conversation. And to give Miss Peterson credit, she did respond the way she ought—politely. He couldn't help but wish she could love him, and maybe with time . . .

He stopped that thought.

"Miss Peterson. I do apologize, but I need to ask you something," he blurted. Her cheeks grew pale and she swallowed heavily, as if she were bracing herself for something awful. He noticed these things now, simply because of Marjorie. Hell, they weren't even all that hidden; he'd simply been blind to them all these years.

"Of course, Mr. Norris." Her gloved hands were folded demurely in her lap, but he noted her grip tightened and her smile was a bit frozen.

"Are you in love with someone?"

Miss Peterson couldn't hide her shock, though she did try to recover quickly. "Oh, no. Why would you think . . . No, of course not. I . . ."

Charles held up a hand, staying her. "Please, calm yourself, Miss Peterson. And please answer the question again, honestly this time."

She looked at him as if trying to gauge whether he actually wanted the truth. "Yes," she said, finally. "I am."

"And he is inappropriate, I gather?"

She dipped her head. "Yes," she whispered. "Terribly so."

Charles furrowed his brow, growing angry at this man for hurting this young girl so much. "Married."

Her head snapped up. "Oh, goodness, no. Nothing like *that*. He's . . . he's poor. A clerk at a counting house."

"Ah."

"He loves me, too. We . . ." She squeezed her eyes shut.

"Enough said, Miss Peterson," Charles said gently. "I will not impose on you again and hold no ill feelings toward you."

Panic filled her eyes. "Oh, no, Mr. Norris. My parents have such high hopes. You mustn't—" She stopped abruptly and flushed. "You don't understand. You haven't heard because you've been out of the country, but there are terrible and untrue rumors going around about me. My mother blames herself for not thinking it through, you see. She wanted to get me away from him and so thought a trip would be just the thing. But a family leaving so abruptly with a tearful girl in tow . . . Priscilla Montgomery was walking by our home as we were leaving. She's such a hateful girl. And now there are rumors that I had to leave the country. That I . . ." She couldn't bring herself to say the words aloud. "And we were gone nine months. Nine. Oh, what was mother *thinking*?"

She blinked back tears, and Charles watched helplessly as she gained control of her emotions.

"You may be my only hope," she said.

"I'm afraid I've no stomach for courting a girl who's in love with someone else."

"Oh, but you must," she said, then stopped abruptly. "No, you mustn't." She smiled at him then, a true smile, and he felt a twinge of loss. She could have been perfect for him.

They ended the ride and agreed to remain friends. And Charles, because he had a soft spot in his heart the size of his entire heart, it seemed, promised to find a better-paying position for the man she loved. One might have thought he'd handed her the moon, for the smile she gave him.

"No promises. And I don't believe you should raise your hopes too far regarding your parents."

"I know. I won't. But my parents love me and they don't like to see me so unhappy. They thought a trip to Italy would make me forget him, distract me. But I still love him. Thank you, Mr. Norris, even if it doesn't work."

You were right. Fielding's ball.

Marjorie smiled at the cryptic note and tucked it into her pocket. "Mother," she called as she entered the house. "Have we gotten an invitation to the Fielding ball?"

She found her mother in the breakfast room, eating a hearty breakfast of fried eggs, black pudding, and kidneys on toast. Dorothea loved breakfast and had announced three years prior that she was no longer concerned about her figure. Marjorie had nearly sputtered out a mouthful of tea, for never in her memory had her mother seemed even the slightest bit concerned about her figure. All her concern was spent on Marjorie's.

"Yes, we cannot afford to miss the Fieldings'," she said. "You may wear your blue, of course. The Crawfords have packed up and gone to the country to prepare for a wedding there." Her mother pursed her lips, a clear sign she was still unhappy that the Crawford girl had nabbed one of Marjorie's potential suitors.

Marjorie's blue gown was a spectacular Worth creation that she had yet to wear. It was a lovely gown with a skirt of the deepest blue tartalane and sinfully expensive Valenciennes lace, which was befitting a young unmarried woman. She wondered if she'd suffer wearing such light fluff for the rest of her life. Still, the dress, with its dark blue lace that accented the light blue bodice and ruffled bustle, was pretty. And it was, of course, Worth. Some days, Marjorie would think about all these gowns, all this money being spent to attract a man. It made her slightly ill to think of it. Especially because she'd known for quite some time that it was all for nothing.

"Good morning."

Marjorie looked up and smiled at her brother, who had apparently escaped the clutches of his valet before he put a comb through his hair. "Good morning, George. We were just speaking of the Fielding ball. I do hope you can come."

George instantly grew pensive. "What night is it?"

"Wednesday. You've nothing planned, have you?"

George slowly filled his plate and Marjorie knew his mind was searching for what he typically did on a Wednesday night. "I will go," he said finally.

"Marjorie," her mother said, slightly exasperated.

"If George doesn't go, who will dance with me?" Marjorie said lightly, and gave her brother a wink.

"Any number of young men," Dorothea said.

"I've been a bit of a wallflower lately, Mother."

"Poppycock."

"And George can rescue me if that happens. That is, if I can drag him away from all the pretty girls."

George flushed red, and Marjorie wondered suddenly if there was a particular pretty girl who caused that blush. Dorothea had said on numerous occasions that no girl would ever marry George—and secretly Marjorie wondered if she was right, for he'd shown little interest in the opposite sex. It would be lovely to see George fall in love and even more lovely to have a niece or nephew.

The night of the Fielding ball, Marjorie arrived with her mother; George very often traveled separately, as he was quite particular about when he arrived and when he left. The Fieldings lived in a grand old house in Mayfair, a lovely neighborhood not far from Hyde Park that had seen better days but was still one of the nicer London neighborhoods. It was, Marjorie's mother said with a sniff, a neighborhood that was attracting merchants and their ilk. But one could not skip the Fielding ball simply because they were neighbors to the fabulously rich merchant Charles Magniac.

"Get your card, dear. I'll meet you at the entrance to the ballroom," Dorothea said, gazing around the room. "Wentworth is here, dear." This last was said in a delighted whisper. A booming laugh came from their left, and Marjorie smiled. "Mr. Norris is here as well," Dorothea said, the brackets on either side of her mouth deepening in displeasure.

"I don't know why you find Mr. Norris so offensive. He comes from a very good family."

"He's loud, his hair is too long, his skin is too bronzed, and his sideburns too full. He looks like a farmer more than a gentleman."

Marjorie turned and found the object of their conversation standing with a few other men. He looked rather dashing to her, but she noted immediately that he was leaning heavily on a cane and that the knuckles of the hand grasping the head were stark white. It was the oddest thing, for at that moment, Marjorie felt the almost overwhelming need to go over to him and lay her hand on his, to let him silently know she understood a tiny bit of what he was feeling. He smiled, he laughed, but all the while gripping that cane so tightly, it was a wonder he didn't crush the metal ball and claw head.

"Yes, Mother, he is all those things." And all those things had been irritating to her at one time. Now, though, she was finding his loud laughter endearing, his palpable energy exhilarating.

She turned her head abruptly away from him. It would do no good if she were to develop feelings for him. It could only end disastrously. A wave of depression struck her at that moment, just as she reached her hand out to take the lace-embossed dance card. She had the sudden urge to jerk her hand back, to refuse to participate in this absurd farce. She was not going to marry, so why was she here, wearing her loveliest gown, her hair intricately styled, her jewels sparkling and inviting stares of both envy and greed? Instead, she calmly took the card and looped the gold-tasseled cord about her wrist. Perhaps with Miss Crawford officially off the marriage mart, her card would once again be filled.

She glanced down at the card and noted the Fieldings had scheduled three waltzes that evening. Perhaps she could save one for Charles; a lady could never decline to dance with a gentleman unless that dance had already been filled. It was a ready excuse to give to her mother, who would no doubt disapprove of her dancing with him.

That thought was still in her head when Charles appeared by their side. "Lady Summerfield," he said with a bow to her mother before turning to her. "Lady Marjorie, I wonder if you would do me the honor of dancing with me during the second waltz."

"Oh, dear, Mr. Norris, you are too late I'm afraid, her dance card is quite full," Dorothea said, with such sugar sweetness, Marjorie wanted to scream. A hundred times her mother had said those same words to gentlemen she'd deemed unworthy of her. And every time, Marjorie had nodded her head demurely and let her mother have her way. Not this time.

"My goodness, Mother, you must be mistaken. We've just arrived, after all. It would be my honor to dance with you, sir," she said, even as she felt her face flush from her obvious rebellion.

She didn't know what had come over her, she really didn't. But Marjorie held up her empty dance card and showed it to her mother to prove her point even as she saw the anger flare in her mother's eyes.

"So it is," Dorothea said succinctly. She was so very angry, Marjorie thought, and wondered if this tiny bit of defiance would be worth it. She would hear a lecture this night. Her mother would go on and on about how she must be more selective, must find a title, must only dance with men her mother approved of, must must must must *must*.

"If that is the case, Lady Marjorie, could I be so bold to ask for a galop as well?" Oh, the cad. He must know her mother was livid. He wasn't smiling, but his eyes held the devil in them. Marjorie heard her mother's sharp intake and felt a warning fissure at the base of her neck.

"It would be my pleasure, Mr. Norris." Both dances required her to be held in his arms and she could almost feel his warm hand against her back already.

She removed the card from her wrist and handed it to Charles, who removed a pencil from his breast pocket, then scrawled his name boldly on the first galop and second waltz. Marjorie took the card back with a smile that was meant to tell him a bit about how brave that small act was. He winked as he bowed again and Marjorie felt her world swirl, her pulse beat a sharp staccato in her throat. A wink and he very nearly had her heart.

When he'd gone, Marjorie braced herself for her mother's scathing words, but they didn't come. And that was a bit worse, she thought. She would get a talking to, but her mother would never make even the smallest scene in public. Marjorie wished she would, if only to get it over with. Instead, Dorothea smiled at her and said, "Let's see if we can get the rest of your dance card filled. With more appropriate gentlemen."

Ah, there it was, a small hint of what was to come. Marjorie returned her mother's smile and looped the dance card back over her wrist.

Before the Grand March started, Marjorie's card was nearly filled, and her mother seemed to forgive her small transgression. Lord Wentworth had requested the first waltz and she thought her mother would explode with self-satisfaction.

"The first waltz," Dorothea said. "Leave the last waltz open, dear. One never knows what will happen."

One knew, Marjorie thought darkly. No doubt her mother would continue her campaign with the poor fellow, who didn't begin to look like he wanted to be in this room with a gaggle of giggling debutantes. But she supposed attending a ball was better than staying at home with five motherless children all demanding his attention. She knew Lord Wentworth would ask her for that last waltz and she couldn't stop the dread that formed in the pit of her stomach.

Lord Wentworth, it turned out, was a pleasant fellow who seemed amazingly cheerful for a recent widower with five children at home. He did have an unfortunate habit of spitting a bit as he spoke, but Marjorie supposed if she kept her distance during conversation she could tolerate him well enough.

"Your country home is in Coventry, is it not?" Marjorie asked in an effort to break the awkward silence as they danced. Lord Wentworth was a tall, thin man with pleasant gray eyes and thinning brown hair. There was nothing at all disagreeable about him (besides the spitting), but Marjorie didn't feel even the smallest twinge of interest in him.

"Yes, it is."

"I toured St. Michael's Cathedral in Coventry once when I was visiting a friend. Perhaps you know her. Miss Anne Barnes? Her father is a squire."

"Of course, I know the Barnes family. Sir Alfred is an avid fisherman and we often fish together. How is Miss Barnes? I haven't seen her in years."

"She married Baronet Redgrave. We still correspond, but she is quite busy with her two young children."

"My goodness. Little Annie Barnes has two children. I've five, you know, and I can hardly believe it."

Marjorie laughed at his bewildered expression. "Five is rather a large number. And they are all quite young?"

"The oldest is ten." His smile became wistful as they skirted the edge of the dance floor. He seemed to realize he was dancing with a potential mother to his large brood, and added enthusiastically, "but you'd never know I have any children. A very quiet bunch. Studious and well-behaved, you know."

"I'm sure they are all good children." She might have added, "with such a father as you," but she couldn't bring herself to do it. She didn't want to flirt with him. She didn't want to give him any hope. As they danced, she saw Mr. Norris standing along the side of the room, his head dipped slightly so he could hear what a young lady, whom Marjorie didn't recognize, was saying. Whoever the stunningly beautiful girl was, she was definitely not on her list. Marjorie tried not to stare at the pair, but couldn't help herself. How could such a lovely young lady have been introduced to society without Marjorie being aware of her? Why, the season was in full swing.

"That's Isabella DeRiccio. Daughter of an Italian duke. But their titles aren't quite so lofty as ours here." Lord Wentworth had obviously noted her interest in the couple, and she blushed at being found out.

"Why is she here, I wonder?" Marjorie said, even though she knew the reason. Why would any single woman attend a ball? More competition in a sea full of pretty little fishes. Her mother would not be pleased. And at the moment, seeing Charles smile down at the lovely girl, Marjorie was none too pleased, either. The Italian was not on her list. And . . . she was completely wrong for him. Marjorie knew what she was feeling had nothing to do with Isabella DeRiccio and everything to do with her feelings for Charles. Her futile, ridiculous feelings.

This was all wrong. This was to have been a grand adventure, a diversion from the boredom that came with every season. She was to have found him a bride so that her brother's debt would be forgiven. It was a lark. But here she was pining for a man she could not have and loathing a girl she'd never met. It was all so unlike her.

"Why is anyone here?" Lord Wentworth said, with more than a little bitterness. "We must pair up."

"Do you not want to be paired?"

"Sometimes, Lady Marjorie, what we want and what we do are two completely different things." He shook his head. "I do apologize, but this being in London and in society after so long enjoying the country has not been easy for me."

The dance ended and Lord Wentworth released her and stepped back. "Why don't you go home, my lord," Marjorie said gently. "London will be here when you're ready."

He looked at her and at that moment, Marjorie recognized his deep sadness. "I have five children," he said, as if that explained everything.

"And right now, I would imagine they miss you terribly and are probably a bit terrified you might actually come home with a new mother for them. I know I would be."

He furrowed his brow and let out a funny little laugh. "I think I will go home. You are right, London will always be here. Just don't tell my mother."

Marjorie laughed. "I do wish mothers would let their children decide their own lives."

He smiled at her, the first true smile she'd seen from him. Now that she saw it, she realized all those other smiles had been false. "I do promise not to tell your mother that you were the one who drove me away," he said. "She is frightfully tenacious."

Marjorie winced. "She will be the death of me. Good luck, my lord."

The galop was about to begin, and Marjorie looked about for Mr. Norris, silly anticipation making her stomach flutter. But he was nowhere to be seen. Had he asked her to dance only to vex her mother? She was about to give up when she spied him through the opened French doors, his back to the ballroom, his hands resting on the terrace railing. He must have forgotten, she realized, or perhaps lost track of the dances while he was talking to that DeRiccio girl.

This had never happened to her. She'd never been left waiting alongside the room while a man who had claimed a dance failed to show up. Frowning, she made her way to the terrace, skirting the ballroom floor and the couples enthusiastically dancing. It was a game to Mr. Norris, she knew that. He couldn't possibly know that he had wounded her a bit by forgetting their dance. Perhaps she should let him know precisely what a cad he was.

Of all nights, why would his blasted leg do this to him? He'd been feeling better. He'd actually danced a time or two just one night before. Perhaps that was the problem; he'd overtaxed himself dancing a bloody waltz. Good God, was he to become an invalid, unable to dance or even to converse with a pretty girl? He prayed the cool night air would somehow soothe his leg, but as soon as he stepped out onto the terrace, he was gripped in agony as his leg seized up. Stumbling, he made his way to the railing and said a short and rather vulgar prayer that he wouldn't scream aloud. It wouldn't do to frighten all those ladies who were his potential brides.

A cold sweat broke out on his body and his arms began to shake. *Don't scream. Don't scream.*

And then, a hand, small and firm, gripped his gloved hand, giving him enough distraction that the scream bubbling in his throat was forgotten.

"Breathe," she said.

"My dear lady," he said through gritted teeth, "if I wasn't breathing I'd be on the floor."

She chuckled and squeezed his hand. "You forgot our dance," she said. "Now you'll have to make it up to me another night."

Charles looked at her and smiled grimly. "Your mother just might kill me if I do." He took a deep breath. "I should not have come this evening. My leg has been hellish all day. I should have known better than to try this. Prajit was very angry with me."

Another searing pain gripped him and he spat out a curse. It hurt like the devil, but even through it, he still felt her hand on his, gripping even tighter. He still smelled her scent, heard her small gasp, as if she were the one hurting. She shouldn't be there with him. Anyone could see them, standing too close, her hand on his. God, she was warm. He could feel her next to him, and he prayed for something forbidden at that moment. He prayed he had the strength to drag her into the shadows and kiss her, consequences be damned.

Finally, the pain subsided and settled into an incessant ache. He could deal with an ache. He could carry on a conversation, even manage a waltz. She released his hand and stepped back.

"I imagine you've seen doctors?"

"Yes. Three. It was a grievous wound. They all say the same thing—that the leg should have been taken. Perhaps they're right. I wonder sometimes if it would have been better to lose it than to suffer this."

She let out a little sound. "Surely the pain will subside in time."

"It has, actually." He laughed at her expression, as if she could hardly believe he'd been worse.

"I'm glad I didn't see that. It's difficult to see you this way. I don't know how you hide it."

He wondered the same thing, actually. When he'd been talking to the Italian woman, he'd nearly cried out and she'd been perfectly oblivious, even as beads of sweat formed on his forehead. It occurred to him that Marjorie had known he'd been in agony. "I obviously didn't hide it from you," he said.

"I knew earlier your leg was bothering you, when you were standing in that group of men. You were clutching your cane so tightly." She looked about. "Where is your cane?"

"I put it aside. It was drawing too much attention."

"For goodness' sake, Mr. Norris, women think canes are quite dashing."

"Do they?"

"Of course."

"Then I shall have to retrieve it—" He stopped abruptly. She was so damned pretty, so *nice*. Why she had been passed by was a mystery to him, even with her brother. He actually found George an interesting character. Surely that alone could not explain why she wasn't married. Surely someone in the *ton* could appreciate her. He knew he did. He *did*. He . . .

"Have you ever considered what it would be like to kiss me?" Her eyes widened right before her gaze dipped to his mouth.

"Of course," she said. "I wonder what it's like to kiss every man I meet."

Now she'd surprised him. "You do?"

"If one cannot picture kissing a man, one certainly cannot picture being *married* to him."

He smiled. "Ah, but you knew that I was not a man you would marry. So why would you imagine kissing me?"

Her cheeks flushed slightly and she lifted her head haughtily. "Why are you trying to get me to admit I would like to kiss you?"

"Because it's all I can think of. Kissing you, I mean. I'd like to someday."

She smiled then, and he nearly groaned—not in pain this time, but from a far different sensation. Something about that smile felt like a caress, one that sent a heavy heat to his groin. She tapped one index finger against her chin as she contemplated his words, then slowly said, "I think that would be . . ."

Lovely, he thought, *please say "lovely."*

". . . a mistake."

Damn. Wrong word.

"And I think it would be a very good thing indeed," he said, aware of how husky his voice sounded. For some reason, all this talk of kissing her was making it difficult to speak.

She wrinkled her brow. "Do you?"

He stepped toward her and she gave a nervous look toward the ballroom. "Not now, you ninny. But someday soon. I really don't know how long I can resist it."

"I think you should try. To resist it, I mean." She added the last in a rush of words.

"Do you really wish for me to resist kissing you?"

She pressed her lips together and backed up another step. "The galop has ended. I have to go meet my partner for the next dance." She continued backing up, the oddest sparkle in her lovely eyes. Just before she entered the ballroom, she said, "As to your question—no, I don't wish you to resist." And then she spun about, her gown swirling around her so that he got an enticing glimpse of her trim ankle. He took a step and felt a sharp twinge in his leg, but he didn't give a damn. He'd suffer just about anything to get that kiss.

The ballroom in the Fielding house was bookended by a gallery and library, both of which were filled with ball-goers who moved from room to room looking for friends or trying to avoid speaking with enemies. A wide hall separated those rooms from Lord Fielding's study (this night set up for card playing) and one of the home's parlors.

Charles peeked into the parlor and frowned when he spied a large group of chattering debutantes, who instantly stopped speaking when he looked into the room. "Good evening, ladies," he said, and nearly winced at the smattering of giggles and instantaneous curtsies that resulted from his greeting. He bowed and continued farther down the hall, hearing the giggles grow louder, accompanied by some fervent hisses for quiet.

After ten years overseas, Charles realized he knew almost no one. His chums were all married, surrounded by growing broods of children, leaving him to wander the halls of balls alone. It was damned depressing. When had everyone become so young?

Or rather, when had he gotten so damn old?

He passed one of the entrances to the ballroom and spied Lady Marjorie dancing with Lord Pemberton, an ancient gentleman who'd outlived three wives already. It might be suspicious had not all of his wives died of natural causes. The old fox was leering at the lady's bosom and she was valiantly trying to ignore him. Charles chuckled, and at that moment she looked up and met his gaze, a smile flashing across her face—one that made his gut feel decidedly strange.

It was one thing to lust after the lady, to flirt and perhaps some-day—someday soon—steal a kiss. It was quite another to start feeling all starry-eyed when he looked at her. Lust could be turned off. Love, on the other hand, could leave him reeling for months, he'd learned. He turned abruptly away and started to search for some pretty young thing to distract him from the lovely Marjorie and her brilliant smile.

After an old-fashioned country dance, it was time for his waltz with Lady Marjorie, and he'd be damned if his leg would keep him off the dance floor this time. The throbbing ache would normally stop him from attempting such a thing, but he wanted to hold her in his arms, even if it was quite proper and in front of dozens of other people. He shook his head, amused where his thoughts were leading. He was every kind of fool, but for tonight he decided to throw caution to the wind and pretend he had a chance with her.

"This is our dance, I believe, my lady," he said, bowing to Marjorie as she stood next to her frowning mother. Marjorie smiled at him prettily as the older woman glared at him. Charles gave Dorothea his most polite and pleasant smile, secretly hoping it was causing the woman's blood to boil. It wasn't as if he were the son of a banker, for goodness' sake. His father was a viscount. He didn't much care for her opinion and enjoyed watching her thin lips press together in distaste.

"I think your mother loathes me," he said with a laugh when they were on the dance floor.

"Oh, it's a certainty," she said cheerfully.

"She does know who my father is, does she not?"

"Of course, sir. I think she objects to your wild ways. Your hair, for instance, is a bit too long. And you seem to laugh rather loudly. It is quite not the thing to enjoy oneself in public. Or rather, to allow others to know you are enjoying yourself. And the title." She sighed dramatically. "Despite your lofty sire, you, sir, have no title. And that is your fatal flaw."

He grinned down at her, watching her expression change, the way her mouth formed the words, her lips pouting as she said the word "flaw." A surge of heat flooded him unexpectedly and his grip on her slender waist tightened just slightly, bringing to the edge of impropriety the closeness with which he held her. She was not a petite girl, so he didn't have to strain his neck or his ears to hear her. Her forehead was aligned with his mouth, so that if he wanted to, he could lean forward and kiss that little frown line that sometimes appeared.

"Stop it," she said, grinning up at him.

He raised a brow in question.

"You're giving me that look again."

"Ah. The I-want-to-ravish-you look?"

She laughed aloud. "Yes, that's the one. I know my mother is watching and will not be pleased." But Marjorie sounded enormously pleased, so he gave her a look so searing no one observing the pair could mistake his thoughts.

And Marjorie, silly, wonderful girl, laughed, delighted with his sense of play. It was at that moment, when he should have been guarding his heart, when the music and dancers swirled around them, that he fell just a little bit in love with Lady Marjorie Penwhistle. He cleared his mind so that particular thought wouldn't be as apparent.

"But I do want to ravish you," he said blandly. "What would you do if I kissed you right now, right here on the dance floor?"

"I'd slap you, very hard," she said sternly, but there was a delighted light in her eyes.

"And yet I sense you want me to kiss you."

"That's not at all the point. If I allowed a kiss without a great show of protest, I'd be forced to walk down the aisle with you. And we both know that would be a disaster. So, yes, I would slap you."

At that moment, another pair of dancers jostled them a bit, causing Charles to misstep. The result was an ungodly shooting pain that all but sent him in agony to the floor.

Marjorie looked stricken, but he smiled grimly, even as his entire body was almost instantly bathed in a cold sweat. He suffered through it, continued dancing, and it was only when the music finally, mercifully stopped and the pain began to subside that he realized, to his horror, he'd been crushing her hand. And she'd been silent, letting him do it, letting him nearly break the fragile bones.

"My God, I do apologize, my lady. You'll be bruised. I'm so very sorry."

She smiled at him and rubbed one hand with the other. "Please do not worry. It didn't truly hurt." She held up her hand and flexed it in front of him to prove she was unhurt, but all he saw was the glaring red marks left by his fingers. "My goodness, Mr. Norris, you look as though you just murdered my kitten. I assure you, I am perfectly fine."

He nodded, but he didn't believe her. Suddenly, this business of finding a wife seemed futile. How could he court a girl if he couldn't even dance with her, if he could hardly carry on a conversation? He wished he could forgo it all and simply pick someone.

He knew, of course, that would never do. He was still just enough of a romantic fool to want to love his wife.

"Who is next on your list?" he asked abruptly, almost angrily, though he wasn't quite sure where that anger came from.

Marjorie drew back, as if the question surprised her, but she answered immediately. "Miss Mary Crandall. Her father, Sir Arthur, was knighted some time ago. It was one of the queen's first acts when she assumed the crown."

"I know the Crandalls. Their son went to school with us. He was younger, but he was an extraordinary cricket player." He stopped momentarily when she made a face at his mention of cricket. He ignored her and continued. "Made first team his first year at Cambridge." He tried to remember what he knew of the family, as he hadn't seen Jonathan Crandall in more than fifteen years. "But since I won't be marrying Jonathan Crandall, tell me about Mary."

"She's a bit shy, but rather nice. She is a patron of the arts and is deeply involved with the London Asylum for Poor Orphan Girls. She is here if you'd like an introduction."

His leg gave him a twinge. "Not tonight. I'm not really good company and I'd like to be at my best if I'm about to meet my future bride."

She scanned the room and he couldn't help letting his eyes drift to the graceful curve of her neck; one dark curl had fallen just behind her ear and he had the sudden image of himself brushing it aside so he could lay his lips there. "Ah, there she is, dancing with Lord Maplewood."

He dragged his eyes away from her curl and followed her gaze. "The girl in the gray dress? With the mousy brown hair?"

Marjorie playfully tapped him on his arm. "She is a very lovely girl," she said.

"No. She's too small." Charles nodded toward a stunning young girl, her golden blond hair swept artistically upon her lovely head. He knew immediately he'd never seen her before. "What of her?" he asked with a nod toward the blonde.

Marjorie frowned. "That's Lady Caroline Stanley."

"Lord Warwick's daughter?"

"Yes. I imagine you know them?"

"My father is good friends with Warwick." He smiled. "Find out about her. Learn if she's promised to someone. Hell, I can find out myself. I'll write to my mother. She'll know."

"But she's . . . so young and her father's an *earl*."

"*My* father is a viscount. Why do you continually forget that? Let me tell you something *Lady* Marjorie, there is not a single mother, with one glaring exception, who would not be overjoyed to be linked with the Norris name and the Hartley title. My family's lineage is pristine and I daresay there are few titles as respected as my father's. I suspect your opinion has been marred by your mother's prejudice. Or perhaps it's your own prejudice that is rearing its ugly head. Lady Caroline is perfect for me." He was angry and he knew he sounded angry, so angry he didn't even care that she looked stricken.

Marjorie knew why she hadn't suggested Lady Mary. It was because she *was* perfect for Mr. Norris. She felt purely horrified by this realization. "Of course she is. I'll introduce her to you tomorrow night. They attend the opera the opening night of every performance and *La Traviata* is opening tomorrow. I'll make certain I'm there." Marjorie felt unaccountably like crying. She'd remembered considering Lady Mary, but had immediately crossed her from the list. And it *was* because her father was an earl, but part of her now realized it was also because she knew deep in her heart that Lady Mary and Mr. Norris would be a wonderful match. And her job would be done. She would have no reason to meet him secretly, no reason to leave notes. No reason to dance with him. No reason to touch him.

"This is my dance, I believe."

Marjorie looked up to see a solemn-faced young man looking at her, his gloved hand extended. Who was he again? She hadn't the foggiest notion. But she smiled and laid her hand in his as he took her to the dance floor.

The rest of the evening dragged on interminably. Charles had disappeared, either heading home or to the card room. She danced all her dances with little enthusiasm, noting her mother was paying little attention to her. Instead, she spent much of the evening glaring at George, who hardly strayed from the side of Lilianne Cavendish, their neighbor in Ipswich. Her father was landed gentry, a squire of good standing, who'd always been a pleasant fellow. George had danced with her twice, and Marjorie wondered if he were more than a little smitten.

Finally, it was time to leave. Marjorie's feet ached almost as badly as her hand did, she thought ruefully. There was a long queue of people waiting for their hats and coats; her mother stood stiff and silent by her side, no doubt still a bit miffed by her rebellion earlier that evening. Some sort of commotion ahead of them was slowing their progress, and Marjorie strained her neck to see what was happening. When she realized what it was, she blanched. Something had happened with George.

Leaning toward her mother, Marjorie whispered, "It's George. I'll see what's happening, shall I?"

Her mother's expression turned even more stony. "Go on."

Marjorie made her way to the front of the queue of people awaiting their hats and coats to find George highly agitated and holding a hat in a hand that shook.

"This isn't my hat, sir. My hat is from Beale & Inman." He jabbed his finger at the silk label inside the top hat. "This hat is from Tollings. This isn't my hat, sir."

The beleaguered footman kept apologizing and trying to explain that George's hat must have been mistakenly given to another gentleman, but George wouldn't—or couldn't—stop objecting.

"This isn't my hat," he said again.

As Marjorie passed by, one man said beneath his breath, "I believe we've established the fact that it isn't his hat. Is he daft?"

Marjorie felt her face flush red as the footman wrested the wrong hat from George's hand, which only created more anxiety in her brother. At that moment, a large manly shape moved past her and toward her brother, who stood now tapping his fingers together in a silent clap of fretfulness.

"Lord Summerfield," Mr. Norris said. "Where do you get your hats?"

George was momentarily distracted and smiled a greeting, first at Marjorie, then at Mr. Norris, who looked down at her and gave her a reassuring wink. What a lovely gesture, that wink. "Beale & Inman. But that hat," George said, pointing, "is from Tollings."

"Well then, I can certainly understand your concern. Tollings is far inferior to Beale & Inman. I, myself, get my hats there. I'll tell you what. Why don't we go tomorrow and get you another hat, just like the one lost this evening? I'd lend you mine, but I noticed you prefer a taller top hat and mine is only six inches. Yours is nearly eight, is it not?"

Her cousin Jeffrey sidled up next to her, apparently drawn by the small commotion. "He's so charming, your brother, isn't he? I must go to Beale & Inman tomorrow and tell them of your brother's great loyalty to their hats."

Marjorie ignored her cousin's words and instead watched with relief as Charles took charge of the situation.

"Seven and three quarters," George said, visibly relaxing. It was as if the embarrassing incident had never happened. Mr. Norris had maneuvered George aside so others could retrieve their hats and coats, and the impatient murmurs had ended. "Tomorrow is Tuesday. I could meet you there at two in the afternoon."

"Two it is, then." Then Mr. Norris glanced briefly at her, and added, "Perhaps your sister can join us."

"She cannot," Dorothea said in a tone so cool Marjorie half expected frost to emit from her lips.

Mr. Norris bowed politely to her mother and turned to George. "I'll see you tomorrow, then, Summerfield. Perhaps afterward we can go to Brooks."

Dorothea took Marjorie's arm rather roughly and hauled her toward their wraps, which were quickly retrieved. Marjorie didn't dare look back to give Mr. Norris a smile of thanks.

The ride back home in the carriage was silent and thick with tension. Dorothea was livid, Marjorie could tell, and sat stiffly across from her. It was rare indeed, that her mother expressed anger toward her. She was often *disappointed*, but rarely angry, and Marjorie felt a bit more trepidation than usual. Still, she had no patience for her mother tonight and was feeling unaccountably depressed about the entire evening. And her hand ached terribly. She'd lied to Mr. Norris about how much it had hurt when he'd gripped her hand, but now wished she'd been more honest. She'd seen little of him at the ball after their discussion about Lady Caroline, and the entire conversation had left her feeling out of sorts. Worse, before departing the ballroom, he'd stared at Lady Caroline as if he were leaving his intended for the evening.

When they entered their townhouse, Dorothea snapped, "I want to speak to you in the parlor."

"I'm tired, Mother. I'm going to bed." Marjorie was sick to tears of her mother's lectures on how she should or should not act. With whom she should dance or flirt or consider as a husband. All she wanted was to curl up in bed and sleep, perhaps for a week or two so she could miss watching Mr. Norris fall in love. She'd just started to turn away from her mother when the side of her face exploded with a burning pain and a loud crack of flesh hitting flesh resounded in her ringing ear.

Marjorie's hand flew to her burning cheek as she stared, stunned, at her mother's enraged face.

"You will not disobey me again," she spat. "I have invested far too much in you to have you throw away all that I've worked for. You will marry and you will marry this year. I shall pick out your husband and you will marry. And you shall never speak to Mr. Norris again. I want you to know what will happen if you choose to marry someone I do not approve of. You will never be allowed in this home again. I will disown you entirely. That is how serious I am about this. Is that what you want, Marjorie? Are you trying to break my heart with your obstinacy?

"I have sacrificed much over the years for you. I have spent money we don't have on Worth gowns and balls and lavish entertainments, all in the name of finding you the best possible husband. And this is the thanks I get. Throwing it in my face, making a mockery of me in front of my closest and dearest friends. Do you not know the comments I had to endure this evening because of your foolishness? Do you not care about our reputation? You will never dance with that man again. You will be a good and obedient daughter as you have been up until this evening. You will do these things because you are a good daughter. Do I make myself clear?"

Her hand still pressing to her face, Marjorie's eyes filled with tears. Her mother, as stern and stalwart as she was, had never struck her.

"Answer me! Do I make myself clear?"

"Yes, Mother."

"This has gone on long enough. I blame myself for my lenience with you. You've become willful and disobedient. I've allowed you to make your own decisions, but that is over. I will decide whom you marry. You have forfeited your rights in this matter this evening by blatantly disobeying me and dancing with that man."

Dread filled Marjorie as she realized what it would mean for her to be married, to be out of their home, to be away from George, who needed her so. Her mind reeling, and feeling her will dissolving, she shook her head. She might have laughed at her mother's expression had she not been quite so terrified.

"I'm not a child, Mother. You cannot force me to do your will. I understand your anger, truly I do, but you cannot force me to marry a man I do not want."

Her mother gave the most horrible smile at that moment, one that chilled Marjorie and was more frightening than the threat of being struck.

"We shall see about that, my dear. Good night."

Her mother marched up the stairs, leaving Marjorie alone to wonder what sort of plan lay behind that threat.

Chapter 6

Forty years earlier

It was June tenth. In just five more days, Dorothea would be on a coach headed for Ipswich and a life of isolation with her widowed Aunt Frances. Each day that passed made her more desperate to find some reason to put off the trip. She even began to pray she'd become desperately ill and unable to travel. Perhaps Lord Smythe would hear of her illness and come to visit, realize how very much he loved her, and beg her to marry him.

She knew such fantasies were ridiculous, but couldn't stop her mind from creating scenarios in which he fell to his knees and asked her to marry him.

Ascot must be perfect. She must look her best. She must wear the most charming dress, the loveliest hat, especially on the first day, when the royal procession arrived. She must stand out. She must make Lord Smythe look at her anew. She wasn't a friend. No, she could be a wife, bear his children. Never a slim girl, she tried desperately to lose weight, and succeeded a bit. Even her maid commented on how her dresses were a bit looser. It was a small triumph.

Her maid tried a variety of hairstyles, finally settling on the one that would be the most flattering beneath a hat. Dorothea practiced her smile, her laugh. She pretended to have conversations with him so that she wouldn't be so nervous when she finally did see him. He would look at her, stunned, and realize she was more than handsome. She was pretty and still young enough. And she had a brain and loved the same things he did. She studied her copy of *Revue Horticole* so they would have something to talk about. She read every article in the *Spectator* about the upcoming race, the competitors, the horses. Everything she did, everything she read, every thought she had in the two weeks preceding Ascot was on how to attract Lord Smythe.

The only thing she had left to do was buy a hat for the first race. It was a terrible oversight not to have already ordered one. She only had four days, after all, until the races. But her milliner, Mrs. Gibson, would accommodate her. Dorothea was her best customer, after all.

Her shop was located just off Regent Street in a charming little brick building. She walked in, her stomach nervous, and she saw it. The perfect hat. She actually gasped, and clutched at her maid's hand.

"Tillie, that's the one," she said.

Mrs. Gibson, a middle-aged woman with blond hair just starting to go gray, smiled as Dorothea walked in. "It's my favorite creation this year, I think," she said, walking over to where the hat sat on a counter. "But I'm afraid it's for another lady."

It was large and high, with big blue bows on each side and flowers adorning it, as if sprouting from the wide brim. Dorothea had to have it.

"I see. May I try it anyway? Perhaps I can have you make one similar."

Mrs. Gibson hesitated, but no doubt remembering just how much money Dorothea had spent over the years, acquiesced. Dorothea picked up the hat lovingly, walked to the mirror, and placed it on her head. Behind her, Tillie gasped.

"Oh, my lady, it's beautiful."

And it was. There was something about the hat, the color of the flowers, the wide brim and high crown that all combined to somehow transform her face. She had never in her life felt so pretty.

"I'll take it," she said.

Mrs. Gibson had come up behind her, looking slightly ill. "I'm so sorry, my lady, but this hat was designed—and paid for—by another lady. Perhaps a different—"

Dorothea shook her head. "No. This one, or an exact duplicate. You must, Mrs. Gibson. Surely you have duplicated hats in the past."

Looking torn, Mrs. Gibson said, "Yes, but this one is so special and designed by the young lady herself... Of course, I will make it for you. You do look lovely in it, my lady. It is, by far, the most charming hat I've seen on you."

Dorothea looked in the mirror again and smiled. This hat, along with her new dress, would make all the difference. What were the chances the other lady would be invited to enter the Royal Enclosure at Ascot?

On the way home, Dorothea was assailed with familiar doubt. She turned to Tillie. "You would tell me if it was absurd, would you not? It was a rather large and unique hat."

"But that's what sets it apart, my lady. And you did look ever so pretty in it. Truly."

Relief flooded her. "Thank you, Tillie." The final piece was now in place.

Chapter 7

The morning after the Fielding ball, Marjorie peered in the mirror, examining the left side of her face, which was still red and slightly swollen. She prayed a bruise would not form. She still could not believe her mother had struck her so viciously. Now she had sore fingers and a sore face. She smiled grimly at her reflection, noticing her smile was a tad lopsided at the moment. Lovely.

Though she wanted to stay in her rooms all day and hide, Marjorie forced herself to walk down the stairs to breakfast. She was hungry and refused to starve herself from fear of another confrontation with her mother. When she reached the sunny room, her mother was there and Marjorie's stomach clenched.

Her mother looked up and greeted her warmly, as if the previous evening had never happened, as if her face weren't slightly red and swollen.

"Good morning, dear. The fish is especially good today." Then she turned to the footman who stood silently by the door and said, "You may go."

Marjorie gave her mother a cautious look. She'd never before asked a servant to leave.

She walked to the sideboard and filled her plate with a scone, eggs and sausage, even though she had lost whatever appetite she'd had. She sat across from her mother, who, as usual, was enjoying a hearty breakfast.

"I've something for you to read," Dorothea said sweetly. "I think you'll find it enlightening." Her mother handed over several sheets of thick vellum filled with tightly written script. It looked to Marjorie like a legal document, and she took it from her mother with some trepidation.

Without touching the food on her plate, Marjorie began reading the words, at first confused about what the document was. Then, it began to dawn on her and her breathing became shallow.

"Oh, Mother, you cannot," she said, laying the offensive pages aside.

Her mother smiled that horrible smile. "Of course, I can. As you can see, my dear, I can and will have your brother's title stripped from him. Whether that happens or not is entirely up to you."

"I don't understand."

Dorothea let out a long-suffering sigh. "I have been very patient with you, my dear. I have let you refuse suitor after suitor. Fine men, most of them, whom you set aside for no good reason. It is your duty to marry well, Marjorie. It is the only thing this life will ask of you, to marry. And now you shall. For if you do not, your brother will suffer the consequences."

The full realization of what her mother planned sickened Marjorie, and filled her with a helplessness she'd never thought to feel. This was no spontaneous act. The document must have taken weeks to prepare.

"If you love me at all, Mother—"

Dorothea held up a hand, stopping her. "This has everything to do with love. Do you think I would go to such lengths for a child I did not love?"

Hot tears filled Marjorie's eyes. "And what of George, Mother? Do you not love him at all?"

"Of course I do. He is my son. But that does not make me blind to the fact he is flawed," she said calmly. "But you, my dear, you are the jewel of this family. The day you were born, I knew you were special. I am fully aware I am not a beauty. Even in my youth I was not. And goodness knows your father was an uncommonly ugly man." She pursed her lips as if tasting something disagreeable. "But you are a miracle. I knew it then and I still believe it now. You could marry a prince if you set your mind to it."

Marjorie could only stare at her food, now grown cold on her plate. Her throat ached from unshed tears.

"Look at me, Marjorie," Dorothea said placatingly. Marjorie forced herself to look at her mother. "You should be the mistress of your own home by now. You should have produced your heir. It is not too late. You are still young enough. Still pretty. Lord Shannock is interested and he is now my first choice. His estate borders ours and he's mentioned you on more than one occasion over the years."

Lord Shannock was a man in his fifties, who had already outlived two wives. He seemed ancient to Marjorie, for although he wasn't terribly old in years, he was thin and stooped, with a greasy, stringy pate of gray hair. And his breath always smelled of onions.

"You are willing to have the title go into abeyance to force me to marry the most onerous man in our acquaintance? If you believe he is such a good man, marry him yourself."

Dorothea's smile faltered. "The title will go to your cousin, Jeffrey. And Lord Shannock wants children, something I cannot give him. But you can."

Marjorie felt bile rise in her throat at the thought of Lord Shannock touching her. "I'll marry, but I won't marry Lord Shannock. I won't, Mother. This is eighteen seventy-four. You cannot force me to marry against my will."

Dorothea smiled. "Of course I cannot. But I can strip your brother of his title if you disobey me on this."

"That's not possible." Even as she said those words, she wondered if that was true. She knew nothing of the legal merit behind the document she held. She'd never heard of anyone losing his title, but that didn't mean it hadn't been or couldn't be done. "Besides, Jeffrey is a toad."

Her mother slammed her hand against the table, making the teacups dance in their saucers. "He has all his wits and that is enough for me." Dorothea took another bracing breath. "Now, my dear, enjoy your breakfast. I believe we should do some shopping before the opera tonight."

This could not be happening. Could not. Her mind whirled, trying to think of a way out, but nothing came. She'd never felt so alone in her life, so completely helpless. Who could help? Perhaps Mr. Norris would know what to do. Perhaps he could give her some sage advice. Surely he would help her if she asked. They were friends, after all.

She lifted her head and gave her mother her most winning smile. "I planned to go to the Christy Collection this afternoon, if that's all right with you."

Her mother pursed her lips unpleasantly, no doubt knowing it was the day George always went to the exhibit. "Certainly. Be home by six so you have time to rest and get ready."

Marjorie stood, her breakfast untouched, and made ready to leave the room. "And Marjorie," said Dorothea, "George need not know anything of this conversation. I don't want him becoming overwrought. You know how he can be."

Chapter 8

George was in an uncommonly cheerful mood as they drove that afternoon to Victoria Street. He'd spent the day with Mr. Norris and was filled with news about their adventures. It was obvious to Marjorie that George had placed Mr. Norris in the category of hero. It was nice to see her brother making a friend.

"This is a fine hat, is it not?" George asked for the third time. "It's smaller than my last one. I wasn't certain I would like the way it looked, but Charles said I looked dashing and I think that I do. The other hat was too tall, wasn't it, Marjorie?"

"I think you look fine in both, but this one is a bit more modern."

"Yes, indeed. More modern. And dashing, I think. I noticed that many of the men in Charles's club had similar hats." He furrowed his brow. "I do hope no one mistakes my hat for theirs again and takes it. I suppose if that happens, I can get another hat, just like this one," he said, tapping the precious hat, which sat next to him in the carriage. "Do you think Miss Cavendish will like it?"

"Are you sweet on her, George?"

His blush gave him away before his words did. "I think she is very pretty and she's awfully smart. She knows nearly as much of history as I do."

"Goodness, a bluestocking."

George nodded. "She's awfully smart. And pretty."

"You should court her, then."

The expression on his face told Marjorie that such a thought had already occurred to him, but he shook his head. "I don't think so."

"Miss Cavendish is very nice. She's nothing like Miss Jones, George."

"I don't think I could bear it if she were," he said softly. "Miss Jones told me she would never marry an idiot. I'm not an idiot. I'm smarter than she is by far."

Marjorie leaned over and squeezed his knee. "You're kind and smart, and any girl would be lucky to have you."

"Miss Cavendish is nothing like Miss Jones. I'll think about it. She is awfully pretty."

"She does seem to like you."

George ducked his head and smiled. "Perhaps I'll ask her father if I might."

Marjorie's heart ached for George and she prayed Lilianne Cavendish's father was as kind as his daughter. She'd watched such cruelty toward George over the years. If she'd been a man, she would have been in at least a dozen fistfights defending him. George did take a bit of getting used to and any woman he ended up with would have to deal with his habits, his idiosyncrasies. But that woman would also end up with a kind husband who was uncommonly devoted. Though they'd known the Cavendishes for years, Marjorie had never taken much note of Lilianne. She seemed painfully shy and was a bit plain. At the Fielding ball, when she'd been talking with George, the girl had lit up and seemed lovely. The more Marjorie thought of it, the more she liked the idea. If George married, she wouldn't have to worry so about him. She wouldn't . . .

She wouldn't have to remain a spinster. She could marry without worry. George wouldn't need her anymore. She glanced at her brother, seeing the man he'd become, not the awkward little boy she held in her heart. Even though he was only two years her junior, she'd always thought of him as a boy who needed to be cared for. But he was a man thinking about marriage. Marjorie reached over and squeezed her brother's hand. "I'm very proud of you, George. And I approve of Lilianne wholeheartedly. She would make a fine countess. And just think, she would be head of the household, not Mother."

Marjorie grinned as the idea took root in her brother's head.

"You mean Mother wouldn't live with us?"

"She'd have her own house, I suppose. Perhaps The Glen would be an appropriate home for her." The Glen was a sweet home in Exeter, one they'd visited only a few times, but one that was quite lovely. And quite far from London and Ipswich.

"Would you live at The Glen, too?"

Yes, Marjorie realized, she would. Drat. She didn't want to live in Exeter, but where else could a spinster daughter live than with her mother? Perhaps her grandmother would like some company?

"I could live with Grandmama Penwhistle. Mother loathes her and would never come visit," Marjorie said, laughing. She did feel a bit guilty at the thought, but Dorothea was not her favorite person at the moment. For years, she'd been a dutiful daughter, obeying her mother without question. And Dorothea had been an indulgent mother, one who, if Marjorie were completely honest, had been a bit too tolerant of her daughter's opinions. At one time, they had been the best of friends, laughing and enjoying the social season, sharing quips and secrets.

But somewhere along the way, her mother had lost her tolerance for Marjorie's fickleness. Perhaps the other mothers who had married off their daughters had made comments. Perhaps the idea that her daughter might just turn out to be a spinster was becoming a reality in her mind. Or perhaps Marjorie was simply sick to tears of constantly trying to please everyone but herself.

She didn't know what had caused the two of them to be at such odds. Marjorie hardly recognized the woman who'd slapped her, the woman who'd hired a lawyer to strip George of his title. For six seasons the two of them had had such fun. Six years. No wonder her mother was losing patience!

If George did marry, Marjorie had to make a decision. Marry or remain a spinster. The idea of not marrying now seemed rather dismal to contemplate. What would she do, flit from relative to relative, slowly becoming what was so pitied among the *ton*—an old spinster? Would she end her days alone, no children, no grandchildren, just dutiful nieces and nephews who visited once a year?

My goodness, if George could find a girl to love, certainly she could find a husband.

"You could live with us," George said, his brows knitted with worry. Oh, bless him.

"No, George. I think this season, if you are successful with Lilianne, I shall find a husband. It's time."

*   *   *

Mr. Norris was waiting at the door when they arrived, looking impatient, energy seeming to emanate from him like an electric current. They entered together and wandered about the exhibit for a while, George exclaiming over the artifacts that in truth bored Marjorie. How he could get so excited about chipped bits of flint was beyond her.

The rooms, with their creaking wood floors, were well lit with gaslight sconces. Very few people were about, and most of the time the three of them had the room to themselves.

"I suppose the fun is in finding the stuff, not in looking at it," Marjorie said, gazing doubtfully at a display case filled with rocks that apparently had been excavated from a cave in France. George gave her an annoyed look and Marjorie wrinkled her nose and crossed her eyes at him.

"What a lovely expression," Mr. Norris said, laughing, and then his expression changed and he grew still. "George, we'll be in Room Two." He grabbed her arm and led her across the hall to the second room, which, Marjorie quickly determined, was empty but for the display cases along the walls. He maneuvered her to a small alcove between two large cases, so that if anyone did enter, they would not immediately see them there.

"What happened to you?" Mr. Norris demanded, his eyes pinned to her cheek. "Who struck you?"

Marjorie had taken great pains before leaving for the Christy Collection to powder her cheek, which had darkened to a slight bruise over the course of the day. Only the most discerning eye would have seen anything wrong, and Marjorie had left feeling confident no one would notice.

Feeling humiliated, she quickly tried to come up with an explanation for her bruised cheek. "I struck it. On my door. It was the silliest thing—"

"No. Who hit you?"

"Mr. Norris, it is none of your concern. Truly."

"Is that why you brought me here? Are you in some sort of trouble?"

She shook her head. "No. It's another matter entirely."

"I should like to know who it was so that I might teach him what it is like to be beaten."

For goodness' sake, the man would not leave off. "It was my

mother. She was angry with my behavior last evening. She has never hit me before, and I daresay she never will again. She lost her temper."

Those words seemed to bother Mr. Norris even more. "It is my fault. I taunted her by asking you to dance with me."

Though this was partly true, Marjorie didn't want Mr. Norris to take any blame for what had happened. "It had nothing at all do with our dance, but everything to do with me. I have so far refused to marry and she has grown exceedingly frustrated with me. She has devised an ultimatum and that's why I asked you here. But on the way I've had some news, so it may all be a moot point."

Mr. Norris bent his head and searched her face for the truth. "Tell me anyway."

"Unless I marry a man of her choosing, she will strip George of his title," she said, her throat clogging as she uttered those last words. Sudden tears were streaming down her face and she found herself pressed up against a warm, firm body, large hands patting her back. He smelled so nice, she thought, even as she let out a sob. "But George may marry and if he does, I can marry and she'll leave me be. But if George doesn't, and it's not certain by any means, I fear she will follow through on her threat," she said in a great rush of words.

"You do know that's impossible," he said, and she could feel the deep vibration of his words against her face. Withdrawing from his embrace, she looked up at him.

"It is?" she asked on a small hiccup.

"Yes. Drat that woman for putting such fear into you," he muttered. "Members of the peerage can have their title stripped only by an act of Parliament. There have been members of the peerage who were madder than any inmate in Bedlam who retained their titles. Peers have murdered and stolen and kept their titles. It simply cannot be done. It was, my darling girl, an empty threat."

Relief swept over Marjorie. She'd known Mr. Norris could help. "She had a document. It looked quite official."

"I've no doubt she went to great pains to frighten you, blasted woman. But think, my lady. Is your mother the sort of woman who would bring such scandal and embarrassment to her family? Such a proceeding would not only reflect badly on the title, but on you as well. You claim she wants nothing more than to have you marry advantageously. Such a filing would immediately ruin your chances of a good marriage." He smiled down at her, and Marjorie was suddenly aware of how alone they were, how close he stood. How handsome he looked in the soft gaslight. How kind he was. Her eyes dipped briefly to his firm lips.

"Then again, if she were to file that document," he said, leaning a bit closer with each word, "you could marry whomever you liked."

His lips were nearly touching hers and she found it suddenly difficult to breathe. "What are you about, Mr. Norris?"

"I believe," he said, pressing the softest of kisses against her mouth, "I'm kissing you."

"Oh."

And then his mouth was not soft, but demanding and hot. She clutched his lapels, trying desperately not to dissolve to the floor in a heap. Something was happening to her, something she'd never felt in her life, certainly not to this astounding degree. Marjorie had experienced a few chaste kisses from her beaus, but this was not a chaste kiss. This was hunger and passion and nearly out of control. This was all the desire that had been pent up—exploding in one painfully sweet moment.

He growled low, his chest vibrating, and deepened the kiss, his tongue touching her sensitive lips. "Open for me," he whispered, and she did, letting in his tongue, greedy and insistent. And more wonderful than anything she'd felt in her life. It shouldn't be wonderful. It should be frightening and shocking and wrong. But when Marjorie pushed her tongue against his and he let out another feral growl, she felt such a rush of heat, she nearly swooned. His hand moved behind her neck and he pulled her to him, slanting his head to deepen the kiss. It was instinct that moved her now, a strange insistence that she do more, feel more. She let out a small sound, of joy or frustration, she wasn't certain. All she knew was that for the first time in her life she felt desired.

He stepped back suddenly, moving to the center of the room, his burning gaze never leaving her, his chest heaving. "Your brother is coming," he said, his voice raspy. "Should I apologize for that?"

Marjorie shook her head, her breathing ridiculously shallow. It had only been a brief kiss. She could have gone on for hours. And yet, she had a feeling she would never be the same. That had not been a normal kiss. It had been heaven.

"I should apologize," he argued, "because I regret it, with every fiber of my being. Now I only want—damn it, my lady, I do not want this." He looked at her angrily, and Marjorie didn't know why. Had she done something wrong?

"There you are," George said, smiling as he came into the room. "You missed the last two displays, you know."

Charles continued to stare at Marjorie as if he were very, very angry. "Your sister and I were discussing tonight's opera. She is going to introduce me to my future bride. Did you know that? And I will do my very best not to fall in love until Lady Caroline falls madly in love with me. And then we shall marry. *That* is the plan."

The plan, Marjorie thought dismally. She had forgotten all about it.

George was oblivious to the tension in the room, and immediately went to the first case and its display of bone knives and harpoon heads. "I'd like to marry someday. Wouldn't it be grand if you got married, too, Charles? And you, too, Marjorie."

Marjorie stared at Mr. Norris, not bothering to hide the hurt she felt, that he should kiss her and then in the next breath talk about marrying someone else. "Yes, I would like that very much, George. Mother has a baron picked out already."

"A mere baron?" Mr. Norris drawled. "My condolences."

Charles spun away from her, from her hurt and sad eyes. "We missed two cases?" My God, he was still reeling from that kiss, from the sounds she'd made. His reaction to her innocent kiss was nothing less than astounding. He felt like a sixteen-year-old boy experiencing his first mad rush of lust. It could not happen again.

"Oh, yes," George said. "The artifacts from Russia and Portugal. And of course Asia. Those are the most fascinating to me, you see. Stone axes from Sumatra, you know."

Charles smiled at George's enthusiasm, wondering at how articulate the man could be when talking about something he loved. "You stay here. Your sister and I will go back and view those displays."

"I'd really rather not." Her voice had an edge to it that he'd never before heard.

"Please, my lady, I'd appreciate your insight."

She gave him a steady look before nodding. "Very well."

As soon as they were again alone, he took her hand and pressed it against his heart, regretting the resistance he felt, a small tug letting him know he had hurt her. She relented, finally, spreading her fingers slowly, her eyes fixed on her hand. "I fear if I kiss you again," he said, "I shall be lost."

She looked so stunned by his words, Charles nearly laughed. "This is my fault, I know. I kissed you. You did nothing wrong. I didn't realize how—" He gave her a pained look. He hadn't realized how a simple kiss could make everything so complicated. He fell in love too easily, and here he was, falling again. It must not happen.

"What didn't you realize?" she asked softly.

"How much I would enjoy it, I suppose."

She let out a light laugh. "Kissing *is* enjoyable. How could you not know that? Surely you've kissed other women."

"Yes, of course." He chuckled when she frowned. "But all those kisses weren't quite as . . ."

"Enjoyable?" she asked, an adorable note of hopefulness in her voice.

"Yes. Enjoyable," he said, annoyed that he found her so charming. "Though that word seems rather tame to me." This last was muttered beneath his breath.

Marjorie withdrew her hand and he let her. It would do no good to draw her into his arms as he wanted. It would do no good to let his mind imagine her in his bed, smiling sleepily at him in the morning. He must turn his mind toward other things, other women. It was ridiculous of him to fall in love—again—with a woman he couldn't have.

The worst of it was that he liked her quite a lot. They were *friends*, and he was teetering on the brink of love. He'd never been friends with a woman; it was a bit disorienting. He had the awful feeling that he hadn't been in love with all those women in the past, but in love with the idea of being married, of having the type of family that he'd grown up with. He wanted it so desperately, perhaps he'd been simply convincing himself he was in love. Wasn't that what Marjorie had hinted when he'd first proposed the idea of her finding him a bride? Or perhaps he only loved what he knew, deep down inside, he couldn't have. His friend John had suggested that flaw more than once. What an idiot he was.

"We'll get you good and married, sir, if it's the last thing I do," she said with an authoritative nod. "You've been such a help to me, it is the least I can do. You've forgiven George's debt . . ."

"Not yet."

She ignored him. ". . . you've helped me understand my mother cannot strip George of his title. You've danced with me when you oughtn't."

"How is your hand?"

She gave him a sheepish look. "It was a bit sore, but it's better now. You know, I've been thinking quite a bit about those pains you get. Is it because your muscle seizes up or is it something else?"

"Most often it's a contraction, a seizing of muscle, as you said."

She gave a little clap. "Good. Well, not *good*," she amended, obviously seeing his frown. "I wake up in the middle of the night with awful leg cramps, especially after a night of dancing. I've found that if I flex my toes back, I can stop a cramp and the pain is quite brief. I've gotten so I can stop nearly all those cramps using that simple method. I wondered if you could do the same, somehow."

Well, damn, just when he was trying desperately not to love her, she had to say something so sweet, his heart melted. "I shall try that," he said gruffly, though he felt it wouldn't do much good. "Thank you. We should get back to your brother. He'll no doubt be vexed with us if we don't view all the cases."

Charles was not a fan of opera. He preferred Alexander Dumas's version of the tragic affair between Violetta and Alfredo. And really, could a woman dying of consumption really sing as well as Thérèse Tietjens? Three interminably long acts lay in front of him, he thought as he entered Covent Garden.

"You loathe opera. There must be a woman involved."

Charles turned, delighted to see Lord Avonleigh and, by his side, Katherine. "I thought you'd be back in the wilderness by now," Charles said, referring to Avonleigh's estate in Northumberland.

"We've another week here before heading back," Katherine said. "I miss the place and we have so much to do."

Charles gave his old friend a searching look. "You're all right on that front then?" he asked. Avonleigh had been in desperate financial straits not long ago.

Graham smiled down at his new bride. "It turns out I married well after all."

Katherine looked at her husband with mock anger and batted him on the arm. "He married me thinking we'd be poor."

"And loved you madly. Don't forget that." Graham turned to him. "What of you? Is it a woman who has brought you to the opera?"

Charles caught sight of Lady Marjorie and he didn't think to school his expression. Even had he tried, he doubted he'd have been successful, for she was stunning this evening. Her dark hair was swept up, allowing a few curling tendrils to delicately caress her pale neck and shoulders. The gown she wore was magnificent, a shimmering gold creation that hugged her figure before cascading down in a series of intricate lace layers. "Perhaps."

Katherine followed his eyes and smiled. "Lady Marjorie is lovely tonight."

Charles started, as if unaware he'd been staring at her. "Is she? I hadn't noticed," he said deflectively. "I'm actually hoping to see another—Lady Caroline, Warwick's daughter."

"Oh?" Graham drawled. "I thought she was still in the schoolroom."

"They all seem that way, don't they? But no, she's an ancient nineteen." Charles let out a gusting sigh. "It's either the schoolroom or widows. Lady Marjorie is helping me, you see. I've been away for so long, I hardly know a soul anymore. She's my guide, so to speak."

Katherine looked delighted with the news. "She's matchmaking?"

"Something like that," Charles grumbled, and seeing the mischief in Graham's eyes, said, "and not a word from you, you besotted fool."

Katherine took Graham's arm. "He is besotted, isn't he?"

"Completely," Graham said, looking for all the world as if he were going to kiss his bride right in the middle of the theater lobby.

Charles scowled at the pair of them. Neither had wanted to get married and yet there they were, staring into each other's eyes as if they were the only two people in the world. Charles had worked so hard over the years to find just that sort of love, and here he was, the last of their circle to marry.

"Perhaps if you stop looking so ardently, you will find love," Katherine said, looking over to where Lady Marjorie stood next to her termagant mother. He wished he were the sort of man who would strike a woman, for if ever a woman needed striking, it was Lady Summerfield. Just thinking of that bullish woman slapping Marjorie with her beefy hand was enough to make him forget his upbringing.

"You can stop your matchmaking right there, Lady Avonleigh,"

Charles said grimly. "Lady Summerfield is a force to be reckoned with and I do believe she would murder any untitled man who dared to court her daughter. Or even dance with her. For some reason, she's taken a particular dislike of me."

Katherine laughed, but they both knew he was not exaggerating overmuch. "I do wish you would go up to them, just so I could see Lady Summerfield's expression."

"I don't wish to witness murder this evening," Graham said.

"But I? I am feeling adventurous," Charles said, a glint in his eye. "Besides, Lady Caroline just joined their group and I've been promised an introduction."

Charles was feeling a bit reckless, though he didn't know why. Joining their little group was perhaps the worst thing he could do, but at the moment he didn't give a damn. As he approached, Lady Marjorie widened her eyes and shook her head just a bit, but Charles ignored her.

"Lady Summerfield, you're looking lovely this evening," he said effusively. She was wearing a dull brownish-gray gown, the color and shape of a farmer's cart.

"Mr. Norris." As greetings went, it was about one step shy of being a cut. She didn't look at him and stiffened considerably.

"Lady Marjorie." He tried to say her name without inflection, without giving a hint of their intimacy. And then he glanced at Lady Caroline, who stood looking up at him curiously, clearly not knowing who he was.

"If you would be so kind," he said to Lady Summerfield. Her good breeding didn't allow her to ignore him completely, so she let out a huff of air and did her duty. "Lady Caroline, please allow me to introduce you to Mr. Charles Norris."

"We've actually met," Charles said. "You had a spotted dog that you tortured by making him carry your doll."

Lady Caroline's eyes widened. "Oh, of course. Your father is Viscount Hartley." She shook her head. "I'm sorry I did not immediately recognize you."

"I've been out of the country these last ten years and you were only a child when I saw you last."

She blushed becomingly, glancing at Marjorie before looking back to him. "My parents and I visited your home just last summer. How is Laura?"

"She is well," Charles said noncommittally, for he suspected his sister was deeply unhappy in her marriage.

"My goodness, I haven't seen her in years. Though I often visit with your brother and his wife. I adore their children. Christopher is a fine pianist, but I'm sure you know that."

"He gave me a concert the last time I visited." Charles felt something inside him click into place. Yes. This was the girl he should marry. She knew his family, was no doubt well-liked by his mother. Both their names began with the letter "C"; that had to count for something. And their children would have lovely blond hair, though lately he'd pictured his children with darker hair. He wondered that his mother had never proposed Lady Caroline as a possible wife, but perhaps she'd simply neglected mentioning her. Or maybe she had and he hadn't been listening.

At that moment, Lady Warwick came up to their small group and Caroline made the introductions. Throughout the happy reunion, Lady Summerfield stood like a statue, her jaw set, her eyes like cold steel. Marjorie, on the other hand, had the oddest smile cemented upon her lips, as if she'd been set in some sort of plaster that didn't allow her to stop smiling.

Marjorie supposed that wearing a constant smile didn't allow anyone to notice that her heart was slowly breaking. It was such a silly thought, but one she couldn't stop from having. Lady Caroline was perfect for Mr. Norris. They practically knew each other well already and made a striking couple with their blond hair. Caroline was clearly no shy miss and didn't seem to flinch at Mr. Norris's laugh. They were chatting about shared experiences, people she didn't know, places she'd never been. Like old friends who were delighted to find one another after all these years.

With the addition of Lady Warwick to the group, the reminiscences only grew more intimate, excluding Marjorie more fully, who found herself slowly drifting away, seeking out other acquaintances to talk with. When she spotted her friend Katherine, she nearly sighed aloud with relief.

"Mother, I'm going to talk with Lord and Lady Avonleigh. Would you like to join me?"

"If you will excuse us?" Dorothea said, but the pair was hardly acknowledged as they left the animated group. Charles never looked her way. He was too intent on staring, with a silly, stupid grin, at Lady Caroline, who wore a matching, silly, stupid grin.

"That would be a good match," Dorothea said when they were away from the group. Marjorie could only stare at her mother in disbelief. Given her prejudices, how could she think Lady Caroline, the daughter of an earl, would possibly be a good match for a title-less second son?

Dorothea gave Marjorie a sharp look, immediately understanding her unspoken words. "She is the fourth daughter. You are my *only* daughter."

When they reached Lord and Lady Avonleigh, Marjorie's mother completely changed. It was rather astonishing to watch. She could be charming and delightful when she put her mind to it.

"I see you are still smiling at your bride, Avon," she said with a small chuckle.

"Yes, ma'am. I haven't been able to stop for weeks now."

"I can hardly countenance that legend now," Katherine said. Somehow, Lord Avonleigh's legendary scowl had led to a tale claiming he would marry the first woman he smiled at—a tale most were quickly forgetting now.

"I knew I was right about the two of you. I said it, didn't I, Marjorie? I said they belonged together the moment I saw that first smile."

Behind her, Marjorie could hear Mr. Norris's exuberant laugh and it felt like little needles at the back of her skull. Then she heard Caroline's tittering laugh and sharp shards of jealousy replaced those needles. In actuality, Caroline had a musical laugh, but to Marjorie's burning ears, it was pure torture to listen to her. Surely she had a flaw. She must.

Alas, Marjorie was fairly certain that her only flaw was that she was free to marry whomever she pleased—within reason, of course. She glanced back at the group, hoping to see concern or wariness in Lady Warwick's eyes, but all she saw was the delight of a mother watching her daughter find a potential husband.

Drat.

The gaslight dimmed for a moment, indicating it was time to find their seats, and Marjorie watched, depressed, as Mr. Norris was invited to the Warwicks' box.

"Would you care to join us?" Dorothea asked Lord and Lady Avonleigh.

"Of course," Katherine said, placing her arm through Marjorie's. "We have so much to catch up on."

The opera began and it took all of her restraint not to look at the Warwicks' box, which was three down from theirs. If she wanted, she could see Lady Caroline's lovely profile and watch as Charles looked—again and again—at the girl sitting beside him. No doubt he was already half in love. Marjorie tried not to look at the pair and through raw determination only gave them two brief glances. Perhaps three.

"Are you in love with him?" Katherine whispered in her ear after Marjorie had oh-so-casually glanced in the direction of the Warwick box.

She felt her face flush and she jerked her head back with near violence. "Shhh," she hissed, and glanced at her mother, who sat just in front of them.

"Are you?" Katherine always had been the persistent sort and not one to follow the rigid rules of English society, which was to be expected given she was an American.

"Of course not," Marjorie said.

Silence for a while as the famous soprano performed a lovely aria.

"Then why do you keep looking over at him and why do you look at him as if you'd like to murder him about now?"

Marjorie turned her head and glared at her friend, who shrugged her shoulders innocently.

"Because he's blackmailing me," she whispered, rather proud of herself for coming up with something that was both the truth and a lie. That was not why she was staring at him, but he *was* blackmailing her. Or rather extorting. But blackmail sounded somehow more dastardly.

As the orchestra played a bridge, Marjorie quickly explained how her brother's poor card play had led to all her problems. And said that she was nothing but pleased that Mr. Norris seemed to have found a potential bride so that she could end this charade, her brother's debt would be forgiven, and she could go on with her life. Throughout her whispered monologue, her mother only turned to give her one annoyed look for talking.

Katherine nodded, as if finally understanding. Then leaned over again and whispered gleefully, "Liar."

Three days later, Marjorie wandered out in the garden, which was fully embracing spring. Tiny rose buds had appeared, and the azaleas were in full bloom. Even their vibrant colors couldn't improve her mood. Her mother had written to Lord Shannock and asked that he come to London "for a visit." Marjorie couldn't gather the energy to argue, for she knew it would do no good. Dorothea would invite the man, he would come, and her mother would begin her assault.

Marjorie supposed he wasn't so awful a choice for a husband. He seemed pleasant enough. He didn't seem to have a foul, awful temper. She could hardly recall him speaking at all. But how could she stand a man who made her suppress her gag reflex whenever he came close enough for her to smell his breath? And he had overlong, and often filthy, fingernails. She could ask that he cut them. And clean them.

"Oh, God," she said, feeling sick inside.

At least Mr. Norris would be happy. Perhaps they would see each other over the years and laugh about their little adventure. He hadn't left a note for her in three days, though she'd left two—two that had remained hidden behind the brick unread.

> *Dear Mr. Norris:*
> *What success! Lady Caroline seems like a fine match for you. I'm so pleased to see you smile. I hope you find the love you are looking for.*
> *Yrs,*
> *M*

And . . .

> *Dear Mr. Norris:*
> *George and I are planning to visit the British Museum tomorrow if you'd like to join us. More rocks and bones, I think.*
> *Yrs,*
> *M*

Feeling a bit despondent, she opened the gate to the narrow lane that divided their garden from the mews, suspecting if she looked behind the brick, she'd find her notes still there. She pulled out the brick and felt a ridiculous surge of relief. Her notes were gone and a new one was there. She lifted it out, her heart doing happy little flips. She quickly replaced the brick and returned to the garden to sit down on a bench to read. Finding her seat pleasantly surrounded by the azaleas that somehow suddenly looked more beautiful than before, she opened the note.

It read:

> *I need your assistance one more time. Please let me know when you can visit.*

It was not signed, but Marjorie knew it was from him. His penmanship was exquisite, yet masculine and bold. A bit like the man, she thought with a grin. She frowned at the words "one more time" but pushed that thought away.

Marjorie ran into the house, calling for her maid, Alice. "We're going out," she announced, heading to her wardrobe. "The green silk, I think." She pulled the gown from the wardrobe and began tackling the buttons until Alice gently took over the task.

"Where are we going?" Alice asked.

"To Bury Street. I've a friend there who needs my assistance."

Prajit opened the door, his eyes widening a bit.

"Mr. Norris is expecting me," Marjorie said.

And to her great surprise, Prajit smiled and stepped back, allowing her and Alice in. He really was quite a lovely looking man when he smiled, though it made her a tad uneasy. "Could you please show Alice to the kitchen so she can have a spot of tea? I'll wait here until you return."

Prajit nodded regally, then led her maid to what Marjorie supposed was the home's kitchen. Mr. Norris's townhouse looked far different in the daylight. What had appeared to be a gloomy, forbidding place was actually quite pleasant and well-lit. The walls were a creamy yellow, colored charmingly by a stained glass skylight in the shape of a compass rose. In moments, Prajit returned.

"If you'll follow me, he is in his study. He has not been feeling well today, *kumari.*"

"Oh, then perhaps I should come back another time," Marjorie said, hanging back a bit. He had asked that she let him know when she was arriving but she'd been in such a hurry to see him, she hadn't given it a thought.

"No, he will be glad to see you. He has not been himself these last few days," Prajit said, and Marjorie's worry only grew.

He led her down the same long hall as the first night she'd come to the house and she recognized the door to the study. Prajit opened it, allowed her to pass, then left without a word, closing the door firmly—and rather improperly—behind her.

And there stood Mr. Norris. Naked.

Not entirely so, she realized a second later. He had on only a pair of drawers so short they exposed everything from mid-thigh down—including the most horrific wound Marjorie had ever seen.

Mr. Norris immediately turned around, letting out a grunt of pain even has he did so. "Bloody hell, Marjorie, what are you doing here? Prajit!"

She stood with her back against the door, wringing her hands together miserably. "I . . . I . . . You wrote for me to come."

"I said to let me know when you *could* come," he growled.

"Yes, you did, but . . . As you can see, I didn't." She stared at his back, as fascinated by it as she was horrified that Prajit had let her into the room when he was nearly unclothed. His back was a series of broad, wide slabs of muscle, glistening in the sunlit room, as if he were over-warm. His hands grasped the desk in front of him and his forearms shook. She noticed his arms, slick with sweat, showed every bit of muscle and sinew, as if he were trying to lift the massive desk instead of simply leaning on it.

"I should leave," she said hesitantly. Of course she should. She should have already left. But what she wanted to do more than anything was to lay her hand on his straining back and try to give him comfort. His wound was far, far beyond what she'd imagined. No wonder the man still suffered. No wonder any wrong movement caused him such torment. And to think she'd suggested stretching out his muscle to stop a spasm. My God, there was no muscle, just a mottled, angry red hole where his muscle had once been.

"I feel so foolish, suggesting you simply flex your muscle. I didn't know."

He turned his head so she could see the hard lines of his jaw before he slowly faced her. As he did, he pulled on a shirt that had been thrown across the desk. It clung wetly to his form as he struggled to do up the buttons.

He gave her a rueful smile. "It actually eases the pain a bit when it's at its worst."

Marjorie looked down at his leg, tears pressing against her eyes. "I'm sorry," she said, glancing up at him. "It's just—I didn't realize how awful it is. May I?" She took a step forward, and he nodded, a small jerk giving his permission.

Marjorie eased forward, her eyes on his wound, her heart breaking for an entirely different reason this time. "It must have been a terrible wound," she said, swallowing heavily, unable to stop looking at his leg.

"It was that. But each week that passes, it does grow better. Though I must say these last few days have brought a bit of a setback." He took his hand and laid it beneath her chin so she would stop staring at his leg. "I'm sorry I missed your notes," he said softly.

"I know you are busy."

"Busy," he said with a note of bitterness. "These last days, I'm afraid, I've been holed up here nearly all hours of the day."

"Why did you want to see me?"

"I don't know how to speak to ladies when I'm alone with them. I become tongue-tied and awkward and it's impossible. I need you with me. I can relax if you are there. You can lead the conversation, nudge me when I make a mistake. Lady Caroline and I rode out two days ago, the day after the opera, and it was a disaster."

"It was as bad as all that?" Marjorie asked, trying to keep the joy from her voice.

"Worse. I was in quite a bit of pain and not in the mood to go riding in the first place. She chattered on and on and I hardly said a word. I could tell she was confused, as I had been so animated the previous evening. In crowds I am different. It has always been that way."

"Tell me about your ride together."

He cringed, as if it had been a brutal experience.

"I was unable to put together more than two words, and suffered from sweaty palms and a jittery stomach. The more I tried to say something witty or even interesting, the more my brain refused to work. I ended up uttering inanities."

Marjorie smiled. "I'm certain it couldn't have been that awful. What did you say to her?"

"I told her that her hair was gold, as if she didn't already know what color it was. And I didn't just say it, I blurted it. Lady Caroline looked at me as if she was trying to understand a man who cannot speak the Queen's English. I can only imagine what was going through her mind. Why can't I relax when I'm alone with a woman? Why must I turn into a sputtering fourteen-year-old with his first crush?

"I should have just let her chatter on. She was quite good at that, fluttering from one subject to the next with hardly a breath in between. She'd been discussing her older brother when she spied a woman walking a fluffy white dog and she immediately veered course and started talking about her dog, which led to a soliloquy about grass, somehow. Whether it was soft or prickly or some such thing. I can't remember it all. But I do remember how desperately I wanted to add to the conversation but could not."

"You did mention the color of her hair," Marjorie said, clearly teasing him, and he smiled grimly.

"Yes, it was a brilliant observation. And it isn't even that color. It's more straw-like in color. More brown, really, with shots of yellow, which combined to make it appear gold. Good God, who cares about the color of her damned hair?"

Marjorie gave him a sympathetic look. "You've never been tongue-tied around me," she said, then held up her hand because she knew what he was going to say. He wasn't courting her so it was entirely different. "Can you not pretend you are not courting her? That she is just a person you want to get to know, not a potential bride?"

"No. I cannot. I *am* courting her. And she *is* a potential bride."

Marjorie colored slightly, annoyed that he should draw such a distinction. "I don't understand your fascination with marriage in any case. You don't need an heir. Why can't you just live your life happily alone? As long as George is at home, I've no wish to marry. And despite what my mother says, I fear I will not marry. Ever."

He let out a sound that was very much like a snarl. "I want a wife. I want to wake up to the same happy face every morning. I want a pile of children waking me up before the sun rises and clambering down the stairs on Christmas day. I want to teach my sons how to fish and watch my daughters braid their hair."

Marjorie turned away from him, clasping her arms around her midriff. She wanted all those things, too, with a longing that was nearly painful. She rarely allowed herself to think of such happy scenes, had conditioned herself against it. "I think," she said, glad that her voice was strong and clear, "that Lady Caroline would be perfect for you." She turned, and her brow furrowed, for something had happened to his drawers. There was something rather large poking inside them. Even as it dawned on her what she was looking at, Marjorie continued to stare, fascinated. And as horrified as she was that she was so fascinated, she simply could not drag her eyes from the sight.

"Hell," Charles said, adjusting himself. "I think I need my trousers on."

As she continued to stare, Charles became even more agitated—and felt himself grow harder. What the hell was she doing, staring at him like that?

"Does that always happen?" she asked, her eyes still glued to his obvious erection.

"Only when . . . no." Only when a lovely woman was in the same room as he. This lovely woman, he corrected silently. He'd been distinctly unaroused when he was with Lady Caroline. He swept his hand through his hair and sought out his trousers, which were draped across a chair on the opposite side of the room. "Would you mind getting my trousers for me? I'm afraid my leg will not allow a trip across the room."

She turned to look at his trousers, for all the world as if she were determining what they were. "May I see it?" She looked a bit shocked with herself, but now, thankfully, kept her gaze steady on his face.

It took a moment before he realized what she was asking. If she had the smallest inkling of what she was doing to him, how he felt, she would not have asked such a thing. He was heavy with need, in agony for her touch, and there she stood calmly asking if she might see him. "Lady Marjorie, I do not think that is a good idea," he said, trying to sound formal.

"I shall never have the opportunity again. As I said, I fear I will not marry and, well, *it* is here. And *I* am here."

"*It* is attached to me and I don't believe we should be having this conversation," he said, aghast. What had gotten into her?

"Very well," Marjorie said, turning and retrieving his trousers. But she held herself away from him, holding them out as if they were bait. She had the most charmingly evil glimmer in her eye. "One peek, then I shall deliver your trousers posthaste."

He steeled his jaw, and in a flash had pulled down, then pulled up, his drawers. "There, you saw."

"That was too fast. I hardly got a glimpse," she said with affront.

"What has gotten into you?"

Something desperate and sad flashed in her eyes so quickly, he was momentarily stunned. And then she smiled and it was gone and he wondered if he'd seen anything at all. "The devil, it seems." She shook her head slightly and handed over his trousers.

He took them, holding them against his chest. "Thank you." Her cheeks were flushed, and she wouldn't meet his eyes. "I do apologize," she said miserably. "I really don't know—"

"There. Take your look."

She looked at his face first, stunned, then slowly moved down his body to the object of her curiosity, her eyes growing wide when they took in his rather impressive erection. She moved a step closer, and by God, he grew impossibly harder as his body reacted to her closeness. She didn't understand what she was doing to him, how every nerve seemed to be on fire and aching.

"Do you," he swallowed heavily, "want to touch it?"

Her eyes darted to his and she let out a small gasp. "Would that be all right?"

"No," he said on a groan. "But if you wanted . . ."

"Perhaps a bit?"

God, yes. "Only a bit." It was beginning to be difficult to breathe and his brain was shutting down. This was wrong, wrong, wrong. He should be turning his back and pulling on his trousers. He should be screaming at her to get out of his study. Instead, he stood there leaning against his desk, pain long forgotten, watching as she approached him, one hand extended and about to touch him. She hesitated just before her delicate fingers grazed the tip and he couldn't stop himself. He gently took her hand and wrapped her fingers around his shaft, shuddering as he did so. He could feel himself swell beneath her warm hand, could feel himself tighten, and he thrust his hips toward her unconsciously.

"Marjorie, move your hand," he whispered.

And then she wasn't touching him and he nearly cried out. "Not *re*move, move. Let me show you." He was long past the point of being the gentleman he should be, so he took her hand and placed it back, showing her how to please him. Wrong, wrong, wrong. But she felt so good and he'd wanted her for so long now. It couldn't go further, he knew that. He couldn't do what he longed to do. He couldn't bury his cock deep inside her, couldn't feel her surround him, couldn't come inside her. "Feels so good." All coherent thought was gone. All he knew was that Marjorie's hand was on him, squeezing gently, moving up and down, making him so close to finding release it was unmanning.

He wasn't touching her. Couldn't touch her lest he lose any control he had. But then she leaned forward, her hand still working him, and kissed his jaw. And that was the end of his resistance. He brought his hands to her shoulders and pulled her against him, finding her mouth and kissing her long and hard, pressing his erection between them, her hand now trapped. He kissed her, devoured her, ached for her.

"I want to make love to you," he said against her neck, his body screaming for sweet release. "I want to show you how."

She stiffened slightly, and he said, "No, not like that. I want to give you pleasure. I want to make you come."

"I don't understand."

"You will. Let me show you."

He kissed her, moving his hips against her, and her grip on his arousal tightened slightly. Had anything ever felt this good before? He put his hands on her firm bottom and pulled her center against his erection, moving rhythmically, making her feel a small amount of what he was feeling.

"Oh." She breathed this into his mouth and he knew she was beginning to understand that something more, something wondrous was coming.

"I'm going to touch you. I'm going to make you feel the way you're making me feel." As he said these words, his hands worked to bunch up her skirts, endless amounts of fabric that hid her from him. When finally his hand skimmed the slit of her drawers, he let out a groan of relief. And when he brought his hand to her center to find her wet and deeply aroused, he nearly found release.

Marjorie was lost in the sensations he was building in her. If she thought about what he was doing, where he was touching her, the words he was saying, she would have fled from the room and never returned. But she'd stopped thinking some time ago. Now it was all feeling. How could something, anything, feel as wonderful as what he was doing to her? Her entire body sang with new sensations, a need she'd only had the barest hints of in the past. Now, as he moved his finger back and forth on her, she could not contain herself. She moved against him, glorying in every new sensation, of the building of something, of this delicious experiment. As he touched her, she touched him, his long, velvety shaft that strained against her hand. If what she was doing to him was anything like what he was doing to her, what a wonderful thing all this touching was.

He suddenly increased his rhythm, both against her hand and between her legs, and she clung to him, gasping, reveling in every movement, thrusting against him and then . . . bliss. Oh, it was positively the single most wonderful thing she'd ever felt in her life.

As she let out a rather unladylike grunt, he turned away from her. Her hand still clung to him and she felt a pulsing surge as he found his own release.

She dropped her hand, and he collapsed a bit against his desk and she collapsed a bit against him. "Oh, my," she said, trying to catch her breath.

"Oh, my, indeed," he said, chuckling. He took a deep breath and then another. He was silent for a long moment until he finally said, "While I did not intend for that to happen, I'm damned glad it did." He gave her a devilish smile. "May I put on my trousers now?" he asked, lifting one brow.

Despite the intimacy they'd just shared, Marjorie blushed hotly. "Of course. I'm so sorry." Now she was simply mortified. What had she been thinking? What sort of woman did what she'd just done? And what sort of woman did Charles—she could no longer think of him as Mr. Norris—think she was? Had she gone mad?

"I'll have none of that," Charles said sternly. "We are two adults and there's no harm done. Your virtue is intact. My conscience, not quite so, but there you have it. Now that we've gotten that out of our systems, we can get on with our business."

Of course. How foolish to think for one moment that what they'd done meant anything other than some animalistic release. She was so mortified, she didn't see the look of longing on his face, the deep regret, and that was probably a good thing. For Marjorie needed a reminder that no matter what, they were to remain friends, business partners. Charles needed help courting another woman. He might desire her, but he didn't love her. And even if he did, it wouldn't matter. Her mother would never allow her to marry him.

"You must allow that you have never acted that way with another business partner." She sounded decidedly sophisticated, as if what had just happened wasn't the most wonderfully devastating experience she'd ever had. She was still keenly aware of how wet she was between her legs.

As she'd hoped, he laughed. "You are correct. And I suppose it shouldn't happen again. I will try not to allow our deep mutual attraction from blinding us to our goal—and that is to find me a bride. And you a husband. Despite what you say, I think you will find one."

Marjorie smiled gamely, even though his words were a bit crushing. It was impossible, she knew that. For as much as she'd like to think she could stand up to her mother, she knew, when it came down to it, she would not. Twenty-three years of being a good and obedient daughter was a habit that would be difficult to break. Still . . .

If he loved her—if Charles told her he loved her and begged for her hand, she'd do it. She'd go against her mother, she'd walk out the door, never to return. It would break her heart, yes, but if he asked . . . would she? Did she love him that much? Or was her heart being muddled by lust?

"We did get a bit sidetracked. So, you'll help me with Lady Caroline? I'm planning a trip to the zoo and perhaps you could come with George."

Marjorie smiled, even as his words caused her breath to stop. Foolish, foolish girl, to think she would give up everything for him. If Charles loved her, would he be discussing courting another girl? And asking for her assistance? Men were such odd creatures. A few kisses, a great passion, and she was ready to leave everything she'd

ever known behind. Those same kisses were not nearly as meaningful
to him.

"Of course. That was our deal, was it not?"

She turned away, and as he watched her walk out the door,
Charles frowned at her back. He didn't like their deal anymore. Not
one bit.

He already felt a deep regret for what he'd allowed to happen. It
would do no good to apologize, though his instincts told him he
should. His biggest fear was that he would never be able to hold her
in his arms again, never truly make love to her the way he longed to.
Hours and hours of lovemaking, days and days. And so, he let her go
without another word.

She'd surprised him. Indeed, he was flummoxed. Why had she
come, anyway, without inquiring first? May I see it, she'd asked. *May
I see it?* He would have wagered his life that Marjorie would never
have uttered such words. He struggled to put on his pants, cursing his
leg, cursing his lack of title, cursing his weakness when it came to
beautiful women with curly, black-brown hair.

She was no doubt mortified by what had just happened. He could
see it in her face just before she'd turned away from him. And he, cad
that he was, had done nothing to make her feel better. He hadn't held
her or kissed her or told her that he was falling in love with her.
Which, if he tried very, very hard, he would be able to prevent. He
would not, ever again, fall in love with a woman he could not have.

Charles was most thankful when Prajit knocked on his door and
entered without awaiting an answer.

"You called, my lord."

Charles gave his servant and friend a withering look. "No, I did
not. And what the hell were you thinking, bringing Lady Marjorie in
here when you knew I was unclothed?"

"You were unclothed, sir?" Prajit raised one eyebrow, but otherwise his expression remained deceptively submissive.

"And you damn well knew I was."

"Yes. Perhaps." Prajit went about straightening the room, placing
a book back upon a shelf, picking up an empty teacup. "You seem in
better spirits."

"I'm not in better spirits," he said, even as he knew he was. Having a woman bring one to heaven would likely help any man's mood. "It was not well done of you to leave her in here with me. I know you are unused to English society, Prajit, but if we were discovered together alone, with me half-dressed, it could have ended very badly."

Prajit raised his brows in question.

"She would have been compromised. She's an unmarried woman and unmarried women should not be alone with half-dressed men. Hell, they shouldn't be alone with fully dressed men." Charles looked at Prajit's carefully blank expression. "Which I am certain you know. Why am I telling you this? Just don't do it again."

Of course, Charles would have to ask for her hand, a prospect he found a bit daunting. He'd been in battle, he'd debated with generals, he'd nearly died. But he was, frankly, terrified to meet Marjorie's mother. Something about that woman made his blood freeze.

Chapter 9

Forty years earlier

The Ascot races were the highlight of the season. Five days of races attended by the highest levels of British society, including the king and queen. Dorothea had been to many Ascot races, but never had she so looked forward to this one—and appreciated being part of a great family. Because her father was a marquess, she and her family were allowed the privilege of sitting in the Royal Enclosure, an area along the racetrack reserved for the titled. It was one of the few times each year when they were all together, though this year only her parents and Dorothea were present. Her sisters, all married, had begged off.

She and her mother were staying with their dear friends, Lord and Lady Chesterfield, for the week. They lived just outside Berkshire, where the races were held, and had the most lovely carriage to arrive in. Dorothea was friends with their daughter, Esther, though she was now living in Cambridge with her husband and three children.

Soon, Dorothea thought, she herself would be a married lady and too busy to attend the event.

The morning of the first race, Tillie smiled in satisfaction as she placed the final hatpin into her coif. "Lovely, my lady, truly."

"My dear, it's true. I have never seen you look so pretty." Her mother stood in the doorway, contemplating her daughter as if she'd never seen her before.

Dorothea gazed at her reflection in near wonder. How could a hat transform her so? Of course, she had lost some weight and her hair was perfection, but Dorothea gave most of the credit to the hat. It was almost as if it were magical.

They arrived at Ascot at one in the afternoon, a full hour before the Royal Procession, and gathered in the garden to await the king and queen. Dorothea, feeling a wonderful new confidence, found herself chatting easily with old acquaintances, gaining looks of approval from her mother. But no matter whom she spoke with, she was always keenly aware of Lord Smythe.

He wore a dark gray morning suit and top hat, and once in a while she could hear his laugh, deep and masculine. Dorothea was desperate for him to notice her, to look at her with widened eyes, to finally *see* her. She tried to stay facing in his direction, and when it appeared he might be looking her way, she smiled brilliantly at whatever was being said. Nearly an hour of smiling brilliantly was beginning to take its toll, and Dorothea was beginning to think he would never notice her.

And then, as if by some divine providence, the crowd separated between the two of them, and he looked at her. There was that stunned and puzzled look she'd dreamt of. There was that smile that made her want to throw herself at him and make a total fool of herself.

Instead, she smiled serenely back at him and nodded her head. He took a step toward her and her heart nearly burst. It was happening, just as she'd prayed it would. Oh, it was happening!

"That's my hat. Where did you get it? Where?"

Startled, Dorothea turned to see a girl—for she was no older than seventeen—glaring at her hat beneath a hat that was the mirror of the one on Dorothea's own head.

"That is *my* hat. *My* design. How dare you!"

"Yours doesn't suit your coloring at any rate," Dorothea said, looking at the child with derision.

The girl's eyes widened, her cheeks turned a deep red, and then, without warning, she reached up and pulled Dorothea's hat from her head, flung it to the ground. And stepped on it, ruining it entirely.

Twenty-eight years of proper behavior, of remembering to do everything with dainty grace, of never losing her temper in public, were crushed along with her beautiful, beautiful hat. She hardly remembered doing it, but Dorothea launched herself at the girl, and before she knew what was happening, they were both on the ground, tumbling and hitting and pulling as the crowd of spectators grew.

"Anne," a man's sharp voice called out. Within seconds, it was over. A man, likely the young girl's outraged father, was removing the girl from atop Dorothea.

Dorothea sat up, stunned, in dawning horror of what had just happened. She heard a giggle, and looked down to see one breast fully exposed.

"Oh!" she cried, trying in vain to pull up her tattered dress and cover herself.

Hot tears filled her eyes as she struggled to gain her feet. A pair of strong hands helped her up, and she felt herself being wrapped in a man's coat. When she got the strength to look up, she saw the lovely blue eyes of Lord Smythe looking at her pityingly. "No one saw," he said softly.

By his side was Lady Matilda, the girl her mother had told her Lord Smythe was courting. "I think the hat looked lovely on you," Lady Matilda said with a tentative smile.

Dorothea looked at her and burst into tears. She wanted to hate Lady Matilda, but how could she when she was so kind?

Her mother arrived, wrapped her arm around her, and drew her quickly to their carriage. Dorothea sat back, her hands still clutching Lord Smythe's coat to her, desperately aware of the scent it carried, of him, of all her lost dreams.

"It's just as well you're going," her mother said softly. "People will forget, my dear. At least I hope they do."

People might forget, Dorothea realized as the carriage brought them back to the Chesterfield estate. But she never would.

"Who was that girl, mother? I don't even know her."

"Lady Anne Wadsworth. She's the daughter of Lord and Lady Dunlop. What a disgrace she must be to her parents."

Anne Wadsworth. No, she would never forget.

Chapter 10

"No." The word was as sharp and final as the crack of a rifle.

While Charles was not surprised by Lady Summerfield's response to his question, he was surprised by the jagged slice of disappointment he felt. It *hurt*. Quite a bit. Did he care for Marjorie more than he'd realized? Good God, he was a bloody fool. It was clear he loved her and just as clear, standing in this ugly parlor facing a frowning Lady Summerfield, that he would not be able to marry her.

"I love her, my lady. And I do believe Lady Marjorie loves me."

Lady Summerfield lifted her chin. "Unless there is a reason other than *love* for a marriage between the two of you, my answer remains the same."

"I don't understand. I know I don't have a title, but my father is a viscount. I come from the finest of families—"

She held up a hand to stop him. "Your family is none of my concern. My daughter, however, is my concern. And she will not marry you. Most importantly, she will not know of this conversation. Is that clear?"

"Yes, ma'am."

"Good day, sir."

"But—"

"John," she snapped, and a large footman appeared almost instantly. "Please escort Mr. Norris to the door."

Stunned and feeling a bit numb, Charles followed the footman out. Not five minutes after he'd arrived, Charles found himself standing on the steps of the townhouse, staring at his carriage. He closed his eyes and tried to release this awful ache. It would do no good to wallow in it. Wallowing had never worked before. He had to move on, to dismiss Marjorie from his mind and pray he could as easily dismiss her from his heart.

"Here, could you post this for me?" Not thirty minutes after his conversation with Lady Summerfield, Charles handed Prajit the note to Lady Caroline asking her to accompany him to the zoo. He wanted to take a look at Jumbo the elephant.

In truth, he hoped Lady Caroline was frightened of the animal so she would sidle close to him. Or perhaps a lion would roar and she would press against his side. That had been the idea, but now it seemed silly and he really didn't want her pressed up against his side. Not with Marjorie there.

Prajit glanced at the address posted on the sealed note and frowned.

"Lady Marjorie and her brother are also coming along."

"Ah, that is good."

"Lord Summerfield is a good chap," Charles said, ignoring the true reason Prajit thought the idea good. Somehow, Prajit had taken a liking to Marjorie. Maybe he'd been impressed with her bravery, entering a gentleman's home in the middle of the night that first time. Prajit would never say anything aloud to him, but he sensed his disapproval of any woman other than Marjorie.

"Prajit, I thank you for your interest in my romantic affairs, but you should know that Lady Marjorie cannot marry me. Her mother would not allow her to marry an untitled gentleman. So you see, your subversive efforts to throw us together are futile."

Prajit looked immediately affronted. "I would never presume to interfere with your personal life, my lord."

Charles stared at him for half a beat, then nodded, not believing a word his valet said.

The Zoological Gardens in Regents Park held a marvelous collection of animals, mostly from Africa, those large and exotic creatures a fascination to a population used to horses, foxes, and small woodland creatures.

It was an overly warm day, the sun beating down on the visitors who walked along the graveled paths. Women holding frothy parasols and men in their straw hats strolled from exhibit to exhibit as the animals, bored and fat, ignored them. Marjorie had seen a few small private menageries but had never ventured to the zoo. Her mother thought such an activity far too pedestrian. In fact, she thought Marjorie and George were viewing an exhibit of Italian masters at the Museum of Art. Strange how lying to her mother had become almost second nature. It was better to lie than to face the wrath and scorn of Dorothea. She and George had been doing it for years.

They waited, she and George, at the south entrance near the Lions House for the arrival of Charles, Lady Caroline, and her mother. From time to time, the air would rumble with the exciting sound of a lion or the trumpet of one of the elephants. Despite her reason for being here, Marjorie looked forward to the day and told herself it had nothing to do with the fact she would see Charles. He would, after all, be with another woman.

"There they are now," Marjorie said, her stomach giving a funny little twist at the sight of Charles with Lady Caroline. Lady Warwick walked happily beside them, no doubt already assembling her daughter's trousseau. Lady Caroline looked utterly charming in a white gown with pale blue accents, the perfect dress for an overly warm, late May day. She was as fresh as a newly bloomed pink rose, whereas Marjorie felt more like the rose that had opened and already lost a few of its petals.

Why had she agreed to this meeting? Why did she go on pretending indifference when she knew her heart was fully engaged?

"Good afternoon, Lady Caroline, Lady Warwick. I'm so glad for such fine weather for our outing. Have either of you been to the zoo before?"

Lady Caroline smiled at Marjorie beneath her white and pale blue parasol. The sun shone through the thin material, giving her an almost ethereal glow. "When I was very small," she said. "I hardly remember a thing except that I was very afraid of the ostriches. Wasn't I, Mother?"

"You were very afraid of everything," her mother said, chuckling.

"Where shall we start?" Marjorie asked, leaning over to look at the map of the zoo George held. "The lions are first if we go to the left."

"Oh, yes, the lions," Lady Caroline said with a happy little bounce. "I had a cat when I was a girl who looked just like a lion. Well, not just, but the same coloring. She had two little white paws, though, and I don't think lions have white paws. I remember one time that naughty kitty climbed the curtains in Papa's library and ruined them. Then we had to keep her outside. What was her name, Mama?"

"Ginger."

"Oh, yes. Ginger. Because of the color. I do like a black cat. I never had one. Perhaps someday. Have you any pets, Mr. Norris? I think a home needs pets of some kind. We've always had pets, haven't we, Mother."

And so she went on, one sentence after another, so quickly that Marjorie wondered if she would faint from lack of oxygen. Throughout her monologue, Charles walked silently, nodding occasionally. As the day went on, he gave Marjorie more and more progressively panicked expressions. He hadn't uttered more than two syllables in twenty minutes; he couldn't with Lady Caroline's nonstop chatter.

George peered over the map constantly, stopping to read the plaques at each exhibit, which slowed things down a bit, but no one seemed to mind. He was fascinated with every detail of the animals, and read aloud each plaque to enlighten the rest of the group. Lady Warwick had attached herself to Marjorie, allowing the "young couple some privacy." As if Marjorie were a co-conspirator in their love. Even though she was supposed to be, Marjorie couldn't help but feel more than a bit resentful of her role.

From time to time, Lady Warwick would give Charles and her daughter a knowing look, and then turn to Marjorie to make certain she was catching how wonderful and charming and perfect they were together.

The elephant exhibit was the final destination, as it was opposite the entrance. Marjorie had no doubt why, for the zoological society had, in her opinion, saved the best for last. Jumbo was aptly named, for he was a massive creature, looking even larger standing next to the zoo's only other elephant, Alice. He stood in the center of his compound shoving straw into his mouth while a man, dwarfed beside the beast, patted his sides as if he were a pet dog.

"He's from Paris, you know," Charles said, finally able to utter more than a grunt because the sight of the elephant had made Lady Caroline, thankfully, quite speechless.

"Really?" Lady Caroline asked, eyes wide. "They have elephants in Paris? I've been to Paris and I've never seen . . . oh, you're making sport of me." She batted him playfully on the arm and Marjorie wanted to smack her hard. Good Lord, why had she agreed to this? Charles stood there, devastatingly handsome in his light brown jacket and cream-colored pants, looking precisely like a gentleman should on a jaunt to the zoo. His hard features softened when he gazed at Lady Caroline, and Marjorie could hardly stand to look at him. When she did, all she could remember was how his mouth felt against hers, how he'd touched her. His low groans of pleasure, his seductive words as he'd moved his hand beneath her skirts.

This was unbearable. Even now, she could feel the warmth and heat of arousal. How could he be so completely unaffected by what had transpired between them? How could he be so utterly callous as to flaunt his desire for another woman *one day* after holding her in his arms? The zoo required quite a bit of walking and she could tell he was beginning to suffer for it. She couldn't quite bring herself to care.

"He was brought from Paris when he was just little," George put in, as he read the plaque in front of the exhibit. "But originally, he's from Africa."

"Do you like elephants, Mr. Norris?" Lady Caroline asked, looking up at Charles as if whatever the next word he said would be wonderful and witty.

He seemed startled to realize she was actually waiting for his answer. He glanced Marjorie's way, and she could see him visibly relax. Suddenly, all bitter thoughts were erased. He might be with Lady Caroline, but he *needed* her. Why that depressing thought was comforting, Marjorie couldn't fathom.

"I find them grand and majestic creatures, and part of me is pained to see such a fine animal put on exhibit. But he seems happy and I've read he is a gentle giant, even allowing people to ride upon him. Would you like me to hoist you aboard, Lady Caroline?"

"Goodness, no, Mr. Norris. What if I fell?"

"I would most certainly catch you," he said grandly, earning a beaming smile from both Lady Caroline and her mother. Marjorie braced herself for another knowing look from Lady Warwick and was not disappointed. "I think you'd look grand riding the lion, too, but I fear you would be too tempting a meal for the beast."

Oh, good God, Marjorie thought. But Lady Caroline giggled, delighted with his teasing.

The rest of the afternoon was much the same. Lady Caroline would say something, Charles would respond wittily, and Lady Caroline would giggle. The repetition of it was extremely tedious. Every once in a while, Charles would shoot her a grateful look, and she was tempted to ask him what he planned to do when they were married and he was tongue-tied and she was not around to give him courage.

The incessant chatter of the happy pair was grating, and Marjorie couldn't wait until the tour was over. No doubt Charles felt the same (but for an entirely different reason), for by the time they made their way back to the south entrance, he was limping noticeably. She told herself she didn't care. And she didn't, until she saw he'd broken out into a sweat that had nothing to do with the warm day. Indeed, the sun had given way to clouds and the temperature had dropped rather dramatically. It looked as if rain was imminent as Charles handed the two ladies up into their carriage.

"George, I'll meet you in our carriage. I need to speak with Mr. Norris privately, if you don't mind."

"Of course. Good day, Mr. Norris."

"Good day, Summerfield. We'll see you tomorrow night." When George was gone, he turned to her. "Thank you. That went swimmingly, did it not?"

"I quit." She hadn't realized that was what she was going to say, but there it was. She quit. She simply could not suffer another day like the one just endured.

"You cannot. Not now. Why?"

"I've done what we agreed. I've found you a bride."

His brows instantly drew together. "I think that's a bit hasty, to be honest. I'm not certain we suit."

"You're perfect together. Good day and good-bye, Mr. Norris." Despite her departing words, she didn't turn to her carriage, even as the first raindrops began to fall. She immediately snapped opened her parasol.

"This is about yesterday, isn't it?"

Marjorie lifted her chin. "I've no idea what you mean."

"Because of what we did. What I did. I am sorry. I take complete responsibility. I should have made you leave, turned my back, done something, anything, to prevent what transpired between us. It was wrong."

"What *transpired?*" she asked, for some reason affronted by his using that sterile word to describe something she thought was wonderful. "You are correct. What *transpired* should never have happened and will never happen again. It was meaningless and will not be repeated. Ever."

He stiffened. "Of course not."

Marjorie ignored the pain and disappointment those words wrought. "So you see why I can no longer assist you."

"Quite the opposite, my lady," he said, looking and sounding angry. "If what transpired was meaningless, which is apparently how you see it, then we should have no problem at all continuing on as before. We should be able to revert to our business relationship without conflict. I place the blame firmly on myself. I flirted with you. I kissed you. I—" He stopped suddenly, and looked away. "I, perhaps, gave you the wrong impression of my intentions." This last was said softly and perhaps hurt the most.

"You did not," she said, proud that she sounded so certain and strong. "However, I feel it is in both of our interests that we have no relationship, business or otherwise."

"But you, my lady, have not met the conditions of our arrangement," he said coldly. "Unless your brother has found twenty-four thousand pounds in his back pocket?"

"I hate you."

He lowered his gaze, then gave her a mocking bow. "I'm certain you do. You will be gratified to know that I will likely ask Lady Caroline for her hand before the end of the season. And then you will be rid of me. Good day, my lady."

"Good day," she choked out, feeling tears threaten.

"Oh, I nearly forgot. I'm attending the May Ball tomorrow evening."

Of course he would be there. As would she. Her mother would never miss attending that grand event. She didn't answer, but walked past him without looking up, fearing he might see the unshed tears in her eyes.

Chapter 11

The next day, she, along with her brother and Miss Lilianne Cavendish, visited Katherine in her suite at Brown's Hotel for tea. Any doubt Marjorie had about affection between her brother and Miss Cavendish was quickly relieved. She was a quiet, composed creature, with brown hair and brown eyes, wholly unremarkable except when she looked at George. Never did Marjorie believe that anyone could love her brother as much as she did, but she was beginning to think it was possible.

On the way to Brown's, the two of them pored over a book describing the architecture of an Egyptian pyramid, gushing about secret chambers and massive dimensions. George had clearly read the book prior to this, and continued to recite facts and figures about the pyramids. Even Marjorie, who was used to this tendency, was slightly annoyed, but Miss Cavendish was more bemused than anything. And when George started to repeat himself, she would gently insert a comment into the conversation, stopping his monologue. She had a way about her that was both gentle and strong.

Brown's Hotel was located in the heart of Mayfair, a grand, four-story structure of light stone, and Marjorie, given her belief that Avonleigh was strapped for cash, was surprised they were staying there. Still, he was a marquess and a marquess certainly could not stay in one of the seedier hotels.

Katherine greeted them as they entered the hotel with her usual exuberance. She wore a gown Marjorie recognized from the previous year, a forest-green creation with cream lace and pale yellow collar and cuffs.

"I thought after tea we could walk to Green Park. That's why I'm wearing green," she said, laughing. "Very clever of me, I know. Besides, it's so lovely and not nearly as crowded as Hyde. I've been cooped up in this hotel for far too long. Graham has been busy meeting with lawyers and investors, and I'm about to go mad from boredom."

Marjorie looked over to the young couple and immediately agreed. There were very few activities when a couple could be alone but also closely chaperoned, and a walk in the park was one of them. She wanted to observe the pair a bit longer, just to assure herself that Miss Cavendish wanted George and not his title.

"That's a lovely idea."

The four walked to a small restaurant within the hotel and were immediately ushered to a table. Marjorie looked around, nodding to Lady Cartwright, an elderly woman who was friends with her mother, and her recently widowed daughter.

"Oh, my, there's Jennie Jerome and her mother," Katherine said, apparently delighted. Marjorie shook her head; she didn't know the girl.

Katherine leaned forward. "You know, she caught the eye of Marlborough's son, Lord Randolph. I'd go say hello, but we really didn't run in the same circles. Still, she is an American . . ."

"Yes, now I recall," Marjorie said, remembering reading something about the American heiress and Lord Randolph. "Aren't they engaged?"

"Yes, much to both their parents' horror. I do sympathize with what they've been through." Katherine hesitated, then rose and walked to the table where Jennie Jerome sat with an older woman. They chatted briefly, then Katherine returned, smiling.

"What a charming girl," Katherine said.

Marjorie eyed the other American girl warily. "Please don't be insulted," she began, then stopped, pressing her lips together. The influx of American girls with money coming in and marrying British titles was a bit disconcerting, particularly for an unmarried British lady.

Katherine waved a dismissive hand. "Don't worry," she said with a laugh. "We won't take all your men. Only the *poor* titled ones."

Marjorie couldn't help but laugh at her outrageous friend. "And you are happy, are you not?"

"Terribly happy," Katherine said. "That was all my father needed to see to give us my dowry. But I do believe we would have been happy without it. Truly I do," she added when she saw Marjorie's skeptical face.

"If one is going to be happy, it is better to be rich and happy than poor and happy."

Katherine laughed. "You sound like such a snob when you talk like that. But I still adore you."

After tea, the foursome walked to Green Park, just down Albemarle and onto Piccadilly, where the park entrance was.

"I like this park better than the rest," Katherine said as they walked through the massive gates.

"And why is that?"

"Because it's just grass and trees and flowers. It's so natural."

"It also used to be a leper colony and a haven for thieves," Marjorie said, looking around the green expanse.

Katherine wrinkled her nose. "Can't you just enjoy a place without knowing every detail of its history?"

"And Queen Elizabeth was nearly assassinated right over there," Marjorie said, ignoring the admonition and pointing toward Constitution Hill. She stopped her history lesson to smile at George and Miss Cavendish, who were walking ahead of them, heads close together in animated conversation.

"I do believe I've made at least one successful match this season," Marjorie said.

"They certainly do seem taken with one another. I'm glad."

"As am I," Marjorie said feelingly.

"And what of you? How goes your matchmaking adventure?"

Marjorie frowned and looked away from her friend, momentarily surprised how much it hurt even to think of Charles. "He seems quite taken with Lady Caroline. Their families are close so it's almost certain that he'll propose before the end of the season." She tried to keep all emotion from her voice, but she must have failed.

"I'm sorry," Katherine said, touching her arm.

"Whatever for? I've been successful. Now George's debt will be cleared and Mother need never know of how foolish he was. But I do blame my cousin in part. He had no business bringing George into such a high-stakes game. Finding Mr. Norris a suitable bride is what I wanted." She could not look Katherine in the eye, so she kept her gaze on her brother as she lied. She stopped walking and looked down at the gravel path beneath them. No, she couldn't lie to her friend any more. "Of course, it's not what I want. You know that."

"Oh, Marjorie. I suspected as much."

Marjorie swallowed, refusing to give in to the emotions that were swarming to the surface. She could not allow herself to show the depth of her despair in such a public place. And so she smiled. "There's nothing to be done. I cannot disobey my mother and he has no interest."

"I can't believe that's true. I've seen the way he looks at you."

Marjorie felt a small spark of anger. "And have you seen how he looks at Lady Caroline? I daresay his smiles are more brilliant than when he looks at me. He's a cad, really. Boorish and loud. I haven't the faintest idea why I like him at all."

"Men can be confusing," Katherine said.

"Confusing? Confounding!" Marjorie felt a rush of tears and quickly dashed them away.

"What is wrong, Marjorie? Tell me."

Marjorie swallowed heavily, trying to get her emotions under control. "I must tell you something," she whispered. "If I don't tell someone, it will fester inside me and kill me for certain."

"Go on."

"We've kissed," she said on a rush. "More than kissed, actually."

"How much more?" Katherine asked cautiously.

Marjorie gave her friend a look of apt misery. "Quite a bit more. And it's my fault."

"You didn't," Katherine said on a gleeful rush. "Oh, and after all the lectures you gave me. Shame on you."

Marjorie was momentarily confused before she realized what she'd said. "No, no. We didn't do *that*. But we came very close." She let out another gusty sigh. "I went to see him to discuss Lady Caroline."

"Alone?"

"I brought my maid, of course. But I didn't only go to discuss Lady Caroline. That was merely the pretense of my visit. His servant brought Alice to the kitchens for tea and then led me to his study and he was, um, rather unclothed."

"He was *naked?*"

"Very nearly so. He wore only his drawers. And his injury, it's just awful, poor man. I should have left, but I didn't. And then, well, his thing, his man thing, it was . . ."

"Big?"

Marjorie buried her head in her hands and nodded, mortified beyond all being that she was having such a conversation. But there wasn't another person on earth she could tell this to.

"You're not going to believe what I did, what I said. I still can't believe it. It's so unlike me. So against everything I've been brought up to be."

"What did you do?" Katherine said breathlessly, and Marjorie could tell she was caught between horror and curiosity.

"I asked to see it." Marjorie looked up at the blue sky and shook her head. "Can you believe I would say such a thing?"

"No," Katherine said with a small laugh, "I can't. And did he? Let you?"

"No, not at first. He demanded his trousers. He was in such pain he was unable to get them himself. They were across the room, you see. I got them and wouldn't give them to him." She said this last in a mortified whisper. "Then he did as I asked. Quickly. I called foul and he, well, he dropped his drawers so I could get a better look. Odd things, aren't they?"

"Men?"

"No, their man parts."

"Oh, yes, quite," Katherine said, blushing.

"Then things got a bit out of hand and we kissed and . . . other things. The next day, I accompanied him and Lady Caroline to the zoo and he acted as if nothing had happened between us at all."

"He is a cad."

"I know!" Marjorie walked a bit farther, hands fisted by her sides, before spinning about to face her friend. "And even though I know he's a cad—and believe me I do know it—I still find myself thinking about him and wishing he felt even the smallest bit of what I feel for him." She crossed her arms angrily. "I love him. I love a cad." She threw her arms up in surrender. "To make matters worse, my mother wants me married this year. To Lord Shannock."

"Who is Lord Shannock?"

"My father's old friend and neighbor. He's onerous. And old. He's in his *fifties*."

Katherine touched her wrist. "Can your mother force you to marry a man you don't wish to?"

"Of course. She can throw me from the house, and then where would I go? And don't you dare say to you." Katherine snapped her mouth shut. "Besides, I don't like going against her. She has been so patient with me. I'm nearly twenty-four and have had all kinds of opportunity to marry. Now I fear it's too late."

Katherine let out a laugh. "Yes, because you are so ancient and pruney."

Marjorie couldn't bring herself to laugh. "Most women my age are well married and mothers by now. You're married and you're younger than I. Don't think that didn't stick in my mother's craw. My unmarried state is something my own mother points out to me daily. I see girls like Lady Caroline and they seem so very young." She looked at her brother and smiled sadly. "I didn't think I'd ever marry. I was convinced of it. But now . . ."

Katherine followed Marjorie's eyes. "If George marries, there is nothing to stop you from marrying. Is that it?"

Marjorie nodded. "I suppose I thought he wouldn't find anyone who understood him as I do. But I do believe he's found someone who understands him more."

The young couple turned just then, their faces alight with pure happiness, and waited for Marjorie and Katherine to catch up to them.

"Marjorie," George blurted, "I'm going to talk to Lilianne's father this very afternoon. We hope to marry."

"That's wonderful," she said, grabbing her brother's hands and giving them an affectionate tug. Then she did the same with Miss Cavendish. "How wonderful it will be to have a sister." Miss Cavendish gave her a shy smile before looking at George, and it was more obvious than ever that she adored him.

"May I speak with Miss Cavendish privately a moment, George?"

Marjorie could have asked her brother to jump over the moon and she had no doubt he'd at least attempt it. She'd never seen her brother so utterly happy.

Marjorie continued down the path, Miss Cavendish by her side. "I love my brother wholeheartedly, Miss Cavendish, and I would not ever want anything to hurt him."

"I would never hurt your brother, my lady. I love him. And please call me Lilianne."

"Yes, I can see that you do. How do your parents feel about this courtship?"

"They approve," she said, with just enough hesitance that Marjorie's worry grew. "They know George is a bit different from other men his age. But they trust my judgment. I think they fear for me, that I will regret my decision, that I don't know my own heart. That what I feel for George is the same as I would feel for a poor, wounded puppy. But it's not like that at all."

Marjorie wondered if the girl was just fooling herself. "George can be difficult at times. He's very set in his ways and can spend hours working on his research. You will not be able to pull him away and it can be frustrating."

"I understand him. I'm very much like him in many ways. I think that's why we suit. I have never felt comfortable with girls my own age and I'm frightened to tears of most men. But when I met George, it was like meeting the second half of myself, as if he were this missing piece of me that fell into place."

Marjorie's eyes burned from unshed tears and she impulsively grabbed Lilianne's hand. "That was beautifully said. There are very few of us who find that person. I'm so happy for you and George that you have."

As they walked back to the hotel, the young couple chattering happily, Katherine said, "I don't think you understand the seriousness of what happened between you and Mr. Norris. Do you know what would have occurred had you been discovered? Scandal, that's what. You would have been compromised and Mr. Norris would have been forced to marry you. And that would have been disastrous. Just look what happened with Graham and me. Found out, shamed, forced to marry. And living happily ever after."

"I don't find you at all amusing," Marjorie said dryly. She had said very much the same thing—without the happily-ever-after part—to Katherine not all that long ago. She'd suspected the couple had been acting indiscreetly and had warned Katherine that a forced marriage would be the worst outcome possible. "Yours was an entirely different situation," Marjorie said, sniffing.

"Oh? How so?"

"Lord Avonleigh was clearly intended for another."

"They weren't engaged. At least not at first," Katherine added a bit sheepishly. "Though when we were caught together, he was engaged."

"See? Entirely different."

"Should you wait until Mr. Norris is engaged before you tell him you love him and throw yourself at him? It worked for me." Katherine let out a delighted giggle.

"You are ridiculous," Marjorie said, but couldn't help smiling a bit. "And it is different. Avonleigh loved you."

"You don't know how Mr. Norris feels about you."

"Of course I do. He's asked me to help him court another woman. If he were in love with me, would he ask such a thing?"

Katherine frowned. "I don't see how he could. Perhaps you're right. But if he does love you, being compromised could be the perfect solution."

Marjorie shook her head. "He doesn't, so it makes no sense to even think about such things." But for the rest of the walk back to Brown's, it was all she could think of.

"You know, Charles, your situation isn't that much different from mine," Avonleigh said, lazily twirling his brandy.

The two men sat in Charles's study, enjoying their brandy and each other's company. Graham was fascinated by the artifacts Charles had collected over the years he'd been gone from England, but more fascinated by the stories that accompanied each item. Charles's glass was empty and he gave a longing look to the half-full bottle on the sideboard. "Oh?"

"You need a wife—"

"Want a wife. Far different."

"Fine, you want a wife, though I can't fathom why you think that's so. Still, it all worked out for me in the end."

Charles gave in to temptation and heaved himself up to retrieve more brandy.

"I wonder how you would feel had you married that Von Haupt chit instead of Miss Wright."

"I daresay I'd feel quite different, at least about marriage. The money, now, that would have been grand."

Charles let out a sharp laugh. "I have found, sir, that money cannot buy what one really wants. A leg, for example. Or a title."

"What need do you have of a title? It's a mantle around one's neck, I say. Duty and worry and worry and duty."

"If I had a title, we wouldn't be having this conversation. I'd be well on my way to be married right now." He cursed under his breath. "Where's John when I need him? He's much better about this sort of thing."

"You mean he's better at thinking like a woman? He's counting all his children. They just had their fifth, you know. Good God."

Charles smiled. He'd come from a family of three and had always been a bit jealous of larger families. He couldn't imagine being an only child. The loneliness must be crushing. Perhaps one made up for lack of siblings with friends.

"For God's sake, get that ridiculous grin off your face," Graham said in mock anger. "If you didn't have a beard, I'd think you were a woman."

Charles poured a large splash into his glass. "Why, because I want to marry?"

"No, because you want to fall in love."

"You did."

That shut Avonleigh up for a time. "Didn't do it on purpose. Just happened. In fact, I didn't want it to happen at all. Wasn't a very pleasant thing, you know."

"Yes, I do."

Avonleigh leaned back in his chair and gave his old friend an even look. "Do you, now. Lady Caroline? No, not her. Too chatty. Too young. Let's see, who does Charles love *now*?" He tapped his head as if massaging his brain for an answer. "Title. Woman. Woman who wants title. Man who doesn't have one." He snapped his fingers. "Lady Marjorie."

"You should work for Scotland Yard," Charles said dryly. "Of course Lady Marjorie. But she has no interest in a man without a title and her mother would kill me if I courted her. Have you met that woman?" Charles gave a mock shudder.

"You're afraid of her mother?"

"Who isn't? I do believe it's one of the reasons the poor girl is not married."

Graham smiled, his eyes on his swirling brandy. "You know," he said softly, "there's more than one way to propose to a girl who's entirely unsuited to you."

Charles furrowed his brow and walked back to his chair. "What do you mean?"

"I would never condone such a thing, believe me. But it worked out quite well for Katherine and me. Quite well indeed."

"She'd murder me if I compromised her."

"Lady Summerfield?"

"No, Lady Marjorie. I could never put her in that position. I care for her far too much to bring that sort of scandal upon her."

Graham placed his still full glass aside. "You misunderstand what I'm saying. What if you both were agreeable to being compromised?"

Charles was stunned by the suggestion. "You mean a planned compromise? One in which we'd both be culpable? She'd never agree."

"Would you?"

Charles was silent for a long minute. Would he forge such a plan if Marjorie agreed to it? It did seem quite like the only way they could be married with her mother's reluctant blessing. Still, the scandal. Charles studied his friend, his very happy, married friend, who had suffered no ill consequences from society for his forced marriage. Indeed, even the most hardened old curmudgeons looked at the match fondly because it was so obvious the two of them were happy. "If she agreed, then, yes, I would. Happily. But Marjorie would never agree to such a thing."

"And how do you know she wouldn't agree to the plan?"

"For one, she told me just the other day that she hated me," Charles said, chuckling. "So you see, I'm fairly certain her heart is not engaged. No more than any other woman I've managed to foolishly fall in love with. I swear I'm cursed."

"I wouldn't be so hasty in your assessment of Lady Marjorie's feelings toward you. Something Katherine said to me makes me think she wouldn't at all be opposed."

That brightened Charles's mood a bit. "Something Lady Marjorie said?"

"Yes." He tapped his head again. "What was it? It was rather obscure and open to interpretation, of course. Oh, yes, I have it. She told me Lady Marjorie was in love with you."

Now it was Charles's turn to set aside his glass. "What? Did Lady Marjorie actually say something to your wife? Or is it supposition?"

"Supposition. But when she accused Lady Marjorie of having such feelings, she did not deny it completely."

"What did she say?"

"Actually, she did deny it," Graham admitted, "but Katherine is convinced she wasn't telling the truth. Apparently she couldn't keep her eyes off you the other night at the opera. And since you cannot ask for her hand with any hope that her mother would agree to the match, you really have no alternative, do you?"

Charles picked up his glass again and took a deep swallow. No, actually, he could think of no other way for them to marry. But Marjorie would have to wholeheartedly agree. And if she loved him as he loved her, then it was the perfect solution.

"You what?"

"I'm engaged, Mother."

Marjorie's heart nearly broke at the way her brother was standing there, looking unkempt and uncertain, his head down. He was a different man when he stood before their mother.

"What girl would say yes to you? Some greedy little thing only interested in your title, no doubt. I can tell you right now, I'll put a stop to it."

"It's Miss Cavendish, Mother."

"The squire's daughter?" She let out an ugly laugh. "Oh, ho, they do have high aspirations, don't they?"

"She loves me," George said, lifting his head in a small show of defiance. His cheeks were flushed and Marjorie wanted nothing more than to have this interview over. "She told me. She loves me. I went to her father and he gave us his blessing."

"I'm sure he did. He's not a fool. I can tell you one thing, young man, you will not marry that girl. She doesn't love you, she loves the title, the idea of being an earl's wife. I will not allow it. It will not happen."

Marjorie couldn't take another word. "You cannot stop him, Mother," she said gently. Despite the awful things her mother was saying, it was clear Dorothea was concerned that George would be hurt. Frankly, Marjorie was surprised her mother was championing her son so ardently. "He is of age and is the head of this family. You cannot prevent him from marrying whom he chooses. I understand your concerns, Mother, truly I do. For I had them myself." She shot George a look of apology. "But I firmly believe Miss Cavendish loves George, that she would marry him even if he were a commoner. And you know you have no power over George and no say in whom he marries."

Dorothea looked at her daughter as if she'd sprouted a second head. "How dare you contradict me in front of your brother? Women who want something can be very clever. Just look at your American friend."

"You *like* Katherine."

"I admire her cleverness, if that's what you mean. One must, I suppose. But I will not allow an equally clever woman to marry my son for self-serving reasons. A squire's daughter, indeed. Really, George, why not simply marry a shop girl or a scullery maid? Certainly not." She looked at George with sympathy. "It's best that you get any ideas of marriage out of your head."

"No, Mother. I love Lilianne and I will marry her. I have her parents' blessing. I would like yours, but if you cannot give it, I will marry Miss Cavendish. I love her. We will marry September twentieth of this year. I love her and I will marry her."

"Don't get hysterical, George," Dorothea said with a long-suffering sigh. "You know it gives me a headache."

George clenched his fists by his sides, and Marjorie knew he was struggling to remain calm. "I love Miss Cavendish and I will marry her. We're to be—"

"Oh, for God's sake, shut up," Dorothea screamed. "Leave me, both of you, now. You've given me a headache."

Marjorie and George were more than happy to leave their mother alone. When they reached the second story landing, Marjorie touched George's hand.

"I was very proud of you."

He ducked his head, his cheeks growing ruddy. "They gave us their blessing," he said, just in case Marjorie needed convincing.

"I know they did and I'm glad. Lilianne loves you very much, as she should. You are a wonderful man and will make a wonderful husband."

George turned toward his room, then hesitated. "Do you think she can stop it?" he asked, sounding very young.

"No, George, she cannot. You are of age and head of this household. You are the Earl of Summerfield and can marry whomever you choose."

He smiled and relaxed, heading to his room to change for the May Ball, but as Marjorie turned to go to her room, she frowned. She prayed Dorothea would do nothing to keep the couple apart. But what could she do, after all?

Chapter 12

Thirty years earlier

Ten years after Ascot, Dorothea Stockbridge bore little resemblance to the young woman she'd been that day. Though she'd traveled home to see her family on occasion, she made her home with Aunt Frances, who continued to thrive at age eighty-five. With both parents now in their graves, Dorothea rarely had the opportunity to leave. Twice a year she would travel to visit her brother and sisters, but the visits were always brief and she sensed her siblings were relieved when she waved good-bye. This past year, she hadn't visited at all, nor had she been invited. So Dorothea spent endless days with Aunt Frances, knowing that someday, should the old lady ever die, she would be at the mercy of her relatives. She felt fairly safe, as Aunt Frances was as hale and hearty as she was mean and miserable. Dorothea often thought it was the devil keeping her alive simply to torment her.

Having nowhere else to go, Dorothea remained in Ipswich in Stonebridge Hall, a drafty old place on the River Orwell, and was reminded nearly every day that she had few other options. She no longer wore the latest fashions and hadn't bought a new hat in nearly eight years. The last was for a garden party, which she'd allowed herself to look forward to, only to be told by her aunt that she looked ridiculous, as if she were a wren trying to be a peacock.

Her hair, which had long ago turned coarse and gray, was constantly pulled back into a serviceable bun. Her dresses came in three colors: gray, brown, and black. She wore the uniform of the over-looked and the expression of a woman whose life was filled with days of duty and monotony. And when she went for walks, as she did each day, she wore a man's coat.

Dorothea loved her daily walks. They were one of the few things her aunt approved of. Exercise, she would often say, kept one alive, and her aunt lamented the fact her painful knees would no longer allow it. Those walks were Dorothea's escape, the only time she could be alone with her thoughts. The only time she could hold a piece of Lord Smythe against her, his coat that she had "forgotten" to return to him. Before she'd made the move to Ipswich, she'd placed it guiltily in the bottom of her trunk and after she'd left home, she'd pulled it out frequently. Too frequently at first. Now it was simply a serviceable coat to wear on a brisk walk.

He'd married Lady Matilda of course, the vacant-headed, kind girl he'd been with that day. She'd read the *Times* issue that described their wedding and would on occasion see mention of them—or their children.

That was, perhaps, the worst of her life. She'd realized after mov-ing to Ipswich that she wanted children far more than she'd wanted a husband. The sight of a woman walking with a small brood always made her a bit sad. It would never happen for her. Time was running out. She was thirty-six years old. Many of her old friends' children were already married or at university.

Dorothea sighed heavily as she crossed the stone bridge to the house's garden. She stood for a moment staring at the old place, hat-ing it, hating what lay inside. Why couldn't she find contentment with her life? She knew women had far worse lives than she did. What was inside her that made her feel as if some great trick had been played and she was living the life someone far less vibrant was supposed to have lived?

With a sense of resignation, she crossed the last few feet of yard and opened a side door. Pulling off her coat and placing it on a wooden peg, she spied a servant hurrying with a tray.

"Sally, where are you off to in such a hurry?"

"Oh, mum, Lord Summerfield's here and in the parlor." She bobbed a quick curtsy and went on her way as Dorothea leaned against the wall in utter defeat. With a quick look of longing at the door she'd just entered, Dorothea began walking toward the parlor where Aunt Frances always entertained guests. Of all the guests that infrequently stopped by, Lord Summerfield was her least favorite.

He was a pompous man in his late fifties whose superior attitude grated on Dorothea's nerves. It wasn't so much what he said, but rather the way in which he said it. He could tell her she looked beautiful (which he never had) and Dorothea would somehow understand he meant the opposite. When he'd first made an appearance, Dorothea had feared that he was visiting with the intention of courting her. His wife was long dead and he had no children, no heir to his great title. Over the years, she'd been relieved to realize that Lord Summerfield seemed content to let his younger brother or nephew inherit his title.

Dorothea had felt foolish to think his visits had initially been precipitated by her. Now she finally understood she had little to offer a man except a dowry, no doubt collecting dust in her father's coffers. She'd come to realize over the years that no man would want her. Not even an onerous, ugly old man like Summerfield. It was a rather sobering thought.

Dorothea entered the parlor, not bothering to even glance in the mirror to be certain she was presentable. From the look both her aunt and Summerfield gave her, she knew she was not.

"Here she is," Lord Summerfield said, standing, his sleepy eyes regarding her. Over the years, his upper eyelids had continued to descend, so it was impossible for the man to open his eyes fully. His nose, looking much like a small tomato balancing above his too-thick lips, was constantly dripping. Dorothea on more than one occasion had had to look away. He held a kerchief in his left hand at all times and would dab at the moisture incessantly but many times to no avail.

"Here I am," Dorothea said with forced pleasantness, and sat down next to her aunt.

"Lord Summerfield, shall I leave?" her aunt asked, and Dorothea felt a shiver of unease.

"No, no." He waved his hand, then turned to Dorothea. "As you may know, Miss Stockbridge, I have been searching for a wife for some time now."

Dorothea hadn't known any such thing, but nodded.

"And I've chosen you."

"Me?"

"I know you are not young, but neither am I. And I'm quite running out of options."

Dorothea looked to her aunt for help, knowing she would get little.

"It's wonderful, Dorothea, though I will miss you, dear. And the timing couldn't be more propitious. I'm going to live with Christina for a time." Aunt Frances thumped her cane to punctuate her decision. "My daughter wrote to me just last week, asking me to come," she said to Summerfield, leaving Dorothea stunned. Her aunt had known she was leaving for a week and hadn't said a word. With her mother and father both dead, she had nowhere to go.

Dorothea's brain had quite stopped.

Summerfield sniffed.

"Of course, I wholeheartedly approve of the match," Aunt Frances went on. "Everything has been agreed to."

"But I haven't agreed to anything."

A heavy silence filled the room.

"Would you please excuse us, madam? I fear I do need to speak to your niece alone, after all."

Dorothea watched in disbelief as her aunt hoisted herself up and made her way slowly to the door, her cane thumping softly on the carpet.

"I do apologize, my lord, but you've never given any indication that you even liked me, never mind wanted to marry me."

He stared at her for a long, uncomfortable moment, as if reassessing his offer. "How old are you?"

Dorothea felt her cheeks flush. "Thirty-six."

He raised one eyebrow and tilted his head as if pitying her. "And how many men have asked for your hand?"

Her cheeks grew impossibly hotter. "None, sir."

"And how many have courted you?"

"None."

"Held your hand? Kissed you? Even admired you?"

Dorothea's throat began to burn.

"Answer me. How many?" He said the words gently, but with an arrogance that was humiliating.

"None."

"None. Not one. And yet you think to refuse me? I am giving you the greatest of compliments. I am telling you that you are worthy of me and the Summerfield title. And you think to refuse me?"

A terrible feeling of inevitability fell over her. "I have not refused you, sir. Only questioned why you asked."

He seemed to calm at her words. "I have asked because I pray you are young enough to produce my heir. You still have your flow?"

Could she possibly bear such humiliation? "Yes."

He clapped his hands together so loudly, Dorothea flinched. "Well, then, it's settled. I'll make the announcement and have the bans read. I think a small affair is appropriate, do you not? Write to your brother and sisters, my dear. Perhaps they can be of assistance in planning the wedding."

He left soon after, full of accomplishment. Before he departed, he took her hand in his and kissed it. She tried to smile, but cringed at the feeling of wetness that remained after he'd withdrawn his hand. When he turned his back, she wiped her hand furiously on her skirt.

Oh, God, what had she just agreed to?

Chapter 13

The May Ball, held each year at the Ashton Estate twenty minutes outside of London, was one of the premier events of the season. To be invited to the May Ball was akin to being invited to a royal ball. The Cavendishes, alas, were not invited, so George refused to go. Marjorie was a bit proud of his stance, but Dorothea seemed, if anything, relieved. She was always on edge that George would do or say something that would cause her embarrassment. And to be fair, Marjorie admitted to herself, he almost always did. As much as she loved and understood her brother, she also understood and loved her mother—even if she didn't agree with her.

Castle Ashton rivaled Marlborough's Blenheim Palace in size and grandeur. As a girl, Marjorie had been bitterly disappointed to learn Castle Ashton wasn't a castle at all, but rather a grand house, much like their own in Ipswich. The Baroque building, designed with painful symmetry, was a favorite of Marjorie because it held such happy memories. House parties there were always lavish and long, and she'd spent many summer days there exploring the expansive grounds. Because of its proximity to London, most people who attended did not stay overnight for the May Ball, and so Lord and Lady Ashton always invited a huge crush of people. Queen Victoria often attended the ball, but this year she was unable to, much to the great disappointment of everyone attending. Still, it was a grand event, one that every high-born young lady in England yearned to attend. It was Marjorie's fifth.

Charles, along with his brother, father, and sister, were invited, though he was the only one who attended. His sister's husband would not leave the side of his ailing mother—a mother who had been suspiciously ailing for the past twelve years. His brother, never one to enjoy society's gatherings, was more than happy to send this younger brother as proxy. Charles didn't mind in the least.

The night air held a hint of rain to come as Marjorie grasped the hand of an Ashton footman and stepped down to the meticulously groomed stone drive. No doubt she would meet many old friends, some she hadn't seen in months. It seemed as if her little group had scattered to the four corners of England. One of her dearest friends, Lenore, had married an American and now lived in Philadelphia. She remembered their tearful good-bye, their promises to see each other at least once a year. She hadn't even received a letter from Lenore in six months.

She wore her best and newest Worth gown—as she always did for the May Ball. The gown was a pale peach with lacy cap sleeves that hugged her shoulders, with a bodice that dipped low enough to reveal the tops of her breasts. Lace that edged the neckline could be fluffed up a bit to provide more coverage, but when Marjorie presented the more modest version of her gown, Dorothea clicked her tongue and pushed the lace down.

"Lord Shannock will be there this evening," she said with a smile. "We want you to look your best."

Marjorie had looked down at herself, clearly seeing her breasts displayed, and grimaced. "Really, Mother, surely he can use his imagination."

"Mr. Worth designed this dress specifically for you to show off your best assets."

"These are my best assets? I rather thought my wit and cleverness were."

Dorothea adjusted the lace a bit more to create the desired effect. "Those may very well be your best assets, but I'm quite certain Lord Shannock will care more for these," she said pragmatically, giving the lace one final tuck.

As she walked up the steps to Castle Ashton, Marjorie released her train, letting it fall artistically behind her. It was a lovely dress, and Mr. Worth had been quite proud of it. Its bustle was modern, a natural shape that didn't call for the sometimes painful cages that his earlier designs had required. Instead of a bell-shaped skirt, the front hugged her legs rather closely. When she'd tried the dress on, Dorothea's eyes had widened with appreciation and Mr. Worth had given her a small bow. Marjorie might not be the youngest debutante at the ball, but she would most certainly be the best dressed.

Marjorie suspected he would mourn the loss of his best customer should she marry this year as her mother wished. Five seasons meant five years of the most beautiful and costly gowns money could buy, and she had no doubt that Mr. Worth would be a bit sad to see her married. She'd still be a customer, but her need for so many new gowns each year would surely be diminished.

Once they were in the grand foyer, Marjorie gathered up her train, looping the satin band, decorated with lace and tiny pearls, around her right wrist. No matter how many balls she attended, this part of any evening was always Marjorie's favorite. It was the part where she would spy old friends, collect her dance card, and feel the tiny thrill of anticipation that this night would be different from all the rest. In her first season, she'd been so excited at the prospect of a ball, her stomach had been aflutter with the possibilities. She had been acutely aware of the attention she drew and had reveled in it.

Now, there was far less excitement, but she still felt a pleasure in being part of something special. Even as Marjorie looked around trying to spot friends, she knew that by the end of the evening, a new and strange hollowness would set in. It was like looking forward to a wonderful birthday only to realize that the only thing that had come of it was being one year closer to dying. Marjorie furrowed her brow. It would do no good to think such maudlin thoughts at one of the season's premier events. Goodness!

"Penny for your thoughts."

Marjorie turned to see Katherine standing next to her. "Oh, Katherine, you don't want to know." When her friend's eyes widened, she remembered their last conversation and quickly said, "I was thinking that balls are becoming rather tedious."

"I always thought they were," Katherine said. "This one, thankfully, will be our last until next year. We leave the day after tomorrow. Graham is champing at the bit to get back to Avonleigh. We have so many plans."

Katherine looped her arm around Marjorie's and pulled her toward the grand ballroom. Outside, the single ladies were standing in line for their dance cards and the two women joined the line. "He's here, you know."

"Who?"

Katherine gave her a small look of exasperation. "Mr. Norris. He's here. He and Graham have already made it to the billiard room."

Marjorie was still stinging from her last encounter with Mr. Norris and wasn't certain she wanted to see the man at all. "Mr. Norris can go to perdition," she said in a low voice.

"You don't mean that," Katherine said lightly.

Oh, but she did mean it. At least she *wanted* to mean it.

Marjorie gathered her card and the two friends entered the ballroom, giving a collective gasp. It was beyond stunning, with hanging baskets of ivy and delicate lobelia, and sparkling crystals that gleamed in the gaslight, making the large room look as if a fairy had decorated the place.

"Oh, it's lovely," Katherine said. "I think I shall have to borrow this idea when we have our first ball at Avonleigh."

"And when will that be?" Marjorie asked.

"Not for at least a year, I would think. Our first priority is to get the mill operating, and then Graham has plans to build a brewery to give the hops farmers a local place to sell their crop."

Marjorie smiled at her friend's enthusiasm, and noted her use of the words "*our* first priority." She wondered if she'd ever feel such enthusiasm over Lord Shannock's interests. Oh, speak of the devil, she thought, seeing the man looking about the room. She swallowed thickly, having forgotten just how unattractive he was. And how jittery. His movements were sharp and distinct, like a lizard darting about for prey. She realized with a start that she was the prey when he caught her eye and started toward her.

"Save me," she whispered into Katherine's ear. "Do you see that thin man coming toward us?" Katherine nodded. "Mother wants me to marry him."

Katherine turned and gave her a sharp look. "But he's ancient."

"He's titled and our neighbor. He was my father's friend, and ever since I came out he's been hinting about a match. My mother put him off because she thought I'd do better, but now . . . Oh, hello, Lord Shannock," she said a bit over-enthusiastically. "May I introduce you to my dear friend, Katherine Spencer, Countess Avonleigh."

"Lady Marjorie." He bowed and a thin blade of greasy hair sprang loose, revealing a bit of bare scalp. "A pleasure to meet you, Lady Avonleigh."

"A pleasure, Lord Shannock. Lady Marjorie was just telling me you are neighbors."

Lord Shannock's bushy salt-and-pepper eyebrows shot upwards. "You're an American," he said. It sounded much like an accusation.

"I am. And you are English," Katherine said, as if playing a parlor game and she'd just gotten the right answer.

"Yes," Lord Shannock said stiffly. "Is Lord Avonleigh here this evening?"

"He is, indeed. I spied him heading to the billiard room not ten minutes ago. Are you acquainted with my husband?"

"My son and he attended Cambridge together."

Katherine smiled. "You seem far too young to have a son the same age as Graham."

Marjorie pressed her lips together so as not to laugh aloud. What a flirt Katherine could be. But Lord Shannock beamed, revealing an awful-looking set of teeth. At that moment, she pictured him kissing her as Charles had, touching her, and she felt physically ill.

"I do apologize, my lord, but I must find my mother. I promised to bring Lady Avonleigh over to her as soon as I located her. And as you can see, I have."

Lord Shannock darted a look about, then bowed again, loosening up that stiff section of hair. "Before you go, my dear, may I be so bold as to ask if you might honor me with the first waltz?"

Marjorie smiled as if delighted. "Of course, sir." She handed over the card and Lord Shannock penciled in his name. Giving the man a small curtsy, Marjorie grabbed Katherine's arm and led her away as if Lord Shannock might give pursuit.

"No, no, no, you cannot marry him," Katherine said when they were out of Lord Shannock's hearing.

"I know," Marjorie said miserably. "But Mother is set. She insists. What choice do I have, really? I haven't had a proposal in three years. I just realized that yesterday. Three *years*. I'd say the chances are fairly slim that I will get another proposal this season. My dance card rarely fills anymore and if it does, it's because George is in attendance."

Katherine squeezed her arm. "It's not time to panic yet."

"Yes, it is. It is the perfect time to panic. Did you see his teeth? Oh, God."

"You're not marrying Lord Shannock," Katherine said, as if it were a certainty.

"I'm not?"

"Of course not. You're marrying *him*," Katherine said, with a nod to their right.

Marjorie looked over and saw Lord Avonleigh and Mr. Norris coming toward them. "Lord Avonleigh is already married," she said darkly.

Katherine laughed. "I meant the other one. The great handsome lummox standing next to my wonderful husband. The great handsome lummox who is looking at you as if you're the sun come out after a long winter's night."

"Stop," Marjorie said. "If you recall, I am quite angry with that great lummox, handsome or not." Despite her words, she felt the tug of a smile because Mr. Norris was looking at her much as Katherine described. If she wasn't careful, she was going to start believing anything was possible.

Marjorie dipped a curtsy to the men and said, "I thought you'd be playing billiards all evening."

"I wanted to, but Mr. Norris insisted we come out and take a couple of turns around the ballroom."

"I don't think Lady Caroline has yet arrived," Marjorie said coolly. "At least I haven't seen her."

"I'm not looking for Lady Caroline at the moment," Mr. Norris said with odd intensity.

Next to her, Katherine moved to her husband's side. "I'd like to see the refreshment table," she said, tugging Lord Avonleigh toward the far end of the room. Katherine gave the oblivious pair a pointed look and Graham caught her meaning immediately.

Marjorie wasn't even aware they had left. She wasn't aware there was a single other person in the room. All she could think of was what Katherine had told her, that she was certain Charles loved her.

And there, not so far back in her mind, was a plan that would make marriage not only a possibility but a certainty.

"Care to take a turn 'round the room with me?" Mr. Norris asked.

"I think not," Marjorie said, his cruel words still ringing in her ears. She might melt on the inside when she saw him, but she would not be a fool for him. She would not make a cake of herself over him if he only thought of her as a lovely distraction from his true purpose.

"I know I behaved terribly yesterday. I apologize most profusely. Please, will you not walk with me?"

He seemed utterly sincere, and Marjorie could feel herself giving in. "My mother would object," Marjorie said.

"Your mother be damned." He was smiling, but the look of determination on his face was thrilling.

"All right then, though I don't truly want to damn my mother."

"Of course not. I'd settle for thwarting her, though."

Marjorie's heart sped up a beat. Something was different about Charles tonight. He was more intense, more serious than she'd ever seen him. They began walking around the room in silence, skirting various groups that had gathered to chat.

"I don't plan to ask Lady Caroline to marry me," Charles said offhandedly.

Oh, her heart nearly stopped as terrible hope filled her. "Oh? You don't suit?"

"We do. But I'm in love with someone else. Deeply and profoundly."

Marjorie could not respond, because in her heart of hearts, she wanted that someone else to be her. But what if it weren't? What if Katherine were wrong?

"Are you not curious as to who has stolen my heart? I would think, as my matchmaker, you would be. After all, it was you who brought my love and me together in the first place."

Her heart stuttered a bit at that. He was being so blasé, so dispassionate. "Who is the lucky lady?" Marjorie said, trying desperately not to sound as if she really cared one way or the other.

"She's lovely. Intelligent. She makes me laugh. I think she loves me, but I'm not sure. I believe I might give up entirely on love if she doesn't return my feelings. I don't think I'd get over this one, should she break my heart."

Marjorie stopped walking and was acutely aware that they were in a ballroom surrounded by people she knew, people who would most likely report back to her mother that she'd been promenading around the ballroom on the arm of the one man her mother seemed to dislike above all others. "Mr. Norris, please do not keep me in suspense a moment longer. Who is she?"

"You," he said softly, with the smallest laugh. He started walking again, and she followed, clutching his arm a bit tighter, her heart near bursting. "I'm hoping you return my feelings, at least a little."

Marjorie wanted to scream with happiness, to throw her arms around him and kiss him and kiss him, but she was in the middle of a ballroom and so instead she smiled politely. "I cannot breathe for loving you."

His steps paused for just a moment. "Thank God."

She squeezed his arm a bit, and the two walked on silently as if they'd just been discussing the weather and had run out of things to say. When they'd gone a full circle about the room, they turned to each other, their secret burning in their eyes.

"I have a plan."

"I know what to do."

They spoke in unison, then stopped. Marjorie spied her mother coming toward them and her entire body tensed. "I have to go. My mother."

"I'll leave a note," he whispered, and then louder, "Thank you, my lady. I'll give your well wishes to Lady Caroline when she arrives."

Dorothea, whose sharp eyes had never left Marjorie as she walked around the room with Mr. Norris, visibly relaxed.

"Mr. Norris," Dorothea said with a nod, "I do believe Lady Caroline has arrived."

Mr. Norris bowed and, giving Marjorie one more look, headed in the direction of the ballroom entrance, where Lady Caroline stood with her mother. But Marjorie didn't care. She didn't care if Charles bent over Lady Caroline's hand and kissed it. Because she knew he loved her, that he had a plan. Perhaps they would elope. Or perhaps he would somehow convince her mother that a title was an inconsequential thing. She couldn't wait to find out what it was. And if she didn't like his plan, she had one of her own.

Yes, getting caught together was fraught with danger and she would have to endure the scandal and her mother's deep disappointment. She recalled how shocked her mother had been when she'd told her about Katherine and Graham putting themselves in danger of being seen. It would be purely awful to disappoint her mother so, but she'd do it if it meant she and Charles could be together.

It would not be easy to face the censure of people she'd known all her life who would no doubt think less of her. Yet she couldn't help remembering how everything had worked out for Katherine. No one cut her. She was at this ball, greeting people she'd met during the little season as if nothing scandalous had ever happened.

Of course, Graham did have a lofty title, and that shielded Katherine from some ill effects. It was also clear to anyone who saw her and Avonleigh together that they were very much in love. Would these same people overlook Marjorie's error when she became a mere missus?

"Did Mr. Norris impart good news regarding his courtship with Lady Caroline?" Dorothea asked. "You seem pleased."

"I am pleased, Mother. Look, the Grand March is beginning. I have promised Lord Shannock the first waltz. He's the only name on my dance card so far."

"Mr. Norris did not ask you to dance?"

"No, he did not."

"And does that disappoint you?" Marjorie was watching many of the guests gather for the Grand March, but she could feel her mother's eyes upon her.

"Not in the least."

"It is good to hear that. I feared you felt far more affection for that man than you should."

Marjorie turned to look at her mother. "I do feel some affection for him, Mother," she said cautiously. "He is a wonderful man."

"Just as long as you don't feel too much, for it appears all his attention is now on Lady Caroline. And what a charming pair they make, do they not? Here comes Lord Shannock, looking rather dapper this evening."

He did look as dapper as was possible, Marjorie realized. Suddenly, she didn't care if she danced every dance with Lord Shannock, because she knew she would marry Charles. They only needed to determine how to go about it.

When Marjorie woke the next day, it was nearly noon. She lay in her bed for a moment, excitement bubbling through her. She sprang from bed and ran to her wardrobe, looking for her new afternoon dress in deep purple with mother of pearl buttons down the front. She was tugging on her corset when Alice bustled into the room, tsk-tsking that her ladyship hadn't rung for her.

"You'll never get the purple on without me helping you, my lady," Alice said, moving behind her and tugging at the tapes. "Your mother's already out and about."

"Really? Do you know where she went?"

"No, I don't. But she has the new carriage if you were thinking of going out, my lady."

"I've nothing definite planned. Then again, I haven't seen the morning post and I have been neglecting my friends, as they mentioned last night. They were so cross with me, and I can't say that I blame them. It was so good to see them and we've made plans for visiting before we leave London in August."

Indeed, Marjorie had walked around the ball as if on a cloud, chatting with friends, happily making plans to attend luncheons and teas. She and Charles did not dance, but all through the evening, they would catch each other's eyes and smile—ever so slightly—so as not to attract undue attention. It had been such a delicious thing to hold their secret close to her. Only Katherine knew what had transpired, and she had been so delighted, nearly giving away everything.

"It's good to see you smiling again," Alice said warmly.

"I have been a bit of a stick in the mud of late, haven't I?"

"Oh, no, I wouldn't say that. But I must say there's been just a bit less sparkle in your eyes these past months."

Marjorie looked in the mirror and smiled at her reflection. Funny, she hadn't realized how off she'd been until now. "I think I'll be smiling a great deal from now on."

"Oh?"

"It's a secret." Marjorie gave her maid a wink and walked out the door, making Alice giggle.

"More like it's a man," Alice said on a sigh after her mistress had left the room.

Marjorie went to the breakfast room and grabbed a scone and napkin, and headed directly to the garden, taking a healthy bite along the way. She had no time for niceties this morning. Humming "The Blue Danube," the music playing when she'd waltzed with Lord

Shannock, she strolled through the gardens and out the back gate. With a quick look up and down the lane, she pulled the brick free, smiling widely when she saw the plain white stationary Charles used.

She opened the note right there, the afternoon sun warming her neck as she bent over the message. It was just two sentences.

> *We need to be compromised. I'll be at the Hartford ball tonight.*

She let out a little giggle before dashing back through the gate. She hugged the paper to her breast before folding it and tucking it into the skirt of her dress.

This was a terrible, wonderful idea. Her mother would be positively horrified, Marjorie thought with rather too little shame. Other than eloping, though, it was the only way—and would cause the least amount of conflict. Confronting her mother would create an ugly scene, and one that might end in more threats and punishments against her brother. Marjorie did not understand why her mother insisted she have a title. Most mothers were perfectly content to have their daughters married to fine young men from good families who had a good income. Charles fit all those requirements. This obsession her mother had was positively unfathomable. Yet, she had gone along with it for years simply to appease her. Honor thy mother. It was something she'd taken seriously. She wanted to honor her mother, wanted to please her. What daughter wouldn't? The thought of disappointing her went against everything she believed.

But if she were compromised, the decision would be taken away from her mother. She could not publicly object, could not argue against a marriage when marriage would be the only solution to stop the scandal. Indeed, marriage would be a blessing, a way to stop disgrace. Wasn't her friend Katherine the perfect example?

Lady Summerfield stepped down from her carriage and gave a sniff. Russell Square was hardly a neighborhood she saw much of. The Cavendishes had rented a pleasant, if small, townhouse on the edge of what one would consider a fashionable address. Country folk often were ignorant of how very important the right address was, and this was not the right address if one wanted to launch a daughter into society.

She walked determinedly up the marble steps, noting with some satisfaction that they were swept clean, and gave the doorbell a hard twist. Within moments, the door opened and a butler was bowing before her.

"Please inform Squire Cavendish that Lady Summerfield is here," she said.

The butler's eyes widened slightly upon hearing the lofty title of the woman standing on their stoop, and he ushered her in with a deferential bow. He seemed momentarily confused about where he should put such a fine lady to wait, then decided on a small, sunny parlor toward the front of the home.

"Would you like some tea while you wait?" he asked.

"Of course not," the lady snapped as she gazed around the room. It was not well-furnished, at least not in a way that the good lady found impressive. She remained standing, eying the worn materials of the settee a bit warily. No, it would not do to sit and make it appear that this was a social visit. It was not.

Within a few moments, a large man she immediately recognized as the squire stood in the doorway, looking at her with a beaming smile, as if he were overjoyed to see her in his home. "Welcome, my lady. What a pleasure it is to see you, and on such a happy occasion as this."

"It is not pleasurable in any way," Dorothea said. "My son will not be marrying your daughter. Clearly you can see it is not a good match, not for either of them."

The squire's smile faltered and his eyes grew slightly colder. "I'm afraid I don't understand. Your son proposed, my daughter accepted, and I gave my blessing."

"It would be quite an advantageous match for your daughter. I imagine giving her a season was quite dear. Many country gentlemen do not venture into London for that reason. How old is your daughter?"

He lifted his chin and tucked his hands behind his back, now obviously quite aware what this visit was about. "Twenty-two."

Lady Summerfield appeared shocked. "And this is her first season?"

"Yes, my lady, it is. We felt she should have one. As I'm sure you're aware, Ipswich is a quiet district without many entertainments for a young girl."

"Young," she repeated thoughtfully. "Yes. And she's managed to find a husband with an impressive title during her first season. Congratulations. But this marriage cannot happen. Surely you know that. Unless, that is, there is a reason it must?"

"I'm sure you mean no insult, my lady, but I must tell you that you *have* insulted me and my daughter."

Lady Summerfield raised her eyebrows as if shocked by his words. "I mean no insult to you or your daughter, sir. I do mean, however, to inject some common sense into the children. Surely the differences in their stations alone would make this match unacceptable."

"Lilianne is willing to overlook the title, my lady, so you need not concern yourself that we are troubled by it."

Dorothea's eyes grew decidedly frostier. "I'm sure you mean to be amusing, Mr. Cavendish, but I assure you I am not amused. Let me get to the point, shall I? My son is an idiot and should never marry and bear offspring. I will not allow it." She looked around the room, taking in the shabby furniture, the worn carpet, silently giving her opinion of the place. "Surely we can come to an understanding that would be profitable to both of us."

Mr. Cavendish's jaw tightened. "Do you mean to pay us off? If that is your plan, I'm afraid you have wasted your time coming here."

A small noise at the door drew their attention and they turned to see Lilianne standing there, her eyes wide. She dipped a quick curtsy. "My lady, what an honor to have you in our home," she said softly. "Father, have you offered Lady Summerfield tea?"

"Lady Summerfield is unable to visit longer, I'm afraid, my dear."

"So," Dorothea said, turning her hard gaze toward Lilianne. "You claim to love my son. I find that extremely difficult to believe."

"I do, ma'am. Lord Summerfield and I have known each other since we were children and we have always been friends."

"Forgive me, but I cannot allow my son to marry a girl of such low birth. Indeed, I cannot allow my son to marry at all. You know he is not right, and that you would force him into such a marriage is immoral."

Lilianne's cheeks flushed and her father let out a sound of protest. "George is a brilliant and wonderful man. The real tragedy here, Lady Summerfield, is that he has a mother who does not recognize that fact."

"Thirty thousand pounds," Dorothea said succinctly.

Mr. Cavendish started at hearing such a ridiculous amount.

"You could give all your daughters—you have three more, do you not?—a season. Surely such a sum would make your life easier."

"It would," the squire said thoughtfully.

"Father!"

"Now, Lilianne, I've not agreed."

"Nor will you," Lilianne cried. "It's insulting and obscene."

"It's a great deal of money," the squire said thoughtfully as Lady Summerfield gave him a self-satisfied smile.

"So we're agreed? Thirty thousand pounds and you end the engagement."

"No, Father. If you do this thing, I will never speak to you again."

The squire looked at his daughter and gave her the most subtle of winks. "It's a great deal of money, Lilianne. We do need to repair our stables. And the kitchens are so out of date, cook is constantly complaining. And your sisters, they were terribly jealous that you got your season, and it will be years before they get theirs."

"I can write the cheque immediately," Lady Summerfield said, opening her reticule. She pulled out a cheque. "Pen and ink, if you please."

"Pen and ink?" the squire asked, as if she were asking for a peach in February. "I'm afraid we have none in the house. Oh, dear. It looks as if we haven't a deal after all." The squire looked near to bursting into laughter, and his daughter beside him gave the smallest of smiles. "Do you truly think I would sell my daughter's happiness for thirty thousand pounds, my lady? I wouldn't do that for a million. Good day, madam."

Lady Summerfield's eyes took on the strangest of emotions, almost as if she'd died, for they were cold and lifeless. She snapped her reticule closed, her cheeks in high color. She marched toward the doorway, head held high, and the coldness in her eyes turned to a hot rage. "If you think there will be a wedding in September," she said at the door, "you are sorely mistaken. Good day."

After she'd gone, Lilianne threw herself into her father's arms. "Oh, thank you, Father. You nearly frightened me to death."

"I wanted to have a bit of fun with the old battleaxe, but I'm sorry if I caused you any distress. What a horrible person she is. Are you certain you want to be part of that family?"

Lilianne nodded. "I adore George and his sister. And we've decided to stick Lady Summerfield in their home in Exeter. We'll never have to see her."

Squire Cavendish smiled down at his daughter. "I can only hope for your sake that is true."

Marjorie hadn't felt so nervous at a ball since her debut. Her stomach was aflutter, her gloved hands shaking as she gathered her dance card. With her mother watching carefully, Marjorie tried her best not to appear too ill at ease.

"Lord Shannock is here already," Marjorie said, looking over her mother's turbaned head. She'd taken to wearing the awful thing after reading an article in the *Times* praising Queen Victoria, who'd worn one to Ascot. "I'll be sure to save him a dance."

"I'm glad you've come around, my dear."

Marjorie gave her mother a weak smile. "I haven't come 'round entirely, Mother, but I do recognize my options have become limited."

"Posh. You could have any man in this room, my dear."

Marjorie raised an eyebrow. "Have you changed your mind about Lord Shannock?"

Dorothea, in a rare show of public affection, placed her hand on her daughter's wrist. "I do want you to be happy, dear, no matter what you may think. It seems my powers to persuade my children to do as I want have been greatly diminished."

"Oh?"

"Your brother is intent on marrying that Cavendish girl and I have no power to stop it. A squire's daughter. Really."

"But Mother, I think they'll be happy together. She's known George all her life and she understands him. He had to get married at some point."

Her mother shook her head. "He will have an heir and I fear the defect will continue."

Marjorie felt her face flush with anger. "You know I don't like it when you say such things about George."

"Your opinion of what I say does not alter the truth of it," Dorothea said succinctly. "I am sorry it pains you to hear plain speaking, but I cannot offer anything else."

Marjorie stifled an angry sigh and tried not to be upset by her mother's words. "Let's not quarrel tonight."

"I wasn't quarreling," Dorothea said almost sweetly. "You were, my dear."

Marjorie gave her mother a brilliant smile. "Yes, it's always so gratifying to quarrel alone."

She would not let her mother ruin what would be the happiest of nights. Tonight she would be engaged. She would know her future stood with the only man she'd ever loved. It might not happen the way she'd dreamt it, but it would happen. She braced herself mentally for the ugly scene that was certain to occur once her mother caught wind of events.

As balls went, the Hartford ball was a small, intimate affair with less than fifty persons in attendance. Marjorie wondered how Charles, who'd been away from England so long, had managed to procure all the invitations he'd amassed. As she looked around the room, she spied Lady Caroline standing with her mother, and Marjorie felt a jab of guilt. She hoped the poor girl wasn't expecting a proposal from Charles, but had little doubt she did. She seemed like a nice girl and Marjorie wished her no ill will—other than to stay quite single for at least another day.

Marjorie looked down, smiling, trying to hide from her mother the complete joy she felt.

She wished Katherine were at the ball, but she and Lord Avonleigh were on their way back to Avonleigh and Marjorie felt a bit sad that her friend wouldn't be there to support her. She was the only other woman she knew who would understand how she felt.

Charles arrived, looking dashing and wonderful, and Marjorie noticed for the first time the reaction of the other women in the room. Particularly, the reaction of the mothers and chaperones. Suddenly it became clear how Charles had managed to be invited to all the best events of the season. He was obviously considered the best of matches. She saw more than one older woman nudge the younger one by her side to indicate his arrival. He's mine, Marjorie silently and happily shouted to the poor, wretched girls who didn't have a chance of winning him.

Charles saw her and his breathing stopped. She was so damned beautiful and he could see the mischief in her eyes as she looked about the room, being careful not to look at him. She loved adventure, and he would be certain every day of his life that she got it. They would travel the world, see everything she'd always dreamed of. When they had children, and they would, they would raise happy little people who had as much joy in them as their mother did. Tonight their real adventure would begin. He could hardly contain himself, hardly walk about the room as if this weren't the most important night of his life.

He was positively giddy. Stupidly so. The only thing he could be grateful for was that none of his friends was about to see him so completely head over heels. He could hardly stop himself from gazing at her as she stood with her mother and a thin, balding man who kept staring blatantly at her breasts. He wanted to punch the bounder, but Charles would do nothing to disrupt their plans. And Marjorie seemed more bemused by the man's frank perusal than affronted, so he let it go. For now.

He strolled about the public areas of the Hartford townhouse, scoping out a room where they could be private for a while but one that most assuredly would mean their eventual discovery. Peeking in a few rooms, he chose a parlor two doors down from the ball and across from a small, dark study. The parlor held a couch—perfect for seduction—and was well lit enough so that, should anyone venture in, he or she would immediately see them. He looked at the room critically, finally deciding that the couch should be moved for better viewing. With a quick shove, the couch now sat directly across from the door. Perfect.

Waiting would be the most difficult part. He would have to act the part of a man who was still searching for a bride, yet he couldn't ignore Marjorie completely. It would seem odd to lure her into the parlor without having exchanged even a word with her. He decided he must brave her mother's hostility and ask Marjorie for a dance. He found the pair at the edge of the dance floor, watching the dancers. As ballrooms went, the Hartfords' was rather small, and could only accommodate a handful of couples at one time. Lady Summerfield noticed his approach before Marjorie, and she stiffened, her square jaw tightening noticeably.

"Lady Summerfield, Lady Marjorie. Are you enjoying the evening so far?"

"Of course," Dorothea said. "Why shouldn't we?"

"Mother, he was simply being polite."

"Of course he was," Dorothea said, as if she had never questioned it. "Where is Lady Caroline?"

Charles smiled at her obvious hint that he should be elsewhere. "I haven't the foggiest. I've come here to ask your daughter for a dance. Perchance, have you an open dance on your card, Lady Marjorie?"

"Indeed I do, sir." Marjorie handed over her card, which had only two dances filled in—both, Charles noted, by a Lord Shannock. If he had his way, they would be the last chance Lord Shannock would be allowed to touch her. He had no doubt that Shannock was the lecherous older man who was gawking at Marjorie in such an obvious way.

"I see you have the next polka free. Shall we?"

The polka immediately started, and Marjorie, laughing, took his hand as he led her out to the floor. Charles would have preferred a waltz, but the polka would serve his purpose just as well.

"I'm not certain my leg can stand this bouncing for an entire dance," Charles said as he swirled Marjorie about the floor. "Two doors down. A parlor. At half past midnight."

She smiled up at him. "I'm afraid I don't understand," she said, and his heart did a little stutter. Had she not understood his note? Then Marjorie laughed.

"Oh, Mr. Norris, you are so easy to tease. Of course, yes. Yes and yes." She was becoming a bit breathless from the dance. No doubt her stays were quite tight. Frankly, he needed an excuse to stop dancing himself; he could feel his leg begin an insistent throbbing that portended real pain if he continued.

"I fear my leg cannot continue, Lady Marjorie. If you will forgive me?"

"Of course." As he led her off the dance floor, skirting the other dancers, she said, "This will not be pleasant, you know."

"Oh, my darling girl, it will be the most pleasant thing I've done in a very long time," he said, and watched as she tried to suppress another smile.

When they reached Lady Summerfield, he released Marjorie. "I do apologize. My leg is acting up again and I had to cut the dance short."

"Your leg, sir?"

"Injured, madam, in Ashanti."

"How awful. My sympathies. Oh, look, Marjorie, Lord Shannock is come to claim his waltz. Have a nice evening, Mr. Norris." Her subtle stress on their respective titles was more amusing than anything else, he decided. Soon enough, she'd be calling him son. He let out a soft chuckle, gave the lady a bow, and walked away.

Marjorie endured two waltzes with Lord Shannock, who valiantly tried not to stare at her breasts the entire time. He did not succeed. It was either that or the poor man had some sort of eye condition that didn't allow his eyeballs to rise above a certain level that just happened to correspond with the location of her cleavage.

But she didn't care. She didn't care that he stared, that her dance card was not filled, that Lord Hartford tread upon her toes twice during their dance, that her mother gloated over the attention Lord Shannock was giving her. She only cared about the ormolu clock on the large mantel behind the orchestra that said it was twenty-seven minutes past midnight. Her mother was talking animatedly with Lady Hartford, which enabled her to slip from the room unnoticed, all the while saying "parlor two doors down" under her breath. She opened the door, and he was there already, sitting on a couch that directly faced the door.

"Come here and allow me to compromise you," he said with a wide grin.

Marjorie bit her lip and quietly closed the door behind her. "Are you quite certain of this? You've thought you've known your heart before, only to find it played false with you."

"You're the only woman I can talk to without stuttering. You're the only woman I can truly imagine being part of my life forever. I love you. Believe it, please."

She gave him a small nod. "My mother might murder you. Be prepared."

"I believe I can fend off one small woman. Now, let's begin the compromise."

Marjorie pressed her ear to the door. "But no one's coming yet."

"I don't care. If I don't kiss you in the next moment, I shall die and your mother will never have the satisfaction of murdering me."

He rose from the couch and came toward her with determination in his eyes. "I think we can be thoroughly compromised simply by

being in this room alone together," she said. "I don't think it's necessary to kiss." Even as she said the words, her arms drifted around his
neck and she pulled him close.

"I think it's very necessary." With a low groan, he pressed his lips
against hers and she melted, right there and then. It was so sudden, so
intense, her knees actually buckled. He lifted her against him and
walked backward, never stopping the kiss, to the couch. She felt
every hard inch of him, including that manly part that pressed against
her stomach, and grew even harder when he lay down upon the couch
with her atop him.

He broke the kiss, gasping for air. "Perhaps kissing was not such
a grand idea," he said, his brown eyes glazed with passion. He moved
his hips, letting her feel just how aroused he was, and groaned again.
"I want to be inside you," he said, lifting his hips again.

She widened her eyes and he chuckled. "Not now, silly girl. But
someday very, very soon." He closed his eyes and she kissed his
mouth softly, loving the way he felt beneath her. He was large, solid,
and so very masculine. Every muscle was bunched, and she wondered if there was a soft part on him other than his mouth. She laid
her head on his chest and listened to his heartbeat for a few seconds
before giving in to temptation and kissing him again. She moved her
tongue against his lips and he opened his mouth, making their kiss
something wonderful and carnal. She'd never known how the mere
act of kissing could be so entirely arousing. When he moved his
hands down to her buttocks, she let out a sound she hadn't even
known she could emit. Heat flooded between her legs, making her
move against him to find some sort of release from the exquisite
pressure that was building there.

He turned then, pressing her against the back of the couch. It was-
n't a very wide piece of furniture, but it could accommodate the two
of them easily enough, even with her small bustle. He lifted his head
and stared at her, moving one hand up and touching her swollen
upper lip with his index finger.

"You look decidedly ravished," he said, moving his finger down to
her chin, to her neck, and finally to the tops of her breasts.

"I'm not nearly ravished enough," she said, ruining her bold
statement with a blush. He dipped his finger beneath her dress and
brushed it lightly against one nipple, making her gasp. She closed
her eyes and tried to control her need to moan, but when he squeezed

her nipple gently, she lost the battle. "That feels rather lovely," she whispered.

His gaze became fierce and he kissed her again, open-mouthed and out of control. Wonderful, wonderful this kissing and touching, but she wanted that feeling again, the one he'd given her the last time, when he'd moved his hand between her legs and made her come. She wanted to tell him that, wanted to beg him to lift her skirts and make her scream. Instead, she pressed her core against his arousal and moved in a rhythm that told him what she wanted.

"Yes," he whispered, moving his hand away from her breast and down between her legs. He pressed his hand there and her breath hitched.

"I want you to—" she said. They both tensed as the door to the parlor opened, then closed.

"Oh, hello," said a man.

Marjorie immediately tried to sit up, but it was impossible, jammed between the couch back and Charles's large body. Charles solved the problem by falling off the couch rather ungracefully and then standing.

"Oh dear," he said, rather like a bad actor. "We've been caught."

Marjorie finally sat up, pushing clothes into place, and peered around Charles to see a man standing in the room, staring blearily at them. One couldn't actually call what the man was doing standing. It was more of a sway, as if he were on the deck of a ship and trying not to topple over from the movement.

"Ah," the man said with an extravagant wave of his hand. "You needn't worry about me. I won't tell a soul." He sought to press one finger to his lips, missed, then found the right spot and let out a rather watery "Shhhh." Even from where Marjorie sat, she could smell alcohol on the man's breath.

"Oh, but you should tell. This is awful, isn't it, Charles?" Marjorie said, feeling a bit of panic building up in her that this dolt of a man wasn't going to tell on them.

"Why should I tell? Didn't see nothing," the man slurred.

"But I'm an unmarried young girl. And Charles Norris is a single man and we've been caught in a compromising position. Why, we shouldn't even be alone in this room together. I . . . I'm so ashamed."

Charles looked at her and lifted one disbelieving brow.

"Ish that a couch?" The man stumbled toward it and Marjorie sat up lest the gentleman sit upon her. He patted Charles's back grandly before plopping down on the settee. He sat, still wobbling, for a few moments before he lay down, feet still on the floor, and closed his eyes. Within a few seconds, he was snoring.

Marjorie folded her arms in pure disgust and glared at the man.

"Perhaps when he wakes up tomorrow morning he'll remember?" Charles offered hopefully.

"He won't even remember being at this ball, never mind finding us together. Really, the man is a disgrace." She let out a huff of air and turned her glare at Charles when he began to laugh.

"You must admit it was rather fun to try to get compromised. We'll just have to try again." He lifted out his pocket watch. "But I fear it will have to be another night. It's already well past one."

Marjorie's eyes widened. "But this is wonderful. My mother will certainly have noticed my absence. And perhaps others have noticed *your* absence and that will be that. Let's go back to the ballroom."

Alas, while they were gone, poor Lady Smythe, who'd been complaining for hours that she wasn't feeling well, collapsed, quite taking up the attention of everyone in the room. No one, not even Dorothea, had noted the couple's absence. Everyone had gathered around the lady, who looked quite ghastly, her face a dreadful grayish color and her breathing audible and harsh. A physician had been called for and was now attending her.

"I wish they had thought to bring her to the parlor," Marjorie said softly to Charles. "That couch there would have been more comfortable than the little settee she's lying on."

He leaned toward her, so close his lips brushed the curls by her ear. "Have you no shame?"

"I used to. But you have been a terrible influence on me, sir."

He chuckled softly, then moved away when Dorothea spied them together. Marjorie went to her mother's side, for she looked terribly upset. "I do hope she's all right," Marjorie said, feeling guilty about her earlier jest.

Dorothea pressed her lips together and Marjorie was quite certain her mother was trying not to cry. "I've known Lady Smythe for forty years. She has always been so kind to me. After your father's death, she visited nearly every week to make certain I was well."

It seemed an odd thing for her mother to say, Marjorie thought, because she'd always had the distinct impression that her mother hadn't cared a wit when her father died. They hardly spent any time together when he was alive, and when they were together they barely uttered two syllables to each other. If they loved each other, they hid it well.

Two footmen, carrying a gurney between them, arrived and helped place the poor lady onto it.

"Where are they taking her?"

"Home, of course. She wants to die in her own bed."

Marjorie watched as the men carried the woman from the room, leaving behind the worried guests. "She may recover, Mother."

"No. I've seen the look of death before. I'll ask Bishop Fraser to say a special prayer on Sunday."

It was late and everyone in attendance was greatly subdued. Many of the guests had already departed, and now it was time for them to leave as well.

"Let's have a nice quiet evening tomorrow, shall we? I find all these amusements so tiring of late," Dorothea said.

"Are you feeling unwell, Mother?"

Dorothea smiled. "Fit as a fiddle. I simply find these late nights draining, particularly without a break in between. "

"Tomorrow is the Westin ball and I promised Theresa I would be there. Would it be all right with you if I went with George? I know he will be there."

"With that Cavendish girl, no doubt."

"They are engaged."

Her mother's eyes, which had held such warmth a moment before, became frosty. "Your aunt can go with you."

"All right. I'll send her a note in the morning."

She hated to think of Aunt Gertrude's reaction should she and Charles get caught together at the Westin ball. She was such a sweet old lady and truly loved Marjorie. It would break her heart.

But she knew Gertrude would understand in the end. Aunt Gertrude had loved her husband deeply and still talked about him fondly. If anyone would forgive her transgression, it was Gertrude. Perhaps it would be better having her mother at home. That way she could break the news herself without the humiliation of her mother witnessing her shame.

A wave of guilt twisted her stomach, but Marjorie pushed it down. After all, if her mother hadn't been so stubborn, she and Charles would not be forced into executing such a drastic measure.

Chapter 14

Fifteen years earlier

Lady Summerfield gazed fondly at her daughter. At eight years old, she was the light of her life, the only thing that made it worth getting up each day. She would stare at her in wonder. How on earth had she and Summerfield produced such a darling, beautiful girl? Her head was surrounded by thick, spiral curls that bounced as she skipped down a hall. And she was always skipping. Always full of joy and happiness. Even at eight years old, she showed the ability to charm both her peers and her elders. Summerfield adored his daughter, indulged her far too much, and showed, for the first time in his life, a softer side Dorothea rarely saw. Watching her husband with their daughter was the only joy she had in her marriage.

When George had been born, Summerfield gave her a beautiful ruby brooch as a thank-you. Red, like their little son's hair. He praised her for giving him a son, as if she'd had anything at all to do with the fact she'd produced a boy. Even as a newborn, his hair had been frightfully bright. What a proud father Summerfield had been. Marjorie had been a good little baby, crying only when she was hungry or wet, and grew quickly into the sweet-tempered little girl they both loved so much. George had wailed incessantly. Nothing could stop it but sleep. He cried when he awoke, he cried himself to exhaustion. They went through five nursemaids before finally he outgrew whatever it had been that was making him so miserable. He was three years old when Dorothea began to suspect something wasn't quite right with their son. Something a tad . . . off. She had Marjorie as an example of what a perfect child should be. And although she tried not to make comparisons, it was impossible not to do so. Marjorie had been able to carry on a conversation at two, while George knew only a few words. Marjorie craved physical affection while George tensed up whenever she drew him into her arms. And he had an odd way of bobbing constantly that drove Summerfield mad.

By the time he was six, the differences between George and other boys his age was obvious. Something was wrong with his heir, something that could not be treated and was impossible to ignore. Little George was an embarrassment to Summerfield. He didn't want to be around the child. He wouldn't allow him to be presented to visitors. And he took every opportunity he could to blame Dorothea for his defective son.

Dorothea spent several hours a day in the nursery even though they'd hired a competent governess. She watched her children learn and was relieved when George showed an unusual proficiency at reading and memorizing. Even at six, he read far better than Marjorie.

"You see, my lady? George is brilliant," their governess, Rebecca, said with a smile when Dorothea entered the nursery one day. "I never even tried to teach him. I saw him with a book and thought he was just looking at the pages, but then I noticed his lips were moving as if he were reading to himself. And he was."

George stood in the nursery, clutching the book in his hands as if Dorothea might pull it away from him, and her heart melted. "That was wonderful, George," said Rebecca. "You are the very best reader I've ever heard."

George smiled. "I know the first three pages already."

Dorothea looked to Rebecca for an explanation.

"He's memorized them, my lady. Word for word. It's miraculous, it is. I've never seen anything like it before in my life."

Dorothea stared at her son. "Show me, George. Let me see."

He reluctantly handed the book over.

"Now, tell me what it says," she asked.

"Where should I start? Which page?"

Startled, Dorothea looked to Rebecca again, who simply shook her head and smiled. "Page two. Half way down." She opened the book, a sea adventure written for children far older than George, and he started. A shiver touched her spine. It was impossible. How could he have memorized the book so thoroughly when he'd never shown any signs of remarkable intelligence before? Even as he recited the words with stunning accuracy, he stared at the floor, his head bobbing as he repeated, word for word, what was written in the book.

"His lordship must be made aware of this," Dorothea said. "It's truly remarkable."

That evening, Dorothea brought George down to visit with his father. She had gushed with enthusiasm about their remarkable little boy who had managed to not only read but to memorize five full pages of text that very day. Summerfield had not been impressed. "A parrot can repeat words, Dorothea. I highly doubt the boy was reading. He can hardly speak, for God's sake."

"I heard it myself, Summerfield. It was astounding."

He let out a scoffing laugh and gave her a derisive expression. "Your moron son can no more read than I can fly. Willing it so, does not make it so. I fear you are so desperate for him to be normal, you have invented this trick to prove you haven't produced a defective child."

Dorothea had simply smiled. She knew what her son was capable of. She knew he was a brilliant reader and she could hardly wait to prove Summerfield wrong. God, how she loathed him. It would be sweet indeed to watch her husband's face as George recited the book.

Now, she smiled at her son encouragingly as he stood in front of his father, the book clutched in his bony little hands.

"Go on now, George. Read for your father."

"It's seven o'clock."

Dorothea looked at the clock. Indeed, it was seven. "Yes, George, it is. Now read."

"I play with my tin soldiers at seven o'clock. It's seven o'clock."

Dread, and a tiny bit of panic, bloomed in her heart. Summerfield let out a bit of mean-spirited laughter.

"You can play with your tin soldiers after you read for Father, George," she said gently, even as part of her wanted to give George a little shake. "Now, go ahead and show Father what a wonderful reader you are."

"It's time to play with my tin soldiers," he repeated in a small voice.

Summerfield brought his hands down loudly on the arms of his chair. "Well. That was impressive, Dorothea. We indeed have a little genius on our hands. Go play with your tin soldiers, George. Go on now."

George immediately left the room, relief evident in every muscle in his little body.

"He can read," Dorothea said.

"Yes, I'm certain he can," Summerfield drawled.

Dorothea spun around and immediately headed to the nursery, anger and humiliation fueling her steps. When she entered, Marjorie was sitting in an oversized rocking chair singing to her doll and George was lying on his stomach carefully setting up his tin soldiers. Those blasted, infernal tin soldiers.

"George, you are to be punished. You purposely disobeyed me."

George continued to play on as if she hadn't said a word, but Marjorie slowly put her doll aside and climbed down from her chair, her eyes wide.

"I'm taking your tin soldiers. I'm taking them and you will never see them again." Dorothea stalked over and swept up a handful and stuffed them in her pocket. George struggled to keep the others in line even as Dorothea brushed his little hands aside and grabbed the rest.

And then he stood and began to scream. High-pitched, ear-splitting, and thoroughly painful.

"Stop it, George. Stop it or I shall shake you."

He stopped, but only to take another breath and let out another scream.

"Mother, give him back his soldiers," Marjorie cried, tears streaming down her face. "He plays with them every night. He has to. It's seven o'clock."

"I know what bloody time it is," Dorothea shouted over her son's screams.

Marjorie tugged on the pocket where Dorothea had stuffed the soldiers. "Please, Mama, George needs his soldiers. Please."

Dorothea looked down at her daughter's tear-stained cheeks, then at her little hand clutching her dress, and slowly calmed. She was such a fool to think George could ever be anything close to what a normal boy was. She reached into her pockets and dropped the sol-diers, one by one, onto the wooden floor. The moment the first one struck, George stopped screaming. He crouched down and gathered them up. And when the last tin soldier was on the floor, he lay down on his stomach and began to line them up, one after another, until they stood in a perfect V.

Dorothea stared down at him and wanted to cry. Part of her knew George hadn't humiliated her on purpose, that he was just an odd lit-tle boy. And she wondered, not for the first time, if Summerfield was right, that it was her fault her son had come out wrong. Had she gone for too many walks? Eaten too many figs at Christmas, tightened her corset too much? Summerfield was always hinting that she was fat and it was obvious he thought her pregnant body grotesque. Watch-ing George play with his tin soldiers that night, she only saw his strangeness and none of his beautiful uniqueness. And somehow, oddly, it was a relief.

Chapter 15

"I understand congratulations are in order for my dear cousin." Jeffrey stood by Marjorie, looking at George and Lilianne with an unpleasant sneer. He'd come up to her at the Westin ball as she waited in the foyer for Aunt Gertrude to return from the water closet. She'd never known anyone to spend as much time there as her dear aunt.

"I'll relay your heartfelt sentiments," Marjorie said, coldly. She turned to her cousin, but he continued to stare at the couple with palpable hostility. "You know they are very happy. Lilianne is a wonderful girl."

"She must be a saint," Jeffrey said. "George is a fine enough chap, but I find it difficult to spend any amount of time with him. All those facts and figures and head bobbing."

"He only does that when he's nervous. You must make him nervous for some reason. Perhaps he sees through your polite façade to the anger and resentment boiling beneath the surface."

Jeffrey laughed. "It is the curse of the second son to be green with jealousy."

"But you are a first son."

"The first son of a *second* son. My father died early because he was racked with envy. Do you know how old your mother was when she had George? Forty. What woman has a child at that age? And your father was nearly sixty. My father, understandably I think, fully believed I would inherit the title. He groomed me that way, you know.

Put a few drinks in the man and he'd begin the same rant over and over. 'You should be the next earl, not that idiot son of my idiot brother.' It got so I could shout along with him." He glanced at Marjorie to judge her reaction. "He didn't much like that." He rubbed at his jaw as if still feeling a long ago injury.

"I imagine it must be difficult for you to know you are the next in line and George is marrying and will soon have sons," Marjorie said, trying to be understanding.

"Oh, do I detect pity from my frosty cousin?" He laughed mockingly. "You don't give a damn about how I feel, and why should you? You have everything you want. Certainly that would change if I were earl. That gown you are wearing is likely worth more than my entire annual income, did you know that? Ah, I can see you didn't. You're so used to having that silver spoon in your mouth, you've quite forgotten that it's there."

Marjorie furrowed her brow. "You sound so ugly when you speak like that."

"Yes, I imagine anything like the truth is difficult for you to hear."

"I have never said or done anything to promote such dislike. And neither has George."

He shook his head, as if he pitied her naiveté. "You were both born, dear, dear cousin."

"That is a terrible thing to say."

"Isn't it now? I am a terrible person." He tapped his index finger on her nose and smiled. "It's best you remember that."

She waved a hand at him, annoyed more than frightened. "Go be a terrible person somewhere else then. I came to this ball to have fun and you are ruining my evening."

He bowed in apology and did as she asked. Watching him go, she wondered just how deep his anger and resentment went. No doubt he'd cursed when he saw the engagement announcement in the paper.

"I don't care for that young man," Aunt Gertrude said, coming up beside her.

"Aunt Gertrude," Marjorie said, rather shocked. "He's practically your relation."

"No blood shared between us, thank goodness, which is why I'm allowed to say such things."

Marjorie laughed. Aunt Gertrude liked everyone, and the fact that she didn't like Jeffrey was quite telling. "He can't help being disagreeable. His whole life he'd been told he is second in line for the title. The thing is, I know George would happily give it to him if he could."

"He'd squander it the same way his father squandered everything that was given to him. He may have been the second son, but he had properties that produced a good income. Now all they have left is that ramshackle estate up in Nottingham. I hear it won't be long before that's gone, too."

Marjorie waved to her friend Theresa, who had been one of her first friends to marry. She hadn't seen her in ages. "I hadn't realized things were so bad," Marjorie said.

"Is that Theresa Billings coming toward us?"

"It's Lady Westcott now, Aunt Gertrude. She's been married for . . ." She paused, counting in her head. ". . . five years. My goodness, *five years*."

"When I was your age, I'd been married for six," Gertrude said with a nod. "And had four children. How many children does Lady Westcott have?"

"Two. A boy and a girl." Marjorie's smile widened as Theresa reached them. Funny, she looked like a woman who'd been married for five years. She was a bit thick around the middle and her dress was decidedly matronly. She was only twenty-three years old but looked much older.

"It's so wonderful to see you, Margie," Theresa said, brushing her cheek with a kiss.

"It seems like ages. I was so happy to get your note. You remember my aunt, Gertrude, do you not?"

"Of course," she said, turning to her aunt. "It's lovely to see you again, madam. Marjorie looks exactly like that young debutante at her first ball, does she not?"

Marjorie was certain her friend meant that as a compliment, but something in her tone was slightly off. Or perhaps she was imagining things. "I don't feel much like a debutante," she said, laughing.

"Marriage isn't for everyone," Theresa replied, and this time Marjorie was certain she detected a tiny bit of smugness. "Why, this is the first ball I've been to in two seasons. Caring for my little ones takes so much of my time."

Marjorie smiled, but her expression had gone decidedly cooler. "You don't have a nanny?"

"And a nurse, of course. And Lord Westcott hints at having more children." Her eyes went to Marjorie's flat stomach and tiny waistline. "Children give one such joy." She looked suddenly stricken. "I'm so sorry, Margie. How thoughtless of me."

"I don't think you were being *thoughtless* at all," Marjorie said, hoping her friend understood that she suspected her small jibes were well-thought-out indeed. She hadn't remembered Theresa being quite so unpleasant. Or perhaps she was being overly sensitive. She wanted to shout to her friend that she was getting married, would be married within the month. Instead she said, "I wouldn't have given up these last years for anything. I've had such a pleasant time, gone to so many parties and balls, it's been one long whirlwind of amusements."

Next to her, Aunt Gertrude coughed.

"Doesn't it get tiresome after a while?" Theresa asked with what seemed like sincere curiosity.

"Yes, but I've a feeling this will be my last season."

"Oh, but you're not so old," Theresa said, her eyes widening.

Marjorie lifted one eyebrow. "That's not quite what I meant, my dear."

Theresa and Gertrude gave a collective gasp.

"Truly? You are to marry? I didn't know that. Did I miss the announcement in the *Times*? First your brother, now you. How wonderful. Who is the lucky man?"

Darn. Why had she said anything? Silly, stupid pride. "Lord Shannock has expressed great interest."

"That old goat?" This from Gertrude, who looked about as enthusiastic over the prospect of her marrying him as was Marjorie.

Marjorie couldn't help it—she burst out laughing. "We'll see, Aunt Gertrude. One never knows what will happen."

After Theresa had gone, Aunt Gertrude sniffed and said, "That girl is decidedly jealous of you. Always was."

"I hardly think so, Aunt. She was gloating about how wonderful her life was."

"Because she is jealous, my dear. Now, what is this about this being your last season? And do not patronize me with news about Lord Shannock. That man has been lusting after you since you were a girl, and if your mother allows his suit, then I will have lost all respect for her."

Marjorie considered telling her aunt, but decided against it. "I was simply trying to put her off. There is no one."

Gertrude gave her a disbelieving smile. "My dear, you are in love. I am not blind. It is that Mr. Norris fellow, isn't it? And your mother does not approve. I do hope you are not planning to elope."

"Who is Mr. Norris?" It wouldn't hurt to pretend ignorance.

Gertrude laughed. Apparently it would do no good, either. "You forget, my dear, that I've been at many balls you have attended. The Hartford ball, for example. Poor, dear, Lady Smythe. I hear she is rallying, though. I found it odd, however, that you were not in the room during all the hubbub. And neither was Mr. Norris."

Marjorie could feel her cheeks bloom with heat, not only from getting caught in a lie but also from remembering what she'd been doing.

Gertrude waved a hand, dismissing Marjorie's discomfort. "I planned to speak to you of that particular indiscretion, my dear, but since you've brought it up, we might as well discuss it now." She looked past Marjorie and waved someone over. Marjorie turned and nearly fled when she realized her aunt was waving over Charles. And he was walking toward them. With a silly and clearly besotted look on his dear, dear face.

"Good evening, Mr. Norris," Gertrude said enthusiastically, drawing the pair to a corner of the room where they could have relative privacy. "My niece and I were just discussing you and how you could manage to get married when Lady Summerfield is so violently opposed to you. Though, I must say, I don't understand her reasoning at all."

Marjorie would have laughed aloud at the expression on Charles's face, but she was too horrified at Gertrude's forthrightness. "I said nothing, Charles," she said, quick to reassure him, then giving her aunt a glare. "Aunt can be quite canny."

Charles darted Marjorie a look, then smiled broadly at her aunt. "How we'll go about it is a secret. And foolproof."

"Not entirely," Marjorie mumbled, reminding him of their failed effort the previous evening.

"The plan is foolproof," he insisted.

"A foolproof plan that doesn't involve elopement," Gertrude murmured. She thought for a moment, then blanched. "No. You mustn't. Really, Marjorie, are you trying to murder your mother? Or yours,

Mr. Norris? You cannot think to . . . to . . ." The poor old lady couldn't even bring herself to speak it aloud.

Marjorie touched her aunt's hand. "I know at first it will be difficult. But I firmly believe this is one time when the ends justify the means."

Gertrude shook her head and tried an appeal to Charles. "My dear young man, have you even gotten up the courage to ask Lady Summerfield? I know my sister can be stubborn, but she has surprised me on occasion."

He gave Marjorie a quick look. "I did, actually."

"You did?" Marjorie asked, completely stunned.

"She refused me out of hand. Which is why we are forced to take drastic measures."

"When did you . . . ?" Her voice trailed off. "Oh. I suppose it doesn't matter when, only that she refused. Does no one tell me anything?"

"She asked me not to and after some consideration, I thought it best."

"She is so opposed to you. Did you know, Aunt, that Mother threatened to strip George of his title if I allowed Mr. Norris to court me?"

"But that's absurd," Gertrude said.

"Not to mention impossible," Charles added, grinning, the maddening man.

"Something's not right here. I know Dorothea can be stubborn and has a ridiculous fascination with titles, but Mr. Norris is the son of a viscount. He has an excellent income." She looked to Charles for confirmation, and he nodded. "Who is your mother?"

"Lady Anne Hartley."

"No, no. Who was she *before* she married your father?"

"Anne Wadsworth."

"Wadsworth. *Wadsworth.*" A look of dawning spread across Gertrude's face. "Eureka, my dear. Your mother loathes Charles's mother." She began laughing, then coughing, waving a hand at the pair when their expressions grew alarmed. "I'm fine," she choked. "Oh, dear. It all makes sense now. She will do everything in her power to prevent our families from merging. Oh, dear. I'm afraid she will never agree to a marriage between you two."

"We already knew that," Marjorie said. "You're saying there's bad blood between Charles's mother and my mother?"

"That's putting it excessively mildly, my dear."

"Was your mother Dorothea Stockbridge?" Charles asked hesitantly, as if he truly didn't want to hear the answer.

"You knew my mother before we met?" Marjorie said, sounding confused.

Charles started to laugh, but it was a laugh slightly tinged with tragedy. "I knew *of* your mother. She's legendary in my family. We even bring her up on occasion just to tease my mother when we want to torture her a bit."

"Is it that awful, what happened between them?" Marjorie whispered.

"It caused such a stir at the time that we all thought your mother and Lady Anne would be tainted with scandal for years and never marry." Aunt Gertrude clucked her tongue.

Charles chuckled softly. "Turns out, though, that was the moment my father realized how much he loved my mother."

Marjorie clenched her fists in frustration. "Would one of you please tell me what happened?"

"Fisticuffs!" Gertrude said with an emphatic nod. "At *Ascot*—of all places."

"They fought over a horse race?" Marjorie asked, flabbergasted.

"Oh, goodness, no. More significant than that. They were fighting over—a hat."

"What?" This was impossible. Her entire future was being ruined by a hat? Marjorie wanted to cry, but laughed instead. How was it she'd never heard this tale?

"It was quite a row," Charles said. "My mother, of course, said Miss Stockbridge started it. Apparently, and this is my mother's side, understand, your mother saw a hat at the milliner they both used. My mother had ordered the hat and designed it. Your mother saw it and asked for a duplicate. My mother was quite a bit younger than yours, you see, and quite a bit spunkier than she is now. She was incensed when she saw your mother wearing *her* hat—at Ascot, no less. She strode up to your mother and demanded to know where she'd gotten her hat."

"She must have known," Marjorie said.

"Of course. But she demanded to know anyway. And you know your mother, she can be rather intimidating. Your mother just stared at my mother and said, 'Yours doesn't suit your coloring at any rate.' And that was it."

Marjorie cringed. "What happened?"

"You have to remember that my mother was quite, quite young . . ."

"What. Happened."

"She snatched your mother's hat off and crushed it beneath her foot. Even as she did so, my mother told me she knew she'd been horrid. She always did have something of a temper. And then all hell broke loose. They ended up on the ground, pummeling each other, surrounded by some of the most important people in society. They were in the royal enclosure, you see. In the scuffle, your mother's dress was ruined. *Very* ruined."

"She was *exposed*," Gertrude said succinctly.

Marjorie wished she could bury her head in her hands but there were too many people. "Oh no. No, no, no. Why didn't either of us know?"

Charles shrugged. "Dorothea is quite a popular name among women your mother's age. I know several. And my mother is so much younger than yours, I never put the facts together."

"My mother didn't marry until she was thirty-six."

"Ah. And mine married at eighteen. So, there it is. We've discovered the real reason for her opposition."

"And now we're truly doomed." Marjorie felt like crying. No one she knew held a grudge the way her mother did. And to think she was in love with the son of the one woman on earth Dorothea despised above all others. At least now her obstinacy made sense.

"None of this changes our plans," Charles said. "I love you and we will marry. We simply have to be compromised in grand style. The more witnesses the better."

"A terrible idea," Gertrude said, but something in the older lady's tone gave Marjorie pause. It was almost as if Gertrude was saying the things she ought, but didn't really believe. Perhaps when the time came, she could with a clear conscience tell anyone who wanted to hear that she had warned the couple not to act rashly.

Charles couldn't believe his bad luck. Of all the women to fall in love with, it had to be with the infamous Dorothea Stockbridge's daughter. In his house, the story was legendary. How many times had his sister donned a hat, only to look askance at their mother and feign fright that she might attack and rip the thing from her head? They'd all had so many laughs over the years. His mother would be horrified to learn that her actions of so long ago had caused so much trouble now.

How ironic was it that when he finally found a woman who loved him as much as he loved her, she would be the daughter of his mother's nemesis. Obviously, it was not a story that Lady Summerfield repeated. No doubt the entire episode was humiliating to her, and he wondered if that were the reason Lady Summerfield had married so late. Had the scandal nearly turned her into an old maid? Had she been forced to marry someone simply to be married?

He thought about her features, the bushy eyebrows, the iron gray hair, the mustache, and tried to picture her young and vibrant. He could not. But had she been? Had she worn that hat thinking how pretty she looked, only to face one of the worst humiliations of her life? And at the hands of his own mother. No wonder she was so opposed to their marrying.

It would be difficult, indeed, to have a mother-in-law who loathed one's family. The wedding would be . . . painful. No doubt the two women hadn't seen each other since that fateful day. He wondered how they would handle the meeting. Over the years, his mother had expressed real remorse over what she'd done—and all over a silly hat.

As her Aunt Gertrude left them to talk with a friend, he could tell Marjorie was upset by the news. He wished he could just whisk her away from this ballroom, from London, and take her home. Instead, he laid a gentle hand on the small of her back to give her just a bit of comfort. It was highly improper for him to do, as they were not officially engaged, but at this moment he didn't give a damn. She looked up at him with gratitude before her eyes grew stony, and he had the distinct thought that Marjorie had indeed inherited some of her mother's steel.

"Let's do it tonight and let's not muck it up. The terrace, shall we say at eleven?"

He smiled, loving the fierceness in her gaze. "Why not right now? I just saw a couple go out there. I don't know who and I don't really care. I only know that we'll be certain to have an audience. It's too early in the evening for them to be intoxicated."

The two walked toward the French doors that led out to a large terrace, then down to a garden where Charles could see the shadows of several people walking about. "Perfect," he said, indicating the garden. "We'll find a not-so-private private spot, I'll kiss you silly, then we'll get caught."

"And be shocked and horrified. You mustn't look too pleased."

"That will be the most difficult part of this entire charade," he said, closing the doors behind them. He grabbed her hand and practically ran down the stairs, loving the feel of her hand in his, loving that she laughed as he tugged her toward their fate. "Let's go to the folly, shall we? That seems like a likely destination for anyone going out for a stroll."

Lanterns, their candles flickering in the slight breeze, had been strung along the paths, lending a bit of magic to the air. Charles could hear the murmur of voices, and smiled. Getting compromised in this crowded garden would be certain.

"How many children should we have?" she asked.

He tightened his grip on her hand. He felt his chest swell to impossible dimensions just thinking about their children playing at their feet as they sat by the fire on winter evenings. He remembered how wonderful his own childhood had been, the long days of fishing with his father or climbing trees with his sister and their good friend John. He wanted his own children to have that same sort of carefree, happy childhood. "Six," he said finally.

"That's quite a lot. How about three? That's a fine size."

"No, it's uneven. We need an even set. We were a family of five and it was always difficult to find seating in a restaurant."

Marjorie laughed, then stopped, stood on her tiptoes and kissed his cheek, a quick gesture that seemed so wonderfully natural. "Certainly seating eight would be far more difficult."

"Very well. Four."

"Four it is."

It was settled. Now all they had to do was get married.

The evening was warm, the stars above them visible through thin, milky clouds. Charles wanted to remember every detail of this night. He'd waited for it for so long.

At the steps to the folly, he stopped. "This will do," he said, drawing her into his arms.

"But we're not even hidden."

"Precisely. Besides, I can't wait to kiss you." He brushed her lips with his and she sighed, wrapping her arms around his neck. God, she was soft and lovely and smelled so sweet. He could stand like this forever, hold her against him forever. He deepened the kiss, and she let out a small sound that acted like a bold caress, and he grew instantly hard. They kissed each other, slow and deep, as if they had all night to explore one another. She tasted of chocolate with a hint of champagne and felt like heaven in his arms.

He smoothed his hands down her back to her behind, round and firm and so very lovely. He squeezed gently and let out a stifled groan as he pulled her more firmly against his arousal. Why he was torturing himself, he couldn't say. He only knew he needed to have her against him, needed to hold her, kiss her. What he truly needed was to have her naked, but that would have to wait for another time. A tantalizing image came to him of her lying in his bed on her stomach, her beautiful creamy bum glowing softly in the candlelight. And then a second torturous thought: Marjorie lying on her back, naked, looking up at him as he entered her, closing her eyes in pleasure, wrapping her slim arms around his neck, moving her hips in uncontrollable . . .

He pulled back. "I'm afraid my imagination is getting ahead of me," he said, his voice ragged. "Our plan be damned. If I don't have you now, I think I shall die. Let's go in the folly. I don't care if we get found out or not."

He grabbed her hand again and pulled her up the steps and then against a column. "I know this is wrong, but I must have you."

"Like before?" she asked, her voice filled with an urgency that made him even more aroused.

"I wish it could be better. I wish we had a soft mattress so I could be inside you." He swallowed. Even just saying the words nearly undid him. "But we cannot. So yes, like before. But better. I'm going to kiss you, darling, where I touched you before." He could see her eyes widen. "I've shocked you."

"No," she said. "Yes. Yes, you have. I didn't know a man could kiss a woman . . . there."

"It feels quite good."

He moved his hand between her legs and she melted against him. God, she was so hot, and he imagined he could feel how wet she was already, even through the layers of cloth that separated his hand from her. "Yes," she whispered, "I imagine it does."

As he'd done in his study, he began slowly pulling up her dress, but this time, she helped, bunching up her skirts even as she continued to kiss him. He found the slit in her drawers and, bloody hell, she was so hot and wet he nearly wept. He touched her slick bud and she let out a soft sound, half whisper, half moan, and widened her legs just slightly.

"Should I touch you?" she whispered against his lips.

"God, yes."

Her hand went unerringly to his erection and squeezed gently.

"Should I unbutton you?"

"If you insist," he said, chuckling as he kissed her neck. "I'm afraid I'm a bit too distracted at the moment." He flicked his thumb back and forth and moved his index finger inside her.

"I can't . . ." she whispered. "I can't think when you do that. I can't unbutton you."

He moved his free hand to his front and made short work of his buttons and pulled down his drawers, allowing his member to spring forward. If she touched him right now he wasn't certain he'd be able to control himself. But she did, and he arched his back and very nearly found release. God, he didn't want her to stop, but he also wanted to taste her. He moved down, kissing her neck, her breast, her stomach, until she could no longer reach him. He pulled at her drawers so he could have better access, so he could lay his tongue against her. Her scent filled him, her sounds urged him on.

"Shhhh. Someone's here."

Startled by the sound of another man's voice, Charles froze. God, so close, he'd been so close to kissing her. But this was what they'd come here for, after all. To get caught in the act of making love. But damn, what terrible timing. With great reluctance, he stood, dropping her skirts as he did. He turned to see another couple, barely visible, standing on the far side of the folly. Doing very much the same thing he'd just been describing to Marjorie. He smiled as he rebuttoned.

"We have company," Charles whispered. Marjorie peered over his shoulder.

"Is someone there?" she asked, her voice sounding overloud in the quiet of the evening.

They heard a muttered masculine curse and the panicked sound of a lady whispering fiercely, "Please, no one can know."

The shadowy couple walked toward them, and Charles instantly recognized both. Mrs. Williams and Lord Seaton. Vera Williams had been married for one month. Lord Seaton had been married for two years.

"We won't tell a soul if you don't," Vera said. "Please."

"Hullo. Didn't know the folly was such a popular spot this evening," a female voice called out from below. The two couples had been joined by a group of several ladies—including Aunt Gertrude, bless her soul. "Lovely evening," Aunt Gertrude said.

"Yes," Mrs. Williams said, her voice shaking slightly. "Lady . . ."

"Marjorie," Charles supplied softly.

". . . Marjorie and I were on a stroll and ran into these two gentlemen." Her voice sounded uncommonly high-pitched, and she cleared her throat. "It is a lovely evening for a stroll. Which is what we were doing. Strolling."

"What else would you be doing?" Gertrude muttered.

Mrs. Williams grabbed Marjorie's arm and began walking back to the house. They were soon joined by the older ladies. Marjorie looked back at him helplessly, and Charles wanted to scream in frustration.

"Thank you," Lord Seaton said feelingly.

Charles just grunted.

"You don't understand. We love each other. Have for years."

"Then why didn't you marry her?"

"She had no dowry to speak of," he said, as if that explained everything. Which, depressingly enough, it did. "I swear, I won't say a thing about the two of you."

"Thank you for your discretion," Charles said with heavy irony.

There was only one thing to do. Compromise her entirely. In her own house. In her own bed.

And be discovered by her mother.

Chapter 16

"You're insane."

"Insane for you."

Marjorie was thrilled and horrified by his suggestion. More thrilled, though. And that was a terrible, wonderful thing.

"What if my mother kills you? We do have guns in the house, you know. Several of them."

"Then I would die a happy man."

She ducked her head and laughed. She must be insane even to consider such a thing. Who knew that becoming compromised was so difficult? Katherine had done it, quite unintentionally, without any forethought or effort at all.

She and Charles were dancing, and any fool looking at them would know they were desperately in love with each other. No doubt her mother would hear of it, but at the moment, Marjorie didn't care. She could see a few of her mother's friends looking at them curiously. Let them look all they wanted.

"Your leg does not seem to be bothering you at all this evening."

"How can I feel pain when all I feel is love?" He grinned down at her, obviously knowing how ridiculous he sounded.

"If you're going to start all that sort of nonsense, I don't think we have a future at all."

He gave her a wounded look. "I thought I was being poetic."

"I'd much rather you be yourself. Gruff and blunt and slightly overbearing." Those were, she realized, the aspects of his character that had displeased her so much when she'd first met him. Now, though, it was everything that she loved about him.

"All right, then. I want you naked beneath me. I want to kiss every inch of you until you make those noises that drive me—"

"Stop! That's quite blunt enough," she said, laughing. "Besides, anyone could hear you. You were practically shouting it."

He shrugged as if saying such things aloud to an unmarried girl weren't completely scandalous. And delicious. Her entire body was on fire for him and it was difficult to school her features so those matrons along the side of the dance floor wouldn't know precisely what she was thinking.

"Tomorrow night."

The music stopped and they still stood on the dance floor. She bit her lip and looked up at him, seeing the man she loved more than anything else in her life. Seeing love and barely hidden passion that made her toes curl. "All right, then. Tomorrow night."

He bowed. "Thank you for the dance, Lady Marjorie," he said.

She curtsied. "You are very welcome, Mr. Norris. I hope you enjoy the rest of your evening."

On the way home from the ball, Marjorie couldn't stop smiling. She watched as the gaslights alongside the road came and went, muted by the fog that had settled over London. She laid her head back on the cushion, loving the sounds of the horse's hooves and carriage wheels on the stone road. It was a sound, in the early hours before dawn, that had always seemed a bit melancholy. So many evenings had ended with disappointment, the ride home silent and sad. But tonight, those sounds held a promise, the carriage wheels bringing her closer and closer to the rest of her life.

"I remember that feeling," Aunt Gertrude said, breaking the silence within the carriage.

Marjorie looked at her aunt questioningly.

"Of being in love, my dear. Of every thought being of one man. It is a rare thing, Marjorie, and can be fleeting."

"Not this time," she said. "Not with us."

Aunt Gertrude let out a small chuckle. "Perhaps. You are both certainly old enough to know your own hearts." She was silent for a time. "What are you planning?"

"It's better you don't know," Marjorie said after a pause. It was bad enough that they'd tried to be compromised by being caught kissing; it was quite another thing to invite a man who was not your husband into your bed. Though her mind screamed to her how wrong it was, her body and heart were not listening. Every woman was taught from a young age that her virginity must be protected like some precious commodity. She supposed there were many, many girls who suffered the results of not following that rule. After all, if a girl became pregnant, she was the one who bore all consequences.

"I suppose you are right not to tell me. I do want you to be careful, even though I like your young man and he seems completely captivated with you."

Marjorie gave her aunt another dreamy smile and the older woman laughed. "You are so smitten, my dear, I could tell you he was a murderer and you'd just smile at me."

Marjorie giggled. "You are probably correct. We don't have a choice. I hope someday Mother understands that she forced us to be in this terrible position."

"Oh, my dear girl, you are optimistic, aren't you? When I was a girl and a parent wouldn't give permission to marry, things were far different. It was off to Scotland and Gretna Green you went. But that was only for girls under twenty-one. You know, you could marry whomever you want."

"I know," Marjorie said with a sigh. "It's just that Mother has done so much for me, I do believe a secret wedding would hurt her even more than what we plan. At least she'll have time to come to grips with it and she'll be able to be at the wedding. I know, given what happened with Charles's mother, that she won't be happy. But at least she can watch me get married. I think she'll come around. She hasn't any idea how much we love one another."

Aunt Gertrude looked slightly startled. "But Mr. Norris did ask your mother's permission. She must have some sort of inkling."

"I don't think she does."

The carriage slowed and stopped, and with the sound of the steps being lowered, Aunt Gertrude, with some assistance from Marjorie, hoisted herself up. "I do believe I'm getting too old for these late evenings. Since you are the last of my nieces to marry, I must say I'll be glad when these chaperone duties have ended." Her aunt gave her a telling look, and Marjorie hugged her.

"You always were my favorite aunt. I shall miss our evenings together."

"Thank you, dear," Gertrude said, patting Marjorie's back. "But I don't think my nerves can take much more."

Five minutes. In five minutes she would be ruined. Well, perhaps it would take a bit longer than that; he wasn't even in her room yet. Marjorie had left the servants' door open and given him strict instructions in a hidden note how to find her room:

> *Once you're in the door, turn immediately right. Go up the stairs to the second floor—quietly, please! My door is fourth on the left.*

It was an unusually taciturn note for her, but Marjorie was in such a state when she wrote it, it was the best she could do. Imagine planning your own ruination.

Charles was such a large man, she wondered if he could do anything silently. She'd left her door open a crack and sat on her bed, staring at it, her eyes wide, her hands clutched together in her lap.

Ruined.

This was what she wanted. Not to be ruined, of course, but the end result of being ruined. The planning of it had been such fun, but now it seemed such a very bad idea. Wrong. What she was doing this night went against everything she'd ever been taught. Everything she'd believed. Part of her wanted to dash across the room and lock her door.

Instead, she stood and paced, her eyes still peeled on that crack in her door, waiting for it to widen and allow him into her room. Where they would make love.

Oh, God, she could hardly breathe. A noise from the hall made her freeze. Then he silently entered her door and closed it with a small *snick*.

He turned with a devilish grin on his face, and somehow that made everything a bit better.

"Are you ready to be ravished, my dear?" he asked soft and low.

Marjorie nodded. "Ready and willing."

Charles chuckled, then took off his jacket and tie and placed them neatly on a chair. He seemed so large in her room, so masculine when everything around him was delicate and feminine. The light from her lamp made him look more devilish than he was. Charles was a wonderful, kind man, she reminded herself. A wonderful, kind man who was about to ravish her.

"I have dreamt of this moment. I don't mean that to be poetic. I had a dream where you stood before me much as you are now. I pray this isn't another dream to torture me, leaving me to wake up alone in my bed."

Marjorie bit her lip and smiled. "This is not a dream." She realized her voice was shaking and she took a bracing breath. "I'm terribly nervous."

Her words seemed to cause him pain. "Please don't be. You are everything I've always wanted. Do you realize how long I've looked for you? I'm thirty-five years old and I've never found a woman who loves me. Are you certain?"

"You had a birthday? Why didn't you tell me?"

"Are you stalling? I asked you a question."

She laughed, her nerves slipping away a bit. "Of course I love you. And this is precisely what I want. I thought it over and realized there is no way for us to be together without hurting my mother. We have our differences, yes, but I do love her. I want her to be at my wedding, even if she's not smiling." She laughed a little, hoping to ease his worry.

He stepped closer and she held her breath. But he only reached up and touched her hair. "I didn't imagine your hair so long. I could swim in it." He slowly moved his hand to the back of her neck and drew her toward him. "You can't know how much I love you."

He leaned forward and touched his lips gently to hers, hardly even a kiss, but it sent a sharp bolt of desire through her. With a sigh, she brought her arms up and around his neck.

He pulled back to look at her, his eyes sweeping her form. "My God, you're so beautiful. I can't believe what I'm about to say."

He pulled her into his arms and released a deep sound of satisfaction as his hands at the base of her back drew her to him, moving the silky material over her sensitive skin. *This is it,* she thought, *he is going to ravish me.* It felt rather nice so far. She could hardly think, never mind speak, but she did manage to say, "What?"

He kissed her cheek, her mouth, the sensitive place at the base of her ear, his hands moving up and down from her buttocks to her shoulders, long sweeping caresses that melted her inside. "Everything about this is wrong," he said, then groaned as he kissed her, long and deep, and he pulled her toward his obvious arousal. "I can't."

Marjorie pulled back. "Can't?"

"Can't do everything wrong. I want you to be a virgin on your wedding night." His mouth and hands contradicted what he said. One hand moved to her breast, his thumb moving back and forth over her nipple, teasing it into a hard nub. What was he doing to her, telling her he couldn't and at the same time making it impossible to stop?

"No, no, no," Marjorie said, kissing him with an open mouth, letting him know how desperate she was for him. She moved her body against him and he let out another low groan. She loved that sound, loved that she knew he wanted her as much as she wanted him. "It's fine, Charles. I don't need to be a virgin then. It can happen tonight. Please."

"No."

She pulled back. "No?"

He looked down at her and she had no doubt that he wanted her, that he loved her, but there was determination in his eyes.

He let out a soft laugh and moved against her again. "I want you more than I've ever wanted anything in my life. But one thing in this ridiculous courtship of ours, I want to be right." He dipped his head and took one nipple in his mouth, giving her such exquisite pleasure her knees buckled. "However," he said, his mouth still at her breast, "I'm not a saint."

"We'll do what we did before?" she asked, breathless.

"And more. But you will be a virgin. I pray." He looked at her, his eyes focusing hotly on her erect nipples, and said, "Let's get that off you."

"My gown? But you said—"

"What I have planned will be much better if you're naked."

Marjorie blushed, but began unbuttoning the tiny ivory buttons, revealing more and more to his burning gaze, until finally she was able to pull the material off her shoulders. With one delicate shrug, the gown fell in a whisper of sound to the floor. And she was naked.

"I'm not a saint," he muttered, then frantically began taking off his own clothes. "But dammit, I should be canonized for this night."

Marjorie watched, fascinated, as more and more of his flesh was exposed, until finally, he stood before her, all muscle and manliness. She bit her lip as she gazed once again at his full erection.

"Your leg is all right?"

"If my leg fell off at this moment, nothing could stop me."

Marjorie covered her mouth and laughed, trying to be quiet. The very last thing she wanted was to get caught now.

"To the bed?" she asked.

"To the bed." He scooped her up and deposited her in the middle, following immediately, his mouth unerringly finding one nipple and drawing it in. Marjorie arched, her hands going to the back of his head. Who knew such a thing could be so incredibly wonderful? Who knew a caress to her breast could feel as if he were touching her between her legs?

One broad hand moved down her side to her outer thigh, then slowly across. "Spread your legs a bit, love," he said, his head coming up so he could watch her. She did, her eyes never leaving his, as she felt his hand move up until finally, finally, he touched that singular place that gave so much pleasure.

He groaned when he found her wet, and groaned again when she lifted her hips, silently asking for more. She couldn't help herself. Nothing could compare to this feeling of being touched by him.

"I'm not a saint," he said again, then moved down, kissing her stomach, the soft curls at the apex of her thighs, the delicate and sensitive skin of first her left thigh, then her right. And then, oh, then the middle, a kiss with tongue and mouth and sucking and she wanted it to go on forever. Her hands moved restlessly, finally resting on the top of his head, exerting a bit of pressure to silently tell him he was doing something very, very right.

Sensations she remembered from that first time flooded her and she was lost. Her hips began moving as the pressure built, and finally she reached her climax, jerking beneath him and trying not to scream out in pleasure.

Slowly, slowly, she came back to earth, her body feeling languid and sated. But she was aware that as limp and satisfied as she was, Charles was still tense and hard.

Poor man.

He moved up, and with a bit of manly triumph, kissed her.

"That was quite nice," she teased. "What can I do for you?"

"A Victoria Cross would be fitting."

"Or a knighthood?"

As they talked, Marjorie's fingers played with the hair on his chest. It made her feel somehow more womanly to be lying next to such a man. She slowly drew her hand in circles, moving lower and lower, until her knuckles grazed his still straining erection. "I could touch you," she said, and moved one finger from the base to the tip, delighting when he closed his eyes and his face grew taut. She wrapped her hand around him and caressed him, much as before, watching his reactions to everything she did.

"You could kiss me."

She stopped, then stared at her hand, wondering if she understood what he was saying. "You mean the way you kissed me?"

"Yes, please."

A giggle erupted from her throat. "I hardly think it would be the same." She thought about it, about the things that happened with a man that didn't happen with a woman, and became quite unsure what to do. She could hardly ask. But perhaps just a little kiss would suffice.

With grim determination, she moved down and kissed the tip, feeling him grow even harder beneath her hand. It was really amazing, she thought, wondering what she should do next. Charles, looking down at her with such incredible heat, supplied the answer.

"If you wouldn't terribly mind, you could put me in your mouth."

"Like a whistle?"

He laughed, sounding pained. "A bit like that, yes."

And so she did, laving her tongue over him, experimenting, gauging how much pleasure she gave by the low sounds he made and the tightening of his body. Then, in a frantic movement, he hauled her up, his hips bucking beneath her, and kissed her, releasing a long, rumbling groan.

Marjorie lay on top of him, feeling him slowly relax. "Good God," he finally uttered. "I can't wait till our wedding night."

She smiled against his neck, breathing in his scent. "I'm sleepy," she murmured.

"Oh, no, do not fall asleep. When we are discovered, we shall both be clothed. Or nearly so. I have no desire for your mother to find us nude."

Marjorie pouted and moved off him, wrinkling her nose when she saw a sticky bit of thick liquid on her stomach. Charles simply grinned and grabbed a handkerchief to wipe it off. "You'll get used to all this business," he said, gazing at his handiwork.

For some reason, that simple statement made Marjorie so happy. She would get used to it, through a long, wonderful life with this man. "I do love you."

He looked up, as if her words surprised him. Then his eyes became suspiciously misty and he looked away, swallowing heavily. "I've waited so long to hear those words. I shall never get used to hearing them." Then he shook his head as if shaking off all that uncomfortable emotion, and with efficient movements, got dressed. Marjorie picked up her gown, smiling at the naughtiness of such an act, and slipped it on, then froze. Someone had tapped softly at the door.

"Don't answer it," he said.

"But isn't that what we want? To get caught?"

"Not yet," he said. "I want to hold you a bit longer."

Another tap.

She gave him a look of exasperation, then grinned. "Go in the wardrobe then. It's probably just one of the servants with a question." She shoved him gently and waited until he was well hidden before putting on her wrap and heading toward the door.

"Hello, my lady." It was George's valet, Mr. Billings. "I'm so sorry to bother you this late in the evening."

"It's fine, Mr. Billings. Tell me, what's wrong?" For clearly something was wrong. George's valet, always pleasant and calm even when George was not, seemed quite upset.

"It's his lordship. I haven't seen him for two nights now. It's not like him. I confess I'm worried, my lady. Do you know where he could be?"

If any other young man had failed to return home for two nights, it would have been of little consequence. But her brother was so married to his routine, this news was upsetting.

"When was the last time you saw him?"

"Thursday afternoon. He was off to the Christy Collection as he likes to do every Thursday. I expected him back that evening, but he didn't return. I didn't want to alarm you then, for he has, on rare occasion, changed his plans. But not seeing him at all today . . ."

"I'm glad you told me, Mr. Billings. He said nothing to you?"

"No, my lady. I was hoping he'd told you something." Poor Mr. Billings looked close to tears.

"I'll make some inquiries, Mr. Billings. I'm certain there is a logical explanation and we shall be very angry with his lordship for causing us such worry." She forced a smile, and he returned a rather shaky one.

"Good evening, my lady," he said, and retreated down the hall to his quarters.

After he'd gone, Charles emerged from the wardrobe. "I heard. What can I do?"

Marjorie shook her head. She had no idea what to do, where to start. George had never done such a thing before. He'd never stayed away for an entire day, never mind two. "I think George is in trouble. Something has happened to him." Tears filled her eyes and she instantly was in his arms, trying to draw strength from Charles.

"Where would he go?"

Marjorie tried to think, but all she could imagine was how upset George must be. What if he were injured and in a hospital? What if he were still lying beside a road?

"To his club. That's where you met him. He goes there Thursday night, but only for one hour." She let out a small hysterical laugh. "One hour. Precisely. Then he goes home. But Thursday night was the night of the ball. He had plans to go with Lilianne. He wouldn't have gone to his club."

"He was there, and quite late, the night I met him. Perhaps he went to the club and got distracted."

Marjorie stepped out of his arms and began to pace. "Jeffrey must have convinced him. George has a bit of hero worship for our cousin, you see."

"Perhaps he met up with Jeffrey again. Perhaps your cousin convinced him to go somewhere."

"For two days? George would never agree. Not even Jeffrey could convince him of such a thing. At least I don't believe so. I have to talk to Mother." Suddenly, it dawned on Marjorie that Charles was standing in her room, late at night and that she most likely looked like what she was—a woman who had just been thoroughly made love to. "I'm sorry this has happened, but . . ."

He held up a hand. "Please, do not apologize. As soon as you've spoken to your mother, I'll leave. She may know something we don't about your brother. I'll stay until I hear."

Marjorie gave him a small smile. "I'll be right back."

Marjorie opened her door and let out a little screech. Lady Summerfield stood there, her hand up as if to knock, her eyes pinned on Charles.

Dorothea was immobile, panting, her face growing redder and redder with each moment. Her mouth opened, then closed, before she turned her gaze to her daughter. "How *could* you?"

"Nothing happened, Mother." Nothing permanent.

"Nothing happened? *Nothing happened?* There's a man in your room, Marjorie Anne. A man in his shirtsleeves and without a tie." Dorothea squinted her eyes and Marjorie thought her mother would faint on the spot.

"Please tell me that is not Mr. Norris standing half naked in your room."

"He's not half naked, Mother."

Marjorie saw her mother's hand twitch and she took a step back. She knew she was provoking her mother and had no wish to feel Dorothea's hand against her cheek.

"We wish to marry," Charles said, stepping forward and laying a hand on Marjorie's back.

"Do not touch my daughter, you cur. How dare you? How dare you come into my home and into my daughter's room and defile her?"

"I dared because I love her and it was the only way to convince you to let us marry," Charles said, his voice taking on a hard tone Marjorie had never heard before. It was rather daunting, but her mother was not a woman easily daunted.

"You *planned* this?" Dorothea's eyes went from Charles to Marjorie.

"We could think of no other way to convince you, and we didn't want the scandal of an elopement," Marjorie said. She had known this moment would be awful, but she hadn't realized just how awful. "He asked for my hand and you refused. I told you I admired him and you forbade me to see him. We love each other, Mother."

Dorothea's breathing was becoming harsh. "I need to sit," she said, and lunged into the room, nearly collapsing on the vanity chair.

Marjorie gave Charles a desperate look, then went over to her mother and knelt by her, grabbing one of her hands. "We know about the hat," she said softly.

Dorothea looked at her with confusion. "The hat?"

"Charles's mother. Ascot. We know."

"Oh, good God."

"For what it's worth," said Charles, "my mother deeply regrets her actions."

Dorothea began to laugh, and Marjorie looked at Charles, her distress clear.

"It wasn't just the hat. It was my *life* she ruined. I was banished to Ipswich to live with my aunt, a terrible woman. I lived with her for ten years, waiting on her hand and foot. Listening to her criticisms. That's where I met your father." She curled her lip. "Every day I was there I thought about Miss Anne Wadsworth, about how her 'actions' ended any hope I ever had for happiness. And she *regrets* her 'actions.' How lovely."

"She was very young, Mother. Just seventeen. I'm sure she had no idea."

"How could she? How could anyone know what her 'actions' sentenced me to?" Dorothea looked at her daughter, then lifted her gaze to Charles. Something changed in Dorothea's eyes, they'd gone cold and frightfully calculating. "This did not happen," Dorothea said, as if stating a fact. "I did not walk in and find you with my daughter. I will never speak of this again."

"Mother, no," Marjorie gasped.

Charles took a step forward. "I'm afraid, my lady, the deed has been done. You see, you did not catch me in the act of undressing. Rather, you caught me getting dressed. I was just about to leave." Charles's gaze was steady, his voice low and clear, and Marjorie had never loved him more than at that moment. He never lied. He'd told her that, and yet he was lying for her.

To her horror, her mother began to cry, soft, hiccuping little sobs that broke Marjorie's heart. "Haven't you ever been in love, Mother? So in love you'd do anything for that person?"

Dorothea looked at her, her face a picture of misery. "Yes, Marjorie."

"What happened?" Marjorie whispered.

"He didn't love me. He didn't." She let out a shaky sigh and briefly closed her eyes. "I know that now. I suppose I knew it then."

"Imagine if he did." Marjorie looked up at Charles and he smiled at her.

"I love your daughter and I will marry her."

"But I want you there, Mother. Please."

Dorothea shook her head. "I'll think on it. You have hurt me, Marjorie. Lying with this man you knew I opposed just to force my hand was very badly done."

"I know." Marjorie, though she felt horrible about betraying her mother, also felt joy bubbling up in her. It was over. They would marry. Though her mother was still upset by what they'd done, Marjorie sensed a softening in her stance, and she prayed her mother would eventually, if not wholly support the match, at least accept it.

Dorothea lifted a still shaking hand to her forehead. "Why did I come to your room in the first place?" she muttered. "I'd heard a commotion, voices. I thought I heard Mr. Billings."

Marjorie's hand flew to her mouth. She'd nearly forgotten George. "It's George, Mother. He hasn't been home for two nights and Billings is very worried. I am too, to be honest. You know how regimented George is. I'm afraid something has happened to him."

"Two nights?" Dorothea asked, clearly startled. "Are you certain?"

"That's what Mr. Billings said."

Dorothea looked at Marjorie, pain etched in her eyes. "Do you think perhaps he's the one who eloped?"

Marjorie felt the blood drain from her face. "I never thought of that. But why would he? They've already announced their engagement."

"Perhaps they thought I would do something to try to stop them."

Marjorie narrowed her eyes. "Why would they think that, Mother?"

Dorothea stood up, quite recovered from her earlier shock. "Because I went to visit the Cavendishes and expressed my opposition to the marriage. Really, Marjorie, if your brother wasn't afflicted the way he is, would we have ever considered his marrying a squire's daughter?"

"Perhaps not," Marjorie said begrudgingly. "But we've known the family for years and her father is a squire. That's not so far down."

"It is for an earl. We'll go visit the family in the morning. You sir," she said, turning a cold look toward Charles, "will leave immediately."

"Yes, ma'am." Charles gave her a cheeky grin and Dorothea's frown only grew more severe.

"And if you touch my daughter again before I make my decision, I shall kill you." She glared at Charles. "Is that understood, sir?"

"Yes, ma'am." The words were said solemnly, like a vow.

"Not even for a dance?" Marjorie asked.

"Not *even* for a dance." Dorothea gave a nod. "Now leave. And Marjorie, go back to bed. We need a good night's rest for tomorrow's business."

Dorothea watched him like an eagle as he left, making sure he didn't so much as touch Marjorie's hand.

Chapter 17

The next morning, as early as was decent, Marjorie and her mother went to visit the Cavendishes. It was nine o'clock, and Dorothea made a comment that the family was just indecent enough to be up at such an hour. Marjorie suppressed a sigh and the temptation to point out to her mother that she'd been up for two hours already.

Their knock was met by the butler, who didn't bother hiding his surprise at finding the pair of them standing on the stoop so early.

"I'd like an audience with Mr. and Mrs. Cavendish. And their *daughter*," Dorothea announced regally. It was clear to Marjorie that her mother didn't expect to see Lilianne at all.

The butler nodded and backed into the house before leading them to a small parlor. "They are having their breakfast, my lady. I'll inform them you are here."

Dorothea sniffed and looked around the room, her distaste clear.

"Try to be polite, Mother," Marjorie said.

"I am always polite."

"Then try to be nice."

Mr. and Mrs. Cavendish, with Lilianne trailing behind them, entered the room, their expressions curious, but tinged with worry.

"This is unexpected," Mr. Cavendish said.

"What's happened? Where is George?" This from Lilianne who did nothing to mask the worry she clearly felt.

"We were hoping you would know," Marjorie said, feeling more desperate by the moment. She'd almost hoped Lilianne had eloped with George. At least then she'd know where he was.

"We were to attend the Westin ball two nights ago. He was to pick me up and when he didn't arrive, I wasn't certain what to think. He sent no word, no note. And I haven't heard from him since. It's so unlike him."

Dorothea sat heavily on a settee and the others followed suit, finding a place to sit. "When did you see him last, Miss Cavendish?" Dorothea asked.

"We went to the Christy Collection together. He—"

"—goes every Thursday afternoon. I know," Dorothea said. "Did he say anything to you? Did you meet anyone there? Think, girl."

Lilianne's eyes filled with tears and her mother, sitting next to her, grabbed her hand to give the girl comfort. "No. Nothing. We met no one. He was excited about the ball. So when he didn't come to escort me, I was a bit surprised. I thought I'd done something to anger him. Which is silly, really, because George so rarely gets angry."

"Are we not overreacting? He is a young man, after all, and young men do inconsiderate things now and again," Mr. Cavendish said.

"Not George." This was said by Marjorie and Lilianne in unison.

"He's a man of strict routine. It's upsetting for George to have his plans altered," Marjorie said. "It's as out of character for him to not go to the ball with Lilianne as it would be for a cat to start barking. He simply would not do it. Which is why we are so worried, sir."

"Oh, God, something horrible has happened to him," Lilianne cried. Then her face cleared. "We must ask his cousin Jeffrey."

"Why do you say that?" Dorothea asked.

"Because Jeffrey is the only person, other than Marjorie and myself, who could persuade him to alter his plans."

"She's right, Mother. Let's visit Jeffrey."

The Penwhistle house in Mayfair had seen better days, showing visible signs of neglect. The flower boxes were empty, the whitewash beginning to chip, and one copper gutter hung precariously from the roof. It was a house in clear need of funds, funds that Charles had a feeling the master of this house was trying to obtain through nefarious measures.

It was but nine o'clock in the morning and Charles hadn't slept since leaving Marjorie and her mother. He was in a foul mood and ripe for a fight. Though he hadn't known George for long, he'd learned enough to realize George's cousin was the only man whom George considered a true friend. Jeffrey was the one who'd convinced George to gamble that night at the club, likely because his own pockets were empty. Only a desperate man would use another's money to gamble with, and Jeffrey Penwhistle was clearly desperate. Perhaps even a man desperate enough to do another harm if it meant gaining a few pounds.

He knocked on the door and waited only a few moments before a butler answered the door.

"I'd like an audience with Mr. Penwhistle."

"Mr. Penwhistle is not in."

"Sir, I appreciate your loyalty, but Mr. Penwhistle is in. I have no argument with you and I realize you are only doing your job. But if you do not let me in to see Mr. Penwhistle, I'm afraid I will have to force myself in."

A small bit of fear crept into the butler's eyes, for he was a smallish man and looked to be in his sixties. "I'm afraid I cannot, sir."

Charles let out a beleaguered sigh. "Really, sir, I've no wish to harm you, but this is a matter of great concern. A man's life might be at stake and I'm afraid you are giving me little choice but to exert force."

The butler's brows snapped together as he considered Charles's words, then said politely but with a band of steel around them, "Very well, sir. If you will wait in the foyer."

Charles stepped in, smiling at the butler, and said, "No need. Just tell me where Mr. Penwhistle is and I'll save you the trip."

"But sir . . . very well. Third door down the hall on the right." Charles was surprised at the butler's easy acquiescence but didn't show it. Prajit might have very well done the same thing if confronted with a similar situation. It had more, he thought, to do with the man's character than loyalty. Charles had come to realize that blind loyalty was nearly as dangerous as disloyalty.

After refusing the butler's offer to take his coat and hat, Charles immediately started down the hall. "And sir," the butler called after him, "he truly is in no condition to have a visitor, if you catch my meaning."

Charles paused, then gave the older man a salute. So, Mr. Penwhistle was in his cups, was he? Why would a young man be intoxicated at nine o'clock in the morning? A feeling of dread filled him as he thought about all the reasons Jeffrey Penwhistle might have to be drunk and how that could be tied to George's disappearance.

When he reached the door, he didn't bother to knock, but entered without warning. The room stank of brandy and a half-eaten dinner, its contents congealed on a plate placed on the floor by the fireplace. The room was dark, thick velvet curtains effectively blocking the morning sun. Mr. Penwhistle was sitting in an overlarge chair, a flask in his hand. He was so drunk, he didn't even start when Charles entered the room, and blearily looked at him with little interest as he flung open the curtains, allowing sunlight into the room.

"Bloody hell," Jeffrey said, shielding his eyes. "Close the fucking curtains, you cur."

Charles turned slowly, realizing with a small amount of delight, that Mr. Penwhistle didn't know who he was, that he might very well believe he was talking to a footman. With the window behind him, he surmised he was only a silhouette. Charles took grim satisfaction watching Penwhistle's expression change as Charles slowly walked toward the outraged young man. Once recognition set in, Penwhistle sat up quickly, if not a bit sloppily.

"I say, Mr. Norris, what are you—"

Charles cut off his words, grabbing his lapel, heaving him out of the chair, and slamming him against the nearest wall.

His alcohol-reddened eyes wide, Penwhistle sputtered, "I say, what's going on?"

"Where is he? Where is your cousin? I know you know." He didn't know, of course, but did have a great suspicion.

"How should I know where he is?" Jeffrey said. But he hadn't been able to stop his brief look of panic before he mustered his look of outrage. Charles knew he was lying, and he felt sick with it.

"What did you do, you little fool?" he said softly. "What did you do?"

"I . . . I . . ." Jeffrey's face crumpled briefly before he managed to get hold of himself, fueling Charles's suspicions even more. "He's disappeared."

Charles took a calming breath. "We know he disappeared. That's why I'm here."

"No, no. We went to a pub together two nights ago. The Lamb & Flag." Charles gave him a look of disgust, and Jeffrey hastened to add, "Yes, yes, I know we shouldn't have gone there but I'm bored with the clubs and thought going somewhere a bit more exciting was in order. Heard there was a good fight that night. George didn't want to go, of course. He had a ball with his new fiancée. A fight broke out—not the one we expected, of course—and we got separated. Couldn't find him and figured he went home."

"You brought George to the Bucket of Blood. Good God, man," Charles said, referring to the pub's nickname.

"Weren't planning to fight ourselves, just watch," Jeffrey said. "No harm in that."

"Obviously there was some 'harm in that'." He pulled out his watch. "Why are you drunk at half past nine in the morning?"

"Like to drink," Jeffrey said with a grin that didn't reach his eyes. "Besides, what else is there to do?"

"You're lying." Charles wasn't certain, of course, but he felt in his bones that Jeffrey was hiding something. What that could be, he had no idea.

Jeffrey gave an exaggerated shrug. "Why should I? One minute he was beside me, the next he was gone. Looked all over. Even went to his house and then to the ball, but he wasn't there."

"Why didn't you say anything to Lady Summerfield?"

"I didn't want to worry my aunt. After all, he could have gone anywhere. Could have met up with some lightskirt and been having a grand old time, for all I know. George is a grown man, even if he is an idiot. You say he's still missing? That is curious."

Perhaps he was wrong, but it seemed to Charles that Jeffrey was lying and actually enjoying himself. He was acting like a man who had just won a contest he'd known was impossible for his opponent to win.

"I was at the ball. I didn't see you there."

"That's not surprising. I was only there briefly looking for George. When I didn't find him, I went home."

"Did anyone else see you there?"

Jeffrey laughed. "What? You're a constable now?"

Charles curled his fist at the other man's derisive tone. "As a matter of fact," Charles said, keeping his eyes trained on Jeffrey's face, "calling the constable is a very good idea. If George is missing, he'll want to talk to you. You are the last person we know of who saw George."

Jeffrey smiled again. "Of course. Call one now. You know, Mr. Norris, I don't really care for your implications."

It was Charles's turn to look innocent. "I have no idea what you mean."

"Really. You barged in here, manhandled me, and demanded to know what I had done to my cousin."

"Yes, I see your point," Charles said, pretending chagrin.

"Why would I harm my cousin? He is very dear to me."

"I'm certain he is. And I'm just as certain you care far more for George than his title."

Jeffrey's expression became stony, but his bloodshot eyes shifted away. Charles had never been so disgusted with another human being in his life.

Charles walked calmly to the door where the butler stood, white-faced and solemn. "Please have someone fetch the constable, Mr.—"

"Stavers," the butler supplied.

"Thank you, Mr. Stavers. I'll stay here with Mr. Penwhistle."

"Yes, sir."

Perhaps the last thing Charles wanted to do was stay with Jeffrey. The man reeked of weakness and alcohol. As he was a betting man, he wished he could place a wager that Jeffrey knew precisely where George was. When he returned to the room, he sat down heavily across from the chair where Jeffrey had dragged himself. He took another swig of brandy, suppressing a gag.

"Curious," Charles said, and Jeffrey sneered and made a point of taking another long draught.

The constable had come and gone, leaving Charles frustrated and angry. Jeffrey, slightly more sober now, was beginning to have his wits about him.

"I'm certain he knows more than he's telling us," Charles had told the constable after pulling him aside.

"I don't," Jeffrey called to them jovially. Apparently Charles hadn't spoken as softly as he thought. "And I'm insulted you would say such a thing. Defamation of character, and all that. Isn't that a crime, sir? Arrest that man." He started laughing, and it was all Charles could do not to stride over to the man and slam his fist into Jeffrey's laughing face.

The constable had seemed more amused than concerned. He didn't understand that George would never have deviated from his set plans to spend the night with some bit of tail. He gave Charles a look of pure disbelief when he told the constable it was a near impossibility.

The constable shoved his pad and pencil into his jacket pocket. "Listen, if we went out to search for every toff who drinks too much and spends the night where he oughtn't, we'd never have time to do anything else." He lifted a hand to stop Charles's angry retort. "Right now all we have is a young man who didn't return home. We don't have a crime. We don't even have a disappearance. It's not as if he's a lad. He's twenty-one. If he wants to go off without telling Mum where he is, that's his business."

"I'm afraid you don't fully understand the circumstances," Charles had said through gritted teeth.

The constable doffed his hat and left the room, completely unconvinced that anything was wrong. Charles watched him go, then turned toward Jeffrey, who leaned against the mantel, looking as if he hadn't a care in the world.

"If I find out you had anything to do with George's disappearance, I will do everything in my power to make sure you hang."

Jeffrey smiled, though it was a bit shaky. "They don't hang a man for going to a pub, last I knew."

Charles took a step toward the other man, gaining slight satisfaction when he saw a glimmer of fear in his eyes. "You'd better pray we find him, Mr. Penwhistle—hale and hearty."

Charles left the room, only to nearly run head on into Mr. Stavers, who was clearly upset. "It's Lady Summerfield and Lady Marjorie. They just arrived, sir."

Marjorie tried to stop thinking of all the terrible things that could have befallen George, but it was impossible. Dorothea was silent; the only indication that she was upset was the way she held her hands in her lap, a tight ball of worry.

"I shall be very angry with George for causing us such worry," Marjorie said, trying desperately to remain optimistic. Dorothea didn't respond.

"He must be here. Where else could he be? I shall have to speak to both boys about this. How foolish we shall feel for being so worried when we find the two of them."

"He'll be here," Dorothea said with certainty. "Where else could he be?"

Marjorie didn't want to answer, didn't want to think of the possibilities. And when, instead of Jeffrey, she saw a grim-faced Charles coming toward them, she clutched at her mother's arm. Dorothea had gone quite pale and Marjorie could feel her trembling beneath her hand.

"George?" Dorothea said, her voice cracking slightly.

"Let's find a comfortable place, my lady. Mr. Stavers, if you would?"

The butler turned to lead them deeper into the home, but Dorothea didn't move. "Tell me now, Mr. Norris."

Charles looked at Marjorie, then back at Dorothea. "I'm afraid I have no news, Lady Summerfield." Dorothea let out a sound of anguish. "Here, let's sit." He pulled a chair from against the wall and thrust it behind Dorothea, who collapsed into it, still clutching Marjorie's hand.

"Tell us," Marjorie said.

"We know little more than we did last evening. Your cousin says he last saw Lord Summerfield at a pub called the Lamb & Flag near Covent Garden, but there are worse places they could have gone. It's a rough place, to be certain, and not one I would have taken George to. Somehow, the two got separated. Mr. Penwhistle says he looked for him, but was unable to find him. He says he didn't know George was still missing."

Marjorie narrowed her eyes. "But you don't believe him."

"Forgive me, but I do not."

"Why ever would Jeffrey lie?" Dorothea said, affronted by the suggestion. "If he knew where George was, he would tell us."

Dorothea stood and walked farther into the house, followed by a rattled Mr. Stavers. "Jeffrey, come here at once," she called out. "This is beyond ridiculous."

"Wait, wait. Mother, please. Stop. For goodness' sake, listen to Mr. Norris. What do you mean, you don't believe him. Why don't you?"

Charles hesitated, and Marjorie had the urge to shake him.

"It's just a feeling."

"Your *feeling* is disparaging my nephew. As I said, if Jeffrey knew where George was, he would tell us. I'm certain of it."

Charles gently pulled Marjorie away from her mother, breaking his promise not to touch her. His strong hand on her arm was immeasurably comforting. "I think Jeffrey knows more than he is saying. Perhaps he is trying to protect George."

"Protect him from what? And take your hands off my daughter," Dorothea spit out.

Doing as Dorothea asked, Charles said, "I don't know.".

"The constable was here and questioned him. Of course, Mr. Summerfield denied any knowledge of George's whereabouts. The constable indicated this was not a matter for Scotland Yard."

"I see," Marjorie said. "Then we shall have to find him ourselves. No doubt the police are not taking a missing young man seriously because they don't understand George. But we do. I know we can find him. And he'll have a very big apology for us when we do."

Marjorie turned back toward the home's entrance, needing to do more than debate whether her cousin knew where George was. She wanted only to find George, to make certain he was well. Charles moved with her toward the door, and Marjorie smiled when she felt his hand on the small of her back. What a brave man to risk the wrath of her mother.

"I'll look for him," Charles said softly. "I don't think you should—"

Marjorie stopped and gave him a level look. "I shall go to the Lamb & Flag myself. You can either accompany me or not."

"Not," Dorothea bit out. "I cannot have the two of you traipsing about London unaccompanied, and I am too weary to go gamboling about London looking for George."

Marjorie suppressed a sigh. "I'll stop at home and bring Alice with me. Will that suffice, Mother?"

Dorothea looked from one to the other, then nodded, and Marjorie relaxed slightly. "London is a very large city, Marjorie, and I think this is a fool's errand. But I do understand your need to not sit at home awaiting news. I'd go if I were up to it."

"Of course you would, Mother."

After stopping at the house to pick up Alice, the three headed out to the Lamb & Flag, an old pub tucked away on a narrow little lane called Rose Street.

"You should wait here," Charles said when their carriage stopped.

"He's my brother," Marjorie responded, pushing her way past

Charles to step down from the carriage with the assistance of a footman. The pub looked empty, the street deserted but for a young boy
polishing a pair of shoes. The boy looked up, his eyes wide in surprise at seeing such a grand lady. When she stepped onto the stone
pavers outside the pub, the boy stood and grabbed the cap from his
head, the shoe forgotten in his hand.

Charles followed her, his face grim. He tried the pub door, smiling in satisfaction when it swung open. Inside, a man wearing an
apron was sweeping broken glass from the floor, no doubt a mess
created by yet another bout of fisticuffs.

"Ain't open," the man said without looking up.

"I'm here for information, not drink," Charles said.

"We're looking for my brother."

At the sound of a cultured female voice, the barkeep's head
snapped up and he straightened.

"Lord Summerfield was here two nights ago. This is the last place
he was seen. We were wondering if you could tell us anything about
that night that could help us find him. He's a tall, thin lad with bright
red hair."

The barkeep furrowed his brow in thought, then shook his head.
"Two nights ago? That was a bruisin' night. Can't recall seeing the
man you describe. It were a real crush that night an' when the fight
started, it cleared out pretty quick."

"I saw 'im. An' I know wha' 'appened to 'im."

The three adults in the room turned to the young lad who'd been
outside polishing shoes. He stood in the doorway, eyes wide. When
the three looked at him, he snatched the hat from his head and shuf-
fled his feet, looking for all the world as if he'd wished he'd remained
silent.

"Tell 'em what you know, Mickey, there's a good lad," the barkeep
said, his voice gentle.

"I remember 'im 'cause I ain't never seen hair that color before.
An' he was tall, too. Acted a mite odd."

Marjorie smiled. "You are a very observant young man," she said,
hoping to encourage him even as her heart stuttered hearing "and I
know what happened to him."

"He was with another toff." He screwed up his face. "Don't remember what he looked like, only that they was together. Once the
fight started, they left. I thought maybe I could shine their shoes, so I

grabbed me kit and followed 'em out. That's when I saw three toughs. They hit the red-headed man with a pipe."

Marjorie gasped and the boy stopped.

"Go on, tell the rest," Charles said, coming over to her and grabbing one hand.

"Then another man punched the red-headed man in the 'ead." Mickey darted a look at Marjorie as if gauging whether he should tell the rest. "He fell and didn't move and the other men all run off. Didn't take nuffink from 'im. I thought his friend had gone to get help, so I waited for the red-headed man to wake up."

"Where is he now?"

The boy shook his head. "He got up and stumbled around a bit. I followed 'im, thinkin' I could let the other gent know where 'is friend went. 'e fell again on New Row and I run back to where it 'appened so I can tell the gent, but 'e never came back. 'e was really in 'is cups so maybe 'e forgot it even 'appened."

"Anything else, Mickey?"

"I went back to where the gent fell, and 'e was gone. I reckoned 'e just went 'ome."

Marjorie felt as if she might vomit. Her brother was injured and alone and missing. She could hardly stand, never mind speak, and it was only the strength of Charles's hand in hers that kept her on her feet.

"You're a good lad, Mickey," Charles said, and handed the boy a guinea.

Mickey looked to the barkeep for permission to keep the coin and pocketed it when the man gave him a nod.

They left the darkened pub, the morning sun nearly blinding them. "Where could he be?" Marjorie asked, feeling more desperate every moment.

"He could have wandered off, senseless. Or he could have been found and brought to a hospital."

Marjorie nodded, though she knew he was omitting another possibility—that her brother could very well be dead.

"Let's go to New Row. It's across Garrick. Perhaps someone there saw something."

"Charles," Marjorie said as he held out his hand to assist her into the carriage. "Why didn't Jeffrey tell us what happened?"

His eyes softened. "The lad was probably right. He was likely so drunk he doesn't remember what happened."

"It seems like a rather momentous thing to forget," she said.

"Indeed."

New Row gave them nothing. The few people they found claimed to have seen nothing, though Marjorie got the distinct impression that at least two of the people they spoke to were lying. It was all so strange and upsetting.

"What's next?" Marjorie asked, feeling more weary than she ever had in her life.

"I'm bringing you and Alice home and then I'm going to check the hospitals," Charles said. Next to her, Alice perked up.

"No. I want to go," Marjorie said, ignoring her maid's obvious disappointment. "Someone that he loves and who loves him should be the one who finds him. Do you understand? I know you're not quite a stranger, but if he's in a hospital or worse, I want to be the one who claims him." Thick tears fell down her cheeks, and she wiped them away with her gloved hands. Charles handed her his handkerchief, and she blew her nose. "I'm not giving up yet," she said fiercely.

They began their search at St. Bartholomew's Hospital, the oldest hospital in London. It was located in the heart of St. Giles, and so was the logical place to begin their search. Charles sat across from Marjorie in the Summerfield carriage, looking at her for any signs of shock. After her bout of tears, she became eerily calm, her face frightfully pale.

"I do wish you'd stay in the carriage," he said, but she simply shook her head.

She had no idea what she was about to face. St. Bart's and other volunteer hospitals were institutions that serviced the poorest of London. The rich could afford to have physicians travel to them; many believed a hospital was a place one went only as a last resort. It was generally known that once you were admitted into a hospital, your next stop was the graveyard.

As the carriage moved around Springfield Circle, Marjorie moved the curtain aside and looked out, her eyes wide. St. Bart's was a series of four imposing buildings that took up an entire square. At the center of the square was a small park with a fountain bubbling cheerfully, though it did little to soften the stark architecture of the buildings that surrounded it.

"Where do we begin?" she asked, and Charles's heart broke to hear the quiet desperation in those four words.

"We should start with the north wing."

The north wing welcomed visitors with a grand archway. Indeed, entering the building was more like entering a wealthy estate than a place that treated the poor of London. The hospital was a monument to good deeds, a demonstration to all that Londoners took care of their poor in great style. The Grand Hall was dominated by a mural of Christ at the Pool of Bethesda, healing the lame. The floors gleamed and the air was filled with the smell of beeswax, which gave Charles a strange comfort. He'd been in battlefield hospitals filled with smells and sounds that would stay with him a lifetime. This place, with its soaring ceilings and tasteful paintings, seemed built to impress. Or fool.

"This looks like an estate, not an institution," Marjorie said, her brows furrowed with worry. "I've never been in a hospital, but this is not what I was expecting."

"Nor I. And I've been in plenty of hospitals, just not here in London."

As they entered, a woman wearing a dark dress with a gray apron approached them. She took in their fine dress, and curtsied a greeting.

"How may I help you?"

"We're looking for someone of our acquaintance who might have been brought here," Charles said. "Lord Summerfield. He would have been brought here two nights ago."

"An earl? Here?" She shook her head.

"He might have been injured or . . ." Marjorie couldn't bring herself to say the word aloud, so Charles softly completed her sentence. "Dead." Next to him, Marjorie flinched.

The nurse looked from Charles to Marjorie. "Please let me look at the register and see if anyone unidentified was brought in during the last two days. If you would wait." The woman indicated a small seating area, and Marjorie moved toward it while Charles stayed with the nurse.

"It's very important that Lady Marjorie not be allowed in the dead house," he said, keeping his voice low so Marjorie couldn't overhear him. "If her brother is there, I don't want her to see him like that. Tell her it's your policy not to allow women. And please check the admittance records. We don't know for certain what happened to his lordship. He may very well be alive."

The nurse nodded. "As you wish. I'll return shortly."

When Charles reached Marjorie, she was already seated, her eyes hollow with grief.

"I cannot believe what we are doing. It doesn't seem real. How could he be in this place?" She shook her head. "He's not here. I know it."

"I hope not," Charles said.

"What were you talking to the nurse about?"

"I wanted her not to dismiss us. I explained how important it is that she also check the record of men admitted."

The nurse returned, her expression unreadable. "Two unidentified males were brought in over the last two days. One is in the south building recovering. The other is here in our mortuary."

"I want to see him," Marjorie said, standing up.

The nurse shot Charles a nervous look. "I'm sorry, it's St. Bart's policy not to allow women into the morgue."

"But I'm his sister. I'll know him immediately."

"As will I," Charles said, gently laying a hand on one shoulder. "I'll be certain. I promise. Please, my lady, I do think it's for the best."

Marjorie gave him a shaky nod, and he drew her to him, kissing her forehead before turning to follow the nurse into the bowels of the building where the hospital kept its dead. The shining beauty of the architecture was left behind as soon as they began their descent.

Charles knew when they were drawing close, for the smell of a decomposing body was not easily forgotten. The closer they got to the small room that housed the bodies, the more certain he was that he'd made the right decision to keep Marjorie away. The nurse pulled a key from her apron and opened the door, stepping back.

"If you don't mind, I'll stay here. I never will get used to this room."

Several bodies, enshrouded by white sheets, lay on a common table. Though it was cool in the basement, it was not cool enough to stop completely the decomposition, and Charles withdrew a handkerchief and held it to his nose in an attempt to stifle the putrid smell.

Six bodies. Charles swallowed down the bile that threatened to erupt, and withdrew the first sheet. An old woman. The second, a tragically young boy with angelic features and white-blond hair. The third, a man in his thirties with a thick black beard. One by one he withdrew the sheets, quickly determining that George was not among the dead at St. Bart's.

"No," he said to the nurse's questioning gaze when he departed the room.

"Then it's to the south building, though I must say if someone had brought in an insensible young man dressed like a peer, I would have heard about it."

Charles climbed the stairs behind the nurse, feeling ill at ease. This was a terrible business and he was afraid the outcome would not be good. It would be heartbreaking to bring Marjorie to see a man who could not possibly be her brother. Though he didn't want to remove her hope, he felt it unlikely they would find George alive. If he were alive, why hadn't they been informed? A member of the peerage drew quite a bit of attention in a place like St. Bart's, or any of the volunteer hospitals where he might have been taken.

When they entered the Grand Hall, Marjorie stood, her eyes wide with fear. He quickly smiled and shook his head, and she immediately sat back down, as if her knees had given out.

"Shall we go see the patient in the south wing?" the nurse said.

Marjorie nodded. She looked so lost, so utterly sad, Charles wished he could make everything better so she would not have to suffer what lay ahead. If her brother were dead, her cousin would be earl. He knew enough to understand that, given the lack of evidence, it would be highly unlikely Jeffrey would be tried, never mind hanged for his crime. He was convinced Jeffrey had hired those thugs, but alas, had no proof and was doubtful Scotland Yard would find any.

As the three walked across the square, thick drops of rain landed haphazardly on the stone walkways, making dark splotches before disappearing. He looked at the sky, seeing the sun in the west, and looked in the opposite direction to see a brilliant rainbow stretching across a dark sky.

"Look, my lady," he said, stopping to stare at the rainbow. Marjorie stopped and turned toward the colorful display, smiling sadly.

"It's too beautiful," she said. "I'd rather it just rain."

Charles understood what she meant. Despite her brave words, he knew Marjorie was imagining the worst had happened to George. Death was such a final, terrible thing, it was difficult to realize that beauty could continue without a misstep.

The entrance to the south building was far less grand. It was a simple lobby of gleaming marble floors and a set of stairs that rose up, then split, to the upper floors. "This is where we put the accident victims. He'll be in the men's ward. If you could describe him."

"Red hair," Charles said. "Tall, thin. But the red hair is unmistakable."

"If you'd wait here, I will see if this patient meets your description."

Marjorie took a step as if to follow the nurse, but she halted her mid-step with one look. "I do apologize, m'lady, but I cannot allow you in the ward."

Marjorie wrapped her arms around herself and nodded. "What if she is wrong? What if she's looking at the wrong man? He could be here, somewhere, and we'd never know."

"George is unforgettable," Charles said.

She let out a small laugh. "It's the first time I've ever been so grateful for his bright hair. If he's not here, where to next?"

"Lambeth, I think."

"If he is alive, he would have sent a note. He would have let us know. It's been nearly two days since he was attacked, if what that boy said is the truth. Why hasn't anyone come to us yet?" She closed her eyes as if shutting off her thoughts.

"He could be unconscious. He could have been brought into a private home and is being cared for by someone who doesn't know who he is. Any number of things could have happened." Charles placed a hand behind her head and pulled her to him. She was so tense, it was like embracing a large wooden doll.

"I want it all to go away."

"I know, love."

The sound of a female clearing her throat drew their attention. "The unidentified patient is in his sixties and bald. Your brother is not here."

As they traveled from hospital to hospital, Marjorie's moods fluctuated wildly, from painful hope to searing disappointment to sickening dread. One moment she was imagining a tearful reunion, the next she was picturing herself standing wearing black beside a grave. She began to fear her brother's body had simply been dumped somewhere—or was being used for scientific purposes. They'd gone to three hospitals, all of which barred Marjorie from entering their morgue because she was a female. Instead, Charles had the grim task of looking at the recently arrived bodies, often stored on slabs in a windowless room.

It didn't feel quite real to be standing outside a room waiting for Charles to return with the news of what he'd found. She would wait outside with a nurse, still, quiet, and stare at the door, praying George would be found and praying just as hard that he not be found. Each time, Charles would appear, smile, and shake his head. At each hospital, they inquired about any red-headed male brought in with an injury to the head. And at each they'd been told no one matching that description had arrived there.

They traveled to Lambeth, Miller, and St. Thomas, leaving each with a growing sense of dismay that George was not in any of them— either in the morgue or in a ward, lying insensible.

"What's next?" Marjorie asked wearily. They had checked hospitals closest to where Mickey had claimed the assault had been carried out and were running out of options.

"Westminster."

Westminster was a massive building across from Westminster Abbey. Looking up at the three-story building, Marjorie had a sense of how impossible their task was. The crenellated top of the building looked more like a fortified castle than a hospital. Marjorie shuddered.

"Alice, you may wait here," Marjorie said, as she had said at the other three hospitals. Alice was more than willing to wait outside, for she'd freely admitted that hospitals made her nervous. Truthfully, they made Marjorie nervous, too.

"It's so large. How will we ever find him?" she asked no one in particular.

Charles placed his hand on the small of her back as they climbed the shallow steps leading to three large arches that ushered visitors through the hospital's entrance. As they walked in, a nurse met them.

"I'm looking for my brother, Lord Summerfield."

"Oh, yes, right this way," the nurse said with a smile, and Marjorie clutched at Charles's sleeve, feeling the blood drain from her head.

"Wait, you mean he's here? Lord Summerfield?"

Startled, the nurse turned back to them. "Unless the young man is lying or confused. Which wouldn't be too shocking given the condition he arrived in. Got bashed in the head, he did. He woke up last night, though, a bit muddled but otherwise fine. Of course, at first we didn't believe him. Imagine a lord being brought here. And him without a spit of clothing on him but his breeches. But he was adamant and we all decided that if he was a lord and he was wearing his finery, it would make sense to arrive with nothing on his back. Thieves, you know. They'll steal anything that ain't nailed down, and that includes a fine lord's clothing."

Marjorie laughed, giddy and lightheaded. George was alive. She kept repeating that over and over.

"He wants to go home, but since he cannot even sit up without keeling over, we thought it best to keep him here. And we weren't completely convinced he were who he said he were."

"What color is his hair?" Charles asked.

"More orange than a carrot," the nurse said, a dimple appearing in her apple cheeks.

Marjorie began to cry in earnest, as if all her fear and sadness left her by way of the tears. "Oh, God, Charles, he's all right."

She sobbed into his chest, and Charles held her, speaking to the nurse over her head. "We thought his lordship might have died, you see," he explained.

"Oh dear, but we sent a note over to his house, just this morning, letting you know he was here. It's not every day we have an earl on our floor, you know."

"We must have left before it arrived. Mother must know by now. She'll be so relieved. Thank you, nurse. Can you take us to him now?"

The nurse smiled and bobbed a curtsy before turning and leading them up a flight of stairs. "He might be sleeping, but don't you worry. Getting bashed on the head can leave you a bit sleepy for a while. The trick is to not let a body sleep too much. Once we started to believe his story, we moved him to a private room as is befitting. Here we are."

And there he was, his red hair brilliant against the white bandage on his head. His eyes were closed, but Marjorie knew immediately he was only sleeping.

She hurried over to his bedside and laid a hand on his shoulder. "George?" His eyes fluttered open, beautiful, brilliantly aware blue eyes.

"You've been crying," he said. "I'm sorry."

"Oh, George," Marjorie cried and did her best to hug her brother.

"Don't be sorry. None of this was your fault." She pulled away so she could look at his dear face. "I was worried sick, though. We feared you'd been killed." She let out a watery laugh. "Obviously, we were wrong."

George looked away, his brow furrowing.

"Do you remember what happened?" Charles asked, coming up on the opposite side of the bed.

"Not everything. I don't remember being brought here. I missed the ball. Lilianne must be terribly vexed."

Marjorie pulled a chair to the side of the bed so she could sit by her brother. "No, she was only worried. As we all were. Tell us what you remember."

"It was awful, Marge. Purely awful. I don't want to think about it anymore. It hurts my head."

"You can tell us later."

"No," Charles said, suddenly on alert. "What happened, George?"

Tears filled George's eyes, and Marjorie made a low sound before squeezing his hand. "What happened?" she whispered.

"We went to a pub. I didn't want to go, but Jeffrey insisted. I was to escort Lilianne to the ball and I needed to get ready. It was six o'clock and I needed to return home, but Jeffrey would have none of it. We went to the Lamb & Flag. That's on Rose Street, you know. I had a beer and Jeffrey had several. Four, down as quickly as I drank the one. Then a fight broke out and I wanted to leave. I wanted to hire a hack. I was to escort Lilianne to the ball and I knew I was going to be late."

Marjorie smiled. "I know how you feel about being late."

"Yes, indeed," George said. "And then Jeffrey started saying he was sorry, but he was supposed to be heir. I told him it was impossible, as I was heir and would soon marry and produce more heirs in direct line. I told him that he couldn't be heir, as my father was the earl. He got a bit angry with me. Jeffrey doesn't like facts as I do. I thought it was rather silly of him to say such a thing and wanted to show he was wrong. And then he told me it was a certainty that he was the heir. That's when I saw the men. One was holding a large pipe. Jeffrey pushed me toward them and the one with a pipe swung. It hit me on the shoulder. Hurts like the very devil." He moved his shoulder slightly and winced. "Then Jeffrey said, 'His head, you imbecile.' And the other man swung at my head and that's all I remembered until I woke up here."

Marjorie looked over her brother's head at Charles, horrified by the story George had just told. Jeffrey had tried to kill George. To actually hear her brother relay such an awful story was devastating. She knew how dear Jeffrey was to her brother. His only friend had arranged for him to be murdered. It was beyond horrifying. She wanted Jeffrey to suffer for what he'd done, and because George was alive, he certainly would. The law would not protect her cousin because he didn't have the safety of the title.

"Are you certain that's what happened?" Marjorie asked, knowing even as she said the words that her brother was certain. He never embellished and never lied.

George nodded, tears falling, trailing into his dear, red sideburns.

"I cannot say how happy I am that some kind soul brought you here," Marjorie said.

"Someone stole my clothes. My green jacket and yellow vest and my best pair of trousers. My hat, too, but I know where I can get another of those."

"I'll buy you one today," Charles said.

"And shoes. John Lobb, Bootmaker."

"Yes, I'll stop by there too. I imagine they have your dimensions?"

"Father's watch is gone. It was a Longines."

"We can check the pawn shops."

The more George thought about all that was missing, the more agitated he became. Marjorie laid a hand on his uninjured shoulder and gave it a gentle squeeze. "George, nothing is lost that cannot be replaced. The most important thing is that you're well."

"But you'll try to find the watch, won't you?"

"Of course."

George closed his eyes. "I'm a bit tired. My head hurts. When can I go home?"

Marjorie stood and found the nurse, who was across the hall tending to another man. "We'd like to take Lord Summerfield home if we could."

"Let me go find the doctor and we'll see what we can do about moving him."

* * *

One hour later, George was in his own bed being examined by the Summerfield physician, Dorothea hovering nearby, pretending not to be worried sick. When they'd come home, she'd been clutching the note from the hospital and said, "Of course I knew you were all right." But her eyes had been suspiciously red.

With George resting, Charles, Marjorie, and Dorothea gathered in the house's main parlor for tea. "I don't think I've ever appreciated a nice cup of tea more," Marjorie said, setting down her teacup. "I am exhausted."

Charles sat across from Marjorie and her mother, wishing he could be alone with Marjorie. As tired as she was, she'd never looked more beautiful. Even after the strain of the day, her cheeks were slightly pink, her eyes bright and lively. He could hardly keep his eyes off her, but every time he looked away, he saw Dorothea frowning heavily at him. She'd made it quite clear that he'd overstayed his welcome, but he'd ignored her when she'd said, "Oh, are you staying for tea, Mr. Norris?" in a way that sounded much more like "Please tell me you're not staying for tea, Mr. Norris."

"We need to decide what to do about Jeffrey," Marjorie said after the three had gone through the ritual of tea.

Dorothea bristled. "We shall do nothing. Our family name will not be dragged through the mud by a trial or an arrest."

"Mother, we cannot let pride rule us and ignore the fact that Jeffrey tried to kill George," Marjorie said, incredulous.

"You mistake me, my dear. I am not protecting Jeffrey. I am protecting your brother."

Marjorie looked at Charles then her mother in confusion. "I don't understand."

"I think I know what your mother means," Charles said, feeling that the tension between the women could result in an argument. "If we go to the authorities, George will be questioned. And he will relay the facts the way George does. And they will note how odd he is and I fear—and I think your mother does too—that they will disbelieve him. Do I have the right of it, Lady Summerfield?"

The older woman gave Charles a look of surprise that was ever-so-slightly tinged with admiration. "They would crush him," Lady Summerfield said. "They would make him look like a fool and discredit him thoroughly. And Jeffrey would get away with attempted murder. I have a better plan."

Charles, who had fostered a dislike for Dorothea, couldn't help but admire her gumption and intelligence. She was right, he realized. Any lawyer worth his salt would make George look like a fool on the stand. He need only ask George about his ancestry, and off the poor man would go, relating his lineage in excruciating detail.

"What is better than having Jeffrey be punished for what he did?" Marjorie asked.

"I remember taking one of my mother's rings as a child. I couldn't have been more than five or six. It was a large ruby and one of her favorites, and I admired it every time she wore it. When it turned up missing, everyone, including me, was questioned. Having that ring, fearing my mother would find it, became unbearable. After only a few days, I tearfully confessed. I suggest we do something of the same to Jeffrey."

"I'm not certain I understand, Mother." An instant later, Marjorie's face cleared. "Oh, what a wonderful idea."

Dorothea smiled. "Precisely. Jeffrey will go mad wondering when and if George or George's body will appear. We will simply continue to act as if George has disappeared. It won't take long before he cracks."

"And the beauty of it," Charles said, "is that Jeffrey will be unable to claim the title unless he admits he knows George is dead. And the only way he would know that is if he confesses what he did. It's marvelous."

"It's diabolical!" Marjorie said, and she and Charles exchanged a look, remembering another diabolical plan they'd hatched together. "Oh, this shall be the most fun I've had since, well, Charles and I cooked up our plan."

Dorothea frowned heavily. "I hardly think this compares with the disaster you two planned. I've never heard of such a ridiculous scheme in all my years."

"It very nearly worked, Mother."

Charles cleared his throat, distracting the two women, who were now glaring at each other. "It's essential that you, Lady Summerfield, appear more irritated than worried by George's disappearance. And you, Marjorie, must appear to be worried sick. I'd like to see your cousin's reaction to all that."

Marjorie waved a hand at him. "He won't care about my worry. The only thing he likely cares about is whether George is dead or alive. If he's dead, Jeffrey is earl. If George is alive, my cousin will know he's in deep trouble."

Charles clapped his hands together, startling the two women. "My apologies," he said, grinning widely. "But my dear, you are a genius."

"I am?" Marjorie asked, looking adorably confused.

"Jeffrey needs to see George. Everywhere. At least he needs to think he sees him."

Marjorie furrowed her brow. "I'm not certain what you mean."

"Have you ever read a story called the 'Tell-tale Heart'?"

Marjorie shook her head. "I confess I'm not much of a reader of fiction."

Dorothea also shook her head.

"In the story, a man commits murder and hides the body beneath the floor. After a while, riddled with guilt, no doubt, he thinks he hears the old man's heart beating, beating. It's a rather gruesome tale, and at the end of it, the man who committed murder goes quite mad."

The two women looked horrified by the tale.

"That's what I want to do to Jeffrey. I want to drive him mad, drive him to confess what he did. He'll think he sees George, but we'll act as if he's seeing things."

This time Marjorie clapped her hands together. "Oh, Charles . . ." Dorothea glared at her. "Mr. Norris," she continued, "that is a marvelous plan. What do you think, Mother?"

"I think I am going to very much enjoy the next few weeks. Only one thing—how are we going to convince Jeffrey that he's seeing George, Mr. Norris?"

"He will see George. Brief glimpses here and there that will require quite a bit of planning on our part. And, of course, we'll have to begin only when George is up to the task."

At that moment, the butler appeared and announced a Miss Lilianne Cavendish was waiting in the small sitting room. "Should I bring her in?" he asked.

Marjorie stood. "Of course. Please do. She must be worried sick."

"What is that girl doing here?" Dorothea asked.

"I wrote a note to let her know George had been found. She was worried sick, Mother, and as his fiancée," Marjorie stressed, "she has the right to see him."

Dorothea stiffened but said, "Very well, but you must accompany her. They are not to be alone."

Charles nearly chuckled out loud because he could almost see the strain Marjorie was under not to say something to her mother about how silly it was to chaperone the couple.

"I'll be going now," Charles said, walking with Marjorie to the parlor's exit. "Lady Summerfield, may I kiss Lady Marjorie's cheek?"

"No."

Charles grinned at Marjorie and she smiled back, evoking a sound of disgust from the older woman.

"Before you go, Mr. Norris, I would like to thank you." It seemed as if the words were forced from her throat, like scraping the last bit of preserves from a jar.

"You are very welcome, Lady Summerfield. I like George very much, and I love your daughter. I would do anything in my power to make certain they are well and happy."

Dorothea gave him a withering look, as if she knew he was being overly nice to get into her good graces. Which he was, of course.

When they left the parlor, Charles gave Lady Summerfield a polite nod, and acted for all the world as if he weren't going to kiss Marjorie the moment they were out of sight. He must have done a good job of pretending, because when he pulled Marjorie into his arms, she let out a small sound of surprise, which he quickly stifled with his mouth.

"I think your mother is trying to kill me," he said roughly, kissing her again. Marjorie pressed herself against him, and he nearly wept with the relief of having her in his arms. If they weren't married soon, he truly believed he would expire. He kissed her, deep and hard, as if trying to get a week's worth of kisses into one. It was frantic and wild and wonderful, but far, far too brief. Footsteps sounding behind them forced them apart. These quick embraces were sweet torture for Charles. "Damn."

"Yes, damn."

He chuckled as they both turned to walk toward the entrance. "Why, Lady Marjorie, such language."

"Sneak into my room tonight," she whispered. "Mother will be exhausted from the excitement of the day and—" She stopped herself. "Why didn't we elope?"

"We'd be married now. I'd have you in my bed every night, warm and soft." He lowered his voice even more. "And wet."

"Stop, you awful man."

"Lady Marjorie," Lilianne exclaimed, coming toward them. She gave Charles a quick, curious look before continuing. "Is George all right? I know you said so in your note, but one cannot always be completely truthful in a note."

"He's fine," Marjorie said, reassuring the frantic young woman. "He did get hit on the head and has an awful-looking bruise on his shoulder, but he's perfectly well." Marjorie turned to him. "Should we tell her of our plans?"

"I'll leave that decision up to you. But it can go no further. Your cousin mustn't suspect a thing."

Lilianne looked from one to the other, her eyes wide. "I'll tell her," Marjorie said.

Next to her, Lilianne smiled. "Perhaps we can have a double wedding?" she asked.

Marjorie let out a small laugh. "That would be wonderful, but Mother is opposed. Men have so much more freedom than we do. And the truth is, I don't want to hurt my mother. She'll come 'round, though."

"I don't think she'll ever approve of me," Lilianne said without inflection.

"Probably not," Marjorie said with complete honesty. "I know she seems like a hard woman, and she is, actually. But she does have a soft heart. Somewhere."

The two women laughed, then bade farewell to Charles.

As he made his way out of the foyer, he heard Marjorie say, "Let me take you to George. I know he'll be happy to see you."

Dorothea walked up to her rooms, past where Lilianne was visiting George. She paused, hearing only the soft murmur of female voices, and suspected that George was sleeping again. Their doctor said it was common for those injured on the head to sleep and that it would help with the healing. Then she heard a low rumble of laughter and her heart gave an unexpected lurch before she forced herself to move on toward her rooms.

If Jeffrey had succeeded in killing George, she would have been to blame. How many times had she thought that Jeffrey would have made the better earl, was the better man? How many times had she hinted as much to him? She was sick with it, this feeling of guilt and remorse. Despite everything, the pain, the worry, and the humiliation of having a son like George, she loved him.

She loved him more than she realized.

No one would know what was in her heart when George had disappeared. No one would believe it if she told them. She knew she'd become a hard, cold woman over the years. She rather gloried in the reputation she fostered as the cold countess. If one didn't feel, one didn't hurt. It seemed like a practical plan for a girl who had been hurt so very, very badly by the circumstances of her life. She realized now such a strategy was wholly a failure.

Her breath hitched as she realized she was about to cry. Again. For goodness' sake, she hadn't cried in years. She hadn't even cried at her husband's funeral, though that surprised no one. She was not a sentimental fool. And yet, when George had disappeared, when she'd feared something truly horrible had happened to him, she'd cried.

George was her son and she loved him. And if that girl made him happy, then she supposed she was going to have to accept her. Privately, of course.

"I'm going to rest before dinner," Dorothea said when she spied her maid darning in the corner of her private sitting room.

"Yes, m'lady." Her maid stood and quietly left the room, shutting the door softly behind her.

And then, Dorothea gave in to the tears of relief she'd been hiding for hours now. They were tears for George, and tears for herself, for loving Jeffrey nearly as much as her son and not seeing what a monster he'd become. It wasn't a long bout of tears. Dorothea would never do something so common as that. When did tears do anything but release of bit of the strain caused by life?

When she was done, she did lie down, something she rarely did in the middle of the day. She didn't sleep immediately, but lay there thinking, thinking about George, her daughter, and mostly about how satisfying it would be to make Jeffrey pay for what he'd done to her son.

Chapter 18

"I'm sorry, sir, but Mr. Penwhistle is not in." Mr. Stavers, the Penwhistles' beleaguered butler, looked decidedly nervous as he stood just inside the door of the townhouse.

"I know. I'm not here to see Mr. Penwhistle," Charles said. "I'm here to see you."

"Me, sir? I don't understand."

"You will soon enough." Charles looked past Mr. Stavers to see a maid peering curiously at the pair. "Where can we speak privately?"

"My quarters." Mr. Stavers hesitated a moment, then backed up to allow Charles's entry before shutting the door behind them. "This way, Mr. Norris."

Mr. Stavers led Charles down one level and toward the back of the home, to a narrow hall before turning into a tiny suite of rooms. The butler's quarters consisted of a sitting room with a single chair and desk, beyond which Charles spied a narrow bed, hardly big enough for a child, never mind a full-grown man. It was almost undignified.

When the door was closed, Charles said, "I've come to offer you employment, Mr. Stavers."

The older man looked stunned, then sat slowly behind his desk, taking in what had just been offered. "But I have a position, sir. I've been with the Penwhistle family for more than thirty years."

"Mr. Penwhistle is about to lose his position in society. I cannot go into particulars at the moment, but I can say without a doubt you may find yourself unemployed in the near future."

Mr. Stavers looked down, his white brows coming together in consternation. "Is it to do with Lord Summerfield's disappearance, sir?"

"I'm afraid so, yes."

"Dear God." The news affected the butler far more than Charles would have thought, for he looked quite distressed. "I have a bit of a soft spot for the lad, you see," he said. "This is terrible news. Terrible."

"It is. Mr. Stavers, my offer of employment is conditional."

Mr. Stavers lifted his head, and Charles had a feeling he was testing the man's pride, something he had no wish to do. "I understand you have certain loyalties to Mr. Penwhistle, and I admire your fidelity. But Mr. Penwhistle has done a terrible thing and I need your help, sir, to make certain justice is done."

"My help, sir?"

"It's nothing too egregious, I assure you. I simply need to know where Mr. Penwhistle will be and when. I promise you no physical harm will come to him. You have my word on it."

Mr. Stavers pondered this for a long moment. "Did he . . . did he harm Lord Summerfield?" he asked softly.

"Yes, he did."

The butler's face tightened, and without hesitation he said, "Then I will help. And I appreciate your offer of employment. But, sir, do you not have a butler? I wouldn't want to take another man's position from him."

Charles chuckled. "I could hardly call Prajit a butler. At the moment, my man is valet, butler, footman, and sometimes maid. But I believe I'll soon be expanding my household and will need a proper staff. I hope you will help me in this endeavor."

"Of course, sir."

Charles held out his hand to seal their agreement. "Very good, Mr. Stavers. If you have a trusted footman, he can deliver the notes. Do you?"

Mr. Stavers didn't hesitate. "I have just the man, sir. And if I may be so bold, if you are in need of a footman, he would do nicely. He's my son, sir."

"And your wife?"

"The housekeeper."

Charles could almost hear the hope and excitement in the older man's voice. He smiled. "Sir, this is truly a banner day for your family. It happens I'll also be in need of a housekeeper. You don't have any other children, do you?" he asked with mock fear.

Mr. Stavers laughed. "Two daughters, sir, but they are well married and off on their own."

"Thank goodness. My house isn't all that big. Thank you, Mr. Stavers. Someday you will know how much this means."

"I don't know if I'll be able to be pleasant to Jeffrey," Marjorie said. "I keep picturing my hands about his throat."

Next to her in the carriage, Dorothea laughed. "I think I'm going to enjoy this far more than I should."

They were attending the opera at Covent Garden. Jeffrey was to be in their box and George was to be in Charles's. It was rather nice that the boxes were nearly facing each other, making it practically impossible for Jeffrey to miss spotting George. Marjorie couldn't wait to see the look of surprise on his lying face.

The past few weeks had been filled with planning and pretense. It was decided that whenever Jeffrey spied George, he would be wearing similar clothes to those he'd been wearing the night he was accosted, a memorable green suit with orange vest. Dorothea, she, and Charles had had quite a lot of fun coming up with various scenarios where Jeffrey would briefly see George.

Not long after they'd devised their plan, Jeffrey had been invited to dinner, where Marjorie and Dorothea sat forlorn, and Jeffrey, the cad, pretended along with them.

"I fear something terrible has happened to him," Marjorie had said. "But the police will do nothing. They say he could be anywhere, with anyone. But I know they're wrong. I know George would never disappear without a word."

"It does seem unlikely," Jeffrey had said before shoving a large bit of broiled beef into his lying mouth.

"We think he may have been shanghaied," Dorothea said, and it was all Marjorie could do not to burst out laughing. This had not been part of the plan, so she was completely taken off guard by her mother's statement. "It may be years before he makes his way back. No doubt he'll write and we'll know he's fine before long. Those Americans are always coming to port and stealing men."

Jeffrey nearly choked. "Surely, that couldn't have happened."

"I'd rather that than the alternative," Dorothea said.

"And what is that, Mother?"

"He could have run off with some lightskirt," she said, and Marjorie dug the nails of one hand into the palm of another to stop from giggling.

Jeffrey had given Dorothea a look of pure disbelief. "Those are your theories? Surely you've realized that something darker may have happened. Have you looked in the hospitals? The dead houses?"

Marjorie gave Jeffrey a level look and used all her willpower not to let him know she knew precisely what had happened to her brother. "We did, as a matter of fact. We found nothing. We've scoured every hospital in the city and found nothing. It's such a relief. And so we've concluded he must have run off—"

"—or been shanghaied," Dorothea put in.

"Or been shanghaied, as difficult as that is to believe."

Jeffrey seemed rather upset by that conclusion, and Marjorie glared at him as he looked down at his plate, only to smile pleasantly when he raised his head. "He could have fallen into the Thames," he suggested.

Dorothea had struck the table with her palm, making Jeffrey start in surprise. "I'll have no more of this talk. George is not dead. I refuse to believe it. I'll have no more talk of this."

Of course, there was more talk of it. Over the next few days, the two women spent an inordinate amount of time with Jeffrey. They explained to him sweetly that they felt so much safer having a man about the house and accompanying them to various amusements. As each day passed, Jeffrey became visibly more and more uncomfortable with all the talk of George. Finally, he pulled Marjorie aside.

"I think your mother must come to the conclusion your brother is not coming back."

Marjorie looked at him as if he were quite mad. "Why ever would you say such a thing? Of course he's coming back."

"Yes, yes. I hope that too, with all my heart, but at some point, you are going to have to acknowledge that he very well may have died. I do hate to say it, dear cousin, but what other conclusion can we possibly draw?"

Marjorie smiled. "That he was shanghaied. Or has run off. I refuse to contemplate that he is no longer with us. As does Mother."

"But at some point won't you have to consider the future of—" He stopped abruptly.

Marjorie tilted her head curiously. "The future of what?"

Jeffrey shook his head. "Just . . . the future," he mumbled.

Yes, this night at the opera would be wonderful. God, how she loathed him. Every time he said George's name, she wanted to shout at him. No, strike him. Hard. In his smug mouth.

"I feel like a child at my own birthday party," Dorothea said as their carriage pulled up in front of the Royal Opera House. "There he is."

Jeffrey stood waiting for them under the center arch. "I don't know how you do it, Mother. You are a far better actress than I."

"I've had years of practice, my dear."

Marjorie laughed and stepped out of their carriage with the assistance of a footman. Dorothea was next, and when the two women were on the ground, they walked toward Jeffrey, who looked dashing in his evening attire.

"Shall we go immediately to our box?" Dorothea said, which meant, of course, that they should immediately go to their box. The plan was for the three of them to sit in the box and have George appear right before the intermission. Jeffrey would no doubt rush off to find him, but George would be long gone.

Marjorie sat next to Jeffrey, her stomach a jumble of nerves. What if Jeffrey failed to notice George? What if he leapt up immediately and gave chase? Worse, what if he saw him and appeared delighted, throwing doubt on George's story.

If the Queen of England were sitting next to Marjorie during that performance, she wouldn't have noticed. By the time the first act was ending, she was so tense, she could hardly breathe. And then, George, his red hair seeming to glow, appeared sitting right next to Charles. Jeffrey was oblivious.

Marjorie looked at Charles, who was clearly waiting for Jeffrey to look up and across the room, but Jeffrey seemed riveted by what was happening on stage. Marjorie hadn't known that Jeffrey was such a fan of the opera.

Then, Charles, bless him, clapped loudly at an inopportune moment, drawing several eyes toward his box—including Jeffrey's. Marjorie ignored the clap, but was aware the moment Jeffrey spied George. He stiffened noticeably and let out a small sound that was difficult to interpret. Jeffrey looked back at Marjorie, as if to see whether she also saw her brother, and when he looked back to the box, George was gone. Marjorie wanted to shout out with joy.

Jeffrey leaned over to her. "I swear I just saw your brother sitting with Mr. Norris. Is that possible?"

Marjorie looked across the theater. "I don't see anyone who looks like George."

"Not now. Before. He was there, then he disappeared."

"I daresay, Mr. Norris would have told us if George had shown up at the opera, Jeffrey," Marjorie said softly. "But perhaps we should investigate during the intermission. Oh, I do hope you're right."

"Yes, as do I," Jeffrey said, sounding vague and troubled.

On stage, a tenor was singing his last note, marking the end of the first act. After the applause, Marjorie stood. "Mother, Jeffrey claims to have seen George sitting with Mr. Norris. We're going to investigate."

"What? George is here?" Dorothea seemed so genuinely delighted and surprised, that for a moment Marjorie thought her mother had forgotten their ruse. "Of course you should go. I do hope it is. Though, why wouldn't he have sat with us?"

As Marjorie was leaving, her mother gave her the most impish smile, almost making her look like a young girl. Jeffrey and Marjorie made their way through the crush of people to Charles's box, only to find him there with an elderly man he introduced as his uncle.

"Was there no one else in your box? I looked over and saw another man here," Jeffrey said, looking a tad worried.

"Another man? No, it was just my uncle and me."

"He thinks he saw George sitting with you," Marjorie said, sounding bewildered. "It gave me such hope."

Jeffrey looked around the small box as if someone might be hiding. "I swear I saw a man with red hair sitting right by you."

"Are you certain it was my box you were looking at?"

"Very certain," Jeffrey said, now sounding angry. He took a deep breath. "I suppose I could have been mistaken."

"We all want to find him so much," Marjorie said with sympathy, but behind her cousin's back she wrinkled her nose in distaste.

The evening was a great success. Jeffrey's confusion was palpable, and over the next few days, it grew even worse. He saw George in a bookstore, walking along the street, in Hyde Park. And in every instance, by the time he was able to investigate, George had disappeared. Making matters worse for poor, poor Jeffrey, no one he was with saw George. He was clearly becoming rattled.

Three days after the opera, Jeffrey came for tea, looking haggard and on edge. They sat in the front sitting room, which faced the street, talking over the clatter of the occasional carriage that went by, for it was a warm day and the windows were open to allow a breeze. Marjorie sat by the window, nibbling on a small sandwich, and her mother sat next to Jeffrey on the settee. They talked of the upcoming regatta and made plans to all go together. Though Marjorie tried to engage Jeffrey in the conversation, he muttered only a few words, then grew silent.

"Are you not feeling well, Jeffrey?" she asked innocently.

Her cousin shook his head. "I haven't been sleeping well. This whole thing about George has me a bit rattled."

"I'm sure we'll have word from him any day now," Dorothea said cheerfully, and Jeffrey gave her a look of complete disbelief.

"Aren't you at all worried that something terrible has happened to him?"

Dorothea looked at him for a long moment, so long that Marjorie was afraid her mother would say something and give up the game. "Of course, I'm worried. My only son has disappeared. But I daresay, Scotland Yard is making progress on the case. They've several investigators looking for clues and whatnot. Apparently, there was an American ship that left port the very night George disappeared and at least one other man was shanghaied. I'm quite convinced George was also taken."

"That is promising," Jeffrey said unconvincingly. "They haven't found anything else?"

"No, they haven't."

Jeffrey wiped his brow, and Marjorie noticed a slight tremor in his hand. A few minutes later, Jeffrey said his good-byes and headed out the door, claiming he had an important appointment.

Marjorie leapt from her chair and hurried to an adjoining room. "George," she whispered harshly. "It's time."

These past days had also taken a toll on George, who disliked his routine being so disrupted. He grew more agitated each day, even though he understood the need for what they were doing. He didn't take quite as much delight in tricking Jeffrey; he simply wanted to end it all and tell Scotland Yard what he knew.

Marjorie tugged George to the open window. "Stand here. And if Jeffrey sees you, wave. Don't smile. Wave slowly, as if you're in a trance." Marjorie looked past her brother and grinned at Dorothea. "This will drive him positively mad."

"Very well," George said. "What if he doesn't see me?"

"Then we'll try something else," Dorothea said, her voice tinged with a bit of impatience.

"If he does see you, he might stop the carriage. As soon as he's out of sight, step to the side and run to the other room."

Marjorie sat back down where she'd been and took up her needlepoint.

"Here comes his carriage," George said, sounding excited.

"Just stand there. Do try not to smile, George. Is he looking? Does he see you?"

Dorothea, still sitting on the settee, whispered, "He's seen him." She started giggling and Marjorie pressed her lips together to stop her own laughter. Behind her, George quickly turned away from the window and awkwardly ran across the room to the adjacent door, barely making it through before Jeffrey came bounding into the room, his eyes wild.

"Where is he?"

Marjorie calmly put her needlepoint down. "Whom do you mean?" she said, looking about the room.

Jeffrey pointed to the window, his face covered with a sheen of perspiration. "He was standing at the window. He was wearing, oh, God. He was there. He waved at me."

"Who, Jeffrey?"

"George," Jeffrey shouted as if they were the crazy ones.

He began moving about the room, looking behind furniture, in places no man could ever hope to fit. Then he stalked toward the door George had disappeared behind and swung it open. Marjorie held her breath, praying George had thought to hide. Marjorie and her mother stared at each other for a long moment, holding their breath.

Dorothea stood, smoothed out her skirts, and walked toward the room where Jeffrey was apparently searching for George. "You are being unkind, Jeffrey," Dorothea said. "You know very well George is not here, and to continually claim you see him is beyond cruel."

Breathing harshly, Jeffrey came back into the front parlor, looking bewildered and defeated. "I swear I saw him. I swear."

"The light can play tricks on the mind, my dear. We all are upset about George's disappearance, but this seems to be affecting you more than I would have thought. Perhaps you feel guilty because you were with him the night he disappeared. I do hope that is not the case, Jeffrey. None of this is your fault," Dorothea said sympathetically.

"No, none of it is," Jeffrey said, still looking around the room. "If only I could get some sleep."

"It has been a strain on us all," Dorothea said.

When Jeffrey had left once more, Dorothea said, "I almost feel sorry for him."

"I don't." George and Marjorie spoke in unison and grinned at each other.

"Either way, it's nearly over. He looks like a man about to snap." Dorothea sighed and grabbed another sandwich. "All this excitement has improved my appetite."

"Mine, too," Marjorie said, taking the last scone. "I think the regatta will be his undoing."

Chapter 19

On the second day of the Henley Royal Regatta, Charles, looking smart in his Panama hat, sat in the stands at the finish line with Marjorie, Lady Summerfield, and Jeffrey, enjoying the bright sunshine and the excitement of the upcoming race. They had already watched a number of races, and now were anticipating the final contest of the regatta, the Grand Challenge Cup. Both banks and the slight rise above the river were dotted with men in their best summer suits and white parasols held by women in their summer finery. A set of opera glasses lay on the bench beside a large basket filled with more food than the four of them could possibly eat.

Jeffrey sat nervously, looking around the crowd as if he might see a ghost. He most assuredly would, Charles thought. Jeffrey was at the opposite side of the bench from him, and would often stand and pace back and forth. The man didn't look well. No, not at all. The past weeks had taken a toll on him. Dark smudges marred his face below his eyes, and the creases on either side of his mouth had deepened. It was all so very gratifying.

"Jeffrey," Charles boomed, delighted when Jeffrey actually jumped. "Who do you have your money on this year?"

Looking slightly annoyed, Jeffrey said, "Thames."

"I've got London. Won the last two years and they look strong again this one. I hope you didn't bet too much."

"I actually didn't bet at all this year," Jeffrey said.

"Good man." Charles winked at Marjorie, who was clearly trying to suppress a smile. They sat inches apart, a frustrating thing for a man who knew what lay beneath all those frothy layers of silk and lace. Dorothea, glaring at him, sat on the opposite side of Marjorie next to Jeffrey, as if daring him to as much as touch her daughter's hand. He did, of course, his pinky finger on hers. He occasionally moved it back and forth, feeling ridiculously aroused by that innocent caress.

He couldn't help but stare at her mouth, her breasts, the outline of her legs. He couldn't stop all his carnal thoughts, not when he knew how she tasted, how she sounded when she came. But he did try to hide those thoughts whenever Dorothea looked his way.

Taking a deep breath, Charles forced himself to look at the Thames flowing languidly by. Spectators lined both banks, but Charles had always preferred the stands. A young girl, curls bouncing, ran after her older brother on the grassy strip between the stands and the river, and Charles couldn't help wondering if he had seen Marjorie when he was a much younger man on this very spot. She wouldn't have been much older than that little girl chasing her brother. It made him feel a bit old.

"Do you think I'm old?" he asked, suddenly feeling unsure.

"Yes. Ancient." The starting cannon sounded and she clapped her hands. "Oh, good. The Grand Challenge has begun." She picked up her glasses and peered through them up the river.

"It's a bit soon to see who's ahead," Jeffrey said.

Marjorie dropped the glasses and stared at her cousin. "I wasn't watching for rowers, I was trying to get a glimpse of the queen."

She handed the glasses to Jeffrey. "Here. I don't much care who wins."

Charles leaned back on his elbows and tilted his head to the sun, closing his eyes. He hadn't felt so warm since leaving Africa. Soon, the wealthiest Londoners would be leaving the city and heading to the cooler countryside.

"Once we're married, we can go visit my brother in Nottingham. Much cooler there."

"I'd like that," Marjorie said, looking back at him and smiling. The large brim of her hat cast a shadow on much of her face, revealing only those lovely lips of hers. God, he wanted nothing more than to draw her down on top of him and kiss her silly.

"We haven't established the fact that there will be a wedding," Dorothea interjected with pursed lips, but there was slightly less bite in her tone lately. Charles had a feeling he was winning the old lady over by helping to plan Jeffrey's demise. The man was in a state of complete nerves. He was continuously looking about, and more than once grabbed up the glasses to examine someone more carefully. No doubt anyone with red hair was enough to drive the man close to the edge.

Like a subtle wave, the crowd's attention toward the race grew, until it was obvious the placement of the crews would soon be apparent. "Who's leading?" Charles asked Jeffrey, who still held the glasses.

"London," Jeffrey said with disgust, snapping down the glasses. "And Thames nowhere in sight. Looks like Eton's coming up, though. It'll be a close one."

Indeed, the crews seemed to be almost even. Everyone on the hill stood, and the shouts of encouragement grew louder the closer the men got to the finish line, the "plish" of the oars entering the water at the catch becoming ever louder. "Come on! Come on, lads, you can do it," Charles shouted, oblivious to the startled look Dorothea gave him.

"He does like his sports," Marjorie said, laughing, then shouted, "Come on, lads."

A shot rang out, marking the end of the race and London's win.

Marjorie stood and took off her hat, waving it in front of her as if to create a breeze. Charles watched as George, having seen her signal, stepped from behind a small group of people, who looked suspiciously like Mr. Stavers and his family, and walked up the hillside until he was standing quite alone, looking down on them.

"Mother," Marjorie said, looking up the rise in the general direction of where George stood, wearing his ridiculous green jacket and orange vest. "Is that Lord Sewall? I haven't seen him in ages."

Dorothea looked up the hill. "Where, dear?"

"There."

Jeffrey looked, just as they'd planned, and turned a frightening shade of gray.

"Oh no, it's not," Marjorie went on. "I wonder why he doesn't come to the regatta anymore? He always enjoyed them so. Do you remember the balls they used to hold after Henley—"

"Marjorie," Jeffrey said, still staring at George. "Look up there. At that man. Do you see him?"

This is it, she thought. Her cousin looked like a man about to break. Marjorie thought back to Jeffrey's words: *I am a terrible person. It's best you remember that.* Had he been trying to tell her something, hint at something that was to come?

"That's not Sewall, Jeffrey. Sewall had gone quite bald the last I saw him."

"No. To the right. Higher up. That man standing there by himself. He's . . . staring at us."

Marjorie squinted her eyes and next to her she thought she detected a small noise from Charles, as if he were stifling laughter. "What man? I don't see anyone there. What does he look like?"

Jeffrey began to sweat, and Marjorie maintained her innocent composure. Everything rode on this moment. If Charles was right, Jeffrey would beg for it all to end. From the look of her cousin, he seemed ready to rid his soul of the guilt that was no doubt eating away at him. No matter what he'd done, Marjorie refused to believe he was purely evil. She'd known Jeffrey all her life, and if George hadn't told her what he'd remembered, she would have had a difficult time believing Jeffrey capable of such an evil act.

His voice shaking noticeably, Jeffrey said, "He's wearing a . . . a green coat with an orange vest. He has, oh God, he has red hair."

Marjorie looked at Dorothea and at him, as if confused. "I don't see anyone like that. Do you, Mother?"

"What? I wasn't paying attention," Dorothea said, sounding bored.

"It's George. By God, you cannot tell me you don't see him. He's looking right at me." Jeffrey stopped as if choking. "He just waved at me. Just now. Right there." He pointed, his hand shaking so badly he could hardly keep it up.

Marjorie laid a hand on her cousin's arm. "There's no one there, Jeffrey," she said, making her face the picture of concern. "No one." She turned to Charles. "Do you see who he's talking about?"

"No," Charles said, pretending to scan the hill. "My God, Mr. Penwhistle, you look as if you're going faint."

"He's haunting me," Jeffrey muttered. "I see him everywhere I go." He looked at Marjorie and Charles as if desperate to get them to believe him. "I saw him at the library, on Market Street. He was walking with that girl he was engaged to."

"Lilianne Cavendish?"

"Yes, her. And I saw him standing in the window at your house. You remember that."

"Yes, I do. But we didn't see him, did we, Mother?"

"What poppycock," Dorothea said, sounding angry.

"I tell you he's haunting me."

"Don't say such a thing," Marjorie said. "George can't haunt you because he's not dead."

"How do you know?" Jeffrey said, looking up at the rise again, then crying out when he realized the man he'd been staring at had disappeared. "He was there. Oh my God. I can't take any more. I can't. He's haunting me."

"Stop saying that," Marjorie said. "It's awful and not true."

"It is true. He's dead and he's haunting me."

"He's not dead. How could you possibly say such a thing? How could you possibly *know* such a thing?"

"*Because I saw him die,*" Jeffrey said brokenly. He lowered his head, and added softly, "I was there."

"What are you saying, Mr. Penwhistle?" Charles asked. "How could you have kept this to yourself and let your aunt and cousin suffer these past weeks searching for him?"

"He was so stupid, so gullible. So goddamn *undeserving*. It wasn't fair."

"What are you talking about?" Marjorie asked, feeling sick inside. For all that she'd hoped and planned for this moment, now that it had come, she truly wished Jeffrey hadn't been involved.

"I was the heir," Jeffrey said, looking from one to the other. "For the first ten years of my life, *I* was the heir. And then he was born. He ruined everything, don't you see? I was the heir."

"My God," Charles said. "What did you do, man?"

Jeffrey buried his head in his hands. "I wish I'd never done it. You have to believe me. I wish I hadn't hired those men. I should have stopped them, I should have stopped them," he said, finally retching on the ground.

"But you didn't." George, accompanied by another man, had come up behind them. "You led me to those men. You left me to die. Why, Jeffrey? I don't understand. I thought you were my friend. My best friend."

"George?" Jeffrey looked from George to the others in the small group. Marjorie grabbed her brother's hand, and Jeffrey's gaze followed the gesture. Realization slowly dawned, until it looked as if Jeffrey would retch again. "You tricked me. All of you."

"Mr. Penwhistle, I am arresting you for the crime of attempted murder. I need you to come with me, sir."

"What?" Jeffrey looked disbelievingly at the man, finally recognizing him as the constable who had been to his home when George had first disappeared.

"Jeffrey, please do not make a scene," Dorothea said. "It's bad enough you vomited in public. I'll send a note over to your mother so she knows where you are. Good-bye, Jeffrey."

"Aunt, what do you mean? What's happening? I did nothing. I never laid a hand on him." Jeffrey looked at the constable who had a firm hand on his arm. "Unhand me, you cur. You've made a terrible mistake. Do you realize who I am?"

"Please come quietly, sir. If what you say is correct, you'll be home by supper," the constable said soothingly.

Jeffrey lifted his chin. "Right, then. Still, I will talk to your supervisor."

"I'll make certain of it, sir," the officer said.

As the constable started drawing Jeffrey away, her cousin looked back at the group with pure loathing, and Marjorie couldn't suppress the chill that crawled up her spine.

Dorothea turned her back on her nephew and the rest followed suit, mentally dismissing him.

"That was extremely distasteful," Dorothea said, looping her arm through George's. "You did very well these past weeks, George. You have restored my confidence."

George smiled, and Marjorie felt tears pressing on the back of her eyelids. She hadn't heard Mother say a kind thing to George in years. Perhaps nearly losing him had softened her a bit.

"And for God's sake, take off that hideous suit of clothes when we get home."

Marjorie stifled a laugh. She never would understand her mother.

Chapter 20

Just thirteen years earlier, Jeffrey Penwhistle would have been sentenced to death by hanging. But in 1861, Parliament decided attempted murder was best punished in other ways and England had ended transportation to distant penal colonies. So at least Mrs. Penwhistle had the convenience of visiting her son in Newgate. No one else visited him.

One month after his arrest, he'd been tried and convicted of the crime of attempted murder. He was, in a word, stunned. How could he be convicted of a crime he hadn't committed? He hadn't laid a hand on George. It had been two thugs—criminals that had disappeared into the bowels of St. Giles. George had testified, but perhaps the most damning testimony came from the constable and Lady Penwhistle who had heard Jeffrey confess to the crime. The jury deliberated for twenty minutes.

Two weeks after the trial, Charles arrived, special license in hand, and demanded to see Dorothea. He'd hardly seen Marjorie these last few weeks, and certainly not alone. The family had been in the throes of a terrible scandal, and had forgone any activities outside the home. They hadn't even ventured into Hyde Park. Charles understood, of course, for the newspapers had been filled with lurid details of the murder attempt. George had become something of a hero, for not only surviving the attack, but for participating in such an ingenious plan to incriminate Jeffrey. The details came from Jeffrey himself, who seemed rather to enjoy his celebrity and who, perhaps, thought by telling his story he would evoke some sympathy. His plan quite backfired, for people delighted in his downfall and cheered when he was convicted.

Charles had not attended the trial that last day. He'd spent it instead searching for a suitable townhouse to purchase. His rented one would never do, and he wanted something that would be airy and comfortable—and large enough for a family of six.

Now that he had a home and the license, he need only convince his future bride's mother that she should wholeheartedly approve their match—in spite of the terrible history between their families.

He was asked to wait in a small sitting room with rose-colored cushions, delicate furniture, and fragile-looking porcelain figurines resting upon every surface. The room made him decidedly nervous; one wrong move and he would destroy some priceless heirloom. He had no doubt Lady Summerfield felt a bit of delight when she told her butler to escort him to this room.

He sat, albeit carefully, upon the edge of a chair, fearing it would collapse beneath him. When Lady Summerfield entered, he stood, causing the chair to move into a small spindly table, which in turn caused the figure of a lady holding a small dog to wobble precariously. Lady Summerfield smiled in satisfaction—or at least that was how it seemed to Charles.

"Thank you for seeing me, my lady."

Dorothea nodded, then sat upon a chair opposite. He couldn't help but notice that she looked nearly as out of place in the feminine haven as he did. She indicated he should sit and he did, smiling grimly.

"To what do I owe the pleasure of your visit today, Mr. Norris?"

"You must know, my lady. I've come to ask for your daughter's hand. Again."

She raised one bushy eyebrow as if surprised. "I told you I would think on it, sir."

"Yes, ma'am, but that was some weeks ago. And now I would like the deed done. I've purchased a townhouse on Piccadilly and procured a special license."

Dorothea tilted her head as if confused. "How presumptuous of you, sir."

"May we stop this pretense, please? You know your daughter and

I will marry, with or without your permission. Marjorie would like you to support our marriage and be at our wedding. It is my whole-hearted wish as well."

The lady's eyes grew sharp and Charles thought he'd made a tactical error. "You behaved very badly toward my daughter, sir. Do you forget I found you in her room? Thankfully, no ill consequence of that evening occurred, so there is no reason to marry. To treat a woman with such disrespect does not bode well for you as a husband."

"Lady Summerfield, I fear I have a confession to make."

Dorothea lifted her chin and Charles took a bracing breath. "Oh?"

"I lied to you before. Your daughter is a virgin still."

Dorothea's eyes grew wide and her fury was palpable. Very much like the evening she'd caught them together, she opened her mouth and closed it, as if she were about to say something so horrid her genteel tongue couldn't form the syllables. And then, she smiled. "I can hardly be angry at you for *not* ruining my daughter, can I?"

"No, ma'am."

"Never lie to me again."

"I will not."

Lady Summerfield stood and Charles hastily followed suit. "St. Paul's is available next Saturday if you are."

There could only be one way the lady had known such a thing; she'd obviously made inquiries. "Yes. Of course I am. Thank you, my lady," Charles said, beaming his future mother-in-law a smile.

Lady Summerfield looked as if she were about to leave the room, but turned, hesitantly. "Will your mother have a chance to be in town in that time?"

"It is my dearest wish that my parents be at my wedding, ma'am."

Lady Summerfield nodded, her expression unreadable. "Very well."

The night before the wedding, Dorothea came to see Marjorie, an awkward interview in which Marjorie assured her she needn't continue when it was clear what the interview was about.

"I sense your marriage will be far different from mine," Dorothea said. "I do hope so."

For some reason, that small admission touched Marjorie. Her mother had never said an unkind word about her father, though she had often wondered if her parents had ever felt love for one another.

"I know tomorrow will not be easy for you, but I'm very glad you will be there, Mother. It would be purely awful if you were not."

Her mother looked away. "I am sorry I put you through so much, that my close-mindedness forced you to act in a way that was against your principles. Perhaps you will understand better when you have children of your own. I only want what's best for you. I suppose I wanted you to prove to the world that you were worthy of greatness. That you weren't an afterthought."

Later, Marjorie would think back on her mother's odd choice of words. *An afterthought.* Was that how she'd felt? As if she should have been grateful for whatever crumbs someone threw her? She'd never thought of her mother as a young girl, in love, with hopes and dreams. She'd known, of course, that Dorothea had married quite late, but had simply assumed her mother was as particular as she was; it had just taken her longer to find the man she wanted.

Marjorie looked about her room, realizing with sadness and a bit of excitement at what lay ahead, and that this would be the last time she would sleep here. She touched her dressing table, drawing her finger over the polished surface, her eyes sweeping around the room. This was where she'd gone when her father had died, to cry into her pillow. It was where as a young girl she dreamed of marrying a duke—or perhaps a handsome prince from some foreign land. And it was where she'd made love with the love of her life for the very first time.

Her maid knocked on her door and she called for Alice to enter.

"I thought I'd lay out your things tonight," she said, moving to her wardrobe where her wedding dress hung. It was by Worth, of course, and since they'd not had time to travel to Paris for a new gown, Marjorie would wear one she already owned, much to her mother's deep disappointment. The gown was one of her favorites, with an outrageous bustle that made it nearly impossible to sit—perfect for walking down the aisle. It was cream with light rose lace, and a modest neckline perfectly suitable for a wedding.

Marjorie climbed into bed, drew her knees to her chin, and watched her maid work. "Are you excited to work in a new household, Alice?"

"Oh, yes, m'lady. It's nice that I'll know so many on the staff, so it won't be too strange for me." Alice surveyed her work. "If there isn't anything else, good night, m'lady."

"Thank you, Alice. Good night."

Marjorie smiled at Alice as she left, glad at least something would be familiar in her new home. Charles had lured a big bit of Jeffrey's staff away, apparently, and it would be nice to see so many familiar faces. "Good night, room," she said, feeling silly and nostalgic.

The two mothers did not speak at the wedding or the breakfast that followed, something that Marjorie wasn't certain she was glad or sad about. At the wedding itself, her mother did not even glance at Charles's parents, a lovely pair Marjorie knew she would come to love. His sister had come, alone; her husband could not leave the side of his ailing mother. Marjorie was thrilled to have a sister, for Laura seemed like such a lively woman. "We've been waiting for Mother Brewster to die for more than ten years. I daresay she won't meet her maker the one week I'm away." Marjorie wasn't sure whether to laugh, but when Laura did, she followed suit.

"I'm so glad you were able to come. Charles speaks of you often. I do hope you are able to visit us in London more often."

Laura looked around the room and smiled. "I think I will," she'd said, softly but with conviction.

Marjorie had understood from Charles that Laura wasn't entirely happy with her situation, so perhaps a few trips to London would make his sister's life more enjoyable.

The ceremony was brief and private, with only family and a few close friends in attendance. It wasn't the grand wedding Dorothea had dreamed about for so many years, but it was perfect. Charles was stunning in his formal black, with his curling hair slicked back in thick waves. Marjorie could almost sense his need to muss it up, but he showed remarkable restraint. George was his best man, and Lilianne, much to Dorothea's disappointment (Marjorie's best friend, Lady Blackwood, was on the continent and unavailable) was her maid of honor. Their own marriage was in two weeks' time and Lilianne, likely thinking of her own upcoming wedding day, cried nearly nonstop throughout the service.

Back at the house, Aunt Gertrude hugged her warmly and said, "My only regret is that I don't have more nieces to get married off. It was such fun, my dear."

"It was the best of adventures," Marjorie said, giving her aunt a kiss. "And now an even better adventure awaits."

Aunt Gertrude chuckled and shook her head. "I wish you could keep this feeling in a box and take it out whenever life gets difficult."

"I think I shall, Aunt. That's a splendid idea."

"You may go, Prajit," Charles said, a bit more harshly than he'd meant to. Prajit hovered just inside the door of his rooms, moving from one foot to the other, as if ready to bound into the room and fight off a tiger. The tiger, in this particular case, was his damnable leg. This day, of all days, it hurt like the very devil after giving him days and days of reprieve.

"A bit of morphine, sir, will take away the edge and allow you to perform your duties as husband," Prajit said stubbornly.

"A bit of morphine will likely have the opposite effect, Prajit." He'd spoken a bit louder than he'd meant to and glanced at the door that separated his suite of rooms from those of his new wife.

He wasn't nervous. No, nervous was far too mild a word. After putting off Marjorie's official deflowering, he felt added pressure to make this night perfect for her. And how on earth could he make things perfect when he was about to hurt her?

His father had thought his fears adorable. "Son, if every husband killed his wife the first night, humanity would have long since been extinct."

Still, there was blood. And pain. And pleasure, for him at least. And God knew he'd spent enough sleepless nights imagining himself thrusting into her. Just the thought made him stir, made him forget the pain in his leg for a moment. Yes, that was just the thing.

"Prajit, I do appreciate your concern about my abilities to perform my husbandly duties," he said, meaning the complete opposite. Prajit either chose to ignore his sarcasm or had not yet mastered the ability to detect it. "But you are dismissed. Until noon tomorrow."

Prajit lifted his chin imperceptibly, then bowed and backed from the room, closing the door quietly behind him. But Charles could still sense his worry. He would be bloody glad when no one worried about him.

Charles tightened the belt around his robe and walked determinedly toward his wife's door. He opened it without knocking, and in hindsight that might not have been the most intelligent decision, for his wife's maid screeched as if he was a madman bent on murder.

"Oh, I am so sorry, sir," Alice said, then laughed nervously.

Marjorie, looking lovely in a frothy nightdress and overwrap, laughed along with her maid. "We'll get used to all this, Alice. You may go now."

"Until noon," Charles said, causing both ladies to start in surprise. "I gave Prajit a half day, so I think it's only fair."

Marjorie flushed from her neck to her cheeks. "Noon, then, Alice. Good night."

"Good night, m'lady," Alice said, dipping a quick curtsy and rushing toward the door.

"Here we are," Marjorie said when the maid was gone

"Yes." Charles looked around the room. "I see you've settled in nicely." Polite. Awkward. God, why was this suddenly so difficult?

"Your leg has been bothering you today. Are you certain you're—"

He held up a hand, stopping her. "My dear wife, if a horde of wild beasts now ran into this room, they would not be able to stop me from making love to you." He sounded angry, he knew, but the last thing he wanted was for his new wife to worry about him.

She laughed uncertainly.

"All right, then." She lifted her chin as if agreeing to some business arrangement.

"Are you frightened?"

She looked startled for a moment. "No," she said. "Should I be?"

Charles shrugged. "I have no idea." He wiped a hand through his hair, making his once-tamed locks spring about.

"Let's find out together, shall we?"

He watched, desire growing with every movement, as Marjorie slipped off her silky robe and draped it over a nearby chair. What she wore underneath took his breath away. It was sheer, leaving very little to the imagination, her dusky nipples and the dark shadow at the apex of her legs clearly visible. He might have already seen her completely nude, but something about this flimsy bit of cloth was incredibly arousing. He grew hard instantly.

"My aunt," she said, blushing again. "Can you imagine?"

"Your aunt wore this gown?" Charles asked.

Marjorie laughed. "No. She bought it for me."

"I love your aunt." As he looked at her, her nipples grew hard, making two obvious points though the fabric, and he groaned aloud. "I'm afraid I'm going to have to throw caution to the wind and ravish you rather more quickly than I'd planned."

She bit her lips and he took two long steps, and putting one hand behind her head, drew her to him for a long, deep kiss that told her just how much he wanted her. His other hand went unerringly to one breast, his thumb grazing her hard nipple. When he pulled away long moments later, she could hardly catch her breath. Her cheeks were flushed, this time not from embarrassment, but from arousal.

"I can't believe I can have you now, anytime I want."

"Any time?"

"Yes," he said fervently, kissing her cheek and moving down to her sweet neck. She arched against him and he pushed his arousal against her, unable to stop himself.

"Even at the dinner table?"

He drew back and laughed. "If you insist. Though the servants might be a bit mortified."

She drew her arms around his neck; he loved it when she did that. It was such a possessive thing for her to do. "Take my gown off," she whispered against his lips before thrusting her tongue inside his mouth.

He was lost then. Lost to the silky softness of her, the small sounds she made, the heat from between her legs, the hard nipples pressing against his chest. He swept his hands down her body, then up again, this time gathering the material and pulling, slowly, over her head. Inch by creamy inch, she was laid bare to his hot gaze, until he was drawing it over her head. She was gloriously naked. He wore nothing beneath his robe, and his erection thrust through the opening, gaining her attention.

"Please," he said. "It is yours to touch whenever you like."

"At the breakfast table?" she asked, the little minx.

"Any—" he drew in his breath sharply as she wrapped her hand around him "—where you'd like."

He lifted her up and she straddled him, her arms wrapped tightly around his neck, her bum nestled against his arousal, and he walked her to her bed. Ignoring a sharp jab of pain in his leg, he slowly lowered her down, following her until he lay beside her.

"You're hur—"

"No. Nothing hurts," he muttered, bringing his hand between her legs. She was always so hot and wet for him. It was enough to make a man think he could conquer the world. She held her breath when he touched her nub, then slowly, as if in extreme ecstasy, released it. He took one nipple in his mouth, suckling, loving the way she moved against his hand, the small sounds that escaped her beautiful mouth, as he worked to pleasure her.

"I want you," she said. "I need you inside me. Please."

He slowly, carefully, pressed his index finger inside her. She was so damned tight, and he closed his eyes against the thought of what it would feel like to press himself into her. He let out a groan as she lifted her hips in an almost desperate attempt to feel more.

"Please, Charles." Her breathing was harsh as he continued to caress her, bringing her closer and closer to the edge. She moved her head back and forth, moved her hips faster, jerking little movements he'd already come to recognize as signs of her impending release. "Oh, please." And then he felt her contract around his finger, and he nearly spent just watching her come.

Slowly, languidly, she came down, opening her eyes and smiling at him. "Why didn't you do as I asked?"

He chuckled and kissed her. "I'm about to, my lady." He positioned himself between her legs, and she suddenly seemed shy and vulnerable. He stroked each inner thigh, urging her legs farther apart. "I'll try not to hurt you, my love."

She nodded and braced herself, which only made him laugh again. "Please relax." He stroked her and watched as her eyes drifted closed. Then he slowly pushed himself inside her, where she was hot and wet and so damned tight. He knew when he encountered her maidenhead and stopped, just for a breath, before thrusting all the way inside.

Oh, heaven.

She didn't let out a single sound. He looked at her, trying to see if she'd been hurt, but she just smiled. "I love you," he said, the words seeming incredibly inadequate for what he felt for his wife. He pulled out slightly, watching her intently for signs he was hurting her, then pushed back in. "Wrap your legs around my . . . yes, like that." He pushed in, then out, every nerve in his body centered on that one spot. When she responded, when he felt her slim legs pull him toward her, when she let out a small sound of pleasure, he could hold back no longer. He thrust, hard and fast, unable to use any of the finesse he'd thought he would. He had no control, his body needed release, demanded it. And so he gave her everything he had, let it go. And when release finally came, he buried his head in the pillow beside hers and let out a long groan of pure satisfaction.

As he slowly came to himself, he first became aware of her soft breath against his cheek, of her hand caressing his nape. "I'm glad we waited," she whispered.

He carefully pulled away, then drew her against him, feeling happier and more content than he had in his entire life. "As am I. Even though it nearly killed me." He laughed again, ignoring the deep twinge of pain in his leg. He could ignore anything unpleasant as long as she was in his arms.

Epilogue

"Grandmama, throw!"

Dorothea picked up the ball and tossed it to her grandson, now two and running about chasing every ball she threw like a small puppy. He had a pint-sized cricket bat and even at so young an age, could swing it fiercely and connect with the ball more times than not.

She had two grandchildren now, and another on the way. George's little girl was nearly two and Lilianne had announced just last week that they were expecting again and hoping for a boy.

Dorothea, finally, was coming into her own. She realized that the first two-thirds of her life had simply prepared her for the best part. For the first time in her life, Dorothea was happy. Purely content.

All those years of worry and fear and living a life she'd loathed had been worth this time, this moment, of watching her grandson, black curls bouncing, chase after that ball. It was the oddest thing, being a grandmother. One didn't worry so much about how things would turn out. That was Marjorie's job, and one she seemed to be doing quite well. Already, little Michael was an intelligent and polite lad, but full of the dickens and as charming as his father.

Dorothea liked Charles, perhaps even loved him. But she liked to keep the man on his toes. It wouldn't do to allow him to completely relax with her. It was wonderful to see her children so happy.

Sometimes, Dorothea would look back and think of the girl she'd been—what a sad little thing. Yet how could she regret anything when it had all turned out so very well?

"Don't wear out Grandmama, Michael," Marjorie called.

Her grandson looked solemnly at her, his little blue eyes wide. "Are you worn out, Grandmama?"

She smiled. "Not yet."

"Are you certain, Mother?" Marjorie asked.

"I'll let you know."

Marjorie sat next to her on the garden bench and leaned her head on her shoulder. "I'm worn out and I haven't even done anything today," she said.

Michael tossed the ball onto Dorothea's lap, then held out his hands to catch it. He didn't more often than not, but he never seemed to get bored trying. A tenacious little thing. Dorothea tossed the ball and it slipped between his legs and bounced down the gravel path.

Suddenly, a large manly shape shot past them, growling fiercely. Michael screeched in delight as his father scooped him up and held him high above his head, a Viking capturing his prize. Dorothea's heart stopped each time he did it, but Michael adored the flight.

Charles settled the boy in one arm. "He'll be playing for the All-England Eleven before you know it."

Dorothea sniffed. "I hope he aspires to more than that," she said. "The North Eleven, for instance."

Charles looked horrified, and Dorothea laughed.

"Mother, don't torture poor Charles like that," Marjorie said, rising up to give her son, then her husband a kiss on the cheek. "We have news."

Dorothea knew already, or at least suspected.

"We're having another baby," Marjorie said.

"Two down and two to go," Charles said, giving Marjorie a kiss that lingered a bit too long for Dorothea's comfort.

Four grandchildren. Four. It ought to make her feel old. Instead, Dorothea experienced a lightness that made her feel like that young, hopeful girl she'd once been.

She wondered what she would say to that girl as she looked in the mirror at the hat shop. Would she warn her? Would she tell her that if only she could endure, she would finally be happy?

No, she wouldn't. Because this feeling she had right now could not have been reached without all the pain and sorrow. She would be a different woman and chances were, she wouldn't have this lightness and air in her heart just looking at her daughter with her little family.

Dorothea had never found love, but strangely enough, love had finally found her.

Read on for an excerpt from Jane Goodger's Lost Heiresses series, debuting this August!

His little shadow was back.

For two days, Mitch had noticed . . . someone. He wasn't quite sure whether it was male or female, but that didn't matter. Out here in the middle of nowhere, where a man could disappear and never be found, a man had to be careful. A man had to make certain his rifle was loaded, his canteen filled, and he listened to his gut. And right about now, his gut was telling him whoever had been watching him for two days was up to no good.

"You wait here, Millie." Mitch patted his mule and tied her to a scraggly white pine. If Millie really got in a mind to escape, the sapling wouldn't do much to keep her in place, but he very much doubted Millie would take a notion to do more than nibble on some grass.

Mitch was no stranger to the mountains of Yosemite. He guessed he knew them better than most. He knew how to walk silently and he knew when to make a noise that might scare a grizzly away. That was one creature he wasn't ashamed to admit he didn't much care for. He'd seen the results of a bear attack and was quite certain he didn't want to be on the receiving end of one of those razor-sharp claws. Other than grizzlies and men with guns, he wasn't afraid of much else. A man who'd seen and done what he had learned not to be afraid.

Whoever was trailing him was high up, likely taking little peeks over the rocks that jutted out above him like crooked teeth. He climbed silently, his boots pressing into the thick cushion of pine needles, until he was pretty sure he was above his prey. He scanned the area, Winchester in hand, fully loaded and ready to fire. Then he saw movement, a flash of hair.

"Well, damn," he whispered, looking at the girl through his sights. At least he thought it must be a girl with that long, pale braid down her back. She was lying on her stomach, no doubt staring at Millie and wondering where the heck the man she'd been spying on had disappeared to. His eyes moved down, following the trail of her braid, until he reached the decidedly feminine curve of her backside. Definitely female.

Now, a man didn't like holding a rifle on a woman or a girl, but he'd learned the hard way that women and girls could be just as dangerous with a gun as a man, so he wasn't about to take chances. If any of his friends back home saw him, they'd probably punch him in the jaw. But this wasn't New York City and that girl was no debutante, so he held his gun on her real careful. She turned her head and he saw the delicate curve of her smooth cheek. Seeing that bit of feminine beauty in such an unlikely place did something odd to his stomach. It was like seeing the first crocus after a long and terrible winter. He eased his gun down. The girl didn't have a weapon that he could see, and he relaxed slightly.

"Looking for someone, darlin'?"

Jane Goodger lives in Rhode Island with her husband and three children. Jane, a former journalist, has written and published numerous historical romances. When she isn't writing, she's reading, walking, playing with her kids, or anything else completely unrelated to cleaning a house. You can visit her website at www.janegoodger.com.

Don't miss these other charming Victorian romances in Jane Goodger's Lords and Ladies series.

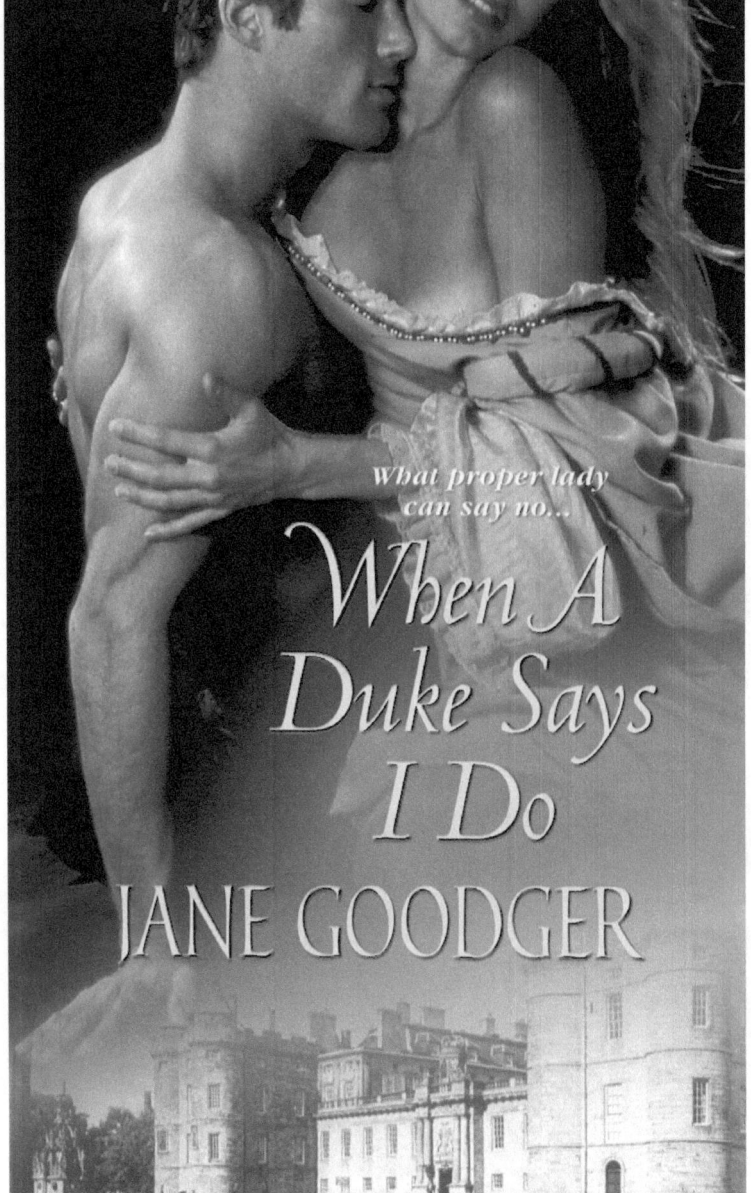

What proper lady
can say no...

When A
Duke Says
I Do

JANE GOODGER

The Mad Lord's Daughter

She couldn't resist...

JANE GOODGER

When a Lord
Needs a Lady

JANE GOODGER